"Agee's landscapes are the Nebraska Sand Hills and the interior of the human heart, and she renders both with equal power, filling the story with stunning depictions of weather, land, rage, and redemption."
—*The San Diego Tribune*

"[*The Weight of Dreams* is] a rich story shot through with sorrow, passion, and a portrait of the disappearing West. Jonis Agee tells a story with a finely tuned ear and a spirit as wild as a Sandhills horse."
—*Tulsa World*

"Agee's descriptions of the backbreaking life of a Plains rancher . . . are so real they make your muscles ache."
—*The New York Times*

"*The Weight of Dreams* is a book you'll want to sink into, its vast and rich landscapes, its broken and hopeful characters, its broad reach through time and space and every hidden corner of the human heart."
—Pam Houston, bestselling author of *Cowboys Are My Weakness*

"An engaging, mysterious and ultimately moving book. Agee knows the geography cold, both physical and emotional. She peels back the stereotypes and with startling clarity allows us to look in on the slow-motion moments upon which whole lives turn."
—Tom McNeal, author of *Goodnight, Nebraska*

"Here's the real novel for horse lovers. And here is a riveting story, shot through with sorrow, passion, a portrait of the disappearing West, a boyhood out of Dickens, and a most satisfying romance. It's Jonis Agee at her best."
—Frederick Busch, author of *The Night Inspector*

"With its contemporary story, this marvelous and haunting novel captures perfectly the history of American Indians and Anglo-Americans in the Midwest. It is an epic that places Ms. Agee among the likes of Louise Erdrich as our best chroniclers of the region."
—Greg Sarris, author of *Watermelon Nights*

PENGUIN BOOKS

THE WEIGHT OF DREAMS

Jonis Agee is the author of seven works of fiction, including most recently the novel *South of Resurrection*, as well as *Bend this Heart, Sweet Eyes*, and *Strange Angels*, which were *New York Times* Notable Books. She lives in St. Paul, Minnesota, where she teaches at the College of St. Catherine.

JONIS AGEE

THE

WEIGHT

OF

DREAMS

PENGUIN BOOKS

PENGUIN BOOKS
Published by the Penguin Group
Penguin Putnam Inc., 375 Hudson Street,
New York, New York 10014, U.S.A.
Penguin Books Ltd, 27 Wrights Lane, London W8 5TZ, England
Penguin Books Australia Ltd, Ringwood, Victoria, Australia
Penguin Books Canada Ltd, 10 Alcorn Avenue,
Toronto, Ontario, Canada M4V 3B2
Penguin Books (N.Z.) Ltd, 182–190 Wairau Road,
Auckland 10, New Zealand

Penguin Books Ltd, Registered Offices:
Harmondsworth, Middlesex, England

First published in the United States of America by Viking Penguin,
a member of Penguin Putnam Inc. 1999
Published in Penguin Books 2000

10 9 8 7 6 5 4 3 2 1

PUBLISHER'S NOTE
This is a work of fiction. Names, characters, places, and incidents are
either the product of the author's imagination or are used fictitiously, and
any resemblance to actual persons, living or dead, business establishments,
events, or locales is entirely coincidental.

THE LIBRARY OF CONGRESS HAS CATALOGED THE HARDCOVER EDITION AS FOLLOWS:
Agee, Jonis.
The weight of dreams / Jonis Agee.
p.   cm.
ISBN 0-670-88233-X (hc.)
ISBN 0 14 02.9188 1 (pbk.)
I. Title.
PS3551.G4W45   1999
813'.54—dc21   98-54893

Printed in the United States of America
Set in Weiss
DESIGNED BY BETTY LEW

For Jackie Agee, who knows what it means to
dream of other places. And for the people of
Rosebud Reservation and the Nebraska
Sandhills, who lead lives as large and complex
as the land they inhabit.

∽ Acknowledgments

I would like most especially to thank my longtime editor and friend, Jane von Mehren, who makes all things possible in my writing life. I would like to thank my agent, Emma Sweeney, who gives wonderful advice and loves horses as much as I do. I thank Lon Otto, who has been my friend, mentor, critic, and anchor for more than twenty years.

A special thanks to Kelly Hogan and Dana Hanna for taking time to share with me their legal worlds and lives in western Nebraska and South Dakota. And thanks to Duane and Darlene Gudgel, who run the best bookstore in western Nebraska and keep their doors open to strangers in need of a good dose of imagination and fact.

Thanks to Kelly Allen, who provided organization, support, and good food during the writing. Many thanks to my friends, who continue to make life interesting and filled with humor: Andrea and Gorman Beauchamp, Tish O'Dowd, Lorna Goodison, Nick and Elena Delbanco, Charlie and Martha Baxter, Heid Erdrich and John Burke, Leslie Miller, Susan Welch, Greg Hewett and Tony Hainault, Juanita Garciagodoy and George Rabasa, Gerry LaFemina, Rebecca and Tom Binger, Connie Baron and Danny Vorls, Jane Barnes and Janet McNew, and Hugh Ledyard.

And to Tom Redshaw and Gregory Page, who gave me shelter in my recent travels, thank you. Heartfelt thanks to Sharon Oard

Warner for listening during those long phone calls. Thanks to John Turner, who made me feel like I could talk about something that mattered again. And thanks to my sister Cindy, whose distinctive voice is a source of wit and inspiration. Finally, I would like to thank my daughter, Brenda, for being such a bright light in my cosmos.

He has returned to this dream for his bones.
The waters darken. The continent vanishes.

—Agha Shahid Ali

I

Chasing the Lightning
(August 1975)

⌾ Chapter One

Ty Bonte kept his eyes fixed on his hands folded in front of him, the knuckles white as he tried to control his rage at being treated like a kid. He had been doing a man's work on the family ranch since he was eight; his browned, battered hands were evidence of that fact. What he really needed was a beer and a couple of shots of tequila to sort this whole mess out. The pills Harney had slipped him in the men's room half an hour ago hadn't kicked up any dust. All the edges were still too damn sharp.

The county prosecutor laid down the yellow pencil he had been using like a baton to conduct the litany of misdeeds and turned to look at the seventeen-year-old sitting at the table across the narrow aisle. "Your Honor, this boy has multiple arrests on his record, including driving without a license, underage drinking, malicious destruction of public property, and assault—I'm not even going to mention the other things he could be charged on."

Ty's mother sighed and even without turning around to look at her sitting behind him on one of the wooden benches that lined the back of the small room, he knew she was shaking her head like a dog with a taste of poison bait in its mouth. Sitting as far from his mother as possible, Ryder Bonte, his father, leaned against the wall, tan cowboy hat dropped down over his eyes as if he were asleep, arms folded, with his faded black western shirtsleeves rolled to the elbow so the blurred tattoo of a woman's naked silhouette seemed to lie along his forearm like a sick lizard.

Ty shifted his eyes to follow the staggering motion of a centipede that had been slowly circling the bare space between the tables and the judge's dark wood-veneer bench, which was dented from an angry defendant's kick. That must have felt good, Ty decided, only if he were going to do it, he'd put all his strength into it and make a big boot-sized hole. Although the courtroom blinds were shut, the sunlight still managed to cut through in yellow bars and had gradually marched across the brown linoleum tiles during the hearing so that now the scuffed and muddy toe of his right boot was caught and exposed in the grid of light. Instinctively he shook his boot, but the light held. The centipede wove toward the prosecutor's table, entering the home territory of the highly polished black loafers. The kind of shoes a Bonte man would never even try on. His wife had money, Ryder had told Ty this morning while they waited like poor relations on the bench outside the courtroom during Harney's session. Old man Rivers, Harney's father, had insisted that the two boys be tried separately.

"And there's strong evidence that he's not getting the controls needed in the home either, Your Honor." Francis Waverly, the prosecutor, swiveled slightly in his chair and directed the room's attention to the father, who pushed his hat up with his thumb and stared back. Waverly glanced at Mrs. Bonte, who was staring straight ahead. Ty shifted his gaze back to the centipede just as Waverly's shiny black loafer lifted and squashed it. Then Ty looked back at his father, whose deeply tanned face burned a shade darker.

Ryder had grown up around Francis and remembered him as a skinny kid who couldn't ride a horse, but had gone to the University of Nebraska in Lincoln and thought he was hot stuff when he came home to Babylon on vacation. The law degree only certified that he was another asshole wearing a face. These days he was nostril deep with the bankers and business interest in town, busy protecting *their* kids while trying to settle old scores on *his* kid's back. In the old days a ranch teenager was expected to come to town, drink a little, raise some hell, spend money, and go home. It was part of growing up until he got married and settled down to the real work of ranching and raising a family. Now, they threw the book at these boys every time one sneezed. Ryder wanted to throw a punch at Francis, splatter that nice white shirt and pale sissy blue suit with some blood, but Quinn Yount, their lawyer, had warned the two Bonte men to say and do absolutely nothing. Last time, they had been fined for disrupting the proceedings and that had put another black mark on Ty's record.

Ryder looked across the room to the left, where the raised platform filled with chairs seated a jury when necessary. Today the blond oak chairs were empty except for the social worker and a visiting county prosecutor sitting beside Red Tibbetts, the lawyer for Harney Rivers, whose case had gone just before this one. No wonder Francis was on his high horse, putting on the show for the out-of-town visitor. Ryder took the worn black checkbook from his shirt pocket and began tapping it lightly on the back of the empty chair at the prosecutor's table in front of him. They were in the middle of haying at home. Neither he nor Ty even had time to shower before they changed clothes and rushed to town for the hearing. He could smell his own sour stink and hoped it bothered his wife and Francis too. He noticed that Francis was looking out of the corner of his eye at the checkbook. They might get down to business after all. Best he could do for the kid was a couple of hundred. Not like Harney's old man, who had rigged a deal so his kid could go to a 4-H meeting and talk about the evils of alcohol and get off without a fine or a note on his record. Harney Rivers Sr. owned the Cattleman's Bank, so that kid could ride free as long as Francis and the judge were in office.

"Do you have anything to say?" The judge directed the question at Ty, who glanced up quickly and away, feeling the shame press against his face like a fat stomach pulling him into its pillowy flesh, making him breathe its musty sweat until he had a rotten sweet smell like a dead mouse stuck in his nose. He shook his head and stared at the black Formica tabletop scratched with angry initials and swear words. He felt like adding his own.

Red Tibbetts, Harney's lawyer sitting on the sidelines, cleared his throat. "Your Honor?"

The judge held up his hand while he wrote notes on the file and stared at them for a minute.

Ryder had heard how the judge spent weekends at an enclave of cabins on the Niobrara River in the breaks northeast of town, playing cards and drinking with the local lawyers, bankers, sheriff, and an assortment of men with money. About once a month during the summer they lured someone from the state offices in Lincoln to come up and spend the weekend floating down the river in canoes, drinking around the campfire, raising hell like real men. Two weeks ago, the lieutenant governor came—almost as good as the governor, who promised a visit in late August. Anytime Red Tibbetts wanted to say something in court, whether he was an official part of a case or not, it was okay.

"Sons a bitches," Ryder muttered loud enough for Francis Waverly to hear but not the judge. Waverly's sissy blue suit back twitched, but he didn't turn around. These lawyers were all a bunch of punks. "Yeggies," he muttered, a word his father had used that had no real definition except to signify people who didn't really work for a living, but lived off the fringes, lazy, no-good, half-evil, half-incompetent, conniving sons a bitches. Couldn't find their own asses in the dark. Damn kid could end up just like 'em too if Ryder didn't watch out. Nothing but backbreaking work kept people on the hard road, his own father used to say as he kicked Ryder out into some cloudburst or snowstorm to work cattle.

The judge looked at Harney's lawyer.

"Your Honor, this boy is just having growing pains. We all remember those days, and I bet his father will be whipping some sense into him before dark." Red Tibbetts smiled at the judge, who gave a short nod and looked at the social worker and raised his eyebrows.

Ryder snorted loud enough for the judge to glance in his direction. He almost hated that the tide was turning in his boy's favor because some fatass lawyer was taking their side for a change. Hell, a person never knew where these lawyers were going to land—going to court was like riding under a tree full of snakes.

The social worker was a stout young woman with cropped brown hair, a square face with a low forehead, and a mean glint in her eye as she looked the Bonte family over. Dressed in pink-and-gray plaid shorts with an elastic waist and a gray men's cotton short-sleeved pullover, she slouched in her chair as if she were a bored teenager in court herself and didn't bother straightening up as she gave her report. "We were hoping to get Ty into the counseling program at the Outreach Center, but it's full right now."

"He don't need more talking to—" Ryder leaned forward and glared at the social worker.

"Please be quiet," the judge ordered in a monotone.

"Your Honor, we'd like to see this boy sent to the training facility in Hastings," the prosecutor announced in his dry, flat voice. "Smashing the window at the Corner Bar was a willful act of vandalism—not to mention the brawl with the two cowboys."

"No! I need him working on the ranch—" Ryder's urgent whisper could be heard all over the room.

"He's needed at home, Your Honor. The Bonte family would suffer great hardship without him this time of year," Quinn Yount, Ty's lawyer, said. "And there's no actual proof about the window."

The judge, a thin middle-aged balding white man in glasses who looked like he might sell insurance on TV, glanced at Red Tibbetts and the visiting prosecutor, then back at Ty.

"Son, you're becoming an embarrassment to your folks. The community is sick of you causing trouble. You've got JAIL printed across your forehead. I see you one more time, that's where you're going. For now, I'm fining you three hundred dollars plus court costs, and I want *you* to pay it. Your father can pay the fine today, then I want a letter saying you've paid him back. You have sixty days. Remember, next time we won't be sitting here holding your hand—"

"Three hundred dollars!" Ryder muttered, "bunch a yeggies . . ."

Ty turned to see his mother stand and ease her way along the narrow bench and into the aisle. He half-expected her to pat his shoulder or lean down and murmur something in that quiet, even voice of hers, at least a word of caution or regret. Anything, really, would have been enough, but his body waited, almost naked with expectation as she brushed past, in her navy blue shirtdress with the little patent leather belt, a whisper of lavender scent against the wood bench behind him. He dropped his hands into his lap, fixing his eyes on the wood grain of the judge's stand and willing himself not to cry. Nobody ever held his hand, he wanted to protest. Nobody even tried. Out of the corner of his eye, he caught the motion of his father standing and winced from the sharp tap of the checkbook on his shoulder as Ryder passed.

"Court dismissed," the judge said.

Turning, Ty saw his mother and father starting to argue in the hallway and Harney's grinning face lurking near the stairs.

"Best stay away from that Rivers boy," Yount said as he shuffled papers into the thick yellow file with Ty's name on it.

Everybody had a piece of advice, but not one of them was worth a wagon of manure when it came down to those nights on the ranch with his father drinking or about to start drinking again. Ty faced that alone, and it was only going to get worse now. Maybe he should just get it over with—ask the judge to send him to Hastings now instead of waiting till the next time. Except for the problem of having no booze, the training school would be a vacation from Ryder and the ranch. He rose and his back pulled from the most recent beating with the belt, for lying about some cattle he was supposed to doctor for pink eye and hadn't gotten to yet. Lucky he'd grabbed the belt when Ryder had switched to the buckle end, as he did when he drank enough. The way it was flying through the air, that big trophy buckle would've torn his back open instead of his hand. Everyone thought Ty had broken the bar window because of the deep cut that almost tore off his little finger, but it was Harney who'd thrown the half-full whiskey bottle after their fight with those cowboys from the ZC ranch, not him. Doc saw him in jail yesterday morning, said the stitches Ty had put in himself were sufficient. Leave an ugly, thick scar though. Then he'd checked the mobility to make sure there was no tendon or nerve damage. When Ty told him it was a roping accident, Doc's eyes flicked with disbelief because of the dark purple stripes crisscrossing his back like a bad night sky. Ty hadn't wanted his lungs and heart checked out. He knew he was breathing a little shallow and hunching over. Doc never said a word though. Wouldn't give him any pain pills either. Probably figured Ty deserved it, being the kind of boy who got examined in jail of a Sunday morning. A boy whose father and mother were so disgusted they wouldn't bail him out until the afternoon, so he would be home for night chores and start work bright and early Monday morning when haying began. It was just natural to take a belt to that kind of boy every so often, the way rank horses needed a good tussle to put their minds on work.

"You coming?" Yount asked, laying a hand on Ty's back so softly it made the boy wonder if Doc had told him. He shrugged off the gesture, put his straw cowboy hat on so it shadowed his eyes, and stood. He was already an inch or so taller than the young lawyer, and it made him feel even more alone, as if he were growing beyond anyone's reach now. He kept his expression empty as he thanked Yount.

"You want to talk about this—or anything—you give me a holler, okay?" The other man's features were so pale they reminded Ty of the late summer hills, subtle shades of tans and yellows in those watery hazel eyes that held a surprising sympathy. It was a little too late for that, something inside Ty said. He was grown now, six one in his socks with a promise of another inch or so to put him over Ryder. He couldn't bring his troubles to another person anymore. His father was right on that count.

Collecting the file and turning to go, Young paused again. "I'm serious about Harney. His wiring's bad, and your family doesn't have the kind of deep pockets old man Rivers has."

Ty nodded and kept his eyes away from the lawyer's. Following Yount, he saw his mother put both hands on her husband's chest and shove him back. Ryder was laughing as she turned on her chunky black patent leather heels and walked down the steep marble stairs. Ty hung back long enough for his father to push his way through the lawyers and clients toward the window to the left, where the clerks sat waiting for payment of fines and news of verdicts they could spread around town. Glancing at the pale green marble stairs his mother had disappeared down, he thought briefly of running after her. Not after *her*, but after her in the same way she had run from Ryder and the ranch several years ago, taking Ronnie and his sister,

Charla, and making it clear that Ty was part of what she was fleeing.
And after Ronnie, his younger brother, died two years ago at the
ranch, where he spent his summers, there wasn't any question of her
ever coming back. In fact, Ty couldn't understand why she bothered
coming to court today, unless it was to look good in front of people
here in town. The thing was, he could never figure out why she
hated him so, even before Ronnie.

It used to drive him crazy, now it just felt like a numb lump, the
way that place on his leg bone felt where he got cornered and
kicked that time by the mare who'd lost her foal. Ended up with
bone chips that had to be taken out, and a huge blood clot that
swelled his calf to three times its normal size so he couldn't walk for
a week for fear it'd break loose and travel to his heart before the
drugs dissolved it. Maybe that was when his mother finally lost interest in him, coming up the stairs with his meals on a tray, standing
there with her arms folded and staring at him like he was doing
these things on purpose to make her mad or hurt her. He was only
twelve. He didn't know what to do about other people's feelings. He
was just a kid.

When she said, "I want you to come to town this winter and stay
with me. I don't want you out here all the time," he'd protested and
argued and finally asked his father to stop her. He couldn't know
that she'd give up on him then, that she'd hate him for giving Ryder
ammunition to use against her, that she'd see her son as following in
the footsteps of her mean, drunk husband. He was just a kid, he'd
wanted to tell her for several years. How could she give up on him?
Now he knew: A parent can decide they don't *like* their child. And
there isn't a damn thing either one of them can do about it.

"Hey—" Harney nudged him in the ribs and laughed at the way
Ty caved away from the elbow. "How soon can you get away from
your old man?"

Looking quickly at Harney, then glancing over to check on what
Ryder was doing, Ty thought about his lawyer's warning about the
wiring in Harney's head. It was true, although you couldn't see it at
first. His light brown hair and almost boneless face, with a regular-
sized nose and evenly spaced blue eyes, were so ordinary that he al-

most stood out. He was stockier and a couple of inches shorter than Ty, without being overweight. In fact, his first two years in high school, he'd been on the wrestling team and had kept the muscular build and quickness that let him dominate in two weight classes until he was kicked out for a string of dirty plays. The strange thing was that he would've won anyway. When the third opponent lay writhing on the floor with an ear half-torn off, Harney had stood panting over him, a small satisfied smile on his face. Harney Sr. had thrown a fit and claimed it was all a misunderstanding, an accident, and had his son reinstated. But Harney Jr. never joined a team or club again. Instead, he had gradually taken a central role in their school as the boy who could put his hands on anything illegal: drugs, alcohol, fake driver's licenses for trips to North Platte and Rapid City, and pictures of stupefying filth.

Ty's mouth was suddenly dry as he pictured the exhausting, hot days of ranch work ahead, with only the few beers he was allowed to drink. He'd have to get away somehow.

"We're haying—but maybe Friday night. I can steal the keys to the truck unless he tries to hide them again. That could take a while, but I'll catch you at the Gas 'n Git just after dark—you better have something other than those pills you gave me in the john—what was that shit, aspirin?"

Harney smiled lazily and shrugged one shoulder. "Worth a try—"

"Yeah well, you owe me, man—"

"Don't worry—" Harney looked past Ty and frowned. "Here comes your old man—just don't be late, we're going to 'Mexico' "— Harney gave his arm a light punch and ambled over to the little knot of lawyers. "Mexico" meant a crazy night of tequila, grass, and looking for girls. Ty could already taste the oily burn and sour salt on his tongue.

"Come on." Ryder brushed past with the yellow receipt for the fine crushed in his fist. He was scowling and walking quickly, landing light on his feet as if he were on his way to someplace important. "Don't even think about getting into trouble again," he said over his shoulder on the way down the stairs. "You're gonna be so damn tired from working, you'll be grateful I let you take a shit. Next time you come to town, it'll be with that letter to the judge saying you repaid me this three hundred dollars at fifty cents an hour. Plus what you owe me for my time today, the gas to drive in here, and the energy to fight your mother." Ryder pushed the big glass door open and stepped outside, pausing to put on his aviator-style sunglasses in the bright light bouncing off the concrete and stone as if they were tin. "Boy, you'll be lucky you even make it to school this fall."

Ty stood on the top step for a moment, glancing back at the courthouse, again considering a plea to the judge to put him away. Then the horn on the truck honked and he sighed and descended the limestone steps. Climbing in, he settled on the torn brown vinyl seat with the exposed springs. Ryder had taken the old red-and-gray striped saddle blanket that usually covered the hole in the seat and bunched it up for the small of his back. Years ago he'd busted his back when he fell off a haystack and it gave him fits during the summer when the work was nonstop. Ty put his hand down on the seat, pushing the stitched cut against the spring so that it throbbed. Staring out the windshield speckled thick with bug debris, he saw his mother standing under the awning of the J C Penney Catalog Store, shading her eyes with one hand, watching them. He couldn't tell even now what she thought or felt. If she changed her mind about him, he'd never know. She was as quiet and unrelenting as the hills they were heading into.

ᘓ Chapter Two

Ty had spent most of the day doctoring a bunch of cows with the scours over on the east range, and now to top things off, one of the two-year-old bulls here in the north pasture had died from what looked like might be a lightning strike. But since it was so bloated and maggot-ridden, it was hard to get close enough to be certain. His horse didn't want to have anything to do with the carcass and kept blowing hard through its nose and trying to back away. Ty kept his legs tight, nudging with his heels. He was on a young mare named Marie he was hoping would make a cutting or roping horse. She was bred the best, but at five she was taking her own sweet time growing up. Had that bulgy eye that kept looking around for trouble. Ryder had warned him about mares with that eye. Good for survival in the wild, bad for work. A palomino, she had extra-sensitive skin that picked up fungus and infected fly bites all summer long, and her pink nose was always peeling. Although her winter coat was a deep gold, in the summer she bleached to a pale runny shade of yellow that always irritated Ryder for some reason. He'd been trying to force Ty to send the mare to the sale barn in Babylon since May, but Ty had stubbornly hung on to her. Now she hopped back and forth on her hindquarters rather than go forward until Ty turned her and had to rein back before she bolted.

"Maybe the old man's right about you, Marie." Ty made her stop now that she was facing the other direction. To stay on the ranch, she'd have to pick up the knack of being useful. She wasn't going to make it otherwise.

The sun seemed to breathe its heat across the hills today, and it arrived in shimmering waves that bore against his eyes and mouth until his lungs felt dried out and he coughed up his own hot breath. He reached for the canteen tied behind the saddle, moving slowly so the mare wouldn't spook. She dropped her head and blew out her breath as if she smelled the water and needed a drink too. Her neck was wet and starting to lather under the reins. "Okay," he sighed, opening the canteen, "let's get you some water." While she walked, he took little sips, letting the water settle slowly in his hot stomach. No point in making himself sick out here.

The meadowlarks and sparrows were silent in the late afternoon heat. Except for the buzz and click of insects in the bunchgrass, nothing moved this time of day. He kept an eye out for the rattlesnakes that lived in this particular little valley where the hills had some rock they could den up in. "Probably even too hot for them," he remarked to the horse. He looked up into the milk blue August sky, where he could just make out the thin white streak of a vapor trail from a fighter jet, so pale it looked like the smear left by a finger drawn across glass. The jet would be from Ellsworth Air Force Base outside Rapid City, South Dakota. He'd gone there once with Ryder and Ronnie and tried to imagine running off to join up after that, but that was another useless dream. They wouldn't take some kid without a high school diploma, and he was so far behind now, he didn't see how he'd catch up. Ryder was making grumblings about school starting in a couple of weeks too, and Ty had been panicked at the thought of maybe having to join the class of kids a year younger than he was and being laughed at or worse, stared at and pitied. That was one thing he shared with his old man—wasn't nobody allowed to feel sorry for him. The thought made him nudge Marie into a trot as they crossed the long valley and headed around the hill toward the little lake in the hay meadows.

He heard the grunting and hopeless neighing before he could make out more than a dark shape against the marsh, but it made him send the mare into a lope. As they got close enough to see the horse's head and upper body, Marie broke stride and gave a body-shaking whinny that ended in a series of short baby cries almost like a whimper. It was Ryder's old roping mare, Marie's mother, a light sorrel with a lot of white that was black with muck. Ty untied his rope and did a flying dismount, letting the reins drop as he ran forward. The old broodmare's hindquarters had somehow gotten stuck in the deep mud along the marshy edge of the lake at this end. It had been so dry the last month the lake had shrunk in size and she'd probably been fooled by the bulrushes and green scum into thinking the edge was safe. From the white-rimmed sweat streaking her neck and chest, her exhausted eyes, drooping ears, and raspy breathing, he could tell she was nearing the end of her struggle.

He shook out a loop and swung once, twice over his head, then threw. It landed around her neck, but he didn't pull until he had it wrapped securely around his saddle horn and could back Marie up. He didn't dare go out there to the horse, for fear he'd get stuck too. Instead, he knelt at the edge where he could squat without sinking in more than a half a foot. "Okay, com'on, Mama, you can do this, you got to help now. Com'on, girl." He kept his voice soft, then stood and pulled on the rope, the sign for Marie to start backing.

The first time the rope tightened against the dead weight of the stuck horse, Marie came forward and Ty had to urge her back again with a tap of his hand on her chest. The horse in the marsh seemed to resist until the rope was up around her windpipe, then she shook her head and strained to come forward, but her hindquarters stuck and she ended up pawing and trying to strike out at the muck in front of her.

"Com'on, Mama, com'on," Ty called and the horse gave a mighty grunting heave, freeing the right hind leg enough to step forward as if over a bush before sinking into the muck again. The brief slack caused Marie to rush back with a squeal and jerk the other horse forward hard enough that she strained to lift the other leg and drag it out for a small step too. Then the mare laid her head and neck in the muck, groaning, and Ty had to stop Marie and go back to encouraging the horse to get up and try again.

They struggled like that for almost an hour, working the mare loose step by step until finally she hit solid bottom in the wet shallows and Ty could loosen the rope. Marie stood, spraddle-legged, head dropped, dripping sweat and panting from the exertion, but Ty knew she'd be all right. It was the old broodmare he was worried about. Lying on her side, coated in mud and salty sweat, she looked about finished, her eyes half closed while she breathed in broken gasps as if her wind had been ruined.

Retrieving the canteen, he trickled water into the side of her mouth until she began to work her tongue and swallow. Then using his hat and the canteen, he brought water to wash off what he could of the mud and cool her down. Gradually, his hands working over her body and his murmuring comfort seemed to encourage her enough that her breathing calmed and she closed her eyes to rest. While she dozed, Ty gave Marie a drink, loosened her cinch, and picketed her to graze. Then he sat down to wait. When the old mare woke up, she lifted her head and began to look around.

"Ready?" He fashioned a headstall from the rope and gave her a pat. The mare looked around again, rolled to her stomach and propped her front feet out before her, then took a deep breath, straightened her hindquarters under her body, pushed off, and stood up in a clumsy rush. She looked at Ty, snorted, and gave a big shake that splattered mud all over him.

"Hey!" He laughed and led her to where Marie was watching them.

———

It took twice as long to get back to the ranch as normal, because the old mare was pretty stove up from her ordeal. At a couple of points, Ty thought about leaving her and coming back with the trailer in case she was starting to colic or tie up, but he kept going. The sun was sitting just above the horizon, pausing as if it wanted one last look around before it left when Ty rode up to the corral where Ryder was just finishing with the evening chores.

"What happened to my mare?" He hurried to take the rope from Ty and lead the limping horse to the water tank, where she thrust her nose in and drank in deep, greedy drafts.

"Found her stuck in the marsh northeast of here. She was about finished." Ty climbed down and worked the cinch loose on his little mare. "Marie here pulled her out." He patted the yellow horse and scrubbed the underside of her jaw with his fingernails. She stretched her head out and pulled her lips back so her teeth were bared and clicking like a dog's in pleasure.

"What were you thinking, old girl?" Ryder rubbed the horse's neck and smoothed some of her mud-encrusted mane over. "Better make her a bran mash tonight," he said and turned to lead the mare from the water tank. "I'll hose these legs and rub 'em down with some lineament. See if we can take the strain out." The mare had been Ryder's best roping horse for years and had thrown some good babies, too, but Ty wasn't surprised that his father didn't thank him. Ty was just doing the job he was supposed to do, his father would say. You don't get thanked for that. Now if the horse had died, like that bull—oh shit, he'd forgotten that he'd have to tell his father about the damn bull. Ty lifted the saddle and sweat-soaked blanket off his horse and hung them in the barn to dry.

They ate a cold, late supper of leftover meatloaf, corn on the cob, canned green beans, and beer. At sixteen, Ty had told Ryder that since he did a man's work, he should be able to drink beer. When his father's back was turned lifting the corn out of the boiling water, Ty managed to sneak a couple of whiskey shots into the bottle too. He got away with it most summer nights they ate on the screen porch, with only the kitchen light casting a dark brown shadow to see by. The wood siding behind the men was speckled with the black shapes of flies that had made it onto the porch during the day and stuck there now for the remaining warmth. Out in the corral, horses stamped against the mosquitoes as the pastures found their voice and a loud throbbing set up. They had finished their plates and were leaning back in their chairs, listening to the night chorus. Ryder poured an inch of bourbon into his glass, lit up a cigarette, took a deep pull that flamed the tip bright red against the dark yard, and let the smoke out in a long satisfying stream between his thin, scarred lips. Ty turned his head away as the breeze brought the smoke into his face. He hated the smell because it belonged to his father, but there was no use saying anything about it; Ryder just laughed at him when he objected.

But as if he saw his son's motion as a challenge of some sort, Ryder said, "Think you'll ever amount to anything, boy?" Ty glanced out of the corner of his eye at the lean, long face with high cheekbones and hawk nose crossed by a light ridge of scar from a fall in a barbed wire fence, and small, nearly black eyes that almost disappeared in the folds of the lids.

In the old days, when this question first came up, Ty had tried to fight him, saying yes, yes he would, and this had only infuriated his father until they ended up in some kind of physical battle. Ty had finally learned to either shake his head or shrug. Tonight he sighed—"Probably not," hating the defeat his father tried to plant so much that inside he was yelling: Yes I will, goddamn it, soon as I get away from your sick fucking face.

Ty's reply seemed to silence Ryder as he finished that cigarette and lit another, filling the small porch with smoke as if to say that even the air his son breathed was his father's, and his father could do anything he wanted with what belonged to him.

Then Ryder surprised him. "Well, you did a pretty good job out there today, son." He stared out at the yard light being battered by a couple of large moths and the usual crowd of small, hard-shelled beetles giving off a series of rhythmical clicks.

First there was a burst of joy in Ty, but that quickly turned to anger at himself for letting his father break through him so easily. How simple it was for his father to praise him, yet he almost never did. Ryder must truly believe his son was a failure then, Ty realized. That was it. And he hated him doubly because when the old man heard about the dead bull, he'd wish he could take back the praise.

"I'm tired." Ty stood up, took one last look at the yard, the dark hills outlined against the night sky around them, and went in the house, easing the screen door shut so his father wouldn't yell about that.

"Don't forget we're fencing that piece along Jaboy's land in the morning, boy," Ryder called.

They found all four strands trampled to the ground and three posts broken at the bottom as if a tank had driven over the fence. "God-damned kids." Ryder kicked at the deep grids crushing the soapweed leaves into pulp and ripping out enough bluestem that the sand threatened to heave over the entire area. "Look at these tracks. Play-ing demolition derby with my fence. Hope to hell it tore up their tires. Better dig the broken posts out, son."

Ty paused on his way to the pickup for the shovel. "Wouldn't it save time to dig the new posts in next to those? Might even strengthen the posts to have supports."

Ryder lifted his battered hat, looked across at the hills of Jaboy's land that always seemed greener, more prosperous than his own. With so much more acreage, they never had to run the cattle so long on any given area; they had men to contain possible blowouts when grass got thin or laid bare like this place too. And with all that money, Jaboy could get a young wife and keep her where he wanted her even if she was an Indian. Hell, he could even afford to marry an Indian, and nobody'd say a word for fear they'd be cut off from the money. It made Ryder laugh to see all the old-time families and rich guys having to tip their hats to a woman they wouldn't hire to scrub their kitchen floors. Which brought him back around to why Jaboy's foreman couldn't just send a crew out here to fix this fence instead of calling him. Sure, it was his fence, the damage on his side, but so what. It was just the boy and him doing all the work, and it cost him three posts and a morning to put this fence back up that was proba-bly knocked down by some wild Indian relatives of hers. His boy knew better than to tear down fencing he'd have to put back up him-self. Least he was that smart. Maybe not smart enough to avoid go-ing to jail someday, but Ryder was going to see to it that there was little time for that nonsense anymore.

He took out a cigarette. "Go ahead—dig the new holes—" He

waved the match out and let it cool before putting it away in his shirt pocket, and cupped the cigarette carefully so the breeze wouldn't catch any sparks.

Hoisting himself up on the tailgate of the truck, his shoulders in the perpetual slump that made his lower back ache, he watched his son strip his shirt off and start with the double-handled posthole digger. Only yellowish stripes from the beating remained on his son's back, and Ryder felt a twinge of regret that he'd had to be so hard on him. There was something stubborn, unrelenting about the boy that reminded him of his father, and when he started hitting him, it was in a way to stop Ty from becoming the renegade his father had been. And his own drinking was part of it too, he had to admit it. But he was cutting down, getting it under control. Only drinking at night now.

His son worked with the fluid efficiency Ryder had taught him, and his tall body was lean and muscular from all the hard work. Ryder could feel his little swollen belly nudging against his chest as he sat there. Doctor said it was from the drinking, but that was a bunch of bullcrap. And if it was, so what? He wasn't running for any beauty contests. He finished his cigarette and carefully ground out the end before putting it in his shirt pocket. Ty's back was glistening with sweat, but he worked silently on the last of the holes. When he put his mind to it, that boy could work better'n any two hired men, Ryder admitted, but he was like a young bull. Had to be watched.

"You check the two-year-old bulls yesterday like I told you?" Ryder slipped off the tailgate with the fence stretcher they called "goldenrod" after the brand name. By using the goldenrod with clamps at both ends and a ratcheting handle in the middle they could tighten the wire, moving one end toward the other along the bar with clicks on the notches.

Ty leaned on the posthole digger to catch his breath, watching his father picking through the barbed strands. "That baldy's dead. Hit by lightning."

Ryder straightened, lifting his shoulders and tucking his chin. "That good one from Bennetts'?"

Ty nodded, keeping his eyes on the old man, whose anger could flare without warning, although he didn't seem so hung over this morning. His father's face darkened and the flesh on either side of the scar across the bridge of his nose stood out.

"Sonofabitch!" Ryder threw the wire down, studied the trampled grass for a moment, and turned to glare at Ty. "You took your own sweet time telling me, boy. You sure it was lightning—not some half-ass deal of yours?"

Ty sighed. "You want me to drag the carcass back?" He wasn't going to let himself be hit again, no matter what, so he straightened his back and held the digger lightly to swing it up in defense. Probably knock the old bastard's head off, but who the hell cared.

"Get your stupid ass over here and help me," Ryder ordered and Ty laid the digger down and came over to stand next to his father.

"We should bury a deadman to hold the fence down here. It's pulling out because of the drop as it runs down the hill," Ty said.

"Too bad you didn't bring along the bull you let die—"

"Too bad you didn't bring along the bottle you crawled out of this morning—"

Ryder swung the goldenrod, but Ty was close enough to grab it and twist it back until his father's wrist crackled ominously and the tool dropped to the ground between them. Ryder's face was doughy as he cradled his right wrist, and he wouldn't look at his son.

He deserved it, Ty thought, but put a hand on his father's arm anyway. "Is it broken?"

The old man elbowed him away.

"Sorry—" Ty mumbled, feeling sick and a little giddy at what he'd done.

"Bullshit." His father's voice was weak as he stumbled over the wire and wove toward the truck.

Ty ran ahead and opened the door for his father, who pushed his son off with his good arm when he tried to help. "I'll take you to Doc's—"

Settled in the cab, Ryder stared out the windshield, the deep creases around his mouth and jaw set. "We're not going anywhere until you finish that fence," he said between gritted teeth. "And you fixed it so you're doing it alone too—now get going!"

"Screw you, old man," Ty muttered as he turned away. He hoped it hurt like hell.

Wrestling the posts into their holes, he used the sledge to drive them down, then set up the box with the extra wire and a board forming an X to add stability. He mounted the wire on the posts, stapling when it had as little give as possible. Although he wore heavy work gloves and was as careful as possible, he still ended up with a couple of cuts from the barbs. The sun was burning his back too, but he didn't dare go to the truck for the shirt he'd taken off. Every once in a while, he'd look out of the corner of his eye through the glare at the silhouette of his father in the truck. He'd tried to warn the old man last time that it was to stop, there'd be no more beatings. Old fart deserved it. But while he felt good standing up to him, his stomach was sick with the possibility that his father would take him to the sheriff as soon as they hit town, and there wouldn't be a thing Ty could do about it. Then that sound of cracking bones came back, it had seemed so loud, like a gun going off almost, and he cringed at the thought that he'd actually hurt his father, who'd looked so wounded holding the broken wrist. He'd fantasized about it plenty, but that wasn't the same. He clicked the last wire up the bar and clamped it to the post. He pushed his hat back and wiped the sweat running down his face on his forearm. Shit, the scrap car wheel he'd brought for the hold-down was still in the truck bed.

"Want me to get you some water from the jug in back?" Ty opened the door and pulled his blue shirt off the seat. As far as he could tell, Ryder hadn't moved and his face was still pale, though now it glistened with oily sweat too. "There's some aspirin in the glove compartment—" It was like talking to one of the hills.

"Have it your way." Ty pushed his arms through the long sleeves but left the shirt unbuttoned, since it was so hot. The burn on his back pulled and stung dryly against the material.

First he wrapped wire around the top of the lower post on the box and fastened the other end to the wheel. Then he stretched it out to find the distance and began to dig a deep hole. It took a while because the thin mat of grass and soil quickly gave way to fine sand that wanted to pour back into the hole, but if he dug deep enough, the flatness and weight would keep the wheel from pulling out, which in turn would keep the fence in place when cattle leaned into it. Carcasses, bones, didn't work as well because they eventually disintegrated. Ty had always wondered if in the old days when the hills were first being settled, in the late 1880s and '90s, they did use actual dead men to hold the fence. Maybe they still did.

Nobody in law enforcement south of the Sandhills was eager to come up here, Ryder told him. His granddad had made his own law out here too and gained a reputation as an evil old man other ranchers avoided. Like father, like son, Ty thought grimly. The people in the hills had a long tradition of settling their own affairs, and the cops had learned the hard way what happened when outsiders tried to interfere. Most of the men here had an instant and stubborn brand of justice they personally enforced. A sheriff who interfered too much wasn't reelected, period. Same with the county prosecutor. He'd always meant to ask his father more about the old days, about the early days when cattlemen were openly ruthless with both Indians and settlers looking to farm. Once his father had told him stories of the lynchings and shootings and mysterious disappearances in the hills as wars raged over fencing of public lands and the Kincaid Act. Where the family had once run cattle over fifty thousand acres, the Bontes now struggled with five thousand. The pictures of his grandfather and great-grandfather showed men with cold, suspicious eyes, straight unsmiling mouths, and plain, somber clothes of working ranchers. The women stared out of the pictures with their pleasures seemingly just as thinned down. Even the children stood formally, rigid with little expectation of life except hard work.

There was the one picture, though, of his great-grandfather Tyler as a boy standing to the left of a table his hand rested on, dressed in a made-over man's dark suit jacket, his brown hair slicked down to the side. On the table stood a very tall crystal candleholder with a white candle, lit. It was an absurd, pretentious picture, obviously taken in some North Platte studio his great-grandmother had dragged the boys to on the annual fall cattle shipping trip. On the other side of the picture, with his arm lying on the table, stood a short blond boy dressed all in white, as if his clothes had been made from his mother's summer dress. In his free hand, the fair boy held a bouquet of wildflowers, and his chin was lifted as if he could see over the top of his taller brother's head to a better future, something he would enjoy. This was his great-uncle Buford, who died in a train wreck on the way home from college in Lincoln years later. His mother's favorite, Ryder said. In the little cemetery in the hills behind their house, his was the white marble marker that glistened out of place against the green in the summer sun and disappeared in the snow of winter. "She hated it here," Ryder said of his grandmother. "Made life miserable for all of us, she lived so danged long. Bonte women never like it here, son. If we didn't need to restock, we'd be plain better off without 'em."

Ty thought of his mother in town and that bastard waiting in the truck as he carefully returned the grass sod, what there was of it, and tamped it down on top of the deadman, trying to restore as much cover as possible so it wouldn't blow away. The old man had been right about women. He hadn't met any girls so far who were much interested in a future of back-breaking work on a lonely hills ranch. They wanted TV and clothes and trips to Omaha or Denver. Girls talked about careers in school these days and looked at him like he was some cowboy trash living in trailers on the edge of town. Even at seventeen, he knew enough not to blame them.

Dumping the posthole digger and goldenrod in the truck bed, he turned back to check the fence again when he heard the engine roar and spun just in time to see the truck bouncing away. He tried to run, but in his boots and with the head start Ryder had, he fell back too quickly, his ankles sore from twisting on the uneven ground.

"Fuck you, you old bastard!" he hollered. Sticking his good hand out the window, his father gave him the finger, holding it high and definite as the truck rolled over the hill.

As the sound whooshed away, Ty bent over, hands on knees, trying to catch his breath and avoid looking at the empty miles ahead of him. The sun had moved so close to the hills, it seemed as he could reach up and sear his fingertips on it, but to the southwest a wall of huge white clouds with blue-black underbellies was tumbling into the hills like boulders breaking loose down a mountainside. The blue-gray mist curtain dropping to the ground beneath indicated rain, and he watched for a moment to see if the clouds themselves were lowering in walls that might suggest tornadoes or straight winds. It'd be an hour or so before it'd hit here, he figured. In the meantime, he needed to get moving. There was a windmill twenty minutes away where he could get some water. He kicked at a clump of soapweed, feeling a moment of satisfaction when several fleshy leaves broke off, oozing sap. He hoped that old bastard was hurting like hell trying to drive with a broken wrist. Grasshoppers scattered out of his way, a few thunking on his boots, depositing a squirt of brown juice before buzzing away. He watched for snakes, but was in such a mood he half-hoped he'd see one he could fight with.

When a shadow fell over him, he stopped and looked up as a horse drew beside him. The rider wasn't much older than him. Dark hair and eyes, deep tan, nice smile. He remembered meeting her once at a horse auction when she'd first married Jaboy. He tipped his hat at her; "M'am."

"I'm Latta Jaboy from the next place over? I came in here to ride this morning and can't seem to find a way out. Guess you fixed the fence—where's—" She looked around for his truck or horse.

"My old man took off with the truck." Ty took off his hat and ran his hand through his hair to loosen the flatness. "The nearest gate's a couple miles down the fence line back there to the south. I'd show you, but I'm on foot—" He put his hat on. She unfastened her canteen from the saddle and offered it to him. He started to shake his head out of pride, but then nodded. "Thank you, ma'am."

"You're Ty Bonte, aren't you?"

He nodded, tipped the canteen, and drank. The water was cold, which meant she'd probably come from the windmill he was headed for. He took another little sip, not wanting to be rude and empty it. Handing it back, he tipped his head toward the thunderheads behind them. "Storm's coming."

When she shaded her eyes with her hand and looked west, the sunlight caught on her gold wedding band. "That's why I have to get home—I hate lightning—" She looked around again, a little like a calf trapped in the branding pen.

"You shouldn't be caught out here either. Why don't you climb up behind me and we can go back to your place and wait the storm out there. Then I can call one of my men to come for my horse and me. Okay?"

Ty thought about having this woman in their wreck of a house and wanted to say no, but she was right about the storm. Sticking his foot in the stirrup, he mounted the saddle behind her, careful not to push too hard against the cantle. The gelding was a stout bay who sank his hindquarters under the extra weight at first, but gradually got down to business as the wind picked up the cooler edge of the approaching front.

"Hang on," Latta said and nudged the horse into a lope.

Ty had to grab her waist to keep from knocking into the cantle as they sprang over soapweed and bounced along the uneven ground. With his big hands around her and pressed close, he smelled a sweet perfume he couldn't describe except as something his mother and sister put in their bathwater.

He thought of his father's face when he walked in and saw Latta Jaboy in his kitchen, but then he realized that Ryder wouldn't be back for hours, maybe the whole night. His father would use the trip to town as an excuse to drink, and maybe he'd even go visit his wife. Not that she'd want to see him.

By the time they'd put the horse in a stall and tossed it some hay, the storm was breaking overhead and they had to run to the house. Inside on the porch, they laughed and wiped the rain off their faces with a towel that Ty suddenly saw was streaked with weeks of dirt. They went to the kitchen, where he made her tea and listened to her talk about the places she and her husband had traveled to in the past three years. There was a tint of sadness about her eyes, he noticed, and in her voice something that wasn't being said behind her stories. He didn't dare ask questions though, as awkward as he was even trying to make her a cup of tea with a teabag he didn't know what to do with once he'd dunked it several times. Finally, they were seated at the table watching the storm lash the windows with rain as hard as BB's.

"It's awfully quiet here without your brother, I bet," she said, looking around at the grease-spattered wall over the stove. "Must be lonely with just you and your father—"

He got up and retrieved a beer from the fridge, popped it open, and took a slug before he sat down again. She eyed him like maybe he was pushing the line here and he looked away.

"Ronnie, wasn't it? I remember him, such a sweet, funny little boy."

He wanted to tell her everything, let it pour out from where it sat choked at the top of his throat. In a minute, he promised, in just a minute he'd tell her how at first he was afraid of the baby, so tiny and helpless like a new puppy. Then he'd gotten brave enough to hold him, to smell his milky skin, and to see his blood beating against the membrane over the middle of his skull. How it took his breath away, knowing that the core of his brother's life was only a piece of skin away from him. From that moment on, Ronnie had become his to raise and protect and teach. They'd shared baths, food, sleep, horses, and the hills they both loved, until their mother took her youngest away to town. It was then that Ty realized Ronnie was the first person he'd ever felt loved him and he remembered the phone calls with Ronnie's small lost voice on the other end that winter, wanting to come home, missing his brother, reciting the bad dreams that plagued his sleep without his big brother to protect him. Then spring and summer came and they were together again, but it was the last time. If Ty had only known—that thought crowded itself up against all the other images of Ronnie, which were so numerous they were like single blades of grass seen from afar, how to take one and separate it from the others? So Ty sat there in the kitchen that afternoon darkened with rain, feeling all the potential of those minutes and watching them slip away into silence.

"You miss him, don't you?" she asked in a soft voice.

Ty nodded and drank. "There was this one time, the year before—" He choked and drank again, waiting for the alcohol to cool his head. "Summer he was seven and I was out with the dogs; we had dogs then, tending some cattle and hunting rabbit for supper. I came on a big mama raccoon that'd just been killed. Got wrapped in some old barbed wire and junk we were using to fill the big wash on the south end. Anyway, I cut off her tail for my brother, then I heard this mewling and turned her over. There was a baby, with these runny eyes looking sad as all get-out. So I packed it home and gave it to him. Wasn't nothing but a ball of fur." He stopped and drank and looked out the window, remembering Ronnie's expression when Ty climbed off his horse and handed him the baby raccoon.

"I bet your brother loved it," Latta said in the voice that invited him to share more. He looked at her face, so open, the eyes without any judgment at all, and felt the words starting to pour out of him. He told her how Ronnie raised the raccoon, keeping it in the old machine shed that was half falling down.

"Everything went along fine and that raccoon grew like a weed. Before long it was almost full grown and would follow Ronnie around like a dog, though we had to be careful to pen the dogs up when he took it out. Then in August Dad decided to take Ronnie up to see Mount Rushmore, the Badlands, Wall Drug, you know— Ronnie had been begging for this trip for two years and it was his birthday present. Surprised the heck out of me, you know—Ryder hates to act like a tourist.

"I had to stay home and mind the place, of course. I was looking forward to the time alone as much as Ronnie was to his trip, I guess." Ty tilted the empty beer bottle, stared at it, then got up and re-trieved a fresh one. He could guarantee his father wasn't coming back tonight. Just had to remember to do chores before he fell asleep. That's what had happened that time with the raccoon. Ty had gotten into his father's liquor and passed out, and the raccoon had taken things into its own hands when it got hungry and thirsty enough.

"So what happened?" Latta's eyes followed the bottle to his lips and back.

"Well, the raccoon got out somehow and tore up the vegetable garden pretty good. Had these long nails and paws that it used like hands, you know. Demolished Ryder's tomato patch. Looked like some kind of war out there, red splashed all over the place and the vines torn apart. You expected to find bodies in a mess like that. The old man was pretty damn unhappy about it too." Ty closed his eyes and drained half the beer to keep away the image of that late-night whipping in the barn, after Ronnie had gone to sleep. That was important, both of them knew, to keep Ronnie from waking up, so Ty had used the towel Ryder handed him to stuff in his mouth so he wouldn't cry out when the strap worked its way up the back of his legs.

"The next morning, Ronnie and I took the raccoon out to the wash and left it. It was time, I told him. But he snuck food out there for a month, until the raccoon stopped taking it. That's the kind of kid he was."

"Sounds like you were a good brother, Ty." Latta smiled.

"Think so?" Ty finished the beer, knowing just what kind of brother he was that day he let Ryder put the kid on the tractor and send him out to cut the hay meadow. He looked out the window to the west where the sky was beginning to lighten. "Rain's breaking up."

∞ Chapter Three

When Ty knocked on the door of her little house in town, his mother greeted him with a half-hearted attempt at a hug that made him freeze. She hadn't touched him in years. Then she made him wait on the little concrete porch while she got the black square purse and white sweater she wore draped over her shoulders and held together with two plated gold bumblebees tethered at either end of a small gold chain. He looked at his boots still caked with mud and manure, and reached down to brush the dust off his good jeans, the ones without even a hint of a hole. She'd called him to come into town to shop for some school clothes and he'd put on a clean white shirt he'd inherited from Ryder. The sleeves were too short, so he had to keep them rolled up, and he couldn't stretch his shoulders for fear he'd rip the arms out, but it was a nice shirt, western cut with pearl gray snaps. And he had on his good trophy buckle with the tooled leather belt he'd won. He'd washed and shaved and dressed carefully, wanting to please his mother, who so rarely wanted to see him.

He looked up and down the four blocks of her street. The small houses sat so close together it made him nervous. He could hear the man next door sneezing in his living room through the open screen windows. The cattle trucks shifting gears up on Highway 20, which crossed the top of the Sandhills from Iowa to Wyoming, competed with the sound of the sparrows cheeping in the maple tree. Everywhere he looked, the houses with their TV antennas and chimneys blocked out the blue blanket of sky overhead. Even the wind had to weave around all this obstruction to get anyplace. Too much shelter, if there was such a thing. Maybe people needed too much for themselves.

"Ready?" His mother came out breathlessly, shutting the door behind her as if she'd been waiting for him. When he started for the truck, she said, "No, let's walk. I have something to show you," and put her arm through his. He felt stiff and proud walking with his mother this way, as if she finally acknowledged him as a man she could trust. He even listened to her talk about the town and the people she knew, and tried to agree with her when she seemed to need it. His mother was a tall, thin woman who looked stronger than she actually was. How his father ever married this town girl, convinced her to move out to the ranch when she'd never sat on a horse, Ty would never understand. Even her hands, the long fingers ending in carefully shaped nails covered with clear polish, were uncallused, unspotted, and as youthful as a woman's half her age.

"Here." She steered right and they walked three blocks east to the edge of town where the little cemetery sat wrapped by a short wrought iron fence. The grounds were newly mowed and clipped in contrast to the road shoulder overgrown with tall grass and black-eyed Susans. Ty slowed, not wanting any part of this, but his mother pressed forward, and he couldn't stop without forcing her to drop his arm.

She led him through the gate and down a narrow concrete walk to the middle of the cemetery and wove among several groups of stones before coming to a stop. "Here it is," she announced and pulled her arm free. "My family, Ty—"

He followed the stones from left to right, reading the names of her grandparents and parents, sister and brother, then— "Ronnie Bonte? But he's—"

"I know, Ty, but I need him closer by. I want you to help me convince Ryder to move him. Please?" His mother turned her gray, tear-filled eyes on him, but couldn't bring herself to clasp his arm again, he noticed. He wasn't bitter that it was all about Ronnie, he'd always known that, but he wasn't going to let her steal his brother away from the ranch he had loved.

When Ty remained silent, his mother collapsed suddenly to her knees in front of the pink marble headstone. "Pray with me, son." He felt so awkward standing there, he had to kneel and bow his head while she prayed long and hard for the Bonte men and especially for the return of Ronnie's soul to his heavenly home, with the implication that it was here in town rather than that godforsaken ranch. This new religious fervor startled Ty, but he kept his mouth shut and made his own silent little prayer to Ronnie, that he was happy and knew how much his brother had loved him. And that he'd stay at the ranch, where he belonged.

On the way back downtown, his mother pleaded her case for moving the body and tried to convince Ty to seek the solace of the Lord. She took him to her plain little church on Main Street, with the elementary school in the basement run by a pastor who looked about Ty's age. The difference was that his skin was pale white and he wore horn-rimmed glasses he kept pushing up on his nose. Shaking hands made Ty aware of how rough and dry his were in the soft, moist clasp of the preacher's. When the man returned to teaching, his mother seemed to brighten, her eyes lighting up as they used to with Ronnie, and Ty felt a flush of jealousy that made him start thinking of a reason to get away. The kids being schooled in the dim gray-walled basement fidgeted in their small chairs and watched him with open-eyed curiosity. They reminded him a little of the men he saw in jail that time he'd gotten locked up. Looking around at the carefully crayoned pictures from Bible stories, he thought how lucky he was to have missed this phase of his mother's life. But when he thought about it, what else was there for a woman her age in a small Sandhills town.

"I have to get going," he whispered to her.

She looked at him as if he were a stranger she'd bumped grocery carts with at the store, and nodded.

"Did you want to come with me—shopping?" He sounded like he was begging for something and it embarrassed him.

"I have too much to do here—" She spread her arms out to the nine children scooting their chairs into a circle. "But wait—" She opened her pocketbook, fumbled for a moment, and pulled out a crisp, fresh twenty-dollar bill. "This is for your clothes."

There was a moment when the bill wavered there between them before he could bring himself to take it. "Thanks." He turned before she could see the tears in his eyes and crushed the bill in his hand. This is what it feels like to get hit by lightning, the voice in his head kept repeating. He took the basement stairs two at a time and burst into the sunlight of the street. The shock waves from lightning can be heard fifteen miles away, he'd read in one of Ronnie's books after that afternoon with Mrs. Jaboy, and he wondered if people across town were listening to the strange sound of what had just happened here with his mother. He imagined the arborescent pattern on his chest, down his body. She had no idea, absolutely no idea who or what he was. She called and it was like a tree getting hit, the sap vaporizing, his skin like bark blown outwards—instant shrapnel. The spark in clouds five miles up couldn't be seen though; no way to prepare. When it struck the ground, it made paths that could melt and solidify sand into glass, that's what he felt in his arms and legs, glass so fragile he might break if he didn't get someplace safe.

"Mr. Bonte, how many times are we going to go through this?" The man at the front of the room was tapping the blackboard with his pointer, making dark little commas in the list of dates and places from early Territorial history. The teacher was right. It was the second time Ty had tried to take this course, and he was already failing again. His face burning, he looked down at the history book open to page 35, the last thing he remembered Mr. Lathers saying. He must've nodded out. He glanced over at Harney, who was giving him the thumbs up. Harney had spent half of last year out in Denver with his uncle after he got in another batch of trouble, and so he was taking the same course.

"Do you have anything to say for yourself, Mr. Bonte?" Mr. Lathers slapped the pointer on the wooden desk with a loud bang that made everyone in the room jump.

Ty shook his head. Couldn't very well tell the whole class about being up all night driving his father up to Rapid City to dry out and turning around and driving the rest of the night to make it to school this morning. Yesterday morning Ty had called his mother to get her to send the doctor out so they could argue Ryder into the truck together. She'd sounded the same as ever, although now there was religion where bitterness used to sit out front alone, which gave a slightly different twist to the conversation. He'd managed to stall her again on moving Ronnie, with the idea that it might be too upsetting for Ryder when he got home. She certainly didn't want the responsibility of sending her husband into another spiral of drinking, she'd vowed.

All the way up to Rapid City, Ryder had slept and drunk whiskey from a bottle he kept on the seat next to him, and generally stayed in a pretty good frame of mind until they pulled up to the front of the tan stone building, when he started weeping and begging Ty not to leave him. "I know you hate me, son, but don't—" Then he'd tried to grab the keys from the ignition and Ty had honked the horn three times on the prearranged signal and two attendants came to get his father. As they dragged him out of the truck, his whiskey bottle fell out and smashed on the pavement. The old man was cursing them all roundly for that as he was led up the walk into the building. Ty waited until his father was safely gone before he got out, took the suitcase out of the back, and followed. He hoped they kept Ryder as long as possible. They could both use the break.

This was his Nebraska history, but he doubted the teacher wanted to hear any of it.

"The Dawes Act, who was Dawes?" Mr. Lathers began. "U.S. Senator Henry Dawes of Massachusetts helped reshape our government's policy toward Indians with the Dawes Act of 1887. The government had originally created the Great Sioux Reservation, as it was called, then reduced it from 21,593,138 acres to 12,845,521 acres, selling the 8.7 million surplus at a dollar fifty an acre on the

open market with the proceeds to go toward Indian education. Giving the Sioux all that land originally had not worked to their benefit,
or that of the general public either. Senator Dawes noted that
among American Indians, 'there is no selfishness, which is at the bottom of civilization.' Self-interest, class, is at the heart of all altruism,
it is the soul of democracy and capitalism."

Mr. Lathers tapped his pointer on the desk and glared at his students as if they were personally going to bring on the end of civilization as soon as class let out. "Therefore, the Dawes Act was
designed to cut the size of the one large reservation in South
Dakota, breaking it up into six smaller ones and creating an allotment system that would provide each Indian family a privately
owned, 160-acre plot. Free land. But they didn't know what to do
with it, couldn't be taught to farm or ranch—so in 1891 Congress
amended the Dawes Act and allowed Indians to lease the land out.
How many of you have family or know people who ranch up there?"

Ty looked out the tall windows at the cloud-scudded deep blue
fall sky. The Indians got screwed out of their land, why not just
come out and say it. Who gave a shit about the name of the rich
fucker who pulled the plug. He was bored by all the games they
played here. Outside the air was cool and hard bright. A good afternoon to hunt some pheasants or bag a deer if chores didn't take too
long. Or maybe he could do half the chores, then hunt, then finish
the rest. He needed to shoe two horses, but that could wait until the
weekend, and change the oil in Ryder's truck—it'd run a little rough
on the return trip last night, and start thinking about moving the
herd down closer to the house for winter pasture. Shut down the
windmills in the outlying pastures, make sure the antifreeze was
okay in both trucks. Pull the plow attachment out and get it ready in
case they got an early snow. Take the screens down and put the
storm windows up. Stack hay bales around the foundation of
the house for warmth. Put plastic sheeting over the screens on the
porch. Don't have to worry that the doghouses have fresh hay this
year. No dogs. Ryder shot them right after Ronnie died. Check the
stalls in the barn for the horses they needed close. Put the water

heaters in the stock tanks. Check the auxiliary electrical pump and oil stove in the basement. He was nodding out again with his running list when he heard Harney's voice.

"Well, my great-grandfather was at Fort Robinson January something—1879 or '80, I forget—when Dull Knife and his band shot up the post and escaped, trying to make it to Red Cloud's camp. We've still got a blanket, a pair of moccasins, and a pipe from the ones my granddad shot." Ty looked over at Harney, whose face was glowing with pride. "The Indians ate their moccasins when they got hungry—"

The girls in the room were rolling their eyes, and some of the boys were grinning, but others were looking out the same windows as Ty. He was on the verge of walking out. He just had too much work waiting for him to sit around here and listen to Harney's bullshit. Indians were his favorite subject, and even Mr. Lathers looked pretty tired of it. The bell rang though, and instead of going on to the next class in biology, which Ty had also not studied for in over a week, he walked straight down the hall and pushed through the double glass doors to the parking lot.

"Hey, wait up, man—" Harney fell in beside him. "Where you going?"

"Home—"

"No, come on, let's go hunting—I got some good smoke and a bottle of my old man's twelve-year-old scotch."

"Got chores." Reaching his truck, Ty pulled the door open and threw his books across the seat. The stack of bills he'd somehow convinced Ryder to sign checks for yesterday before they left sat on the dash ready to be mailed. He'd have to remember to go to the post office and pick up stamps.

"Man, you are getting to be a real asshole, Ty—" Harney gave his shoulder a shove and Ty sprang around and grabbed his shirt in his two fists and shoved him against the truck so hard his head banged back against the glass.

"Don't you ever put your hands on me," Ty hissed.

"Okay, calm down, enough—I was only kidding." Harney shook his plaid shirt loose and brushed at the sleeves. "See what I mean?

You're wound tighter than a cheap watch. You could use some R and R, don't you think?" Harney's eyes glittered like shards of smoky blue glass as he reached into his shirt pocket and pulled out a couple of joints. "Thai sticks—dynamite stuff."

Since they both had their rifles and ammunition in their trucks, they went up north of town into the hilly breaks of the Niobrara River to hunt turkeys and anything else they could scare up. Climbing up and down the steep hills, they took pulls from the whiskey to bring their heads back in line after the dope. Harney was shooting at NO HUNT-ING and PRIVATE PROPERTY signs, fence posts, metal gates, and any bird or squirrel that moved in the cedar and oak trees around them. Ty tried to walk behind him as quietly as possible, which was hard, since his boots kept catching in the bunchgrass and downed tree limbs. Twice he fell to his hands and knees and both times rechecked that the safety was on the gun. The third time his toe caught in a gopher hole and he dropped the gun altogether. When he stood up, his ankle hurt like a bastard and he half wished the gun would go off. Harney threw his rifle up and shot at a pair of squirrels playing overhead, missing them but showering the boys with bark.

"Christ almighty! How the hell are we going to find any game when you're staging world war three with the fucking signposts? I can guarantee every turkey within fifty miles has taken cover, and we probably won't see another deer until summer." Ty threw the empty bottle down. "Fuck it, I'm going home."

Harney leaned on his gun laughing. "Wondered how long it would take to get you mad again. Relax, I know where we can find something worth our time and trouble. Come on—"

"Shoulda known you weren't serious when you left your dog at home," Ty muttered. Harney loved that yellow Lab so much, it usu-ally spent the day in his truck outside school waiting for him like a faithful girlfriend. At lunchtime Harney would take it down the street for a hamburger or share the school offerings if they were de-cent. He always appeared at 1:00 classes grinning and brushing the yellow hairs off his shirt and pants. Ty liked Harney with his dog, but the girls their age thought it was just weird. In fact they thought both boys were strange, and that was another thing they had in common.

At the bottom of the next hill, they found three rustic log cabins sitting along a small creek that fed into the river a quarter of a mile away. Without saying a word, Harney lifted his rifle and began firing at the three windows facing them. Glass popped and splattered out in slow motion, drifting like metallic snow to the ground.

Ty closed his eyes and shook the explosion from his head. "No, man—" Ty let his rifle slide down. "This is baby shit." He didn't want to admit that he was probably too stoned to hit anything.

Harney stopped firing but kept the gun nestled against his shoulder. "Know who owns these?"

Ty shook his head, which felt sloshy and heavy like an overripe watermelon.

"Fucking county prosecutor, that judge, and some other asshole, I can't remember who—but they're all buddies." He aimed for the upper part of the window he'd shot, where the glass was divided into four parts and shattered each in sequence. "I figure they owe us."

Ty thought about last summer with Ryder, working off that fine, lifted his rifle, sighted in, and squeezed the trigger. The wood siding made a soft plunk. He closed his eyes tight, opened them, and tried again. This time the window's upper frame exploded with slivers and the window cracked.

Harney grinned at him and squeezed off a quick round, making the glass pop apart. Ty nestled the rifle against his shoulder and fired twice, and this time a window came apart as if a fist had been shoved through it.

"All right!" Harney crowed. "Let's go inside."

They were on the front porch when they heard the rumble of a truck bouncing down the road across the creek. Running evasively from tree to tree, the boys turned and sprinted into the cover of trees, zigzagging clumsily up the hill. Ty couldn't remember if he'd clicked on the safety, but didn't dare stop to check. Everytime he stumbled, he tried to keep the gun ahead of him and Harney to the right in case it went off. "Stupid, dumbass behavior," his father's voice chanted in time with the spinning blur of trees and rocks. Ty's lungs roared for air by the time they topped the last hill on their hands and knees and scurried to the road. Sinking down beside his truck, Ty checked the gun—bullet in the chamber, safety off. He was damn lucky. His head pounded against the thud of his heart, and whiskey-laced bile rose up his throat. He swallowed and fixed his eyes on a fence post, not daring to close them.

"Man," Harney panted. "That was close." He shucked the last shell out of his rifle and put it in his pocket. "Too bad we didn't have time to pick up the empty shells."

"Think they saw us?" It was dawning on Ty that with Ryder in detox and his mother in religion, he would rot in jail if they got caught.

"No, relax. We were fucking deer. Never ran so fast in my life— you either, I bet—let's go crack some brew at my place and catch some more action after dark, okay? I have to check on my dog."

Ty looked up at the sun settling against the western edge of the hori-zon and thought of the drive and chores ahead of him. "Can't, I'm really late now."

He waved as he climbed into the truck, careful to lay the gun on the floor where it wouldn't draw attention. He'd have to clean it and put it in the rack at home, and start carrying Ryder's good rifle in the truck in case they tried to track down the weapons. By the time he was pulling up in front of his house, he had already given into the nagging uncertainty at the back of his mind. Even Ryder would be right this time: A man didn't go blowing out windows in revenge— that was kid stuff.

A week later Ty was sitting in the back of the history classroom watching the sun that had shone bright enough in the morning that he'd left his jeans jacket at home and the girls had even come to school in short skirts and bare legs like it was still August. By noon the sun had gradually disappeared, and just after lunch, the wind had shifted. Now the sky scummed gray, and grew darker and darker un-til he could feel the cold settling into the classroom as the first sprin-

kles of snow began to fall. Ty knew about these early Sandhills bliz-
zards and immediately got up and walked out of class while Mr.
Lathers and the other students silently watched.

At the ranch he managed to corral some of the horses and throw
a heater into their stock tank. He drove the two tractors into the
three-sided shed so he wouldn't have to dig them out too. Then he
started to drive the truck up to shut the fences to the west so the cattle wouldn't drift too far for help, but he had to quit when the whiteout came. He barely made it back to the house. The storm blew for
two days. The phone went out, then the electricity, so he had to
turn on the auxiliary pump in the basement. As soon as the wind
started howling and it grew so dark it was as if the sun had been
swallowed by the storm, he wished they still had the dogs so he
could let them into the house for company. He wasn't in charge of
anything now and had to force himself to read and sleep so he
wouldn't be tempted to go out there and do something stupid. The
night of the second day, he stuffed tissue in his ears, curled up in Ryder's chair, and pulled a blanket over his head to shut out the terrible
noise of the house battling the wind outside. He squeezed his eyes
so tight he saw pinprick explosions of yellow and red light that hurt,
and then he cried.

When the storm finally stopped toward dawn of the third day, he
woke up in his father's chair, frightened by the sudden silence. He
prayed he hadn't lost any cattle as he quickly dressed and prepared
coffee. Then the real work of digging out began.

After three hours of plowing paths to the barns, pastures, and
stack yard, he went back inside to warm up, change into dry clothes,
and grab a quick sandwich. Lucky he had kept a couple of horses in
the barn, although they'd been without water and grain during the
storm.

The sun shone like bright ice on his face as the horse lurched
through the fresh snow, stumbling belly deep into drifts, breath
roaring, and falling to its knees a few times. He didn't dare get off
for fear he'd wear himself out too, and they'd never reach the cattle
stranded in the far pastures.

It was late afternoon when he found the main herd packed tight against the northeast fence line. Blinking out of snow-crusted faces, they began to grunt and low and shove toward him. As soon as he herded the leaders onto the narrow trail he'd broken, the other cattle strung out behind with little urging and headed toward the ranch.

When they were well started, Ty rode back to the lumps remaining behind. One calf had been strangled in the fence, its tongue hanging in a pink icy petal, while its legs had become tangled. The streams of blood had frozen in long ribbons unspooling into the snow. An old, barren cow they meant to cull anyway had been crushed into the corner, her head twisted up, black eyes frozen open in a sheath of ice, lips rimed white against the worn yellow teeth. While she was struggling between the crush of bodies and the barbed wire, her belly had caught and ripped. The long, bloody intestine ropes and spilling stomachs draped the wire and pooled on the other side of the fence.

Those were the worst. The others had simply suffocated or frozen. Dismounting to check the bodies, he found two still barely alive, their eyes dull and glazed, so weakened they wouldn't make it back before nightfall. Lying there, they'd freeze before dawn. He took his rifle off the saddle and shot them. The bullets thunking into their heads produced a strange silence that he realized was the last whisper of disappearing life.

When he drove into town four days later to see about getting his phone service restored, he somehow felt older than the kids he saw walking toward the high school. Their families made the world safe for them in a way he would never experience, and that safety kept them younger and freer than he would ever be again. He had left the final remnants of childhood in his father's chair the last night of the storm.

He never returned to school. When the authorities contacted his mother, they arranged for Ty to study at home for his GED. Neither his mother nor he told them about his father. Instead, they all agreed that Ty was incorrigible. Chronic truancy. Although nobody expected him to finish, the program was so easy that Ty was done by the time Ryder was released from detox in early December. His mother called, surprised, when his diploma arrived in the mail and told him he could get it when he came in on the weekend to help her string lights and put up the Christmas tree. He cringed at the thought of the gifts she'd have waiting for him to take home.

For many years his mother had insisted he come in from the ranch the day after Thanksgiving and spend a whole day stringing lights along the roof line, down to the porch railing and over to the big maple. When Ronnie was alive, it was even fun, but usually it was a tedious job, sorting the strings of lights and testing each bulb, as his mother insisted. This year she was adding a big blue star to the front of the house and Ty made nine different nail holes in the wood trim of the roof line before she was satisfied with its position. If he were a decent son, he'd go get the wood filler and fix the holes before they invited rot, but since she couldn't see them and he hated Christmas as a general rule, he left them. When the star was hung, he felt vaguely satisfied by the black dots peppered around the point. Then his mother plugged it in without warning him; the sudden explosion of light almost startled him off the ladder. Maybe she knew what he'd done up there, he thought.

Inside, he was responsible for putting the tree up and stringing the lights, but she never wanted him to hang the ornaments. That was her job, hers and his sister, Charla, and Ronnie's when he was alive. Again, Ty didn't mind. She had always made it clear that the ornaments came from her family and were a part of her, not the Bontes. Even before she left the ranch, Ty couldn't remember Ryder touching a single one. The last Christmas they'd spent together though, he remembered the fight between his parents that ended with his mother standing at her beloved tree, with tears streaming down her face, pulling beautiful antique glass balls off the tree one by one and smashing them on the floor until Ryder grabbed her hands.

When he'd finished stringing the lights and she'd approved the tree, his mother took him into the dining room, where they were to sit and have a cup of Christmas tea and some cookies. He'd have to stop at the café and grab a burger before the drive home. He could never understand why his mother imagined he wouldn't need a real lunch after a morning's work, but looking at her thin arms with the blue veins lying so close to the surface it seemed like her skin was transparent, he knew she hardly ate herself. One of the things she'd held against the Bonte men, Ryder told him, was that they ate so much. She hated cooking.

While he drank the weak tea and wolfed as many as he dared of the tiny cookies shaped like wreaths and trees and bells colored green and red and coated with stale sprinkles, his mother left to get the presents she'd be sending to the ranch. The cookies themselves were tasteless, but he was too hungry to care. If she'd hurry, he might even have time to see what they had at the book exchange. He considered trying to convince the librarian that he'd turned over a new leaf so he could get a card, but remembered the way she'd pronounced the "lifetime ban," like he was an Olympic athlete caught in a drug scandal. It was only a goddamn box. So the side got a little dented, and they had to spend the money to cement its legs in place so nobody else would tip it over. They should've done that to start with—at least until he and Harney left town. He thought of the cabins they'd shot up. Nothing said about that, thank God.

He looked around his mother's prissy dining room. Too much pink and gray and lace. The wood floors were too shiny, everything was too shiny. He shuffled his stockinged feet under the chair. She never allowed his boots in the house. Hell, she barely allowed *him* inside. Sometimes he could understand how his parents drove each other nuts. Ryder out there stewing in his own personal brew of anger and hatred. There had been only that brief moment when Ronnie was born that the family flickered on and seemed to burn steady like the flame in a good kerosene lamp. Throughout his short life, his brother had had that effect on them—a brightening even his sister had experienced, as distant from the Bonte men's world as she always was—so that when the light was eclipsed, the darkness they had all fallen into was deeper and more terrible than anyone could have imagined.

"Here's your certificate, son." His mother started to lay the GED paper on the table but noticed the crumbs surrounding his plate, which she had to clean up first. Sweeping them off with the side of her hand into his plate, she disappeared into the kitchen. So much for more cookies, his stomach growled unhappily.

"All right now," she said as she reappeared. "I've put two shopping bags by the door with some things for you." She handed him the manila envelope with his diploma and continued standing, her signal that it was time for him to leave.

"I have some people from church coming over this evening to decorate the tree," she said as he stomped into his boots, cold from sitting on the porch. She handed him the bags and waved him off like he was collecting trash for the county dump outside town.

As soon as he was safely down the block and around the corner, he stopped the truck and went through the other part of their holi-day ritual: ripping open the paper and ribbons to sort the presents. He'd learned from experience that there was no point in bringing all that crap out to the ranch. There were two new shirts for him. One in a bright neon yellow and blue check he wouldn't wear to clean the septic tank, the other a conservative blue flannel he could use. Three pairs of boot socks he needed, some underwear, a pair of jeans, a cheap leather vest with fringe they must have had on the bargain rack at the western store for a year, a thermal underwear top that was a size too small, a fiber-filled vest he could use, and a pair of wool-lined work gloves. There was the usual box of candy canes for a tree she imagined they put up, the box of cookies she figured no family could go through the holidays without, and finally the big box he hesitated to open because it would contain a Pendleton wool bathrobe or shirt for his father. He put it on the floor of the passen-ger's side and drove to the poor box of her Evangelical Church two blocks away.

He dropped the candy canes down the chute and heard them land with a thunk that meant they were probably broken. Well, what did people expect? He held the checked shirt up, shook his head, and threw it in, followed by the fringed vest and the thermal underwear top. With every item he tossed into the poor box, he found himself getting more and more pissed. Where were those damn cookies? He flung the empty boxes and paper around the truck until the box of cookies surfaced. When he grabbed the flimsy shirt box they were in, it bent open and spilled a couple of cookies onto the seat.

"Goddamn you!" He beat the box on the hood of the truck until it flew apart, sending pieces of cookie showering across the truck and into his face. He didn't stop until the box was mangled flat and the cookies ground into crumbs. Brushing himself off, he looked around the little parking lot to see if he'd been noticed. It was a cold day though, and almost nobody was on the streets walking or driving. The sun shone weakly in the pale sky, warming nothing.

Now he did something he'd never done before. He collected all the empty boxes and wrappings and pushed them into the poor box too. Before he could stop himself, he filled his arms with the clothes he had planned to keep and dropped them down the chute also. Everything except his father's present, which sat alone on the floor in its cheap red and gold poinsettia paper with the extra creases that said she'd recycled it from last year. Every year he had to make the decision about his father's present. If he took it home, his father would fly into a rage, threatening to go to town and make her take it back. A few days later, Ty would find the shirt or robe out in the barns or machine sheds, already ripped and ruined from being used as a rag. Almost always he'd open his father's box, making sure it contained the usual, and drop it off too.

The longer he stood there staring at the box, his pulse pounding in his ears and throat from his fury a few minutes before, the tireder he grew with his whole life. Things had worked fine while Ryder was gone, but now that he was back, they'd gone to hell again, and Ty didn't even have school as an escape every day. He was feeling ugly about the world in general. He nodded— "Okay." He was taking the box home, unopened.

Ty got home too late for chores, but made the macaroni and cheese they'd have for supper when the old man came in. He put the box in the middle of the kitchen table, while he drank a beer from a stash he kept in his truck. Usually he didn't drink in front of the old man when he was fresh from detox, but Ty felt perverse tonight. Perverse and sick of the game.

"You get a real kick out of this shit, don't you?" was all his father said, picking up the box and throwing it outside in the snow.

II

Carrying the Weight
of Dreams
(August 1997)

∽ Chapter Four

"That gray with the bow might work for ya." Danny Bladstrom sucked his teeth again and squinted at the seventeen-hand gelding peering suspiciously from the back of his stall. "Lay him up a few months, he'll be good as new. Just a little bow he popped last Sunday in that fifteen-hundred-dollar claiming race, wouldn't you know. He wasn't climbing no ladder to the stars anyway, so—easy keeper, handles good. Just ain't much of a racehorse. Too slow. My grandson can outrun him, and he's only been walking a year." Danny rubbed the small of his back and stretched until there was a popping noise, then lifted his cap and pushed his short blond hair off his forehead, burned a permanent eraser pink like the rest of his face. "Got a big stride the way you like." He glanced sideways at the tall lean man beside him.

Ty was tired after a week on the road looking for resale horses in backyards, remote farms, auctions, and now here at the track outside Minneapolis. Lucky it was Monday, the one day of the week they didn't have races. Least he didn't have to negotiate crowds and cars. Canterbury Downs, what genius came up with that name for a track in Minnesota? He sighed and Danny shook his head, thinking he'd lost the sale.

Leaning against the metal stall post though, Ty watched the horse watching him. Usually he got a feeling from an animal, something that said yes or no, sometimes even an image of a weakness or problem. This one said discouragement. Ty grimaced and folded his arms. He had enough problems in his barn right now, and judging by the size of that bowed tendon, this one would need to be laid up the rest of the summer and maybe into the fall before he could even be ridden to find out if he was good for anything. But racetrack rejects were his weakness. The track, with so many hopeless cases and the killers a quick phone call away, always broke his heart. Who knew what a horse might turn into once it left the track and started living a normal horse life. Some became decent, useful citizens, while others had minds or bodies too destroyed by the harsh early training and racing and never made it back.

Danny sucked again and added a little click in his cheek. "All right, you take the bay mare and the brown horse, I'll throw this one in. He's eating me outta house and home anyways."

Danny had made a good deal, getting rid of an extra mouth, but he also knew if anyone would give the horse a fair chance, the kid would. He'd known Ty for over twenty years and still thought of him as that beaten-down kid who drove an old truck into the stable area at the track in Omaha, looking for work one spring day. He'd been a quiet kid then too, with a load of something on his shoulders he took out on the work of cleaning stalls, hot walking, and grooming. He never said anything about family or where he was from, but he carried a pistol in his jacket for three months. Danny had guessed the kid was from western Nebraska by the license plates and the Sandhills silence most of those cowboys carried. Danny bought stock from a few breeders and trained for a couple more out there. He wasn't getting rich, but he wasn't starving and the boy had seemed to understand that from the git go. Understood stock too, though racing was new to him then. He'd grown into a wide-shouldered, narrow-hipped man who still wore a lot of silence, though the hurt was buried too deep to see anymore. Looking at the serious face, a person might miss it if he hadn't witnessed the bad sleep and hollow eyes of the boy.

"You got your rig here?" The two men walked down the line of stalls so Ty could get another look at the bay mare and the brown gelding. The mare had never broken her maiden, grew up too late, but she'd do something now she hit her growth spurt. The gelding, well, he belonged to his oldest client, the widow of an old Lutheran farmer down by Mankato who ran a home-raised horse every year, no matter how poorly it did. At the end of the summer season, she always ordered them sold and sent him another one in the spring. The brown was too quiet. Just plain mellow, as were most of her horses. She babied them, he complained, took the fire out of them.

The two men stepped outside into the shade of the lone maple tree. The midmorning sun had heated the asphalt and sent waves shimmering off the roofs of the long shed rows. They squatted in the shade, resting on the heels of their boots. Ty lifted his straw cowboy hat, rubbed the sweat off his forehead with his arm, and re-settled it. Danny pulled a bag of tobacco out and stuffed his cheek with a thick plug. Ty smiled in that lopsided way of his that made his weathered face echo a boy from someplace a long time ago. "Chewing now?" he asked.

"Wife made me give up the cigarettes. Safer this way too. Won't burn the darn place down." He held out the chew, but Ty shook his head. Danny looked curiously at him. "Still teetotaling too, I s'pose, so you won't pop a beer with me."

Ty nodded, looked at the ground, and picked up a stick that had blown off the maple in last night's storm and poked at a pile of leaves and twigs that had been a squirrel nest.

"Didn't swear off women, did ya?" Danny spit to the side and wiped the excess off his chin.

"Not really. Just haven't come on the right one lately, I guess." Ty smiled and pushed a pinecone toward the nest. As soon as they'd built the track a few years ago, the long row of pine trees marking the edge of the property had promptly started dying, the trees turn-ing orange like dominoes falling one into another, as if to protest the acres of green rolling pastures disappearing into the tan and orange buildings designed to look like a cross between Taco Bells and me-dieval fortresses. The first time he saw the dying pines, Ty had this fleeting impression that the developers had spray painted the trees to match the new color scheme.

"Quit working and go to playing some, you might have better

luck. But I guess you see plenty of females around horses these days. Used to be just the men here at the track. Now we got the jockeys, trainers, owners, groomers, hell, everybody's a woman! Not that I'm complaining, you understand. So what about it? You want them horses in to-go boxes?" Danny asked.

Ty watched a big, rangy chestnut with three white socks walk by with a four-foot overstride. He nodded at the horse.

"He'll cost you the farm right now. Supposed to be the next Cigar. Wait a few months, he'll be in the back sheds with the rest of the puppy chow. Vic Nickles is already pushing him too hard. Next race or two should tell the tale, then Vic will really start training on him."

"Like to get him before that happens." Ty let his eyes follow the horse with the big stride, noting the good shoulder and hip. He'd make a jumper.

"I'll call you if he breaks down fast enough to save his life. Believe me, you couldn't touch him for under a hundred thousand today. Vic is screwing the owner's wife."

Ty poked the grass at his feet with the stick. It was an old story, horses used as collateral for all kinds of deals that made money in one way or another at the track. Sometimes by winning races, but most often not. He may have been a green seventeen-year-old kid when he started at the track, but it hadn't taken him long to figure the lay of that land. After a couple of years, he'd gone on to rodeo-ing. Riding rough stock for another couple of years and getting banged around pretty good, but not doing well enough to make it pay. Then he'd started working for Big Swenson, the rodeo stock contractor, driving and eventually, by the time he was twenty-seven, managing one crew on the road the whole season. He used to think about how his old man would get a good laugh out of seeing his harsh discipline paying off, but no matter how large, the responsibility for his own crew and animals always seemed lighter than it ever had been on the ranch.

Whenever he got a break from the road, he trained horses for roping or barrels, broke out babies, and saved money. He saved every single dime he could, sleeping in the stock trucks or camping out while other men spent what they had on motel rooms, until he had enough to rent a small place in the Kansas Flint Hills—a tiny, rundown house, an old dairy barn, and forty acres of pasture. Gradually, he was able to buy it and start adding on more land. He'd had the place for ten years now, making a living as a horse dealer and trainer. Not getting rich. Over the past five years, he'd branched out to include horses for English style riding too, hunters and jumpers, and those people seemed to be willing to spend a lot more money.

The jumper people didn't care so much where their animals came from, long as they could get the job done. That was what Ty liked, so he made sure to sell them horses they'd find useful, and now it was beginning to pay off. Last week he'd even gotten a call from someone in Texas who specialized in reiners and hunter-jumpers. Well, the gray and the brown both had the size for jumping if they had the scope and heart, and the mare was just classy enough to be a small hunter if she didn't get too much attitude on her. He'd put her on Regumate to control her cycling as soon as they got home. Maybe show her to Eddie if he was around when he stopped by his place northwest of Minneapolis to pick up a couple of his washouts.

"Guess I'm taking 'em, Danny." He stuck out his hand and they shook.

"You won't be sorry. And I'll keep a look out for some others when we close this meet and move south."

"Better get loaded then. Got to go to Eddie's for a couple I got a message about—Dusty's old ponying horse and some rank four-year-old nobody can get broke."

Danny spit. "Dusty's the Salvation Army of this circuit. All heart, no brains. Can't hold it against him though, he's taken a few of my cripples too. Want to stop for a bite before you hit the road?"

"Thanks, but no. Got a ways to go yet." He dragged a rundown heel through a shallow puddle of water and looked around once more. He missed the track and he didn't. He'd understood it all too soon, that's what had happened. And there were too many memories keeping him restless. Whenever he called his mother over the years, it was one sorry piece of news after another. Ten years ago, it was that she was divorcing his father. Next, his sister had a car wreck and banged up her legs. Then cousin somebody has cancer, and the bottom fell out of the cattle market. His mom stopped asking him when he was coming home a good fifteen years ago, and he figured it must have finally sunk in that he couldn't. Sometimes he dreamed that the outstanding warrant was lifted, that what he'd done all those years ago was just a mistake, that he was free again. He never spoke to his father, but as far as he knew, the old bastard was still out there drinking and cursing himself to death because Ty ran away and Ronnie was partly his fault too. Sometimes on a clear day, it seemed like it might have been all his father's fault, putting an eight-year-old on that tractor after the kind of wet spring and summer they'd been having. Ronnie was small for his age, couldn't handle the work Ty had carried when he was eight and nine. He used to try and tell his father that, but he wouldn't listen. Neither would Ronnie.

"Wanna bring the rig around to this entrance to load?" Danny asked, a curious light in his pale blue eyes as he watched Ty's expression go distant.

Ty backed the nine-horse in place and went to lower the side ramps and make sure the hay nets were out of the way. He'd recently traded this rig to Eddie Nyland for his old dually truck with the six-horse, having to throw in four of his best prospects too. Eddie was becoming his best customer, and always seemed to have equipment and cars to trade or sell. Horses too, but his were usually on the way down the food chain, not on the way up like Ty's were. Eddie's clients were mostly well-off people in Minneapolis–St. Paul who didn't mind trading for bigger and better horses every year or two. And he had a way of making it happen. Ty didn't like that end of the business and often felt sick when Eddie unloaded some of the latest casualties of the show horse wars. Sometimes Ty could rehabilitate them, and Eddie would change their names and recycle them, but lots of times they had a worse life ahead of them.

True to her nature, the mare tried to load herself and Ty had to run up the ramp after her while Danny leaned against the maple tree laughing. "Forgot to tell you about that," he gasped. "Started slow, but now she thinks she knows it all. Does anything once, she wants to run the show. She'll be driving the truck by sunset, so watch it."

The gray stamped and snorted, wanting hay while the brown looked lazily out the window and the mare pawed and looked around for anything she could pick up and throw at them. "Two more, then we're going to Kansas, Dorothy," Ty said and went down to pay for the horses and secure the ramp.

"Nothing much happening here. Think I'll ride over to Eddie's with you. You can drop me off on your way back." Danny crawled into the cab beside him and stretched his short legs out while he played with the ten-position adjustments for his padded seat. "Getting above yourself, boy?" He looked back at the sleeping loft behind them.

"Got a deal from Eddie," Ty said.

Danny nodded wisely. "Yeah, right. Hope he put a new serial plate on it. Somebody's gonna miss a rig like this." He fiddled with the knobs on the CD player. "You must be doing pretty well now to afford this, no matter how cheap it was. Knowing you though, Eddie had to take out a bank loan to afford the bargain you made."

"He's not complaining."

"Not yet. You won't be either till the cops show up. That's why I don't do business with him. You shouldn't either, Ty. Eddie's kind of chickens always come home to roost. Here—" He pointed to the road by the last row of stalls.

"I remember." Ty swung the truck easily.

"Sweet," Danny said.

Eddie's place sat at the top of a mild hill with the barns flanking either side of the large indoor arena. The Cape Cod style house, off to the left side, looked out of place in the sea of green grass and big oak trees. Everytime Eddie scored with a rich client, he added on to his house, so that it seemed to ramble off in back like an ever-growing locust trying to walk out of a sequence of tight shells. As usual, the grass and weeds everywhere were neatly trimmed, the fences painted white, nothing broken or discarded sitting around the barnyard like it was at most stables. Eddie understood that you had to look like money to make money, and always laughed at Ty's little Kansas farm.

They pulled the rig around to the back of the barn and went inside, but the lights were off and the horses were lying down or standing against the back walls with their eyes closed in the cool dark. The horses he was to take would be at this end of the barn, where the discards waited, close to the big double doors in case they had to be dragged out at the end of a tractor chain and a winch. The equipment was shabbier at this end too, without the matching or color-coordinated blankets, buckets, and stall guards that marked the bigger, successful horses. The end stall held a couple of old wooden cots, two stained and ripped blue nylon bags, a lopsided tan card table with two scarred gray metal chairs, and a dirty red plastic cooler that meant Eddie's barn help was living there.

"Where is everybody?" Danny asked. "They know you're taking the horses, right?"

"Yeah, sure." Ty looked around at the dark stalls. The ponying horse was a big sturdy white Appaloosa gelding with lots of spots who stuck his head out of his stall to watch them. Next to him a bony sorrel was hacking away like he had pneumonia. Ty stuck his head in and saw the wet dirty sawdust the horse was standing in. The fumes were strong enough to make him back away into the better air in the aisle. Obviously, Eddie wasn't around or he'd be having a fit about the dirty stalls. Next was a used-up lamer with an old bandage around its back leg and two badly swollen front ankles. Ty shook his head at the tired, broken look in the horse's eyes, and Danny whistled through his front teeth. "End of the line for that one. Couldn't even finish the claimer, the one the gray bowed in. Cheapest race of the day." The other stalls for rejects were empty, and they gave off a dead moldy smell that had a kind of lonesomeness to it, as if all the failed horses that had spent their last hours here had left something behind.

"This must be the four-year-old," Danny called from the dark a few stalls away as a head flashed out and teeth snapped the air over his head. "Need rabies shots you plan to work this one. What's your name, Rover?" He didn't bother trying to pat the horse, who backed up and kicked the wall several times, making their ears ring.

"Saddam Hussein's idea of a kids' horse?" Danny spit a brown glob on the aisle.

Ty rubbed the back of his neck and grimaced. "The message said—"

Danny held up his hands. "Don't tell me, I know. You were always a sucker for sad stories. Just make sure I'm in your will—no, don't do that, I might inherit the son of a bitch. Why don't you just make me your life insurance beneficiary instead."

"Hello?" A woman called out from the doorway.

Ty walked back into the light and nodded toward his rig. "I'm Ty Bonte. Supposed to pick up a couple of horses?"

"Eddie said to tell you to take the others too." She folded her arms across her chest and rocked back on one heel. She was medium height with short brown hair cut boy style and brushed behind her ears. Her face wore a controlled, nervous fierceness with a lot of energy stored in the big brown eyes. When she was relaxed, it would be a comfortable face, without harsh angles, Ty decided. There was some cushion to her hips, thighs, and chest that he liked, and muscles in her tanned arms. Rocking on her heels, she wore dirty jeans and cowboy boots and a man's black T-shirt with a swab of green on the shoulder where a horse had wiped his mouth on her. But the longer he looked at her, the more familiar she seemed, although she didn't appear to recognize him. He thought she'd been here before when he'd come with horses, but he must be wrong, he decided.

"I'm taking the two Eddie left the message about, Dusty's App and the rank colt." He folded his arms too.

"Dusty's on his way to the hospital with damn heart failure. He's not coming back, believe me, and I'm leaving too." She unfolded her arms and rubbed her hands on her thighs while she looked nervously into the dark stalls around them as if she expected someone to pop up suddenly and stop her. "Eddie's off showing for the next month, so unless you want to leave these other two to starve or be killed, you'll put 'em on the damn truck too."

She pushed past him and he felt the urge to grab her arm, make her listen to him.

"Well, I'm sorry about Dusty—" Ty said.

"Me too," Danny added and spit again.

"Here." She opened the coughing horse's stall and led it out. "You take this one." She fastened a lead on the halter and handed it to Danny, then opened the next stall door and began to pull out the hobbling lamer.

"That sorrel is sick, I can't have it in my van," Ty said.

"It's just heavey, now don't be a pain in the ass." She waved Danny on. Smiling, he walked the horse past Ty.

"Better be," Ty muttered.

"He's a good little horse," she said, opening the App's door. "You take these two, but come right back and help me with the colt. He's a handful."

"Right," Ty said and ignored Danny's grin as he loaded the two horses beside the mare. He hadn't even bothered to argue about the broken-down gelding; it would probably end up at the killers anyway. "We'll put the colt in front there by himself," he said as he went down the ramp.

"Not by himself," the woman said. "He goes with my horse, Bobby."

Ty stopped. "No."

"Look, Dusty said you'd do it, he promised. Bobby and I need to get out of here too."

"No." He shook his head. "Unh-uh."

She walked past him with the big dark brown horse and was up the ramp before he could stop her. "He rides best on the outside, so Satan can ride in a double-wide stall next to him." She backed her horse in and fastened the chains on either side of his halter. He looked at them as if to say, see, I've been taking this kind of attitude all my life. Ty wouldn't look at Danny, who kept his head turned toward the empty paddocks as if there were a carnival about to unload out there while she swept past them and trotted into the barn again.

"Can I get some help with this horse?" she yelled, and the flurry of thuds and banging hooves that followed brought both men running.

"You okay?" Danny asked as she picked herself up off the aisle floor.

"Hard to get that halter on, have to sneak up on him and then he gets pissed, but if one of you grabs that rope, we'll be off."

The two men looked at each other. "Satan?" Danny said.

"Okay." Ty sighed and edged into the stall and plunged back out as soon as the horse spun and kicked at him, grazing his left shoulder with a hoof.

"How long has he been in there?" he asked, rubbing his shoulder.

The woman looked at the ground and rolled her lips. "Well, maybe a week or two. We couldn't catch him."

"You have a dart gun, you could try to tranq him," Danny said. "Seen that on *Wild Kingdom* couple a times."

"Perfect," Ty said. "I'm trying to get home tonight. How long you think this rodeo's gonna take?" The horse looked over his shoulder at him and flattened his ears.

"All right." Ty turned and walked down the aisle.

"He's leaving, right?" the woman said.

"Naw, he's getting ready to play cowboy," Danny said. "That boy don't quit on nothing. Say, what's your name?"

"Dakota."

"North or South?"

"My dad's folks moved to Iowa when he was a kid, but he missed home so much he named me for it. North Dakota, over by Standing Rock Reservation."

Ty reappeared with one rope over his shoulder and holding another in his hand. "Okay, now open the stall door when I say so and get ready." He shook out a loop. "I'll throw him, then we'll ease his troubled mind. You hold this—" He handed the syringe to the woman and hoisted himself high enough on the next stall so he could swing the first rope. It took him only one try to get the neck and after he'd passed that rope to Danny to hold, he roped the front legs and pulled the horse down. When it was on the floor of the stall, both men jumped in and quickly hobbled it, keeping clear of the hind legs. While Danny sat on the head, Ty caught the hind legs in another loop and pulled them tight to the front legs so the horse couldn't move enough to hurt them or himself. After the shot, they left the horse down until the tranquilizer took effect. When his breathing calmed and his eye started to look sleepy, Ty went back in and got him up. Enough of the fight was gone that he could be led and loaded with only a few balks and half rears.

Ty rubbed his hands on his jeans and began rolling up the thick sisal mat on the ramp. "Hate having him ride that way, but don't have much of a choice."

Danny helped him slide the ramp into its slot and close the doors. One of the horses inside stamped and shifted its weight in a series of creaks and thuds. Ty wiped his face on his shirt sleeve and glanced at Dakota climbing down from stowing her things in the tack area at the front of the trailer. She still looked familiar. "Satan, huh? Why don't I ever ask the barn names before I buy them?"

Danny high-fived him. "You don't want to know. She going too?" He nodded toward Dakota climbing in the truck. "Told me she's from Iowa, name's Dakota something—"

Ty climbed halfway into the cab and stopped at the sight of her pushing his stuff over on the seat to make room. "I'm dropping you off in Iowa, right?" When she kept staring straight ahead, he repeated, "Right?"

"Whatever," she muttered as Danny climbed in and she had to move over. Picking up the papers, thermos, pliers, and work gloves next to her, she threw them on the dash.

"Yeah, right." Ty settled into the driver's seat, shifted, and slowly eased on the gas, listening for any scrambling or trouble on the intercom to the back where the horses rode. Although the seat was wide, he could feel the extra heat from her body next to his, and it made him inch against the door. Last thing he needed was to get mixed up with some stray girl.

Leaving Eddie's farm, he pulled onto the county road and started to plan his route home to Kansas after dropping Danny in Shakopee at the track. There was always that jaunt through the corner of Nebraska, no matter how he sliced it, which meant driving extra careful. And not stopping, especially for the weigh stations, where his license would be checked and the warrant could pop up. He listened carefully to the CB through Omaha to Lincoln and south to Kansas, and sometimes spent hours in rest stops waiting with the rest of the outlaws for the weigh stations to close. State cops along I-80 were tricky too. One time outside North Platte they'd put up a sign saying MANDATORY DRUG SEARCH TEN MILES just before an exit ramp and then searched all the vehicles that made desperate dives off the highway. State court threw out the arrests, of course, entrapment, but it worked for a few days.

When they dropped off Danny, they checked the horses again. The rank colt was dozing with his body pressed against the big brown gelding, who watched them through half-closed eyes. "Hope that colt keeps riding good," Ty said as they closed the small door on the van. "Least that horse of yours has a decent outlook."

"Just don't drive like a cowboy and we'll be fine," Dakota said and nestled herself into the corner with her head against the glass.

Ty thought about how nice it would be to dump her in Iowa, except then he'd have to manage the colt alone. Well, it wouldn't be the first time, and it was sure a cheap enough horse to unload someplace and leave if it got to be too much of a pain. He looked over at the girl, who already seemed to be drifting off before he could ask her where in Iowa she was going.

It was the middle of the night by the time they circled the outskirts of Des Moines. Dakota had woken up an hour before just long enough to tell him she wasn't stopping in Iowa, but going all the way to Kansas. When he'd tried to question her further, she'd muttered "whatever" and dropped off to sleep again. He'd lost a lot of time hiding out at a truck stop in Mason City until the cops closed shop, and now he was going to have to make the Nebraska leg in the morning unless he had to hole up again. Luckily, the horses were still riding well, even the colt, who had to be feeling the effects of the tranq wearing off.

The long stretch from Des Moines to Omaha was a particularly dark and lonely drive up and down the deep rolling hills, with only

Dakota's light snoring, the sticky hum of tires on asphalt, and the occasional static burst from the CB to keep him company. Something about the moon flooding the fields white in this stretch always reminded him of that January night with Harney driving up to Rosebud on the county road from Cody. It had snowed earlier and the wind was blowing so hard the car had bucked and weaved as it got hit broadside by the powerful gusts. The tires had hesitated on the snow-packed road, used only by cars fleeing Rosebud Reservation all afternoon and evening for the stores and bars just across the border in Nebraska, then back again. Ty could still see the long white streaks of snow blowing across the road like fog, which made it impossible to believe anyone would be walking on a night like that. Then there they were, right in the headlights, staggering backwards into the wind, arms stuck out hitchhiking. Their heads were wrapped in rags tying down the greasy gimme caps, and even in the dark and snow, their faces wore the unfocused look of drunkenness. Harney, driving, hit the steering wheel with the palm of his hand. "Oh yeah"—he'd laughed and looked over at Ty. "Let's take 'em."

Ty pushed away the drowsiness the memory of that night always brought with it, as if he could sleep it away and return to his life before. Now the moonlight made the leaves of corn glitter like rows of knives guarding the land from the dark shapes moving across it, and in the distance, the rows marched up and over the hills like endless armies in perfect formation. The soybean and alfalfa fields alternated in dark plushness that seemed to disguise huge trapdoors capable of opening and swallowing anything that dared move across their surfaces. At night, the land here changed, reaching back to its ancient ancestors like dreams leading to nightmares where everything human is slaughtered and eaten. Ty had had these dreams and turned his eyes back to the safety of the white lines, wishing again and again that he were back in the Sandhills, where the land used to welcome him at night. The soapweed stalks firm and resistant against the sky, while the grass clung in stubborn clumps to the thin soil. Having been away for so long he understood the edges of that life, where to grow anything at all was a struggle and in the struggle came some dignity and pride. Here, everything seemed to grow and flourish too easily. Minnesota, Iowa, Wisconsin, the flat fertile regions of Nebraska and Illinois and Kansas—they made him nervous, as if any moment he would look over his shoulder and see the end coming at him.

He looked at Dakota again, turned down the CB to listen for the horses in back, and satisfied, glanced at his side mirrors just as the flashing lights of a trooper swung up alongside. His stomach leapt and he gripped the wheel with both hands, resisting the sudden urge to swerve into him, and eased off the gas, preparing to downshift when the car swooped on past, swept up the hill, and disappeared over the top. By the time they reached the top, the cop car was a pair of red pricks of light winking in a black distant sea just before it vanished. He exhaled and the woman beside him murmured, "That was close," then fell back to sleep.

The Flint Hills were a big and quiet land, Ty had discovered, the occasional ranches and farms tucked away in distant valleys screened by a few trees as if their lives were too private for any stranger on the road to share. And this was exactly what had attracted him. In early spring, the air filled with the smoky haze of burning pastures as the ranchers took turns firing the land, but the black sooty stubble was quickly replaced by new green shoots of big bluestem, with patches of Indian grass and switchgrass in the upper lands, grama grass and cordgrass in the moist lower and bottomlands, and bright colored mazes of wildflowers, such as purple spiderwort, wild pink primrose, and orange milkweed, sprouted everywhere. And in spring, Kansas skies cleared to that promising blue interrupted only by the long skids of high clouds or the heavy-bellied rain clouds advancing from the south like giant fists to tear at the land with flooding rain and hail, shaking winds and tornadoes. "Tornado Alley" lay from Texas to Omaha, with Kansas directly in its path, a fact that made him keep an eye on the cloudy horizon while he worked and each summer sent him a few times into the shelter of the storm cellar dug into a small hill to one side of his house.

Most days in July and August, like today, the extreme heat lay like a tired dog panting breathless against the skin, and everything stood still, sweating in place, swollen with sleep and irritation. On the farm, the horses would be quarrelsome, sluggish in their work af-

ter ten in the morning, kicking out and flattening their ears at distur-
bances. Along the roadsides now, dust coated the drooping leaves of
grasses and low sumac and catclaw brier bushes in between the sunflowers, goldenrod, and white aster. The greens were beginning to
fade, and within a month, the hillsides would begin to brown into
heaving waves of yellows and tans and burnt oranges that were as
thrilling to his eye as the new greens of spring. Still, it made him
homesick, he admitted, and let his foot relax on the gas and eased
back in the seat.

He'd made two more layovers to avoid the troopers and it had
been midafternoon by the time they crossed the Nebraska-Kansas
border. Ty was grateful that Dakota had never questioned what he
was doing during those long waits at rest stops. At least the day was
mild. The horses were riding easy. He glanced at the blue-white
cloudless sky through the windshield. They were getting a break
there too. Careful to avoid looking to the west, where the sun stood
like a phosphorescent basketball that could blind him to the road, he
peeked out of the corner of his eye at the woman beside him. She
was definitely someone he'd met before, but he was never much
good at faces or people. Stock, yes, he remembered every horse he'd
ever bought or sold, ridden, or got bucked off from. And cattle. That
had been one of his real strengths on the ranch, something even his
father had had to admit. He could keep track of a thousand head at
a time, remember which had a cut to be treated, an infected udder, a
bad tooth. Not to mention bloodlines. To this day, he carried most
of the ranch breeding lines in his head. Couldn't get rid of them, in
fact. Sleepless nights, he'd start with the foundation stock and move
on through the years, from his grandfather's first bull with the first
twenty head of cows he could afford to start the ranch, on down
through his father's and then his own small herd he'd left behind.
They hadn't really been his, he never bothered thinking of them as
his. They were supposed to be for Ronnie and him to start their own
business someday, something his father had tossed at him in a rare
good mood, but that dream had died quickly.

He was glad to see the sign just ahead for the turnoff to the first
of a series of county roads he'd be taking. Slowing, he made the

turn. Half a mile farther on he pulled into Bob's Stop, an old two-pump station at the intersection with a road so obscure it didn't have a sign. No matter how many different ways he figured it, he always seemed to need gas here on his return from the north. Setting his brake and shutting off the engine, he rested his arms on the wheel and leaned across it to stretch his back.

Dakota sighed and he noticed how her purse, three books, and backpack were beginning to take possession of the seat. "We almost there?"

"You're not staying with me," he announced and, opening the door, climbed down. He opened the caps on both tanks and began fueling. From the trailer, he could hear the muffled thumps of the horses stamping lazily at flies and chewing hay. Although it was quiet, he would check on the rank colt before they took off again. Looking around, he saw that the station was empty except for a nondescript black pickup, banged around enough to have driven right off some nearby farm or ranch. The two repair bays were dark and empty too. Must have lost their mechanic. Maybe the station was closing. The chipped yellow forty-gallon Pennzoil drum beside the pump overflowed pop cans and paper onto the cracked, oil-stained cement. A breeze picked up a wadded candy wrapper and rolled it under the truck, then brought it back and sent it toward the garage area to his right. When the breeze died, the only sound was the whishing of tires on the highway half a mile away and the loud, double-noted flute call of a meadowlark standing on a post across the road. He felt good and almost smiled as he pulled the nozzle from the first tank and stuck it in the second without spilling a single drop down the truck's dark blue finish. He closed his eyes and leaned against the fender listening for the full gurgle.

When he opened his eyes again there were two big Kansas line-backer boys, corn fed and beef solid, on either side of him. "Watcha hauling?" the one with the shaved head asked, wearing a broad, foolish grin that didn't match his small, mean eyes. The fumes of a day's worth of beer drinking spread out in front of him like an invisible fog as he reached for the hose when Ty started to replace the nozzle.

"If this is a dance, I want to know who's asking," Ty said.

The blond crewcut on his other side, wearing no expression at all, raised a beefy arm and shoved him casually with stiff fingers against the trailer, knocking off his hat. He banged the bruised shoulder the colt had grazed with its hoof, which pissed him off. He kneed the baldy as hard as he could in the balls, and crouched below the fists that swung at him, moving quickly through the space emptied by the man on the ground. Out in the wider area between the building and the pumps he turned, facing his attacker, and kept his weight on his toes and bent his knees. Ty didn't think he could take them both, so he'd better hurry up and put this one down.

Blond crewcut, who had a big scar across his wide nose that laced across one cheek to his ear, patted the air in front of him as he advanced to Ty's right. "We just want the rig."

"What about my horses?" Ty asked, stepping back to keep the gap from closing and wanting to look over his shoulder to see if the gas station attendant was calling the sheriff or, better yet, coming out with a .12 gauge to get a piece of it. He prayed that Dakota would have enough sense to either stay in the truck or slip out the other side and take off.

"What do you think?" Blond crewcut smiled. He was the smart one. His eyes flicked to the left, and shaved head climbed to his feet and moved over, leaving an opening that led to the truck. But that's what they wanted, Ty figured, and felt the sweat sticking his shirt to his back. They had him boxed in pretty good. Only one way out.

"Can't give up my rig and horses, man." He started to walk toward crewcut, who straightened in surprise and took a step back. "You see how it is, that's my business, that's how I pay the bills, you wouldn't want to deprive a man of his livelihood, would you?" He was closing the gap and shaved head to his left looked anxiously at his buddy, trying to figure out what to do, but crewcut wasn't panicking, he was just a little confused. He wanted him, but he wanted to call the dance. If Ty could just get through him, he might be able to get to the pistol grip shotgun he kept under the seat on this side.

"Stay there." Crewcut held a hand up, but Ty kept coming. "Okay." The man reached for him, but Ty sidestepped and kicked his knee hard enough to drop him grunting. Baldy had been waiting for the right moment and rushed at Ty, scooping him up in a bear hug and crushing the wind out of him so quickly everything went hazy for a moment, and then was on him with fists that felt like ten-pound hammers punching his insides against his backbone. The guy should've gone for the face, but he hadn't gotten over his football training and kept his contact to the body. Ty fought with his feet and arms, finally managing to butt heads, clap baldy's ears hard, and chop viciously at his throat so he went down grabbing for air.

Ty yanked the truck door open. "Move!" he yelled at Dakota and stuck his arm under the seat and pulled out the loaded shotgun and quickly shucked a shell up in the chamber. As soon as the two men heard the double snicking of the shotgun, they froze.

"Back off!" he yelled. "Back the fuck off now!"

"Come on," crewcut whined.

"Get inside, get in the station there," he ordered the men. "Now!"

"Got to pay for the gas," Dakota said behind him.

"Fuck that, they can't protect people pumping gas," he said.

"Go on, open the door and get in there." He waved the gun at the two men.

"Feel sorry for that attendant, but he's on his own. Need to get in and get rolling," he said, never taking his eyes off the men reluctantly backing into the station office, crewcut with the bad knee leaning on shaved head.

Ty snapped the padlock on the door shut and headed back to the truck.

"Let's go." He climbed in and put the shotgun on the seat between them.

"Wait." Dakota jumped out, sprinted to the black pickup truck, and stabbed the two nearest tires repeatedly, then ran back and jumped into the truck as it was rolling away. "That was fun," she said, laying the long hunting knife on the seat between them.

Ty turned onto the county road and felt the shotgun slide into his thigh. Some woman, carrying a pig sticker big and sharp enough to take the head off a horse. He'd have to file that information close to the front where he'd remember it.

"Your horse trading always this adventurous?" she asked, twisting nervously in her seat to look out the side window.

"Sometimes. Usually I keep a gun on me when I'm loaded. Got sloppy today."

"That why we kept laying over?"

He glanced quickly at her but kept his mouth shut. When he saw a rutted dirt road branching to the right, he slowed and eased the truck onto it. He never painted his name or address on the sides of his vehicles just because of this kind of thing, and he could only hope these men had chosen him as a random target. It'd seemed that way, relying on their muscle instead of coming armed for the hijacking. But he'd mix it up some, and see if he could lose them now in case they found a way out of the station and tried to follow. The road was washboard and he had to pick up speed to keep on top of the ridges, but that was dangerous on dirt. He hoped the horses were riding okay. Hadn't heard anything out of that colt, but he couldn't stop now and check. If it didn't make it, well, it had earned its fate.

On either side of the road tall weeds and an occasional bush crowded in with dust-coated leaves, and once in a while when there was a break in the brush, he saw glimpses of the green grass or cream rock outcroppings in pastures with cattle drifting slowly toward the place they'd chosen for the night. The sun was a fierce orange-red ball to the west, taking its time as it spread the last burn across the landscape. He had to head east in a bit, but with luck this road would connect to another before he had to go back to blacktop.

Ahead of them a spray of blackbirds was pecking the road, and he wanted to blow the horn to get them up, but he was afraid the colt would startle, so he took his foot off the gas, letting the truck slow gradually. Finally, at the last minute, they took off, swooping and parting in front of his grill as if they were liquid. One stalled frantically and flew up almost into the windshield, close enough for him to see the missing feather in the middle of the wing and the tiny beak parted in panic before the bird somehow spun loose of them and churned away. Both Ty and Dakota let out a breath when it disappeared, looked at each other, and laughed. She held his eyes a moment too long, then made a point of looking away. It wasn't the color of her brown eyes so much as that brief catch they made inside him, as if they'd given him just this much of her and no more. But it was a lot deeper than he'd seen in another person for a long, long time. Hell, he was half-surprised to see his own face shaving in the morning, the mocking eyes saying, "You again?"

Ty stepped on the gas.

"Thanks for saving our necks back there." She settled back against the seat.

"Nobody's stealing my horses or rig—"

"You handled yourself all right." She looked at him, taking in the lean muscled body, the long legs in worn jeans, and the thick fore-arms. His weathered face was covered in brown hide with tiny pale wrinkles at the corners of his eyes and mouth. His dark straight hair hung shaggy at the collar, and wouldn't stay pushed behind his ears. There was a flat halo around the top part of his head from his hat. "Lost your hat," she said, and he nodded and reached a dirt-grained hand up to push the hair back on the side of his head. He had those big ears too, but at least they didn't poke out at the world. The top of one ear was notched like a steer or something. His humped nose looked like it'd been broken more than once. She wanted him to turn toward her so she could see those eyes again, but he didn't. She thought they were black, but nobody had black, so they had to be such a dark brown they looked black, like a deer's, shiny and deep.

She glanced at his dim reflection in her side window. She'd re-membered him from the time he delivered that bay gelding one of Eddie's buddies in Tulsa had kidnapped. Later she and Eddie had to swear it had never even been in the barn, though its halter with the nameplate hung in plain sight by the wash stall. The state police knew they were lying and she'd vowed not to let Eddie involve her anymore. Lot of good that did. She looked over at Ty. Just how far into it with Eddie was he? He acted pretty straight. Looked it too. But you couldn't trust a man's looks. No, she'd keep quiet about the past and try to disappear before Eddie made another buying trip to Kansas. She wasn't sure she could trust Ty to hide her if he showed up.

She turned in her seat so she could watch him for a few minutes while she pretended to be surveying the countryside. His chin had a slight dent in the middle, not like Kirk Douglas's though; she didn't much like that big groove thing that looked like a birth defect. He had a wide mouth, with smile lines and generous lips. She didn't like those skinny-lipped bastards, seemed like their mouths always told the story of their hearts, or maybe it was Eddie she'd learned that from. Ty was all right looking, maybe even better than that, but there was something in his manner that said don't get too close. And he wasn't bothering to hustle her for whatever he could get like it was second nature, the way guys often did. It made her want to sting him like a mosquito to get his damn attention.

She stretched her legs out in front of her and shook them to loosen the cramps from the long ride. She'd meant to get out at the gas station and walk around, pee, grab something to eat. She'd starve with this one in charge. He'd only given her a few minutes at the McDon's off the interstate outside Omaha, and that food had gone right through her system in an hour like always. The famous disappearing hamburgers. But mostly she was thirsty.

"You got anything to drink back there?" She nodded toward the sleeping compartment, which probably had a small fridge too.

He shrugged, which made him grimace. "You can look."

"What's wrong with your shoulder?" She reached for him and he shied like a horse that'd been beaten.

"Colt clipped it and that banging around back there didn't help none. It'll be okay, just needs to rest. Nothing new." He slowly raised one, then the other shoulder, tipping his head each way. "Guess you can get me something too."

"Beer?" She smiled.

"Pop'll do fine. Don't think there's any beer back there."

"We'll have to fix that," she murmured as she climbed up into the loft.

When she handed the open can of Diet Pepsi to him, she noticed the scars on his knuckles, the thick rope around his little finger, and the unevenness of the bones that said the middle one had been broken. So he'd been a bad boy, which accounted for the way he handled himself in the fight back there. Suddenly she wished she'd put on some clean clothes for the trip. She'd really made him take her on impulse, she was supposed to go with that Lauren guy to Florida, but he was only a trainer-in-training, translate groom, and she'd had her doubts whether he could stick it out long enough to even make Florida. It was better for the colt to have Bobby around anyway.

She'd taken care of Dusty's horses for eight months and they'd gotten under each other's skin in a way she hadn't let anyone or anything in a while. Not since she left that whole crowd at the Mason City spring show a year ago, packed her show trunk, managed to lift it up into the back of her pickup herself, put Bobby in the trailer, and took off. Since then, she'd had to sell the truck and trailer after the truck broke an axle, and ended up like the rest of the derelicts on Dusty's doorstep one day. He took both her and the horse in, and she tried to return the favor by keeping his failing enterprise going months longer than it should've. They both knew it was coming to the end as soon as the Canterbury season closed; Dusty just hurried the inevitable along by collapsing at the hot dog stand a week ago and she'd had to call Eddie to come help her. The paramedics were pronouncing Dusty dead as she finally forced her way through the little crowd, but she hadn't told Eddie or Ty that. They might have refused the horses and sent them to the killers. Ty certainly would have refused to take her and Bobby. Then she thought of the rank colt and what Eddie would do when he came back from the road showing and discovered the horse missing instead of dead as he'd planned. She began to feel the black hopelessness coming over her, and tried to shake it off as they headed down a hill toward a small wooden bridge. Ty braked gradually so they rolled slowly onto the bridge.

"Look—" He pointed toward the gap in the land, and she saw the small brush filled canyon and the stream that rushed along over rocks, glistening in the late afternoon sunlight. Kansas, how the hell could this be Kansas?

"Beautiful," she murmured, feeling the drowsiness that came over her like a blanket, as if sleep were the only form of comfort she could find. The cab was hot too. He'd explained he couldn't run the air, some glitch in the electrical, so the open windows were blowing warm air on her face and she closed her eyes against the dryness.

When she'd been silent for a while, Ty glanced over and found her asleep. Her mouth was slightly open with a little dribble of spit caught on the lower lip, and he had to stop the urge to reach over and clear it with his thumb like he used to do for Ronnie. Her face had that slack look kids got when they slept, that way they gave themselves so completely over to it. Grown-ups usually never slept that way, he'd noticed, they were too tense. He tucked the gun and knife under the seat so that when she started to slide toward him, he let her collapse against him, liking the head on his arm. After a while, he lifted his arm carefully and eased her down so her head rested on his thigh. She immediately curled on her side, tucking her arms into her body, her back against the seat. He looked down. Her eyelids were trembling with some dream, a tear was starting in the corner of her eye, and he wanted to put his arm around her and stop whatever it was, even though he probably couldn't. He'd said she couldn't stay, but he didn't have a clue how to stop this woman from doing anything she set her mind on. He smiled at the image of Danny back in Minnesota; he'd come along to Eddie's to watch the show. Hell, he might have put her up to it for all Ty knew. Married people were always trying to get other people in the same fix.

He flexed his hands on the steering wheel. He'd broken the middle knuckle that last winter night with Harney. He remembered trying to shake the unreality out of his head that kept making things seem distant like in a dream, nothing a person actually did. They'd started the night smoking dope, then they had all those beers back in Babylon, and Mick had slipped them a bottle when they'd gotten up to leave. Harney and Mick liked to sit around bragging about how much Indian ass they could kick. After a few pulls of whiskey, they'd driven around town, empty that late, cold January night, then somehow ended up on that half-paved back road to Mission on the Rosebud Res. Everytime they hit a hole or snowy bump on the patchy old blacktop, the barrel of the revolver deep in his coat pocket had jabbed him in the side, like it was asking him what the

hell he was doing there. He'd thought about his father's mean ass
back from detox, making life hell on every living thing now just to
show that he was still a bastard, drinking or not. His mother wasn't
about to leave town and come out there and stand up to the old man
either. When he'd left the house that night after a particularly vicious argument that came close to blows, he had taken the gun with
him. He wasn't sure who or what he was going to use it on, but he
knew he was going to do something. While Ty had run the ranch
single-handed all fall when Ryder was in rehab, he'd thought almost
daily of how he'd like to blow the old man's brains out. Sometimes
he'd imagined what the pistol would feel like up against his own
head, and once when he was almost blind from booze and pills, he'd
put his head back against the truck seat and forced the barrel between his teeth. The tart metallic taste was still on his tongue when
he'd woken up the next morning with his head wedged under the
steering wheel from passing out.

That January night the headlights had bounced across the two
men staggering beside the road and passed on into blackness before
Harney could put on the brakes. He stopped, shifted, and backed
up. "This is gonna be good," Harney had muttered and slowed to a
stop beside the two men. The bigger of the two drunks had braced
himself on the car and grabbed the window glass as it slid down, as
if he wasn't going to let it go. Ty had put his hand in his pocket, the
tips of his fingers caressing the cool metal until he worked the gun
out of the cloth lining and held it between his legs, ready.

"No," Ty whispered and eased his foot off the gas as he approached
the dirt driveway to his place. It was too late to go through all that
again. What was done was done. Cornering, the rear wheels slipped
on the soft dirt at the edge of the culvert, caved the bank and tilted
the trailer, setting off a terrific scrambling and banging. Since he was
so close to home, it took him only a couple of minutes to pull up and
park at the top of his drive. By the time he turned the ignition off,
Dakota was out the door and running back.

"Be careful—" he yelled and jumped out to help her open the doors and pull out the ramp.

Bobby was down, lying with his legs under the colt, who was prancing nervously, trying to avoid stepping on him. The real problem was the halter and tie chains that were strangling Bobby, hung at such an odd angle, with his hindquarters pressed into the corner, that they couldn't get him up or create enough slack to unfasten him.

"Hurry—" Dakota whimpered as she knelt in front of Bobby breathing in loud, choking gasps.

"Get out of the way—" Ty half-lifted her up and to the side, and reached to unhook the colt, which shied and scrambled back.

"Here—" Ty moved over to make room for her. "You do that while I lift the chest bar—same time—ready? One, two, three—"

As soon as the colt realized that his head was loose and the way in front of him was clear, he dropped his nose and blew hard, then carefully stepped over the other horse's legs and allowed himself to be backed to the side while Ty dragged Bobby's hindquarters out of the corner far enough so the halter could be unhooked and the horse could climb to his feet.

"We'll unload these two and check your horse for injury outside where the light's good. Lucky it happened so close to home," Ty said.

"They were fine till you started showing off—"

Ty glanced at the tears in her eyes and the small cut on her horse's cannon bone, producing a thin stream of blood down the leg. They were damn lucky, but he wasn't going to press the point. It had been a long haul, they both needed sleep. And the horses needed to get out in the pastures and be horses again for a few days, let the Flint Hills lull their bodies. Then he'd start work on breaking that rank colt.

∽ Chapter Six

Before he left the house, he peeked in at Dakota, who slept with her door open now, as if she finally trusted him not to bother her. She slept all out, sprawled in a T-shirt and shorts, her mouth a little open the way it had been in the truck that day. The bedroom was a jumble of clothes and debris he didn't care to identify as he backed away from the doorway. No telling where she kept that knife, which she'd handled back at the gas station as if it wasn't the first time. In retrospect, that hijack deal seemed weird. Usually there was some sense of danger or the signs of a setup when he knew he was going to have trouble on the road. This had come out of the blue, utterly. He'd been keeping weapons handy since that day, in case they showed up again. He had the knife in his boot, and the shotgun he kept in the tack room now. He'd loaded a big syringe with enough tranq to knock down an elephant too, and kept that handy on a windowsill in the grooming area. He hoped to hell Eddie hadn't gotten him into something again. He'd warned Eddie after the kidnapped horse that had brought the state cops around. Eddie had called that time and asked him to pick up a horse in Kansas City and bring it to some backyard place in St. Paul. For an old girlfriend, he'd said. Maybe the rig was still too hot, maybe those guys had tracked it down like Danny had warned. Shit, he'd broken his own rule with Eddie, taking the rig, but his old truck was breaking down regularly enough he didn't dare take it on the road anymore. Best not to drive the new rig around more than necessary, he decided.

The converted cow barn wasn't the fanciest stable, but it was neat and clean. He used the milk holding room at the entrance for shelled corn, the clean-up area on the other side of the thick concrete wall as a wash stall; on the other side of that was his grooming area, with cross ties and rubber mats on the floor in case somebody got rambunctious enough to fall down. Across the aisle was his tack room, which was now being swept clean and dusted on a daily basis by Dakota. For some reason it worried him that she would see his bed in disarray, so every morning he made it, the first time he'd done that since leaving the family ranch.

He walked down the aisle past the ten stalls that needed cleaning for the horses that came in after a few hours of grazing, the ones that couldn't take the flies and heat. Hunter-jumper people liked their horses slick and fat as hogs. No sun-bleached coats. Where he had always cut the manes short, Dakota had been going down the line, pulling and thinning them to lie flat and even. She shaped the tails and clipped the fetlocks, ears, and chins so the horses looked show ready. Though he wasn't intending to let her stay, each evening he found himself eating supper with her, both of them dead tired and silent, promising himself that he'd talk to her in the morning. A person couldn't kick someone out after they'd put in such a hard day's work. And he was getting used to having her around—maybe even more, liking her here, although she never seemed to return his interest.

Three years ago he'd built an addition of ten more stalls to the fifteen already in the barn while he added the indoor arena to the east side. He'd worked a deal with the local pole barn builder to cut costs, trading him a front loader and dump truck he'd gotten from Eddie for a couple of particularly good hunters he'd rehabbed, and sharing in the work. He'd leveled the site himself, and added the indoor footing later. He'd hauled in layers of wood chips and compost until he had a spongy surface that wouldn't jar the legs, yet didn't give so much it interfered with motion or made a horse strain to pull its feet out. While he was growing up on the ranch, they'd used their horses for work and kept them pretty much like the cattle on the range. As his business changed, he learned a new language of horse care.

Past the stalls was another open area, where he stored bales of hay for daily feeding. He used a one-story shed to the right of the barn for storing the rest of the hay. He'd planned on growing all his own grain and hay by this time, but sales had been up and down, and the barn addition had set him back enough that he hadn't been able to finish buying the extra land he needed. Guttman next door didn't mind waiting for the purchase. They'd made an agreement years ago that as soon as Ty could, he'd be buying everything up to the old man's buildings a mile down the road, but he'd do it piece by piece. Now Ty worried he wouldn't get it done before the old man died and there'd be a hassle with the family. Guttman kept saying not to worry, but Ty *was* worried and wished they had some kind of purchase agreement on paper, though neither man was used to doing business that way.

Behind the barn he'd split the huge field into individual pastures to accommodate the various moods and problems of the horses. The long-termers were in the biggest areas, and the short-run stock in the smaller so they could get exercise and relaxation without running off their weight. Eddie had taught him that. Mares separate from geldings. A baby-sitter with the silly young horses. The older, less dominant horses together. He walked to the big pasture and lifted the gate open, then shut it. The sun was already hot enough to make the back of his neck burn. He liked the way it made his muscles loose though, spreading itself through his body so his legs felt strong and his shoulder didn't ache a bit. He swung his arms out and grabbed some air, yeah, that was fine. Down by the creek some birds were setting up a commotion in the big cottonwood tree. He looked hard, a hawk was sitting there at the top on that dead limb poking straight up. The bird ignored the smaller birds flying at it, working up their nerve to peck the back of its head or wings. But the hawk was bluffing too, and in a moment, it spread its wings and lifted up, then drifted out across the creek, followed by three small birds, sparrows maybe, swooping and pecking, driving it from their nests.

When the hawk finally flapped out of sight, the birds flew quickly back to the tree and disappeared with a few final angry squawks. A pair of dickcissels hopped on and off a cedar stump a couple of yards to his left uttering an occasional guttural note, but otherwise there was only the steady churn of grasshoppers, bees, and crickets riffling along the light shushing breeze. He took a deep breath and let the nutty grasses and sweet green blooming of alfalfa from the low lying field next door fill his chest and head. The smells were so strong he could taste them as the green hills rolled out empty of trees and houses as far as he could see to the horizon.

He scraped the toe of his boot in the dirt clumped up by the horses at the gate where they stood waiting when they were ready to come in. It was dry. He'd have to remember to turn the sprinklers on in the arena so they weren't riding in a dust storm. Maybe he should have Guttman cut that alfalfa now. It was blooming, but he didn't want to let it get bitter and lose nutrition in case they didn't get rain soon. The summer had started so wet, then it just stopped, like someone turned off a spigot. Almost a month of dry weather. The creek was way down, just a trickle. In the eleven years he'd been here, he'd never seen it dry up completely though, so he wasn't worried. You had to expect this kind of thing in Kansas. The prairies got every extreme of weather, summer and winter. The people who settled here had the right temperament for it too. Hard-bitten Christians and self-reliant atheists, with only as much idealism as a person could afford who was about to be knocked down by the god of climate. As the early settlers used to say, "In God we trusted, in Kansas we busted." He squinted at the pure, unrelenting blue sky that was turning white with heat, and checked the empty horizons to the south and west. Another prairie habit. You learned to pay attention to what was there, your future was coming from that direction.

"What's up?" Dakota came through the gate behind him, still wearing the clothes she slept in, her hair matted flat on one side of her head and sticking out on the other. He smiled.

"What's so funny?" she asked and ran her hands through her hair, pulling both sides out as if to equalize them. It didn't work. There were sheet creases on her cheek and her eyes were still swollen from sleep. He had to fight the urge to put his arm across her shoulder, and made himself a promise to talk to her sometime today about her plans.

"Thought we'd get western today." He looked down the pasture to where Bobby and the colt were grazing.

"What's that mean?" She sounded cross this morning, as if blaming him for her sleeping so long.

"We'll collect the colt and do some training."

"Why don't you let me catch him."

Ty shrugged and nodded. "Need to turn the sprinklers on in the arena before we work in there."

She sighed. "Who was your slave last year?"

His head jerked up. "Listen—"

"Never mind, I just woke up. I'll take care of it on my way to the house to change." She turned and was gone.

He started to follow her but caught a glimpse of something moving down the far hill toward the creek. A coyote? No, too thick and short. A pig? With those spots, at least they looked like spots, but the sun was turning everything white and black at a distance. No, maybe it was a dog.

It *was* some kind of dog, he realized as he crept closer, and it wasn't particularly afraid of him as it stopped drinking and stood staring at him, mouth open, tongue out panting. Didn't look rabid, eyes calm, mouth clear. When Ty was ten feet away, it seemed to lift itself, raise its ears to points, and draw its lips to reveal big fangs. If it growled, he was going to back away, but the dog was silent, watching him. He put a hand out, palm down, and spoke in a low, soothing tone as he moved forward. "Easy, it's all right, boy." The dog was squat, like a wrestler, with a broad chest, short thick neck, and big boxy head. It had a skinny tail that had been still long enough to make Ty uneasy, but as he talked, it began to wag, once, twice, then back and forth like a metronome. There were white splotches on the legs, across the nose so the black looked like a mask across the face, the tips of the ears, the back, and the tip of the tail. A clown dog, he decided as he stopped two feet away on the bank and squatted. He stretched his hand slowly to the dog, and it watched him with a curious expression. Not afraid, just curious. The dog sniffed his hand, then flicked its tongue across his fingers. Before he could offer to pat it though, the dog sprang at him, knocking him flat on his butt with its powerful body, and began licking his face.

"Stop, okay, all right, I like you too," he protested, patting the dog in big solid thumps with one hand while he tried to push it off with the other. Sitting up, he held the dog like an anvil on his lap and stroked its head. Must run forty or fifty pounds, he decided, a female, pure muscle too. He felt the bumps of ticks on the tail and head. "Who are you?" he asked the face in his hand, and the animal sprang up and gave him a love nip on his neck. "Whoa, no teeth," he ordered and the dog dropped to all fours, ears folded flat as petals on its head. "Okay," he said, and rubbed the head, which immediately came right back up to his chin with more tongue.

"All right, let's see if we can find you some food and maybe talk Dakota into giving you a bath, huh?" He stood and started to walk away, and the dog froze. He stopped and looked over his shoulder and patted his leg. "Come on, then." The dog bounced up ahead of him and began to run circles, so he kept bumping into her; when she tired of that, she went bouncing up the hill, detouring occasionally to follow a scent here and there, but not letting him out of her sight.

He found Dakota in her old jeans and dirty yellow T-shirt working on the stalls. "Look what I found," he announced as the dog swung into the stall knocking into her and spilled the forkful of straw and manure she was lifting toward the spreader in the aisle. "Sorry—" He grabbed her before she fell down, and snatched the fork away from the dog's back. Her arm was thinner than he remembered and he looked at her face. Was it thinner too? Wasn't she eating or something? Her jeans seemed to sag in places he didn't remember from a week ago. They ate at night, he knew that, but he was used to one meal a day. Coffee in the morning, a piece of bread or something at noon maybe, then whatever he could slap together at night, soup or macaroni and cheese from a box, cereal sometimes.

He wanted to ask her if she was eating, but she pulled her arm away with a look that said watch it, buster.

"Thought you could give her a bath, she's full of ticks. Probably got fleas too. I'll pick up some wormer next time I go to town."

Dakota leaned tiredly on the pitchfork, gazing down at the dog, who was now sitting obediently at her feet. Her eyes had dark circles under them, even though she seemed to be sleeping a lot. Was she sick?

"Look, let me finish the stalls." He reached for the fork, but she held on and their hands overlapped for a brief moment before they both let go and the fork fell, banging the dog on the head. There was a frightened yelp and the dog shot out of the stall and started down the aisle.

"No, wait, come on back, girl," he called after it. "Come here, come on," he coaxed as the dog stopped at the doorway, looking over her shoulder at him. He dropped to his knees, and held out his hand again. "Come on darlin', come on, nobody's gonna hurt you, come on." Finally the dog turned and began walking slowly back to him. "Good girl," he said, and the dog trotted up and began licking his face and hands.

"Looks like you should be giving the bath," Dakota said and the dog looked over at her and sat down again. "Well, at least she knows who's boss." She laughed, and the dog wagged its tail and put its ears back in a way that made her face and body look pleased.

"All right, dog show's over." Ty stood. "Look in the wash stall for the flea and tick shampoo I use on the horses. Soon as I finish the stalls here, we'll start on the babies."

"Yes, master." Dakota patted the dog and gave a hand signal that brought it to its feet, standing ready at her left knee.

As Ty started to go out to get the colt, Dakota caught him and, with a scowl, took her bucket of corn and called to Bobby, who came galloping up to the gate, followed by the colt. This time she extended the bucket to him too, and he plunged his nose in long enough for her to snap a lead on his halter.

"The thing with him is not to let him hit the end of the lead, it drives him nuts. You have to keep the rope slack and he's okay," she explained as she handed the colt over and took her horse.

The colt looked at him like it'd just as soon take a bite out of him as follow, but Ty ignored him and walked through the gate with the corn in the bucket rattling encouragement.

"Least he can do is start earning his keep," he said as he cross-tied the colt, making sure the ties were long and loose.

"What's that mean? I'm not?" She stopped in the aisle and looked at him.

"I'm referring to the horses." He picked up the softest brush he could find and touched it to the colt's shoulder while patting him all over to get him used to being handled. Gradually, he worked the brush over the horse's body, checking the legs for swellings and cuts, even brushing the tail, but always being careful to stand to one side so he could get out of the way quickly. The trouble came when he reached up to lift the halter so he could brush the head. The colt went straight up and struck out, caught and spun Ty into the wall, sent the brush clattering away so Bobby standing next to him jumped and spilled Dakota off the short stepladder she was standing on to clip his bridle path.

"That's it," Ty said as he brushed himself off. "You okay?"

Dakota nodded and reset the stepladder. "What're you gonna do?"

"Break this sucker or die," he said, reaching for a lariat hanging on the back wall.

"Just stay out of the way," he ordered when they turned the colt loose in the arena with the rope rigged through his halter and around his hind legs and body.

"This isn't the only way," Dakota said and reached for the rope in his hand.

"Stay out of it," he said and cracked the lunge whip to get the horse running.

"Don't," Dakota pleaded, but it was already too late. Ty pulled the rope and the colt fell, shocked and still. "You've hurt him," she cried and started running across the arena.

"Leave him alone." Ty grabbed her shoulder and shoved her away. "He needs to learn the facts of life before it's too late. You want him to go to the killers? He's useless as he is now."

"But he's scared and hurt," she yelled.

"And he's a thousand-pound bully!"

"Screw you!" she said and moved around him to the side of the horse.

"Leave him alone, Dakota, he has to think this out for himself, or he won't get the point."

"You're just another macho asshole, like all the rest of them." She turned and walked away.

"You can leave anytime you've a mind to," he said. "Sooner the better."

She stopped and half-turned toward him, biting her lip. There was something in her eyes like fear and he was immediately sorry. She turned away and kept walking.

"Now you've done it, you dumb shit," he muttered as he knelt beside the colt to check the ropes that needed to hold him down for at least an hour. "You're not hurt, are you?" He was afraid of what would happen if the damn thing had somehow managed to hurt itself. Ty had done this enough times to know how to make it work, and although the horse was breathing hard, it was fine as far as he could tell. The panic in its eyes was beginning to dull even as he watched. Maybe it wouldn't take that long. A nice big colt like this, it'd be a shame for it to end up in a can.

He spent an hour driving the tractor in circles around the colt, flapping blankets and sacks at the horse, making it tolerate every noise and quick movement he could think of. He even got the dog out of the tack room and chased it around, throwing a stick and watching it do wheelies and bouncing straight up as it ran. The horse was soaked with sweat, but there was resignation in its eye by the time Ty returned to it.

Kneeling beside the head, he began on the halter again, lifting it and moving it around, although the horse grunted as if it were being beaten. Something terrible must've happened with this halter, Ty realized as he ran his fingers through the forelock and over the ears. That's when he found it. A large lump where there shouldn't be one, right behind the left ear, a swelling the halter or bridle would rub. When Ty pressed the lump, the horse bellowed in pain. Dakota was running through the door just as Ty was getting ready to holler for her.

"What are you *doing* to him?" she demanded angrily.

"Get me scissors and that first-aid kit right inside the tack room. Hurry up." He sat back on his heels and patted the colt's shoulder. "Sorry, buddy. Should've checked this first." He hoped he hadn't ruined the horse, he really hoped he hadn't. Not only for the colt's sake, but his own too. He could just imagine Dakota's expression.

When she returned with the equipment, he clipped away enough of the mane and forelock to get a good look at the area. It was some kind of abscess or injury, soft though, like infection. He could call the vet, but it meant a long wait and having to throw the horse again or tranquilize it, and the colt had already had enough trauma for one day. Might as well get on with it while he had the chance. With the small scalpel he kept in the kit, he opened the top of the lump and ducked to avoid the infection that spurted out with the release of pressure, then began to drain in a long yellow stream.

"Jesus," Dakota whispered from the other side of the horse.

The dog lay behind her, watching. The colt groaned again, but didn't struggle against him as he poured some Betadine into the wound and used the scalpel to open it more. Then the tip hit something hard, and as he probed, a roofing nail lifted out and stuck to the opening. "Look at that," Ty said.

Dakota leaned over the horse. "What the hell is that?"

Ty picked it up with the scalpel and held it out for her. "Nail. Short enough so it wouldn't hit the vertebra, but enough to cause infection and pain. Must of been driving him crazy. Lucky he didn't kill someone or himself. Poor guy. Hard to say how far down the infection runs. Guess we'd better put a tube in there. Go to the tack room, look in the box marked A, and you'll find some plastic tubing. Cut about a four- or five-inch piece and bring some tape and packing; you'll see some penicillin too, bring that and a syringe. Fast as you can. We'll have to get him up soon. I'll try to clean and open this enough to do the job."

The colt was listless as they got him up and led him back to a stall with a rope around his neck, since he couldn't wear a halter. The tube was draining gunk down his cheek and slipping off the Vaseline Ty had coated the skin with so it wouldn't stick and tear the hair.

"You make a pretty good vet," Dakota commented as they stood side by side leaning on the stall door and watching the colt nudge the water bucket with his nose.

"Learned most of it working rough stock for Swenson on the rodeo circuits. Couldn't afford time or money calling vets every time something happened. Local vet clinic lets me buy what I need. They're not overly fond of horse calls."

"He going to be all right?"

"Have to worry about colic or founder after our session. Let's give him a bran and molasses mash and watch his water intake. See if some of your babying helps." He glanced at her out of the corner of his eye. She wasn't smiling.

"Guess we need to talk later." He sighed and turned toward the house. "I'm going to town now. You need anything?"

"No," she mumbled as he left.

"I'll take the dog—" he called.

∞ Chapter Seven

Jerusalem was ten miles southwest of his place, and Ty had to take a dirt road to the blacktop, then weave around a bit before it led straight into the middle of town. Whereas Cottonwood Falls, farther to the south, was relatively famous for its picturesque county courthouse perched on a rise at the end of Broadway, Jerusalem had had no such vision when it was built. The town had been a passing-through spot for the trail herds and pioneers of the 1800s, not even a rest stop except for the sick and injured, who found a little water and an abundance of the Jerusalem artichokes that gave the place its name, not its biblical reference, as later settlers believed and cursed it for.

Now the town wore the exhausted look of the dry land around it. Half the businesses had fled, leaving the local bank, single bar and restaurant, small café, combined hardware store and grocery, dusty family clothing store, feed mill, and old plumbing and heating supply store turned pizza parlor that had gone broke and now was divided into stalls of goods for sale by women who produced crafts over the long prairie winters. Four years ago the younger son of one of the old settler families had returned to Jerusalem to open a tiny bookstore in the front of the building, and that was where Ty headed as soon as he parked his truck under one of the two remaining elm trees that used to line the street. The dog stood on the seat watching him without expression. Since it was early afternoon on a weekday, Ty was the only person on the street. Heat radiated off the cement walk and limestone buildings like a steadily pumping furnace, but at least the Towne Mall, as they called their little enterprise, had air-conditioning. As he entered, the thick spice of cinnamon, clove, and artificial lilac from the back stalls sprang on him and he had to almost fight his way through to the odor he preferred—the inky steel and paper smell of new books.

"Logan—" he touched the brim of his cowboy hat at the lanky gray-haired man in white western-cut shirt, jeans, and boots who leaned against the counter reading. Ty wondered if he ever sat down.

"Mr. Bonte, what can I do for you?" Logan Woods smiled and shook Ty's hand.

"Cookbooks?"

"Okay." Logan came from around the counter and crossed the aisle to a small section of domestic arts books. There were five cookbooks, three of them offering old-time range and homestead recipes. The one Logan pulled out looked a little used. "This one has some pretty good meals in it. Used it once or twice myself." He handed the book over.

"*Cooking?*"

Logan shrugged. "You need something more complex?"

Ty laughed. "Been living on macaroni and cheese so long, probably wouldn't recognize anything better."

"Know what you mean. Without Marlys I woulda starved by now."

It had been only a couple of months after his return to the area when Logan Woods had started seeing the single schoolteacher, and within the year they were married. Logan being so much older, it surprised the local boys, who hadn't thought of the odd, skinny man as their competition. Marlys was a tiny woman in her twenties who had come to Jerusalem to settle, she'd announced at the first school meeting. Her ambition in life was right here as teacher and librarian. Only Logan had taken that part seriously. The younger men had wanted a wife they could drag off to their farms or ranches to produce kids and cook. Logan wanted a woman he could talk to.

"Got anything fancier?" Ty asked, keeping his eyes away from Logan.

"Here's an international one from *The New York Times*. Won't be able to find all the ingredients though. Well, for some of them maybe." He pulled the book and handed it over. "You trying to impress somebody, Ty?"

The books suddenly felt heavy and ridiculous and he started to hand them back, but Logan kept his hands at his sides. "No, well, I mean, there's someone staying out at my place and—"

"Better take both these then. Women don't like starving. Been my experience they put up with a lot less in that department than a person would think. They got appetites all right. Marlys, as tiny as she is, can out-eat me most days of the week. And cranky as a dry cow when she doesn't get her food on time. Here, let me ring those up—" Logan finally took the books and walked back to the counter. "Got a couple of other books you might like over there—Ron Hansen, he's from Nebraska, and that Louise Erdrich book there. She tells a good story."

Ty picked each up and turned them over. Logan kept a running catalog of what each customer liked and bought. He'd once even stopped Ty from buying a book he'd already read but couldn't remember. Ty wondered what sort of thing Dakota read. Maybe the woman, Erdrich. "I'll take this one." He handed it over.

"Uh-huh." Logan smiled.

"What's her name?" he asked as he wrapped the books in brown paper and tied them with string, something no one in town could understand, now that plastic sacks were so available.

"Dakota Carlisle, but you don't know her—" Ty could feel the heat mount his throat and spread to his ears.

"Well, bring her in, Ty. I'm sure Marlys would appreciate a new face. Where's she from?"

"I don't know—I just hauled her horse and—" It sounded strange, and he could see from the amusement of his friend's face that he was enjoying it.

"Hauled her too?"

"It's not like that—" He tried to pick up the package but Logan hung onto it.

"Buying her presents, cooking for her. Come to town the middle of the day with the sun shining and not running into the hardware or vet first? You know what Marlys would say—"

"I can imagine." Ty succeeded in getting the package away. "She's just passing through, Logan." But as he left, he realized that she'd never said where she was going. And she had that darn horse with her. Surely she wasn't going to ride out of here. The dog watched him as he passed the truck and waved. He liked it more for not whimpering or slobbering the half-closed windows. Just waiting. He'd be foolish not to keep a dog like that, he decided as he went into the café two doors away and sat down at the counter. It took a minute for Terri to push tiredly through the swinging door from the back room, where she sat at the little table and watched soap operas when things were dead. She used a gray, almost dry rag to brush the crumbs away from his elbows and raised her eyebrows at him.

"Coffee, black," he said and half-turned to look out the big, smeared front windows. Years ago he and Terri had gone out a half dozen times, had barely made it to bed for the first time when her soon-to-be-ex had broken down her door and grabbed her half-naked body out of his arms. The husband had been trying to untangle her loose bra enough to strangle her when Ty had gotten his jeans fastened and pushed the man away. Terri had given them both what-for then and Ty had left the couple arguing about the fine points of separation. None of them spoke to each other if they could help it after that; it'd been seven years now. He vowed he'd say something someday. She clunked the cup down, spilling enough that he knew she was still pissed about something. What? That he hadn't called her again or gone back there? It just wasn't his kind of trouble, he should explain to her. He took a sip of coffee, bitter and lukewarm from sitting all day. Probably saved it for men like him on the off-chance one of them would show up. She and the ex were still soon-to-be and playing out the same melodrama weekends in every bar between Jerusalem and Cottonwood Falls, from what he heard. Be better if she'd stay home and clean up this place. He grimaced at the fly specks on the mirror in front of him. An old strip of flypaper almost solid black with tiny bodies hung in the corner of the mirror as if it were important for customers to get a three-hundred-and-sixty-degree view of dead flies. The red Coca-Cola lettering was buckled and chipped along the top of the mirror, and he noticed that the big new dispenser on the counter said RC and Diet-Rite instead of Coke.

Unwrapping the books, he started looking for a recipe he thought he could manage. Beef Stroganoff. Sounded good, sour cream he could find. Canned mushrooms and sliced beef. Red wine, well—he didn't want to go to the liquor store, five years since he'd been in one. Could he trust himself now? Maybe he could ask Logan to buy it. Logan was the only person he'd ever confided much of his history to—including the outstanding warrant that kept him out of Nebraska, though he hadn't given him the specifics.

Ty's tub took half an hour to fill. Dakota could boil the water on the stove faster than this. And when she'd first turned on the faucet, it had coughed orange and piss yellow before clear water came out. While it was filling, she went out to the overgrown yard and looked for camomile. She found an old white T-shirt in the kitchen worn thin enough it tore easily, and knotted the camomile in it to scent the bathwater.

She'd been discovering his clothes everywhere, and had spent the past couple of hours cleaning and straightening as best she could. At first she wasn't going to do it, get caught like this again. But she couldn't help it, she decided, she wasn't the kind of person to sit around in a mess. And for a man who took his barn work so seriously, he was awfully sloppy in the house. Lucky he didn't smoke or drink hard. That made a kind of mess she didn't much like.

She'd cleaned the bathroom last, scrubbing the faded yellow linoleum floor with vinegar and then finally some Mr. Clean she found under the stairs in the old dugout basement. She'd hated sticking her hands in the half-dark and pulling out the bottle. It must've been left from the previous owner, she decided, as she surveyed the array of household items a man like Ty wouldn't know to get. So far, she hadn't noticed any urge to dispose of anything. He specialized in empty containers, rags, and sacks. After she'd scrubbed the layer of hair and dust off the sill beside the tub and opened the window, which stuck like it hadn't been touched in years, she'd put a mayonnaise jar of Queen Anne's lace and sunflowers on the ledge, and now she leaned there, resting her chin on her arms while she breathed in the hot grasses outside. The outline of the hills seemed to sharpen like blue pencil lines as the hot haze made them almost disappear in the distance. She'd seen that happen in the Grand Canyon too. The way the rock lost detail and grew gray and distant in the heat as far as the eye could follow. She imagined sound would echo that way if you could actually see the way it spread and volleyed the voice over and over, in shades of repeating gray. It was so still now she could hear the dusty plop of horse hooves stamping flies at the pasture gates.

She'd been trying not to think about what had been going on at Eddie's, how he'd called her from Detroit, where he was showing that week after she moved Dusty's horses into the barn, to tell her to be on the lookout for "The Sandman," who was going to take care of that rank colt. She hadn't said anything, so he'd just assumed that she was back on *the team*, as he called it. After all, she'd moved back to his barn, and he'd forgiven her for abandoning him in Mason City, Iowa, the previous fall. As soon as they hung up, she'd called and left a message on Ty's phone to pick up a couple of Dusty's horses at Eddie's. She just hoped he'd be checking in if he was gone. He was the closest out-of-state dealer who still seemed independent of Eddie though he traded with him. It had worked out better than she imagined. Ty had shown up the next week. Making him take the others had been spur-of-the-moment really. Since Eddie'd be gone for another couple of weeks, she figured she had a little time to figure out the next step. For now she was going to let her body slide down, close her eyes, and relax in this hot water.

The old clawfoot tub was still in good shape, and it was long enough for her to stretch out and adjust the water with her toes. Maybe she'd make him build a shelf along the side of the tub for the shampoos and things. Put a set of shelves against the wall by the sink for towels. Right now he used an orange cardboard box printed with TIDE in big black, water-streaked letters. She'd taken the towels off the top gingerly and shaken them to get the spiders out. The corners of the bathroom were littered with husks of insects below the webs bridging the angles, but she'd been careful all over the house to avoid directly killing a spider. Bad luck, her mother always said. Her mother had had a grocery cart full of those beliefs her own mother had carried with her from a pioneer upbringing. No wonder she had taken off as soon as she got the chance; her family had been on the move for over a hundred years.

Still was. Except now she felt like maybe she'd reached the end. Stuck in the middle of Kansas, no place left to go. Dusty had been the turning point, better than any man she'd found at the track or on the horse show circuit. For the first time, she let the grief of losing him come rising up her chest and salt her throat and nose, bringing tears to her eyes. She cried for a while, hugging her arms around her stomach, shivering in the cooling water. Although she'd acted tough telling Ty and Danny, she was awfully sorry for Dusty, whose last worries had naturally been for someone else—for her and the horses he tried to save.

She sat up and let some of the water out, then ran the hot again. As warm as it was outside, the little house seemed to have trapped a permanent chill, smelling like starchy old dust and the humid shaley clay just beneath the floor.

As she lay back and put the hot washcloth over her breasts, it occurred to her that the real change in life with Dusty had started a month ago, when that rank colt had shown up. He'd grown edgy, worried. Hadn't been able to sleep or eat, and she watched him drinking more than usual too, without much effect. His face had grown gray and ragged. She should have done something maybe, but she didn't know what. He'd never mentioned heart trouble, and he almost never wanted to bother other people with his troubles. He saw the good in every bad thing, and every bad horse too. And people, she had to admit. He'd taken her on after she'd left the show in Mason City with enough gas money to get to the Missouri-Arkansas border, where he was laying up his horses till the season started. The axle on her truck broke; her credit cards had been canceled by her husband, of course. Her husband had run off with the second cousin he'd met at a wedding up North while she was on the road. It only seemed fair that he'd take his money with him. She still owed money on Bobby too, though Eddie had had a plan for that also. She traded the twelve-year-old trailer for stall board on Bobby while she slept in the cab of the truck dead behind the barn and looked for work.

But it was really the rank colt that ruined things. It was too good for them, she'd told Dusty the day it arrived from Eddie. Sixteen-three-hand bay with a white star and white ankles all around. A four-year-old, he'd told her, but she'd looked at his upper lip, seen the tattoo that showed he'd raced, and figured it out. A three-year-old. A very, very nice one too. Never been broke, Dusty announced. Rank. But according to the tattoo, he'd raced. She didn't contradict Dusty, she just watched things more carefully, especially since it came from Eddie. Wasn't there anyone above board in the horse business, she sighed. What about Ty? Well, what about her? She hadn't told him anything about the colt. Hadn't had a chance really. Before he'd rushed headlong at the horse this morning with that rope business. She'd heard of a flying W that threw the horse down, but never actually seen it before. She'd been furious all day because of it too. Even though they'd discovered the source of the colt's problem, she hated the way he'd hung his head and plodded along to his stall afterwards. When she'd checked on him before her bath, he was standing with his head in the back corner of the stall, refusing to eat. It was such a goddamn waste, what they did to these horses.

Who was the colt though? The papers were coming, Dusty had promised. Papers were always coming in these deals. Lost or maybe tied up in a divorce, any number of stories people told. She could take the tattoo number, write the Jockey Club, send in the money, find out. Then what? "Better mind your own business and look out for yourself," she said out loud and looked at the water, tan with dirt. She'd better get a move on before Ty got back from town. She wanted to be clean and fresh and relaxed when he walked in the door. Act like nothing big when he saw the clean house. She'd put on the pale blue Mexican shirt she'd stolen from her husband, a pullover with the long opening down the front that she could wear without a bra so he would see the hint of breast between the sewn flat ruffles when she turned her body or leaned forward. It made her feel good and she was tired of not feeling like anything.

She'd fallen asleep on her bed, the only messy room in the house, he noticed as he tiptoed out. The rest of it looked better than it had in years. He found two cardboard boxes of his junk by the back door and laughed. When he opened the refrigerator he'd bought two years ago when the old one sputtered and died the hottest day of summer, he was looking at clean, empty shelves. He unpacked the groceries, filling the fridge for the first time in recent memory, and noticed that she'd even peeled the consumer savings sticker off the front and scrubbed the smudges of his fingerprints from the handle area.

He put the cookbooks on the counter, then moved the one he wasn't using to the top of the fridge. He got out all the ingredients the recipe listed and tried to figure the order of events, the way he did every morning with the horses. The rice was a problem. They were out of the minute stuff at the store, so he'd gotten the dusty bag that looked hard and hopeless, though he read the instructions several times. He had no idea how long the meat would take, so he didn't know whether to start the rice now or later. What if he forgot? And pans, he always kept the two he used most on top of the stove, but they were gone. He began to look through the cabinets for the first time in ages.

It was the door banging shut that woke her, and forgetting about all her plans, she stumbled out into the kitchen just as he was washing his hands at the sink. She rubbed her ear and looked around while it dawned on her. "My clean kitchen—"

"Sorry, I was just fixing dinner." He turned to the stove. "Sit down, you can have a glass of wine." He reached for the bottle.

"I'm not awake." She yawned. "What *is* all this?" She looked at the brown spots of gravy on the floor and the sink stacked with pans and dishes she had left clean a few hours earlier. This was the problem with men. They made work. She pulled a chair out from the table shoved into the nook, and sat down sideways, leaning her back against the wall, pulling her legs up and perching her toes on the chair edge. The dog trotted over and rested its chin on her toes. She scratched its head. "Guess we should name this critter."

"Figured it was time we started eating better. When I'm alone, I forget. Got some cookbooks. See?" He lifted the one with grease-spattered pages from the counter and pulled the other off the top of the fridge. "Bought stuff for breakfast and lunch too. Lots of food—"

"Cookbooks?" she asked as he poured the red wine all the way to the top of a jelly glass and handed it to her. She spilled a drop on her knee before she managed to sip it down. She swiped at the wine on her leg and took another drink. "Aren't you having any?"

He looked at the bottle as if he'd really like to, but shook his head. He was wearing a stained white dish towel around his waist, with the ends tucked in his belt. His pale green T-shirt was splotched with sweat and flour. It made him look harmless, she decided, like a ten-year-old boy trying to please his mother on her birthday. No wonder mothers couldn't give up their sons.

"I turned the babies out again. You forgot them," she announced and regretted it when his face looked like she'd slapped him.

"Thanks." He turned back to the stove, lifting the lid on something, letting out a puff of steam, and plopping it back down with a little bang.

"Don't know what you did before I showed up." She drank and smiled at his back. The wine felt good, and she wanted to stir things up a little. Pretend he hadn't told her she could leave this morning.

"House looks nice," he said, lifting the bottle of wine, then putting it back down on the counter and turning toward her again. "You look nice too, washed up, huh?"

She ran her fingers through her hair, lifting and letting it drop. It'd been wet when she fell asleep, so she hadn't had time to straighten the curls and waves out of it. "When's that stuff gonna be ready?"

"Soon as I set the table, I guess." He opened the cabinet door in front of him and took down plates, then got the silverware out of the drawer on the other side of the sink.

"Hope this is edible," he said, lifting the lids off two pans and scooping piles onto the two plates. When he put the plate in front of her, she had to admit it smelled good. The dog licked its lips several times but stood politely out of the way.

"This is a lot." She picked up her fork, then set it back down to wait for him. He went to the fridge and pulled out two little plates, each with a leaf of iceberg lettuce, a canned pear, a mound of cottage cheese, and a maraschino cherry bleeding pink on top. She almost started laughing it reminded her so much of something her mother would serve, thinking she'd done them all a big favor. In fact, she had liked it as a kid. It was just, growing up, you learned to despise food like that. He sat down, glanced shyly at her, smiled, and picked up his fork. She waited for his first bite before trying hers. It was okay, really it was okay. A little salty, but not bad at all.

They didn't talk while they ate. They never did, she noticed. Too tired. Except they'd both had some time off today, so maybe they could talk, but they didn't. She poured herself another glass of wine and leaned back to let the food sink in and her head follow the meandering of the alcohol. The dog sat watching them for a while before giving up hope and wandering into the living room for a nap.

"She already had her dinner," Ty said, eyeing her resigned departure.

"That was good." Dakota lifted her glass to him and drank with her eyes closed.

"Gotta fatten you up," he said and put his fork down.

"Thought you wanted me out of here." She drank again, watching his face.

He picked up the fork and put it down again. Looked at her for a moment, letting his eyes linger on hers, only his weren't readable they were so dark, then he looked away, licking his lower lip with the tip of his tongue. She pulled on the bottom of her shirt so the opening came halfway down her chest, and pushed the sleeves up over her elbows.

"I'd like to meet the son of a bitch did that to the colt, wouldn't you?" He tipped the chair back so his head rested on the half wall behind him, his legs splayed as he watched her through half-lowered lids.

Very cute, she thought. Okay—she turned in her chair so she was leaning against the wall sideways to give him a glimpse inside her shirt. His black eyes went there immediately and she smiled. The wine was heating up her skin and she could feel her hair start to curl along her face and neck.

"Did Dusty or Eddie ever say anything to you about the colt?" He clasped his hands behind his head, keeping his eyes on her.

Suddenly she was embarrassed and turned in her chair, facing the table again, feeling how the neck of her shirt gaped open and wanting to stick the wadded paper towel down there to cover up. "No— not really." She thought of the phone call about "The Sandman" coming but couldn't tell Ty about that or the fact that they'd actually stolen the horse from Eddie. They still had a week or so, she figured. She'd know in another week whether she could trust him. In her head she could hear the nagging voice that warned about lying and rationalizing because she didn't want to cause trouble, get yelled at, maybe kicked out. "He's an awfully good-quality colt."

"Yeah." He watched her.

"Going to geld him?" She couldn't look at him anymore, but it didn't stop his eyes from doing what they were doing. She could feel them all over her skin and she wanted to get up and leave. Leave the whole thing. Ride off on Bobby. Let Ty sort it out with Eddie. The colt was better now, probably saved his life, finding that nail. Eddie wouldn't—then she remembered the others.

"I'll wait and see. He might be okay now. When I brought the horses in, he perked up and started to nibble. I checked the drain, seems to be working good. Gave him a carrot and he didn't seem too mad at me. Hate doing something to an animal doesn't need it." He wouldn't take his eyes off her. She kept peeking to check.

"Yeah, well—" She pushed the colt and Eddie out of her mind and let her eyes sweep down his legs while she pushed up her sleeves and pulled the back of her shirt collar to raise the gap in front. He was barefoot, she realized with a shock, and his feet were these big, long, knobbed dead-white objects that seemed to have no relationship to the deeply tanned skin of his arms and face. His second toe was longer than the big one and that meant something, but she couldn't remember what.

"Why don't we go in there on the sofa where it's comfortable. Dog probably needs to go out too. I'll clean up later." He waited a minute and then stood, reaching across for her hand and the bottle.

They sat side by side on the sofa, propping their feet on the battered tack trunk he used as a coffee table. It had been monogrammed with PTB in cream, red, and tan on the dark blue vinyl front. "Eddie gave me this, client left it when she moved out." He nodded at the trunk. Dakota remembered how Eddie stole everything he could lay his hands on at shows. Once he even took a stack of four-by-fours and a tractor tire he found behind a barn at the show grounds in Des Moines.

Ty poured more wine in her glass and out of the corner of his eye watched her bring it to her lips. They were quiet for a few minutes, staring out the picture window at the dusty mauve twilight. Barn swallows circled in and out of the open doors of the stable and indoor arena as if they kept forgetting something before they went to bed. Like black arrows they dove and skipped as if they were being flung from a giant, unseen hand. The hundred-foot cottonwood in front of the house began to fill with crows arriving one and two at a time with a clattering and squawking that required a constant shifting of the others along the limbs until the tree seemed to realign its clotted shape in the failing blue-black of the sky.

She felt his fingers on her shoulders as he put his arm along the back of the sofa. It changed everything with a kind of thrilling numbness. She didn't move, not even for the sip of wine she wanted. Finally she heard him sigh and felt the whole hand as he inched closer until their hips were touching, and she found herself tucked in under his arm where the musky scent of horse mingled with his sweat. It was a good, clean sweat from working, almost as sweet as it was acrid, like apple cider vinegar. She took a sip of wine and felt his lips on her hair, heard the deep breath he took, or maybe felt it as his ribs pulled in and his chest rose. She sipped again and he let it out. The numbness was being pushed away by the tingling in her skin, as if she could feel the oxygen in the blood under the surface rushing along, making her breathless. She sipped again and let her hand holding the glass follow its urge to rest on his thigh. It was right next to hers after all. Right there. She heard his sharp intake of air. She let her little finger rub the material of his jeans an inch up, an inch down. Her nail made this little buzzing sound. She felt his hand on her stomach below her breasts. She finished the wine and he took the glass. She leaned back against his arm, his skin hotter than hers against the back of her neck. She closed her eyes and they sat there, fragile, both of them afraid to move while the clock in the kitchen clicked off minutes and the peepers in the high grass along the edge of the driveway began to throb on one after another.

He lifted his feet off the trunk and her hand brushed the inside of his thigh. It startled both of them, and yet she turned as he reached for her face, and their lips met tentatively. She held her breath, and their mouths opened a little while his hand found the back of her neck, bringing her closer. With the other hand he pulled her shoulder so she had to turn, and he lifted her legs across the top of his thighs and she could feel him waiting there. He kissed her chin, her throat, and she opened her shirt and put her hands in his hair. Then he was lifting and lowering her to the floor, on the gray-blue carpet she'd cleaned so carefully, so long and hard, as if she had already imagined the way her bare skin might pick up gravel and dirt but now felt only the soft scrap of the patterned tufts as he pulled her shirt off and raised himself above her while he watched her first unhook the buckle, then unbutton his jeans.

In one slow but complete gesture, he tugged his T-shirt over his head and descended, his lean hips resting lightly on hers, while their chests met and held fast with sweat as they kissed once, twice, then fought their own flesh to get closer still. He reared back, braced on his fists, and looked at her until she began to inch his jeans down.

She closed her eyes as he began outlining her breast in closing circles with his finger until he tapped the very tip of her nipple once,
twice—she arched up to meet his mouth and he caught her against
him, burying his head in her chest. She licked his salty neck while
he sucked and she let her hand touch the hardness between his legs,
pull his underpants down and let it out. He caught both her nipples
in his fingers, and took her mouth with his, pressing himself against
her until she reached for her own shorts. But his hands moved past
hers and fumbling at the button, yanked and popped it, bursting the
zipper open so it tore at her skin as she struggled out of them with
her underpants. Suddenly they were skin on skin from their faces to
their bare feet, resting on each other, and the shock stilled them,
making their breath catch and hold in shallow sacs while they
waited for the sweet honey buzz in their heads to seep down their
bodies and seal them into each other.

∞ Chapter Eight

As soon as they hit the gravel road in front of the farm, Dakota pressed for a trot. Bobby had a long, smooth gait she could find with her seat bones when she relaxed and let the countryside flow by her. The big back sent enough heat radiating up her bare legs that she began to warm up and enjoy the grasslands unraveling on all sides of her. That first day they drove into the Flint Hills, she wondered how she'd ever be able to stand the emptiness, and what seemed like wallpaper uniformity in the repeated patterns of hills and valleys, green grass and blue sky. Now, after only a few weeks, her eye was beginning to notice distinctions. She drew a deep breath, there it was— scissory grasses, sweet clover, and something mustard sharp from the wildflowers. They passed a clump of sumac whose leaves were fading pink along the edges, breaking through the green. The squirrel grass glistened with spider webs of dew drops. Around her the hills had a wet pale green sheen that dropped into mist-soaked valleys that would sharpen and turn yellow-green by midmorning with late summer heat. The dusty leaves of the goldenrod and sunflowers had that droopy, tired green they got in August, a dark drained green. She knew the difference between May and August just by the greens, and she imagined them as some kind of giant clock without the unnecessary specifics of second hands.

She nudged with her heels and Bobby broke into a rocking canter that was easy to sit as the hooves plopped softly in the dust. This was the pace he could maintain around a jump course, letting the fences come up in stride. He'd been able to place anytime she could keep her nerves from interfering. "Stay still, don't move, don't jump on his neck, let him do the work," Eddie had yelled in the warm-up areas. "Keep your hands up, stay out of his mouth. He's not the Concorde, but he'll take you around if you let him." Once, after she'd jerked his mouth in the middle of a combination and jumped on his neck, making his hind legs crash down on the last rail, Eddie had called her "Jack the Ripper" and refused to train her the rest of the afternoon. Not that he had any love for the horse, but Eddie had almost no patience for mistakes of any kind, especially those that stopped a horse from doing its job. He was a complex man, she had learned over the year she was with him, one who could show compassion for a horse one minute, then—

Bobby had been bought as a fancy show horse for a lot of money but didn't pan out for one of Eddie's rich clients. A washout for the Amateur division at 3'6" but fine over fences at the lower levels. Gradually, the horse's status had fallen so low he was living at the far end of Eddie's barn, often forgotten or ignored. The owner wanted him dumped, and needed her money out of him to buy the next horse. All of this happened just when Dakota started working at the barn. It wasn't until much later that she heard the story of how Eddie and the owner had given Bobby huge shots of artificial Adrenalin one day and lunged him for an hour trying to induce a heart attack for the insurance. They were getting ready for something worse when the owner broke down crying and stopped it. After that, Dakota had started buying him on time. Jeff, her husband, had told her he didn't care what she did as long as she supported herself. A year earlier, they'd met in a St. Paul bar during Winter Carnival and married on impulse, and when both of them quickly realized the mistake, they'd stayed together by keeping separate lives. He paid for the little house and groceries and she negotiated the used pickup, and later Eddie gave her the trailer. By mucking stalls, grooming, and managing the barn at shows for Eddie, she could just squeak by.

Eddie hated Bobby though, and when he convinced her husband to put the insurance on him as an investment, she knew it was time to leave.

"Bobby." She leaned down and hugged him, burying her nose in the short mane smelling both nutty and acrid. He snorted and arched his neck and cocked his head around to look at her as he bounced a stride and changed leads. She glanced quickly behind them at the dust flying out in a long thick cloud. They'd end up choking to death if anybody passed them. Grasshoppers scattered like gravel pinging into the brush just ahead of them. Then a gray rabbit hopped into the middle of the road ahead, saw them, and froze. "Go on," she whispered. The rabbit waited another moment, then hopped off, disappearing into the dusty brush on the other side. To her right, she saw mist rising from a pond and a couple of ducks who gave muffled quacks as they glided across the surface, ghostlike.

At a distance she saw something trotting along the road with its nose in the weeds. Coyote? No, as they closed the gap, she saw it was a dog. Damn, Bobby was scared of strange dogs. "Easy," she murmured while Bobby's ears worked back and forth. "He's not going to hurt you." She tightened her legs around him and set her hands to bring him to a trot, then turned him around toward home.

Glancing back, she saw that the dog was a scrawny shepherd collie mix of some sort, big and brown and shaggy with a collar of black hair around its neck like a lion. It followed them without seeming too interested.

"Oh shit," Dakota muttered and tried to loosen her legs and seat to relax the horse, but they were fighting each other and she bounced hard against his jerky, uneven stride. She let him up into the canter and finally a flat gallop.

When they came to the driveway, she had to yank his mouth hard until he broke into a stiff trot that bounced her up against his withers. "Slow down," she growled. At the top of the drive she pulled hard enough to bring him panting to a walk and twisted around to check on the dog, which had apparently given up interest. She patted Bobby's rump and loosened her legs. He heaved a big sigh and snorted hard. Their new dog waited with wagging tail and tongue hanging out at the gate to the yard. Taking a step sideways, Bobby cocked his head and eyed her. "Big baby." Dakota slid off, her arms slick with sweat. "So much for our relaxing jaunt," she said. The insides of her legs were sticky with wet brown hair. The dog came over and swiped at the drying sweat with its tongue. "Stop—" She laughed and shoved at it with her foot while Bobby pulled at the reins.

Suddenly the dog stiffened, ears and tail erect, lips drawn back as a deep growl rumbled from her broad chest. Dakota whirled around just as the brown dog she'd seen on the road ran toward her with its ears flattened, teeth bared. The two dogs met in a tangled ball of white and brown snarls, snapping and biting.

"Stop it! Here, stop, no! No!" She yelled as much at the dogs as Bobby, who began to back and rear until finally the bridle slipped off and he ran toward the barn. The dogs were bleeding now and she didn't know whether to stop them or go after her horse. "Stop, goddamn it!" She tried kicking at them, and although her foot found flesh, it did nothing but cause some slashing teeth to graze her ankle. Quickly looking around, she saw that there was a stack of old fence lumber by the gate. She grabbed a broken piece with a jagged end, then thought better of it and threw that down for one with a smooth end, which she banged on the ground next to the two dogs, trying to distract them. Their dog had the stray on its back as she cut off its air with her throat grip, digging deeper into the thick collar for more purchase, but never releasing it. The battle was silent now, and Dakota realized she had to hurry. Jamming the board between their bodies, she jostled the smaller dog off the stray, but couldn't get her to break her grip. If anything, the dog took a tighter hold with her big jaws and long teeth.

"Come on, come on." Dakota put the board down and reached in with her hands, trying to unlock the dog's jaws.

"Dakota, don't—" Ty yelled and the stray twisted and clamped its teeth on her hand. It was like being caught in a sewing machine, the needle pushing through layers of skin and tendon and nerve, over and over again.

"Help! Ty—he's got my hand!" She kicked at both dogs now, and then felt the stream of water from the nose on her legs and arms as Ty began to squirt them. Finally he shoved the hose in their eyes and noses until the dogs were choking and both released their jaws. She stumbled back, blood bubbling from the ragged holes in her hand. The dogs stood, shook themselves, looked at each other, and backed up a few steps.

"Get in there—" Ty ordered their dog, who slunk through the gate and ran to hide under the porch. "Go home, Scout, you piece of crap—get outta here!" he yelled at the other dog, squirting it with the hard spray until it took off at a limping trot down the drive. Ty turned to her and seemed to notice the small streams of blood for the first time. "Aw shit, I'm sorry—here, wash it off so we can see how bad it is."

She held out her hand with the four punctures on each side but couldn't stop it from shaking as the water turned pink. "It's not too bad," she said, trying not to let her voice crack.

He took off his T-shirt and quickly wrapped it around the bubbling wounds. "Think you need a doctor?"

She shook her head. "You know that dog? Doesn't have rabies or anything, does it?"

"Yeah, that's Logan and Marlys's dog, Scout, from down the road. He's had his shots. We better clean this up good though, puncture wounds infect like crazy. What'd you stick your hand in there for anyway?"

She tried to pull her hand away, but he hung on and led her to the house. At the steps, she stopped and turned toward the barn. "Bobby's loose—"

"He won't go anywhere, not at breakfast time." Ty opened the door for her and she had to admit he had her horse pretty well pegged.

After they'd cleaned and bandaged the hand, arguing over the details every step of the way, he made her take a pain pill and go back to bed while he did chores. She wasn't used to being treated this way. She was too independent usually to accept anybody's help. It had been like that growing up in Divinity, Iowa, too. Even in high school, where she'd been a maverick, she'd felt alone all the time. The boys were mostly interested in cars, drinking beer, and getting laid, in that order. Some of them cared about farming, and they were just as bad in a different way, and none of them cared about anything she cared about. She'd left the night of graduation, and written her parents only sporadically since. She had nothing to offer them, and the feeling was probably the same, she figured. Although lately, since she'd run from Eddie, she felt herself becoming more aimless, slower to pick herself up again. Then Dusty's death, and now this— her hand throbbed, but it felt almost good.

At noon she woke up to find three big sunflowers dripping with tiny black bugs, sitting in a ten-pound coffee can on the crate beside the bed. He'd pushed the clothes and debris into a pile in the corner. And there on the bed beside her was a new book. Well, she sighed, at least she'd have something to read. Outside the heat was making everything quiet except for the whistling of a bobwhite over and over. Then it seemed like the heat itself was making a kind of shushing noise that turned everything drowsy and heavy until even the bird hushed and she fell back asleep.

For the next two weeks, Ty made her take it easy with chores, reminding her that he'd done it all alone before she came. At night, they made love carefully and thoroughly, sleeping later into the mornings than either one of them had in years. The horses settled easily into the new schedule, as if lulled by the same sense of well-being. Nobody worked too hard, everything seemed to go on vacation. The couple of times Ty and Dakota went to town together, Logan Woods teased them until they grew embarrassed to enter his store. At first there'd been a little tension over the dog fight, but even that resolved itself, with an agreement that both dogs would have to be watched more closely and when the opportunity was right, they'd have to be reintroduced so they could become decent neighbors. Finally, it was agreed that they'd all get together for supper on Monday night at Logan and Marlys's place.

Ty had just finished mucking the stalls Monday morning, and the horses he was going to work were waiting in the two paddocks closest to the barn. He looked at the dirt floor of the aisle. Usually he waited to rake it until he'd worked the horses so the barn was orderly for the rest of the day, but he had a feeling today, and after a sip from his coffee cup he kept on a little shelf with the radio by the doorway to the grooming and tack area, he went to work. At the racetrack and later the show barns, he'd seen how the elaborate paisleys or geometric stripes rather than the churned, haphazard dirt pleased the eye. It conveyed a lot to the customer to see that dirt neatened too.

He put the finishing swirl in and hung up the rake with the rest of the tools, out of the horses' way with his shoeing tools. He should take a look at that colt's feet now that it was coming around. He called a shoer only if there was a complicated problem. Growing up on the ranch, he'd learned to be self-sufficient in just about everything. He could repair most machinery, as well as take care of most livestock needs. As for the human end of things, well, living with his father, there hadn't been much chance or need of that. The old man drove everyone and everything away. His sister had ended up moving to Pierre, South Dakota, after high school and marrying an insurance salesman. His mother was still living in Babylon. Nobody saw the old man if they could help it.

"Oh hell," he swore and went to get the colt. Fill in that place with mind-breaking work; he'd learned that at home from his father. Hadn't worked there though, had it, he reminded himself grimly as he snapped a rope on the colt's halter. If he hadn't hooked up with Harney and found drugs and alcohol, who knows what would've happened? Maybe something even worse.

The colt bumped his back and pushed at his gimme hat with its nose. Ty could feel the hot breath on his neck as it snorted. "Here—" he shoved the colt's neck over and laughed. Fastening only one cross tie because the colt was still jumpy, he went to work brushing the dark red bay coat. Even though he was shedding his summer coat, a new shine was coming on after the treatment and healing, and the colt was finally starting to get over being head shy. Ty could thank Dakota for that. She spent hours with the colt, leading him to the best grass, patting and talking to him. Babying him with carrots and apples. He was getting to be a pest like her other horse, Bobby, who seemed to be experiencing some jealousy over the colt. But he noticed that Bobby was enjoying his new role in the big front pasture as the kindly bully who scattered the younger or smaller horses when it pleased him. They all needed to be horses once in a while, he had reminded Dakota last night when she worried that Bobby was getting out of shape.

That had brought up something else. They were sitting at the kitchen table, finished with the roast Moroccan chicken they'd made together. With her hand, she couldn't manage alone, but she could tell him what to do while she read the recipe. He was enjoying it, and he thought she might be too, but he couldn't tell for sure. She was different now, didn't have so much attitude. Quieter. She didn't have another place to go, that was clear. No money either. He'd finally done a thing he was ashamed of: checking her purse when she was sleeping. Just to see, he told himself. What? That she was who she said she was? He knew he'd seen her before, but she didn't talk about herself and he couldn't ask questions. Never had. Too afraid they'd get turned back on him. He had to be careful, he'd argued with himself while he riffled through the scraps of paper and found the letter from her mother, which he read. It sounded a lot like the letters from his mother. The weather and the garden reports and a bunch of small-town gossip. Didn't her mother know her daughter was penniless and homeless? Well, not so much now, he guessed.

Dakota didn't tell any of those stories people usually did. The ones about their pasts, their marriages and friends. And he was relieved not to tell his. They acted like they'd been together for so long they either knew everything about each other or didn't care. Maybe she was afraid. She didn't know anything about him. What kind of woman was she, moving in with a strange man?

He had brushed the haunches so long, the colt did a nervous jig, picking up the near hind leg and slamming it down hard as he peered around and snorted. "All right," Ty said and picked the straw out of the long black tail. Cleaning the hooves, he noted that they were chipping and needed shoes. Not today though. Finally, he brushed the mane, working his way up to the ears and forelock. The colt stood stiffly, braced against the pain it imagined was to come, but gradually relaxed under the soothing touch and blew a long sigh out of its nose, lowering its head for Ty to check the scabbed wound. "Good boy." He took the ears in his hands and gently stroked up. The colt's eyes half-closed and his head lowered to rest against Ty's chest.

"My friend Flicka," a voice behind them announced. "The story of a boy and his horse."

The colt flinched and stepped back, banging Ty's chin with its head. Ty put a hand on its shoulder to calm it and looked toward the doorway, where two men were standing silhouetted dark in the morning sun behind them. When they came forward, he recognized Eddie.

"You didn't call," Ty said.

"And you don't write, but I was in the neighborhood, decided to stop in and see what you had on blue light special this week." Eddie was a small, compact man, with longish blond hair, handsome according to the attention women paid him, and usually wore a gray Stetson as his trademark. He was a good rider and decent trainer, but most of all, he knew how to make money off horses and people. It had its own kind of appeal, Ty had decided. Maybe it was sexy getting hustled. At least it was fun. When Eddie turned the charm and mouth up, nobody was better at getting a laugh or a dollar.

"My friend here's looking for some horses." Eddie didn't give him any of the usual signals he used when he brought clients. In fact, Eddie had never brought another person without calling first. That was their agreement, as much for Eddie as for him, so they could pre-arrange pricing and commissions.

Ty nodded at the man and clipped the lead on the colt, then unsnapped the cross tie. It was a familiar face that stunned him into silence. Harney Rivers.

"Don't I know this colt?" Eddie stepped up and started to put a hand on the colt's halter, but it jerked back and stood braced, eyes wild and nose pointed toward the whitewashed ceiling.

"No." Ty started forward with the colt, forcing Eddie out of the way. What the hell was going on here, Eddie showing up unannounced with him. He walked the colt past them out the front door to give himself time to think.

"Sure looks familiar." Eddie's confident voice followed him.

After he'd put the colt in the front pasture, which was mostly a hill leading to rich bottomland grass and the creek, he turned to find the two men coming out of the barn toward him.

"What else you got these days, Ty?" Eddie grinned at him, eyes sweeping the pastures surrounding them. This was the clue to show the worst horses in the barn first before the big-priced ones, but since he hadn't called, the horses were all out in their pastures.

"What're you looking for?" he asked, keeping his eyes on Harney. He was still shorter than Ty by an inch or two, but his body had thickened, and his flesh now wore a comfortable sense of well-being and power. He didn't look soft though, and only the slight puffiness under the eyes and around the heavy jaw told of a possible weakness for drinking. The fleshy nose and lips would've been ugly on another man, but on Harney they were almost cruelly sensual. His pale blue eyes were neutral, indifferent as glass. His brown sun-streaked hair was cut longish on top and short on the sides in what Ty could imagine was the latest style in the city. Eddie's hair was neatly trimmed too, he noticed, almost as if they used the same barber. It was Eddie's way to carry the trappings of money so rich people would feel comfortable around him while he stole from them.

His gaze went back to the eyes—"Harney."

"How you doing, Ty?"

"What're you doing here?"

"Old man died and I moved back from Denver. Took over the bank, running the ranch, raising horses, and so on. Nice place—" His arm swept the land and Ty couldn't help remembering the strength in that body.

Eddie's face wore a puzzled grin.

"Ty, I'm looking to build up my foundation stock and thought you might have something I could use. Anything young, well bred. Like that colt, for instance."

"He's not for sale." The voice behind them made the men turn as

Dakota walked out of the barn, a .22 cradled in her good arm, the dog trotting alertly beside her.

"Dakota," Eddie said, his smile uncertain for a moment. "Hallucinate another distance?" He nodded toward her bandaged hand. She stared at him and he shrugged, turning back to Ty. "She sometimes rides like she's on drugs, especially to the oxers. I used to tie her stirrups to the girth to keep her feet from touching the horse's head when she found those distances to the fence. Pig farmer one day, Olympic star the next, never a dull moment when this little girl's riding."

"Go to hell, Eddie." Dakota nudged the gun at him.

"You hunting squirrels or just glad to see me?"

"Like she said, the colt's not for sale right now. I got a couple of other horses, and some two-year-olds I'm just breaking out." Hell, that's where he'd seen her, at Eddie's one time. Why hadn't she said anything? It was the hair. She'd had blond hair then, straight as straw, and he'd hardly noticed her because she kept ducking her head between her slumped shoulders. He'd figured she was one of the local teenage wannabe girls who hung around stables to take care of horses they couldn't possibly afford. Eventually those girls grew up, married, had their babies, and got on with life. He'd been wrong about Dakota.

"Take 'em all, long as the colt's in the deal." Harney smiled and that was the thing that reminded Ty most of the old days, because the eyes never went along with what the mouth did, they stayed flat and empty as china marbles. There was a scar across the left cheek bone Ty didn't remember, and he wondered if someone had finally tagged him.

"No," Ty said, and he could hear the after-echo of Dakota's voice lagging a half breath behind his. He didn't like being pushed around and he didn't like someone trying to buy him. Eddie should know better, but when he looked at him, Eddie was watching the colt, which had taken to racing and rearing at imaginary enemies coming up the creek. The bay coat glistened like fresh beet juice in the sun, and although the horse was still tucked up lean at racing weight, the muscles were beginning to take on some thickness from the corn and rest. The horse stopped and trumpeted, bringing the horses in the other pastures to alertness. There were a few anxious whinnies, followed by the thud of horses starting to run as the contagion swept the fields.

"No big deal, man," Eddie said, turning toward the barn. "Thought he came through my barn. Let's have a look at some others. Can you ride?" he asked Dakota. "Guess not, huh?"

"What'd you do, belt her one?" he asked Ty out of the corner of his mouth.

Ty ignored him and went to bring up some horses. He'd probably slept with her too. It pissed him off. Harney and Eddie were both asshole jerkoffs. Good time to raise his prices.

"Hey Dakota, you still owe me a couple of thousand for Bobby," Eddie said as he loped a big, lanky gray thoroughbred past them, almost a perfect match to the horse with the bowed tendon Ty had brought back from Minnesota.

"I let the insurance lapse," she called out and Eddie laughed, pulled the horse up, backed it a few steps to get its attention and balance it again, then moved right off into a canter again.

"His head still look as big as a suitcase out here?" Eddie called from the far end. Luckily Ty had watered the arena footing yesterday, so there was no dust to compete with the tan twilight. He hated turning on the lights in the daytime. Usually he would for Eddie, but he was pissed.

"Passable. He's no Breyer model, but the way he carries it and with that long neck, he'll do," she said. Ty looked at her. These two were more than client and trainer. Now he remembered her unloading the horses that one time a year or so ago while Eddie and he had done their business.

"Call him Samsonite," Eddie muttered as he loped past them again. "I better try him over some fences, see if he can lift those knees. Set up that X with a couple of trot rails and then some of the small stuff with ground lines."

"He hasn't been over anything yet," Ty called as he moved out to put the jumps the way Eddie wanted.

"You always baby 'em too long, Ty." Eddie pulled up the gray and backed him again. "It's Come-to-Jesus time, fella." He laughed as the gray shook his big head in frustration and gave a little buck as it moved into a canter again.

Eddie worked the horse over the first stages of jumping, trotting in over the rails laid flat for balance and collection, then up over the low X in stride. When the horse got comfortable, Ty pulled the trot line and raised the X and Eddie cantered back and forth, then moved on to the brush box, the coup, the wall, and ended with the small oxer. Finally he pulled up in front of them. "He's brave. How's he look?" he asked Dakota.

"He's got a little paddle on the left front, but he's not a channel swimmer. Tucks his knees pretty cute. Looks like he wants to use his back, but it's long and he's not used to it. Nice adult horse. Might go amateur or jumper. Not fancy enough for juniors." She leaned the rifle against the back wall.

"Get up and take him around at a trot, will you?" Eddie slipped off and began adjusting the stirrups.

"No, I'll do it." Ty reached for the horse.

"I'm fine. Give me a leg up," she said to Ty. Eddie smiled, but not so much this time as Ty lifted her on the horse.

"Be careful," he muttered, unable to stop himself. She glanced at him and smiled while she settled in the saddle. It was the first look with any affection she'd given him this morning. He smiled back and squeezed her foot and patted the gray's sweaty neck.

"Trot and canter," Eddie ordered, and Ty noticed a different, harsher tone in his voice. Dakota was a little paler the second time around the arena, and Ty knew her hand had to be hurting. There'd been a bit of initial infection and it was slow in healing.

"Trot the X, then take him around," Eddie called.

"She can't jump," Ty said.

"She's fine. Tough as nails, watch." Eddie pointed his chin toward the fence Dakota was approaching in her half seat. They went over it smoothly. "She's got great balance. Rides off her leg. Probably do it with two broken arms." As they watched, the horse swerved from the line for the next fence. "Steer, goddamn it," he yelled. "Christ, how many times do I have to tell you that?"

They watched silently as the horse took the fences, not quite with as much authority as with Eddie. Harney kept quiet the whole time, his eyes following Dakota. Ty made sure he kept track of Harney for just that reason. When she pulled up, Dakota's face was white and Ty moved quickly to help her off before she fell. On the ground, she leaned against the wall, but pushed Ty away when he tried to comfort her.

"He'll do," Eddie said, "what else you got?" He glanced at Dakota out of the corner of his eye as they walked the horse back to the stalls. When they had passed by, she squatted down and leaned her head back, with her eyes closed against the pain.

Chapter Nine

Usually after trying horses Eddie and Ty drove to Jerusalem for supper at The Wagon Wheel, a place with a separate bar and dining room for family eating. Local weddings and celebrations that didn't go the church route were held there too. When Eddie suggested it though, Ty hesitated. Dakota wouldn't want to go, and they were supposed to have supper with Logan and Marlys. That would have to be canceled. Business always came first, even when it involved Harney Rivers, he guessed. Dakota had been unusually quiet after her ride, and had disappeared toward the end when it was clear they were going to try every horse in the barn except hers and the colt. Eddie had tried to talk his way onto the colt just for a quick canter, but Ty had remained stubborn. In the end, Eddie shrugged and went on to the others.

Finally, they agreed to go without her, Ty promising to bring her back some food and Eddie not smiling at all as they climbed into the rented Continental. Ty wanted to find out more about Dakota anyway, and he was mad at her for not telling him she'd worked for Eddie.

The Wagon Wheel had so much business that even on a weeknight there was a crowd of noisy people, music, and clattering dishes. They were seated in the bar close enough to the big TV in the corner that they could watch Monday night football while they ate. They waited ten minutes for the waitress until Harney got impatient and Eddie volunteered to get the drinks.

"Pepsi," Ty said and caught a flicker in Harney's eyes.

"Jack over ice, and bring Ty something a man would drink," Harney said, smiling.

Ty kept his face neutral and kept his eyes on the television. "Bring the Pepsi."

"You've given up your wild and wooly cowboy days, huh?" Harney leaned forward in his chair and took out a cigar from his inside jacket pocket. He rolled it in his fingers like a pencil.

"What're you doing here, Harney?" Ty watched as he put the cigar in his mouth, lit it from the matches on the table, puffed, and studied the smoke as if it were giving shape to his thoughts.

"Eddie mentioned he knew you, you had some horses, thought I'd check it out. Just doing business, Ty, that's all." He took another puff and let the smoke dribble from his lips onto the table between them. "Sorry you didn't want to sell that colt, but there are always other horses, I guess. So how have you been?"

"You gave them my name. Is that how come you can go back and I can't?" Ty glanced at the bar, where Eddie was finally putting in their order.

"Wasn't like that, Ty. I was just a kid. The lawyer pried it out of me, then made me tell the judge. Your record was worse than mine, and the judge was that shithead old fart we got the time we broke the window at the Corner Bar."

"*You* broke that window."

Harney grinned like the seventeen-year-old Ty remembered, and tapped a fat ash into the ashtray. "Details—we were both stoned and drunk, we were both there. What difference does it make who does what?"

"Not that night, Harney—"

Harney's eyes went cold, the pupils contracting to hard points. "You had the gun, my friend, don't forget about that—"

"Yeah, well you—"

"Here we go—" Eddie put a scotch on the rocks in front of Harney, a gin and tonic at his place, and a Pepsi in front of Ty. Then he gave each of them a shot of tequila. "One won't hurt, Ty," he said as he sat down. "Drink to faster women, stronger horses, and more money than God." He knocked his shot back. Ty hesitated, seeing the old look of amusement and daring on Harney's face, then picked up the Pepsi and took a swallow.

Harney shook his head and chuckled. "She's got you on a pretty short leash, my friend." He drank his shot in a single swallow, then lifted his scotch in a mock toast and sipped, winking at Eddie as if the two of them shared a secret.

Ty glanced down at his shot. What the hell was he doing in this position? Eddie knew he didn't drink anymore. The guy was being a super prick, probably pissed about Dakota. Who knew what had happened between those two, but he'd sure find out before the night was over—even if it meant having to get drunk with these assholes. He could feel Harney's mocking eyes on him, challenging him like in the old days. Here it was then, here it was. He shouldn't do this.

He saw his hand reach for the shot glass. He could already smell the tequila, oily, medicinal, and sweet, as he lifted it to his mouth and felt the liquid cool, then heat sliding down his throat and hitting his stomach with a soft explosion that spread and bloomed inside him. He wiped his lips with the back of his hand and looked at Harney, who lifted his scotch and drained it in one long drink. Ty knew Harney was thinking about that night, because he was. Why was Harney really here? What he needed to do, he decided, was have a few drinks to loosen Harney up and find out why he showed up after all these years. Maybe Harney planned to tell the police where he was or something—maybe the state cops would show up with guns drawn for a shoot-out, maybe—he raised a finger for the next round of drinks.

They ordered steaks and drank some more and Ty couldn't quite remember why he'd quit drinking five years ago. It felt good. It felt real good. His mind felt clear, really clear for the first time that he could remember. And he must've been wanting to do this, it was so easy once Harney had challenged him. The room clanged with noise, cheers shot up when the Chiefs scored, and he found himself betting with the other two men. Then the lights were dimmed, a sign it was nine o'clock, and spotlights came on the dance floor at the far end of the room, where couples got up and moved to the country music a DJ was selecting. The bottles along the bar glowed like jewels of amber and emerald and diamonds, and the mahogany wood of the bar gleamed deep red approval. Even the smoky walls plastered in browning swirls seemed part of the nervous jigging he felt in his body, as if his cells were packed with bees buzzing, trembling with need to get out. Harney was smiling all the time now, his face melting into the boy he'd hung out with. Even his cigar smoke smelled deep and satisfying as it hung over the table.

One of the times when Eddie got up to use the phone or go to the bathroom, Harney reminded Ty of the time they'd put pepper in the bull feed at the rodeo and watched a bull go crazy, kicking and ramming down the fence and scattering the spectators and cowboys. They both laughed. Then Harney's face got serious. "This isn't about bringing the police in here, Ty. I would never do that. Hell, I'd just as soon we forgot the whole thing ever happened. You got yourself a nice setup here, and I respect that. I really do. And I'm back in the Sandhills again, got a wife and family there. Businesses. Last thing I need is that story coming alive again. You know how people in small towns love to talk a person down. I'd be as hurt as you if we had to go through it all over again." He grinned. "I really did just come for the horses, buddy, and to see you, of course. We had us some big times, didn't we?"

"Yeah." Ty's mind felt slow, like swimming through dough. The food disappeared. He couldn't remember if he'd ordered something for Dakota. "Dakota's food," he said out loud and Eddie, who was suddenly back, smiled at him.

"She's a piece of work, man. Swiss watch. Got her timing, but once you find it, she goes off regular as a clock."

"I'd like a slice of that," Harney said.

That word—Ty stood and half-fell across the table, shoving Harney so the chair tipped, spilling him back onto the floor. Eddie was pushing him away before he could jump the other man, and Harney stood shaking the bouncer's hand off his arm. "He's just drunk," Eddie explained and dragged Ty out the door.

"Don't talk about her," Ty said, pulling away, ready to fight them both now.

"Get in the goddamned car," Harney said.

Ty shook his head.

"Okay, stay here, you dumb fuck." He climbed in and started the engine. Eddie stood beside the open passenger door, shrugged at Ty, and climbed in. The car spurted back and roared down the street.

"Son of a bitch." Ty started after them, then stopped. He was drunk. But Dakota—

"Something wrong?" Logan stood behind him on the sidewalk.

"Lost my ride." Ty stumbled back and sat down hard on the curb.

"Lost more than that," Logan said. "Well, come on. After you all canceled on us, I decided to work late at the store ordering books. Have to get home, though, before Marlys makes me sleep in the chicken coop." He looked more closely at Ty. "On second thought, wait here while I get the truck."

The house was quiet when they drove up. Lights off. Ty had no idea what time it was. He hadn't worn a watch in years and the dashboard clock had stopped permanently at seven.

"How's that little girl doing?" Logan asked as they sat there watching.

"Okay, I—"

"Ty?" Dakota called softly from the porch.

"Here." Logan clicked the interior lights on and she stepped to the edge of the porch, where they could see the bright glint of moonlight on the barrel of the rifle. The new dog appeared at her side and growled deep in its chest, ears high and alert.

"What's going on, Miss Carlisle?" Logan was already out of the truck by the time Ty fumbled the door open and fell out. The dog came bounding off the porch, barking so loud it sounded like a much bigger animal, and hit the gate with its full weight, shaking the whole fence.

"Eddie and Harney came and started pounding on the door a few minutes ago. Just about scared me to death. You didn't see them?" She came down the walk toward them. "Hush now," she ordered the dog, whose barking subsided back to growling.

"No." Logan stopped and looked at the gun. "Didn't pass a soul on the road. You all right?"

She waved the barrel at Ty standing with one hand on each side of the gate to the yard, trying to stay steady. "Your friends stopped by to say they'll be over for the horses first thing in the morning." The dog jumped up and tried to lick Ty's face but wasn't quite tall enough, so she settled for his knee.

"Well then, here you are." Logan turned toward Ty. "Need any help?"

"Nope," Ty said and tried to walk straight to the house, having to swing around Dakota and bumping into her in the process, then getting his legs tangled with the dog, who was trying to herd him.

"Careful you don't get shot there, buddy," Logan said and headed for his truck.

"Thanks," Dakota called. Logan paused and turned back.

"You need any help, my number's in the book. He's not been like this—"

"Yeah, okay." She sighed and turned toward the house.

Looking at Dakota, Ty wondered that he'd kept his hands to himself those first two weeks. Her face—well, it was interesting, pretty. He even liked how her hair went every which way. And that scar on her eyebrow, and mole down on the inside of her thigh. He felt the numbing heat rising up his hips into his stomach. "Come here—" He reached for her and succeeded only in grabbing her shoulder and turning her toward him in the doorway to the kitchen, but it was enough. Leaning down, he kissed the back of her neck and could taste the salty dust of the arena. He opened his mouth and bit lightly right where her shoulder started. She moaned and leaned into him and he pulled at the oversized T-shirt, hearing in the distance a tearing sound as he worked it off her. She was naked to the waist. It surprised him and he suddenly grew awkward in his clothes, his hands too big and clumsy for touching. She stepped back as his hands dropped.

"You're drunk and you stink," she said, her eyes gleaming in the dark.

"Not so much," he said, certain it was true in some way he couldn't explain.

"I'm not fucking some drunk." She bent and grabbed her T-shirt and left him standing there.

"Oh sure—" He didn't know what he was saying and tripped into the trunk on the way to the sofa. "Goddamn lights," he muttered. "I pay the goddamn bills, where's the goddamn lights?" he yelled and felt stupid and self-righteous.

"Here—" She appeared in a blinding glare as she switched on the lamp next to the sofa, then went around the room turning on all the lights, repeating the gesture in the kitchen, bedroom, and bathroom.

"Satisfied?" Wearing another T-shirt, she stood at a safe distance from him, while the dog cowered in the bedroom doorway. She kept staring at him with those eyes that made him feel dumb and undeserving and maybe even hated. He couldn't muster nearly that much energy. Lying on the sofa made him sleepy and he wanted her there with him, on top of him or at least beside him. Was that too much to ask?

"Come here," he murmured, shielding his eyes from the light with his forearm. He patted the few spare inches of sofa beside his body. "Come on, I won't do anything." He was hoping he could keep that promise, he really was, but he felt that tightness start in his jeans again.

"Take your boots off," she said, tugging with her good hand.

He sat up, quickly yanked them off, and let them thump on the floor. He took this as a good sign, maybe his jeans would be next. He lay back down, covering his eyes again. He felt the sofa sink beside him and he moved over on his side facing her, but he kept his eyes closed. Felt better that way.

"That guy with Eddie was creepy," she said.

He wanted to ask her about working for Eddie and not telling him, but he could feel her breathing in her body, the way her skin came and went just a little bit where his arm lay against her side. He didn't want to open his eyes, but he thought the soft mound of flesh at his elbow was her breast. He hoped so, imagined so. He concentrated on picturing the nipple, and his stomach gave little jerks. He had to slow his own breathing down or she'd get scared maybe, turned off.

"You know that guy?" she asked.

"Years ago," he whispered, hoping her eyes were closed too, because there was no way she wouldn't notice what was happening down there.

"He tried to come in here." She shivered.

He opened his eyes and looked at her. "What'd you do?"

"Had the gun ready. I do that when you're not here sometimes. I just had a feeling and I was right. The dog growled a lot, which helped. Eddie tried to talk me into it too. I almost had to shoot over their heads to convince them."

She was biting her lower lip and there were tears in her eyes. Ty scooched up and put his arms around her. At first she resisted, but then she relaxed and he held her and stroked her hair while her breathing roughened and shortened, then calmed.

"I have to be careful," she said in a dead voice that worried him. "Being alone, you know, I look easy to some people. Things happen—" Her voice caught and his arms tightened automatically. As upset as she was, he couldn't very well start grilling her about Eddie and the past.

"It's okay," he murmured. He wasn't sure he wanted to know the rest. Some things, some things were just better left unsaid. "Don't worry."

She was quiet for a while and he wondered if she'd gone to sleep. He couldn't see her face from this angle, and her breathing had slowed. He stopped stroking her hair and was getting ready to lift them both off the sofa when she moved her arm across his thighs, hugging his legs. The weight of it pressing down made him so suddenly hard, he groaned.

"Here," she whispered and untangled herself. Reaching back and up, he turned off the lamp, then inched his body down while she knelt on the floor beside him. First she unbuttoned his shirt, using her fingers on his skin, scratching lazy circles all the way down his chest and stomach. He closed his eyes, letting it do its work. When she pulled the shirt out of his jeans and opened it, the air hit his skin like another skin, and her tongue licked him in a long trail from his nipples to there. She took his hand and put it on himself and pressed down. It was so close, his breath caught. He felt the buttons on his jeans release and her fingers inside and he would do anything, anything she wanted if she just didn't stop. And she didn't.

It was the banging on the door that woke him and he stumbled up with his shirt around his waist to cover his nakedness. Eddie was grinning on the other side of the glass.

"Just a minute," Ty said and went to get his jeans, hating that his bare ass was hanging out to the world. He looked around the living room. She must've gone to sleep in the bed. He thought he remembered her on top of him, but maybe that was wrong. He pulled on his jeans and sat to put on his boots. There was a hole in the sole of one, and the stitching on the inside of the other was tearing. He should take them in for repair. Then he'd have to wear sneakers, and he hated to do that. He'd gotten trained to the idea of owning one pair of boots at a time from his father. You wore them till the leather patches on the leather patches wouldn't hold anymore. Duct tape worked too. What he needed was a new pair of boots.

He looked longingly at the coffeemaker in the kitchen as he headed out. Eddie was leaning against the rented car, sipping coffee from a Styrofoam cup. Harney was nowhere in sight. Ty blinked in the morning sun and rubbed his eyes while a headache started bumping the very top of his skull and drained down into the bones of his face as if he'd smashed his head, though he couldn't remember doing it. His mouth was dry and he couldn't work up enough spit to take the crackly catch out of his throat.

"You look rough, man. Here—" Eddie reached behind him and picked up another cup of coffee he held out to Ty.

"Thanks." Ty took it, pried off the lid, and sipped at the burning liquid. His hand was shaking.

"Women like that—" Eddie gestured toward the house. "They're pirates, man. Always looking for the next ship." He finished the rest of the cup. "Can't tame 'em. Just hope you get away before they whack you."

Ty knew for sure then she'd slept with Eddie too. He tried not to let the feeling of that cloud over him. "Screw it," he muttered and drank some more coffee. What he needed was aspirin for the headache, but he didn't want to go back in the house right now. "Where's Harney?" He looked around again. The horses must be pissed, it was at least an hour late for their breakfast and turnout.

"At the motel. So, let's get it done. I got to get on a plane."

As they walked toward the barn, Ty asked, "What's he doing here?"

Eddie shrugged. "Called me about some horses. You know—"

Ty looked at him, but Eddie was such a smooth liar, there was little clue. Maybe that twitch in the jaw or the blue vein on the side of his neck that jumped. Ty had always assumed Eddie was lying or about to lie, though, so he hadn't spent enough time observing him to know for sure when he actually was. Now it was important he find out.

"He's not taking any of the horses, is he?"

Eddie shook his head. "Not unless you want to sell the bay colt, like he said."

"Why that one?"

Eddie shrugged. "Nice horse, I guess."

When the horses heard their voices, they began to nicker and stamp, and one kicked the stall boards with four resounding bangs like a gun going off. Ty automatically picked up the handles of the wheelbarrow he left full of corn every night for the morning feeding. The corn kept them fat and slick and without the attitude oats put in them. He fed good hay to make up any nutritional imbalance.

"How'd he get your name?" Ty asked as he dumped a ten-pound coffee can of corn in the first feed slot and watched the youngster dive its nose into the bucket, then lift, dripping pieces of corn and chewing happily.

"I don't know, for chrissakes, what difference does it make?"

Ty shrugged and moved on down the line of stalls. While he was graining, Eddie went to the bales of hay waiting in the aisle for the morning feed. Breaking them apart, he gave each animal two flakes. If a horse was very skinny, he gave it three.

The feeding done, Ty took the hose and filled the buckets with water up and down the aisle. Have to remember to scrub the buckets today, he decided. Maybe Dakota could manage that with a plastic bag on her hand. Then he thought maybe he wouldn't ask her, it was such a stupid, dirty job. He looked at Eddie raking the leftover pieces of hay into the stalls. She'd slept with him.

"Ready?" he called and Eddie walked toward him with the rake. Hanging it beside the other tools, Eddie noticed the mended handle and broken spike of the long-pronged fork Ty used to muck the stalls with. "You are the cheapest son of a bitch." He laughed. "Only things worth stealing around here are the horses and your rig."

They walked into the tack room, which, in addition to the saddles, bridles, and trunks of equipment, held the cot he'd been sleeping on and a couple of old brown corduroy easy chairs beside a battered gray metal desk he'd dragged out of the Jerusalem town dump a few years ago. Dakota had washed the windows and kept the concrete floor swept clean. It was enough of a difference that Eddie looked around nodding. "Sure miss her at my place. That woman keeps a tidy ship." Then he noticed the bedding on the cot where Ty had slept when she first arrived, and grinned.

"You know, I almost got hijacked coming back from up there in August. Ex–football jocks at a gas station just over the Nebraska border. Wanted the truck and trailer."

Something flickered in Eddie's eyes. He sat down on the desk chair while Ty remained standing.

"Should I be worried?"

Eddie looked at his hands, turning them over and rubbing them on the neatly ironed and creased jeans he sent out to the laundry. "It was an awful good deal, Ty. Got to expect a little trouble. But don't worry, I'll straighten it out. Guy in Louisiana I got it from just needed to unload it quick. He'd had it buried along with some heavy road equipment and the cops were making noises his way. Stupid bastard had to spend a whole week digging up that shit all over his farm. Missed a piece anyway, so the cops busted him. You'd think he'd draw himself a map or something. Runs okay, doesn't it?"

"Yeah, but it's not worth going to jail for. And I don't like being held up either." They looked at each other for a long moment, as if measuring the dishonesty each was capable of.

"I took care of the serial numbers." Eddie dragged the center drawer open in a series of metal squeels and pushed it shut again with both hands. "It's clean. You got your bill of sale. There's no reason you should be having any trouble. Maybe needs a paint job. Deal like that doesn't come along every day, Ty." He lifted his feet up on the desk and put his hands behind his head.

Ty nodded. He'd gotten sloppy that time. He knew better than to take any of Eddie's bargains without real careful scrutiny. He sighed. It was his own fault really. Trying to get by on the cheap.

"You buying horses or what?" Ty went to the window that looked out the front of the barn toward the house. Was she up yet? The dog wasn't out and it always waited for her now. He leaned his hands on the windowsill and his head gave a vicious throb, then settled back down to an ache that made his whole face hurt. Maybe rain moving in. His cheekbone always hurt when a front came through. Damn bulls he was hauling up to Denver that time. Started arguing in the trailer on that mountain road. By the time he'd stopped and gone back to straighten things out, they'd busted the door loose and two unloaded on top of him and his face. It was Rodeo in the Rockies that afternoon. He'd driven the stock to the show grounds and directed the unloading with hand gestures, a bloody shirt tied around his face, hurting so bad he couldn't speak. Finally they put him in a car and drove him to the emergency room. Broken jaw, nose. He took a week off from work but caught up with the stock in Cheyenne. Lived on painkillers and booze the rest of the summer. That was a fun time.

"What about that colt?" Eddie finally asked.

Ty shook his head.

Eddie sighed. "Okay, I'll take the big gray, the sorrel mare, the chestnut two-year-old with the two white hind socks, and the ugly brown horse. Might come back for the other chestnut two-year-old later. And I'll see if there's a customer for anything else. Usual terms?"

Ty turned and nodded. "Just bring 'em back in one piece this time."

"You'll call me if the colt—"

Ty nodded. Not before he'd done some research, however. "Where's Harney say he's living now?"

Eddie looked at him for a long moment. "Out in Nebraska, has a ranch in the Sandhills somewhere, he said. He's loaded, you know, really loaded. I did a D&B on him. He could afford to buy this place fifty times over and give it back to you, Ty. What's the deal with you two?"

"Nothing. Just don't bring him back here, Eddie."

Eddie pulled an envelope of money from his back pocket and handed it to Ty. "Partial down payment. Minus a thousand Dakota owes me." He grinned. "Figured you might like to drive a nice Corvette instead of that trashed-out truck too."

Ty almost took the challenge about Dakota's debt but thought better of it and shook his head. "Need the money this time. And I don't want a bunch of people chasing me down the highway either."

Eddie shrugged. "Good deal. Ask Dakota. This one's clean as a whistle. Took it in trade myself."

Ty's hands tightened into fists. "I need the cash."

"Sure, I'll wire it soon as these puppy dogs sell. I'm good for it, man, you know that." He held out his hand and Ty shook it quickly. The sooner Eddie was gone the better. "I'll send a truck for the horses. Hang loose, man. Enjoy her." Eddie gave his shoulder a mock punch and left.

From the window, Ty watched him walk to the car, then saw Dakota come out of the house, wave, and go to talk to him. His head pounded wildly. She didn't look mad this time. She even smiled and touched Eddie's arm. At least the dog showed some good taste, standing apart, tail and ears stiff. Ty turned away and stomped back into the barn to take the horses out to pasture. Sensing his mood, they walked quietly beside him with no playing around. Once loose, they moved a short distance away, stopped, and looked back at him.

When he got to the bay colt's stall, he stood and looked through the bars. The horse lifted its head from the hay and pressed its nose against the bars and blew. Ty leaned and blew into its nostrils and they did it again, the hot moist air soothing. Then the colt dropped its head to eat again and Ty started for the house.

There was a whole bunch of stuff he wanted to say, but when he saw the breakfast she'd made, he couldn't do more than sit down and stuff his face with eggs, bacon, pancakes, and toast while she smiled at him from the other end of the table. They used to eat like this on the ranch when he was a kid and his mother was still around cooking even though she hated it.

His headache began to smooth out after the second cup of coffee, and he glanced over at Dakota. She was studying her fingernails, putting each one in her mouth and nibbling a little or cleaning, he couldn't tell which. "I didn't know you and Eddie—" He couldn't say it and she caught it, looking at him quickly with surprise in her face.

"Yeah, so?" Frowning, she studied a nail.

"Well, so, what's the deal?" He poured another cup of coffee and ran his fingers through his hair and pushed it back behind his ears. He felt his face—needed a shave or he'd tear her skin up. If—but she'd lied to him.

"No deal at all. I worked for him and left. What's your problem?" Her lips looked swollen and pouty, and he thought about what she'd done last night.

"Just, well, he's not your type, is he?" God, he hated how dumb he sounded. She'd run for sure he started in with this crap, and he couldn't blame her.

"What type would that be, Mr. Bonte?" Her eyes were cool as she stood and began clearing the table, bringing the dishes to the sink.

"Forget it—" He sighed. Talking with women always ended up in some game he couldn't begin to understand. They kept the rules to themselves, letting you know only when you were losing a point or finished. He'd had only a few tries with them, and they all came to this same weird place through talking he never quite got a handle on. Better to keep your mouth shut, he warned himself.

"Look." She turned from the sink to face him. "I'm not a virgin. That's not news. You have a problem with who I am, you say it now. Eddie was not my finest hour, but that's not because I slept with him. Which yes, I did. Happy now?" She yanked the hot water faucet on and stuck a plate underneath, splashing herself.

"I got no problems with anything, Dakota. Things just, well things have been happening since you came—I'm just trying to figure it all out." He paused, taking a deep breath, at the bottom of which he found an anger that surprised him. "This is my home, I stay out here in the middle of nowhere for peace and quiet. Minding my own business. I don't want a load of shit coming down on me for something I don't know about. So I guess what I'm asking is, what the hell is going on?"

He stood and in four strides was at the sink, turning the faucet off and grabbing the plate out of her good hand. It slipped and dropped, shattering on the linoleum, one shard stuck upright like a white knife blade. "Who are you? Why didn't you tell me we'd met at Eddie's?"

"I'm the woman you keep wanting to have sex with, you dumbass cowboy. Who the hell do you think I am?" She threw the dish sponge, splatting his chest with hot soapy water, stalked to the back door, yanked it open, and ran outside.

He followed and grabbed her arm, turning her toward him. "I paid off your horse, doesn't that mean anything?"

She stared at him for a moment before walking away. At the end of the driveway, she slipped under the unpainted board fence into the pasture, and crossed into the hay field that divided Ty's place from his neighbor. The last cutting had been made a week before and safely stacked in the barn for winter. Now the field was a pale yellow stubble with bare ground underneath from the lack of rain. Here and there she saw the feathers of a nesting bird or the torn-up skin of a snake that had been caught in the mower or baler. At the far end of the field, a cloud of blackbirds burst out of the cotton-woods, circling and eddying at the approach of a long stream of birds coming from the north. Following the birds with her eyes, she couldn't discern any end, as if they were a black speckled river pour-ing across the world, weaving over trees and dipping down along the fields, following the flow of a different, invisible land.

The dog galloped up beside her and she threw her hand up to sig-nal it on, watching as it zigzagged across the field with its nose to the ground.

The gold leaves of the cottonwoods shook in the gusts of wind coming up from the west and south with a damp smell cutting into the hot dry of the field. Looking across the hills, she could see the great blotches of clouds passing between patches of sunlight that seemed to weaken and hesitate before the encroaching shadows. She slowly turned in a circle, catching her breath at the three hundred and sixty degrees of horizon that dwarfed trees, buildings, and her. It was a relief, how unimportant a person became out here, and she'd missed this feeling over the past few years when she lost track of time spending days and nights inside barns and show arenas.

Once when she was a little kid in Iowa, she'd gone out to her mother's family farm on a Sunday morning and sat in a pasture watching the horses she couldn't catch. There, miles from anywhere, she'd heard church bells ringing clear but muffled, as if they'd come from a great distance. At first she thought it was God in Heaven, like they promised at church, and she'd felt that moment of wonder and expectation looking at the scattering high strings of clouds in the pure cerulean sky for what was next, angels, fiery chariots, some-thing. Then she realized that it had to be simply a church on earth whose bells carried for miles for some reason she was too young to understand. She never forgot it though, or the momentary hope she'd had, and she never told anyone else. For the first time, she thought maybe this was the sort of thing a person like Ty would un-derstand. She looked around for a place to sit, but the stubble was too uninviting so she circled around back toward his place. Really, she'd walked away because he'd paid Eddie for her horse. It made her ashamed at how her heart lifted. Now she really truly owned Bobby.

~

Ty was lying on the sofa again, a bottle of aspirin on the trunk beside him. She felt a little surge of pity for the hangover he must have. She'd ignored that before. No wonder he was acting like a pissant. She stood there for a moment watching his chest rise and fall as he slept. He didn't know much about women, that was obvious. Never been married, that he'd mentioned, but she wasn't sure, since they hadn't actually talked about marriage. Maybe it was time to talk. Look what this Eddie thing had already done, and that could've been cleared up so easily. They'd gotten too close with too little information. Well, she hadn't planned on anything like this happening, she had to admit.

She looked at his mouth, the full lips parted slightly. A little-boy mouth, with the gap between the front teeth she found so darned endearing. He was inexperienced and open in certain ways, like a boy, but there was something guarded in him too, something he held back. They were the same that way, she guessed. Too much history packed too tight inside the head.

She looked at the long, tapered fingers on his battered, stained hands. The knuckles scarred from fighting, the crooked little finger, and something inside her started to let go, and she fought it, kicking the trunk loud enough to make his eyes startle open. His lips closed as he looked at her with those watching dark eyes.

"I'm sorry, Ty—"

He got up gracefully, a man who took his body for granted. Not like her pudgy husband or Eddie, who had to work out all the time to keep fit.

"And—thanks for Bobby. I'll work and pay it off as soon as—"

He put his arms around her and pressed her face against his shirt, which stank of cigarettes and booze and sweat from last night, but she simply breathed through her mouth and lifted her head. Their lips met hesitantly, as if they weren't sure of the distance that had formed between them and maybe they'd have to relearn everything about each other. He caught her lower lip with his teeth and she pressed into him.

After a while he said, "Made some money today. Why don't we go to town, buy some food, invite Logan and Marlys over for supper, and stop at the vet clinic for the shots and wormer I ordered?"

She nodded and he added, "Who knows, maybe there'll be a treat for you too—"

"In that town? I doubt it—"

"You never know, darlin'—"

She laughed because it pleased her that he called her darlin' and went to change for town, promising herself that as soon as they had a few minutes of peace, she was going to tell him everything. She loved him and couldn't help but believe that he was falling in love with her too. And she knew now that she could trust Ty to take care of the colt, to keep him alive no matter what Eddie tried to do.

∽ Chapter Ten

The walls of what passed as the town's historical museum were painted a lifeless tan about the shade of the dusty road out front of Ty's place. On the wall behind the counter hung a barbed wire display, and the other walls were covered with blurry reproduction photos of pioneer and frontier days in Kansas. Unsmiling men and women with the flat landscape spilling out around them. Dirt street towns lined with small wooden buildings. Cattle, horses, cowboys. Nothing that looked newer than the Civil War, as far as she could tell. Her mother loved that war, owned videos of *Gone With the Wind* and *Gettysburg* and anything else she could lay her hands on about the period. Books she read and talked about endlessly. Two brothers, her ancestors, had gone to Missouri to occupy the borderlands during the guerrilla war. One was killed near Liberty by Bloody Bill Anderson's men. The other took his revenge on the civilian population and came home with a sack of souvenirs the family had passed awkwardly down the generations, uncomfortable with their personal nature. Her mother had inherited the things without explanation and had begun her own reconstruction as a winter project once the bank had taken their farm and they moved into town to live.

Her father had gone to work at the feed mill, and began to disappear almost immediately, a little at a time, she came to realize later. The ground corn and crimped oats powder that coated his clothes and face, clinging even to his eyelashes by the end of the day, was the disguise behind which he was ceasing to be. After a while, he would go out with the other men to the bars after work, but still come home for supper, then later not until well after the women were asleep. Dakota couldn't forget her mother those long winter nights sitting in the recliner with the TV sound turned off, the gray-and-white images flickering across her legs as she studied the maps and books, tracing the battles as if her own war weren't being lost night after night there alone.

After twenty minutes, the lady behind the counter stood up from her desk and asked if Dakota needed something. "Not really," she muttered and left. At the curb out front, she looked up and down the street for Ty's truck in case it had escaped her before. It wasn't there. "Oh shit," she muttered and panicked. What if something had happened to him? She looked again, more slowly and carefully in case she had missed it the first time. Nothing. She didn't have so much as a quarter for a phone call either. She didn't want to go back inside and ask for help. Then she noticed the building with the books in the window across the street. Of course, Logan Woods.

He was standing with his elbows on the tall counter, cropped reading glasses on his nose, staring at a catalog. When the Christmas bells on the door jangled, he took his time, putting a pencil under one line to mark his place before he looked up. Recognizing her, he smiled.

"Have you seen Ty?" she asked, unsuccessfully keeping the worry out of her voice.

His eyes sharpened. "What's wrong?"

"He drove me in, but now he's gone. You haven't seen him?" She glanced around in case he was hiding behind some shelves or in one of the other booths.

"I closed for a while to run an errand. Just got back. Must've missed him. Sure he's not at the vet's?" He took off the glasses, folded them up, and put them in his shirt pocket.

She felt a momentary relief. "Oh yeah, maybe he's still there. Got hung up or something. Can you call for me? I don't have any way back—" She tried to keep her voice calm, but the words were too fast, and she knew he knew she was panicked. He seemed to be moving awfully slow, as if that would reassure her.

While he called the clinic and waited on hold, she picked up some books, pretending to read the cover copy but glancing out the big front windows in case Ty drove up. She shouldn't have—but it stopped her, what? What had she done? She'd apologized, they'd kissed and made up.

"He hasn't been there," Logan said, coming from behind the counter. "Why don't you sit down and wait a little while. Ty wouldn't strand you here. Something must've come up. He'll be back, and if he doesn't come in a while I'll close up and we'll drive out to his place. Okay?"

She nodded, feeling distinctly wrong about this.

Ty had stopped at the four-way intersection on the way to the vet clinic a mile outside town when he felt a bump and started to move forward despite his foot on the brake. The rearview mirror was filled with the huge silver-and-blue cab of a stock truck pushing him until he came to rest bumper to bumper with a new bronze dually pickup. Ty shoved his door open and jumped down.

"What the hell do you think you're doing?" he demanded as a short, bowlegged man got down from the cab of the stock truck. Then he saw the shotgun and, turning, saw a long-hair in a gimme cap getting out of the dually with a pistol pointed at him. "That god-damned Eddie," he swore under his breath.

"Get back in the truck," the man with the shotgun ordered. He lifted the gun and Ty felt his muscles sag. A shotgun tore a body up something fierce.

He turned and climbed back in and sat with his hands on the steering wheel, trying to figure out what to do next. This was his old farm truck, used only for local runs, so there weren't any weapons stashed. Not even the knife in his boot. He was blocked in, bumper to bumper, and his truck was too old against these bigger, newer engines. He'd never be able to power his way out. Maybe they weren't going to kill him, he reasoned, maybe they just wanted the rig at home. Sure, that was it. But this was an awful lot of firepower for something one or two men could do while he was gone to town. He had a very bad feeling now. It wasn't just the rig, then. He squeezed his eyes shut and reopened them as the passenger door opened and a medium-built guy with thin, shaggy, collar-length dishwater blond hair and beard climbed in beside him.

"Follow the dually," shaggy-hair said with a gun held loosely across his legs. With lips obscured by the scraggly tan beard, he had a nondescript face except for a small growth on the cheek and thick-lensed wire-rim sunglasses that only partially hid the empty eyes looking back at Ty. "Keep your eyes on the road," he ordered and patted the gun.

They took the horses one at a time, parading them in front of his eyes as he stood tied to the first stall, his arms stretched and fastened to the iron rods on either side of him. They hadn't bothered doing more than that, but he knew what was coming. Leading the horses by him, they smirked and occasionally said something among themselves and laughed. When he tried to kick out at a horse, hoping to spook it, they simply came back and fastened his legs to the lower boards. His hands were cold and numb from the tightness of the baling twine they'd wrapped several times around them, and he knew it was a bad sign. He didn't waste energy cursing them though, he was trying to think how to stay alive here. Locked in the tack room, the dog didn't waste time barking or howling, but instead threw its solid body against the door with a steady thumping. If only it could get loose, but what could it do against armed men?

When they led Bobby out, he finally said something. "That's not one of mine. You don't have to take him—"

It was shorty with the big head and wandering eye who stopped and shrugged. "Take 'em all. That's the orders." It was nothing personal with him, and that scared Ty even worse. He would kill with the same indifference and expect the victim to understand. Business was business. Ty struggled, but the baling twine was so strong it had to be cut with a knife. It never split of its own accord.

The last horse was the colt, and they didn't take him out to the truck. Instead, they put him in the stall across from Ty, so the two of them were staring at each other, the colt with his head high, pawing and shifting back and forth as the strangeness of the situation began to sink in. Ty opened his mouth to comfort the horse, then stopped himself. Maybe if the colt caused a ruckus, slowed things down or something—but what? He'd been thinking of Dakota hitching out or getting a ride and stopping this, but that wouldn't work. They'd hurt her too. No, he had to pray she didn't come back, had to speed it up so they were done and gone before she made it back.

"Easy, you're okay," he soothed and the colt paused, ears alert, listening to him.

"You always were good with the horses," the familiar voice said as it came through the grooming area toward him. "But you are one dumb son of a bitch." Harney stopped, his hands in the pockets of his western-cut tweed jacket.

"Guess so," Ty admitted. He'd never have thought of this.

"Should've given me the colt, Ty." Harney went to the stall and looked in. "A fine animal, truly."

He looked behind him and nodded. Shaggy-hair still in his green tinted sunglasses walked up to the stall, trailing a couple of thick yellow electrical extension cords whose ends had been stripped away to expose the wires hooked to alligator clips. Ty had heard about this.

"Don't—he hasn't done anything." Ty tried to keep his voice reasonable.

Harney's eyes flared. "Should've stayed out of this, Ty. Horse was supposed to be dead over a month ago. Used the roofing nail to make him unmanageable. He was supposed to have an accident then. Your friend Eddie had it all arranged with The Sandman." He nodded toward shaggy-hair. "Next thing I hear he's missing. Stolen. Can't bring the police in though, can I? And I can't have him trotting around here after I've faked the insurance claim. A hundred and fifty thousand for his tragic demise. He's tattooed. Somebody might figure it out."

Ty shook his head. "Let him live, Harney. He can stay here. I won't sell him, I promise."

The Sandman started to open the stall door, and the colt snorted and backed into the corner, his head bouncing up and down, ears flat, eyes wild with fear. The man dropped the cables and held out his palm, filled with lumps of sugar, as he edged his way toward the colt. As soon as the man lifted a hand to the halter though, the colt spun and kicked out, catching him in the stomach and grazing a knee. The man staggered back and threw the sugar at the horse. "Sonofabitch—" He backed into the aisle and slammed the door as the colt hammered the stall boards hard enough with his hind feet to produce a loud cracking in the wood. The man bent over, holding his stomach and retching. Then he straightened and limped to the wall where the rakes hung. He took down the one with the broken prong and repaired handle.

"No!" Ty shouted. "Here, let me calm him down—" He struggled with the ropes while Harney stared at him for a moment, then nodded his head.

It took ten minutes for his hands and feet to start working again, and the first rush of blood from his massaging was almost more painful than the numbness that had set in, but he used the time to try to figure out how to save the colt and maybe even himself in the process. If he could get to the syringe full of horse tranquilizer on the window there in the grooming area, or take the pitchfork and get the dog loose or jump on the colt and ride off—all of his ideas seemed so absurdly inadequate, he felt more despair now that he was loose than when he had been tied up and it was all in the what if.

"I'm gonna just shoot you both if you don't get a move on it, Ty." Harney held the shotgun now, standing a careful distance away from him.

"I still don't think you have to do this—" Ty picked a brush out of the bandage box on the stall. He slid the door open and crooned to the colt, whose ears twitched back and forth in confusion.

"Think again. Eddie had to do some pretty fast scrambling when the colt disappeared. He found a reasonable look-alike, offed him, paid off the vet to certify it, then the insurance company wants to see the tattoo. Said the vet should've produced more evidence it was the colt. Now we can't very well take the upper lip and leave the horse, can we? And we're back to the problem of a live horse and a big payday."

Ty glanced at Harney's bland face, which could have been watching golf for all the emotion it betrayed.

"But finally"—he sighed—"I paid for The Sandman's work, and now he's going to produce it. Quality control, Ty, key to successful enterprise."

Ty patted the colt's neck and fumbled with the clip on one of the cross-tie ropes. The colt dropped his nose and blew softly on Ty's cheek, then licked him. The stall door was open enough that if he spooked the colt, he might bolt out of there and run over Harney on the way down the aisle. The men had left the back door of the barn open, and if the colt could just make it out there, he stood a chance of running out of rifle range.

"You could fake the tattoo, Harney—put it on a horse that died of natural causes and—"

Harney's burst of harsh laughter startled the colt into shifting his weight back as if to rear, his front hooves dancing. Instead of trying to calm him now, Ty elbowed its side so the colt spun and half-bucked, then circled the stall. This wasn't what he'd intended. He had to get the colt thinking forward, sheer panic, not obedience.

"What the hell are you doing in there?" Harney yelled as Ty edged the stall door open wider and began to inch toward the back of the stall so he could flush out the colt like a bird flying straight into Harney, who was moving closer to get a better view of the commotion.

Ty hated what he had to do next, but he cursed under his breath and slapped at the colt's head as it came around the stall at him. The colt bellowed in rage and spun, heading directly for the open space with Ty right behind it, but the door slammed into its head, knocking it back into the stall. Ty felt the hooves knock him back and down, and started to go out when his breath wouldn't come.

"Get the water buckets," shaggy-hair ordered shorty, who was leaning in the doorway with the pistol dangling from his hand.

"Just shoot him, Harney." Ty shook his head to clear the grogginess. They'd retied him to the opposite stall and somehow drugged the colt enough to cross-tie him.

"I told you, I've already paid The Sandman, you want me to waste money? Besides, a person should always stay open to new technology, Ty. Next time I'll know how to take care of a problem like this myself. Won't have to rely on Eddie or someone else who'll screw it up. And, as you know, I'm a hands-on kind of guy." He looked at his hands and back at Ty. "I could just shoot you too, but I'm not going to." They stared at each other, the pictures of that January night they shared between them now. "I know you went back for them. Just delayed the inevitable, Ty. They're drinking themselves to death as we speak, so what was the point? I never held it against you though."

There was sometimes a strange backlight in Harney's eyes that flickered on and off while he talked, like a caution before a blind intersection. The only time it ever really calmed in the old days was when he was with his yellow Lab. Now it blared on as he picked up the ends of the extension cords.

"Okay," he said to the men, who dumped water buckets on the colt while it jumped around shivering. Then shorty used a bucket of corn to bring the head down so he could clip the wires to the ears, while shaggy-hair clipped a cord to a thin metal rod he quickly inserted in the horse's anus and jumped out of the way as the animal started snorting and shaking its head and kicking out with its hind feet.

"Don't—" Ty shouted, and the men quickly left the stall as Harney inserted the plugs in the sockets.

It took twenty minutes for the horse to die, and Ty kept his eyes closed though he couldn't drown out the sounds of agony clanging against his head with the memories of that other time with Harney. He dreamed about that night only in slow, black-and-white motion, soundless, but now the grunts and moans and cries broke through the silence he had kept that night stored in, came flooding back with the hopeless anger he felt surging through his hands and legs against the ropes. He had to stay alive, he kept telling himself, no matter what, he had to come back and get Harney for this.

Sending the other men on with the horses, Harney pulled on Ty's heavy suede work gloves and began hitting him over and over, breaking his nose, opening a deep cut over his eye that flooded his face with blood, flaying his cheek to the bone, pounding his ribs, his stomach until he felt things begin to cave, give way. Ty kept thinking of Ryder trying to break him, the way he broke the animals around him, and how Ty had learned to build a hole his mind went to, separate from the body that was being punished. It was a hole made out of barn boards, a heap so tall and thick it was as if the barn itself had collapsed in an effort to help Ty resist Ryder's belt and fists. He crouched there like a small animal, his heart pounding, his breath coming in halting gasps, but safe, unseen and safe. He must be quiet, he told himself, Ryder will get tired and go away. Shhh, he whispered, shhh—

"So tell me, Ty," Harney panted. "What was my colt doing in your barn?" He grabbed Ty's hair and banged his head against the bars, producing a pain that spread down his neck and across his shoulders in waves. "Why'd you take it? Ty?" Harney dug his fingers into his jaw and pushed his head back so far that, even through the pain, Ty thought his neck would snap.

"Answer me!" Harney banged his head again, and Ty felt red and black flood the backs of his eyes.

"Nobody—" Ty whispered and tried to see through the red mist of his swollen eyes.

"Nooo—" Harney slammed his head again. "Are you setting me up? Is the insurance company involved, is that it?" Harney dropped his hands and stepped back.

Ty tried again to see out of the slits of his eyes and could only make out the dark form moving away from him. Then it suddenly reappeared, moving swiftly toward him, and he instinctively braced, shutting his eyes and lowering his head.

"Oh, to hell with it—" Harney said, and sharp spikes drove through Ty's chest and stomach and overrode all the other pain, startling him awake and dropping him down into the black blood in the snow. Before he let go though, he saw himself raise a pistol and squeeze the trigger, with a loud rushing sound that burned away all four faces and bodies of that January night in one long white explosion.

It took more than two hours for Logan to wind up business at the store and finally agree to drive her out to the farm. As they slowed for the driveway, Dakota saw that the pastures on either side were empty even though it was the middle of the afternoon. Ty's old truck was parked by the house, the driver's door hanging. She felt a raw space open in her stomach.

"Drive right up to the barn, hurry—"

Logan stepped on the gas and then had to brake quickly, with the truck nose at the wall of the barn, as Dakota jumped out and stood looking around, one hand on the door as if she were afraid to let go of her only means to escape the bad feeling starting to grip her. "Ty? Ty—" she called. Logan came up behind her. "Something's wrong, where are all the horses?" Out the other end of the barn, she could see the pasture gates swinging open in the wind. Then she heard the steady banging on the door of the tack room, followed by loud barking. When they ran inside and opened the door, the dog rushed out and disappeared into the twilight of the barn beyond. They could hear it whimpering ahead of them.

"Let me go first," Logan said, walking cautiously past the blacksmith tools along the wall of the grooming area. The box that held the nails and extra shoes was lying on its side, and the rakes and shovels that usually hung along the wall were all on the ground. Lo-

gan bent to pick up a shovel and Dakota reached for the hoof knife
with the curved end. They moved quietly through the doorway.

"My God." Logan threw down the shovel and ran to the figure
slumped against the first stall.

"Is he dead?" Dakota whispered as they stared at the broken
pitchfork thrust into Ty's body.

"Quick, call 911, get the Doc too," he ordered as he felt along the
wrist and then the neck for a pulse. "Hurry—"

When she returned, they decided to untie his legs first, then his
hands while Logan held him, so they could lower him to the ground
without jostling the pitchfork too much. They'd both seen cows and
horses with puncture wounds that were fine until somebody pulled
the piercing object out.

They were trying to wipe some of the blood from his face and
talk to him when the rescue squad roared up, followed by the doctor
and the fire truck. There was a debate about the pitchfork removal,
but as soon as they had hooked him up to IV's, oxygen, and heart
monitors, they decided not to risk pulling it. One lung had obviously been punctured, and they couldn't tell if it was from the broken ribs or the fork. They clipped the handle in half, the heart
monitor went crazy, and they had to stick him with ephenephrin to
bring it back. They strapped him on the stretcher and walked him to
the ambulance for County Hospital.

"We should medivac him down to Wichita." The doctor paused
while the rescue workers set up for the ride. "But I don't think he'd
make it right now. We'll have to get some X rays, see what the damage is internally. Never saw anything like this before—God only
knows what a pitchfork can do to you."

"It was already missing a prong—I cleaned stalls with it—"
Dakota said.

He looked around him. "The sheriff will be here any minute. He
was out on a dispute between neighbors west of here when the call
came. He's alone on Thursday afternoons while the deputy goes
down to Wichita State to take college courses. You coming with
me?" he asked Dakota, who nodded numbly, then looked at Logan.

"I'll talk to the sheriff and call Marlys to meet you at the hospital

when she's done at school. I'll come as soon as I'm through here."
Logan put a big hand on her shoulder, then drew her to him and
hugged her. "Ty's tough, Dakota, stick with him. He'll pull through,
got that cowboy blood." He smiled grimly and pushed her toward
the doctor.

There had been so much confusion she hadn't remembered to look
for Bobby, but now in the waiting room, she tried to figure out what
had happened out there, where the horses had gone. She thought
she remembered the big trailer and truck still parked by the side of
the barn, so it wasn't those guys from the gas station again. Who?
Eddie? It wasn't him. He'd never get involved in something physical
with another person. He only hurt horses. For money. But there was
something about the colt. First he'd been hidden at Dusty's, then
The Sandman was coming for him. It had to be Eddie—she'd go up
there and kick him to death. He knew who did it. Eddie made it a
point to know. It was her fault. She shouldn't have stolen the colt. At
the very least she should've warned Ty about the colt and The Sandman. The feeling of blame lifted a whole part of her up and away, so
she was light with emptiness as she walked down the hall to the
emergency area again, where they were still working to determine
the extent of Ty's injuries.

A nurse in a blood-spattered mask looked up and their eyes
locked for a moment but she couldn't read anything. The woman's
rubber gloves were streaked with blood as they wrapped around the
handle of the pitchfork and started to pull, and Dakota had to look
away for a moment. They'd cut his clothes off, those worn-out boots
kicked into the corner, the hole in the bottom staring at her with re-
proach as if somehow she had something to do with this. When she
looked up again, she saw his bare legs were so covered with deep
purple lumps it shocked her as if she had glimpsed something obscene. It made the bile rise up the back of her throat.

She turned and paced back down the hall to the empty waiting
room. Concentrate on something else, don't let the negative energy
flow toward him, she urged. Her horse. Someone had taken her

horse, the only other thing in the world she loved. It made her feel both angry and helpless that she couldn't leave and find Bobby because Ty was here, and it was her fault. "Shit, oh shit," she muttered, hugging her injured hand against her body and turning back toward the emergency room again, knowing that each time she came to that room, she might hear or see something her mind would refuse. We can do that, she argued, we can decide not to agree to the horror.

She swallowed the bile again and rested her shaking hand on the door frame. They should have curtains over the doorway, they shouldn't be doing this so publicly, anyone could see it, anyone could see—she felt hands on her shoulders and a voice behind her said, "Come on, Dakota." She hadn't realized she was crying until Marlys handed her a tissue as she led her to the gray-and-white plaid sofa.

"I know it's scary for you," Marlys said and put her hand on Dakota's shoulder again and pulled her into a hug. Dakota tried to resist, but couldn't. There just wasn't anything strong enough inside her for this moment. She was so alone and Ty was in there dying and she already missed him so much it choked her throat tight, and she coughed out the sobs she'd been holding.

"How is he?" Logan asked, his straw cowboy hat in his hand. He turned and walked down the hall, hesitating at the door to the room Ty was in, then going on to the nurses' station beyond.

"They haven't said anything, nothing—" Dakota gasped out and sat back, her hand covering her eyes.

"He's going to make it, you have to believe that." Marlys's voice trailed off unconvinced as she looked anxiously down the hall.

"I should've been there to help," Dakota whispered and sat up straighter.

"No—"

Logan walked back in, putting his hat on, then taking it right back off and tossing it on the yellow oak table next to the sofa. "Still waiting to fly him out of here. May have to fly someone in with equipment instead. I told them to do that. Seems our doc is holding his own in there. Used to be an ER doc in Kansas City, seen his share, they told me. Just not exactly like this, I guess. Sons a bitches." Logan threw himself into a chair, sprawling his thin limbs out tiredly.

"I should've been with him," Dakota said again, trying to concentrate on the silver oval championship buckle Logan wore.

"From the looks of what they did to Ty and that colt, you should be real grateful you weren't, little girl."

"The colt? What'd they do?"

"Electrocuted him. Cut his upper lip off. Figure he was tattooed. Came off the track that last load out of Minnesota, right?"

Dakota nodded at the half-truth. Bobby— "Did you find any other—"

"Nope, just the colt. Must have loaded up the others. Barnyard too messed up to sort the tire tracks. Started to rain too. Must've had a big livestock hauler. What'd you have there, fifteen, twenty head?"

"Seventeen," she mumbled, trying not to cry again.

"Well, they probably hauled the others to the killers—" He stopped and bit his lower lip. "I'm sorry. Ty had some pretty nice stock, maybe they're selling 'em out of state, we don't know anything for certain, not yet."

"He just sold four head to Eddie Nyland this morning. They were supposed to be picked up—maybe he—" She shook her head.

"Who's this Nyland?"

"He wouldn't try to kill Ty. He's a horse trainer I used to know—" She noticed Logan's eyes focus on her more closely, and she tried to keep her eyes on the gray wall behind him. Couldn't they find a happier color for a waiting room? Then she remembered the weird guy with Eddie.

"There was a guy with Eddie yesterday. Gave me the creeps. They used to know each other, I guess, Ty and him—his name's Harney something. Had a lot of money, I could tell. He was interested in the colt."

"Harney what?" Logan leaned forward.

"I don't know—Ty would know—" They all looked down the hallway, where the beeping signals suddenly became more frantic and someone yelled. They got up and ran to the doorway in time to see paddles laid on Ty's bare chest and an electric shock jolt his body. The monitor calmed, and nurses and doctors stepped back to surround him.

"That was close," someone said. "Okay, we're clearing the lung now," someone else said and Dakota could see reddish fluid slide down a tube into a waiting bag. Then a nurse came toward them pushing a cart of bloody towels and tools and shooed them out into the hallway.

"It'll be a while longer," she advised. "Hard to see all the damage with the contusions and massive swelling from a beating like that. Far as we can tell, the fork narrowly missed the stomach and liver. Broken ribs, we're not sure about the spleen yet, one kidney might be in trouble, and there's the problem of infection. His face, well, we can't tell yet. Broken jaw, nose, maybe the orbital bone around his left eye. Cracked left collarbone, other one broken. The list goes on—but he's holding his own now, so you folks take it easy, get some food in you, be a long night yet." She pushed the cart past them down the hall.

Logan walked them back to the waiting room and flipped on the TV hanging high in the corner opposite the sofa. "You two sit here, I'll go to the cafeteria—any preferences?"

"I don't know—something cold," Dakota said.

"Coffee," Marlys said. "And get us salads, sandwiches, something light, dear."

Twisting on the sofa and bringing her knees up under her, Marlys asked, "Is there someone we should notify?"

Dakota shrugged. "He never mentioned a family. We never talked much, really—"

"I know. He used to talk about the Sandhills in Nebraska as if he missed them, but never anything about his family. I have the impression he had a hard time of it, don't you?"

"I guess, I don't know, like I said—"

"Well, I guess if the time comes we can find somebody—"

They sat there in the terrible presence of knowing what time that would be.

Forty-five minutes later, the team from Wichita flew in and went to work, but Dakota, Logan, and Marlys stayed in the waiting room.

It was ten o'clock when they took him into the ICU, and the rest of the night was spent in the upstairs waiting room taking turns sleeping while they watched Ty through the window. He had a fifty percent chance of making it through the night. After that the odds went up.

Everything was whispery white and that was pleasant, Ty decided, he liked it. Then the noise got louder and more irritating, someone calling his name. He fought it, not wanting to leave the dream he'd been having, but it was pulling him up, faster than he liked, and with a snap he was awake, his eyes opening but not seeing good. What was wrong with his eyes?

"Do you know where you are?" a man's voice asked him.

"No—" The idea scared him, and he started to reach down and push himself up in the bed. Not his bed—and it hurt bad to move and talk. Could hardly talk, jaw wouldn't open.

"You're in the hospital. Do you know your name?"

"Can't see good—" he whispered.

"Your left eye is taped, the other one is swollen almost shut. Do you know your name?"

"Ty Bonte," he mumbled, "when—"

"You're at County Hospital outside Jerusalem. You've been here three days."

"What happened?" he managed to ask.

"You were badly injured, but you're going to be okay. Don't worry. Just sleep, now."

The next week he woke intermittently, but couldn't seem to move or stay interested in much. He felt something bothering him each time he woke up, but then they gave him something for pain and he went back to sleep. Then one day he woke and they didn't give him a shot, and he knew he was going to have to make it on his own. When Dakota and Logan showed up the next morning, he could tell from their faces something was wrong. They told him about the horses, about finding him beaten and stabbed, and he couldn't look at them any longer. The screams of the dying colt echoed in his head under their words. He closed his eyes and pretended to go to sleep. That night he told the doctor not to let anyone else in to see him. The doctor gave him a sharp look, wrote something on the chart, nodded, and went away. The next day they got him up for the first time.

When Dakota sneaked in to see him that evening, he tried to pretend he was asleep, but she grabbed his hand and squeezed until his thumb knuckle cracked. "I know you're awake, Ty."

He opened his eyes and she loosened her grip. There were tears on her face despite the smile wavering on her lips. Her hair was clean and curly, wisping around her face the way he liked. She looked so sweet and vulnerable he pulled his hand away. He'd screwed up, failed her, failed the horses too.

"I'm so sorry," he whispered and turned his head so she wouldn't see the tears trickling down his own cheeks. A nerve was severed under the right eye and when a tear slid over the numb place, it was an odd empty pocket the flesh around it tried to make up for by being extra-sensitive. He wondered if she could see it—if his face hung or looked dead now. They hadn't suggested that he look in a mirror yet, so he probably had his answer already.

"How's the dog, she get hurt?" he asked.

Dakota swallowed a small sob in her throat. "She was fine when we let her out—that day, but she—"

Ty wiped at his eyes and turned his face toward her again. "What?"

"She took off as soon as the ambulance came up the drive. The siren must've spooked her." Dakota smoothed a little area of sheet with the side of her hand. "Logan's been checking every day, but she hasn't shown up. I think she's gone, Ty."

Ty felt the urge to make some remark about his being the kind of person who couldn't even keep a dog, but he didn't want the argument. "You better go too—"

She nodded and rose to kiss him, but he held up his hand.

"I mean *leave*—go back to Iowa or Minnesota, wherever—" He

knew that if she wanted to argue, he couldn't raise his voice with his jaw wired shut.

"Ty, don't—please?" She reached for his face but pulled her hand back when he turned his head away again.

"There's nothing here for you—"

"No—"

"Go!" There was no mistaking the anger even though his voice was muffled. "I don't want you—" His throat closed on the last word, "here," but she was already gone.

They released him two weeks later in early November after a bout of infection from the punctures, and Logan drove him back to the house, neither saying anything on the way. He still hurt every time he moved, but he'd already made up his mind to ignore it. Twice the first day, he was on the verge of fainting by the time he made it to the bed to lie down. At least Dakota was safe, he kept reminding himself, though he missed her with a different kind of pain. He hadn't wanted to tell her that he'd let her down, that he was unable to protect her horse, the colt, anything, it seemed. It was Ronnie all over again. He felt a deep shame, almost as if he deserved the beating, deserved losing Dakota.

When Marlys and Logan showed up at dark with a pot of soup, he thanked them at the door and shut off the lights before they had their truck turned around and headed back down the driveway.

The place was so strangely empty without the noise of the horses that he began to hear sounds he'd never noticed before. Boards creaking as they shrank in the late fall cold, mice skittering in the walls, the last of the leaves on the bushes rustling against the bedroom window. Sometimes at night he thought he heard footsteps in the dead leaves under the cottonwood by the back door. He'd get up, grab the pistol and rifle he kept handy all the time now, and turn off the lights before he moved the shade slightly to peek out the window. Once in a while there was a deer or Logan's dog, but never what he imagined it was—Harney and his men.

He hated this about himself, this fear or whatever it was. It made him remember that January night with Harney twenty years ago, when they'd gone looking for drunk Indians on the road to St. Francis. They'd found them all right, staggering, ten miles from home. When Harney stopped and Ty had rolled down his window, the bigger one leaned in—the ragged scarf covering the lower half of his face had slipped down, and the stench of days of drinking beer, cheap wine, and whiskey had spewed into the car's interior. Ty had turned his head away. Despite not wanting Harney to think he was pussy—that was so important in those days—he'd asked, "You sure about this?"

Harney had nodded and grinned. He was almost bouncing in his seat, like that time they went out hunting and ended by shooting up those cabins. Then he'd leaned past Ty and called to the two men to get in. When the man went to grab the handle to the back door, Harney stepped on the gas, sending him sideways against his friend. Harney stopped a few yards away and waited while they caught up. "Get in," he said, barely able to keep his face straight while he repeated the same trick, only this time the drunken man had hung onto the window and run alongside the car a few steps before he tripped in the snow and fell, letting go as he went. Ty remembered that hand on the glass, the fingers that had seemed too delicate, like a child's with the fingernails ringed in dirt. Like his brother's maybe, and maybe that was why he'd turned to Harney and said, "Stop it."

Harney had slammed on the brakes, fighting the car as it shivered and threatened to spin. The drunks were more cautious now, waiting without touching the car until the back door swung open and they could climb safely in, filling the interior with the stench of old alcohol, sweat, and stale cigarette smoke. Ty had rolled the window up, leaving a crack to suck out the smell. The Indians mumbled thanks and leaned back in the warmth. Keeping the revolver in his lap, Ty half-turned in his seat to take a better look at them. The smaller one closed his eyes as the frost melted off his eyelashes and trickled down his round cheeks. He had full lips and a small pointed chin and enough scars to suggest he was no stranger to fights. There was a dark ugly bruise or birthmark high on one cheek that became visible when his head rolled loose and the snores started. The other man kept staring straight ahead between the front bucket seats at the road in front of the headlights, and when his eyelids slipped down he would shake himself back to the same unfocused stare. His face was lean, deeply scarred by acne, with the shadow of a mustache on his upper lip. He was just a kid. Ty felt his stomach shiver as the Indian continued to ignore him and fight his body's urge to sleep in the warmth of the car. Turning back he noticed Harney smiling as he steered the car slowly down the road, then reached over and punched the Super Tramp tape up extra loud.

Ty had opened the window more to suck out the smell and let the fresh icy air cut the sound that boomed against the walls of the car. He remembered wishing he were in his pickup, driving back to the ranch even though the heater had broken and the only music was Reservation radio or the station in Babylon, which played only old country, nothing close to the rockabilly he liked. He was supposed to be up early to ship cattle, what the hell was he doing out here at this time of night? He'd glanced at the clock, one in the morning. Christ. He'd hardly even get to bed, and from the way his body was starting to get that light, tingly feeling like every cell was going to sleep, he could tell he was going to be hungover. The old man would be cursing the whole time, kicking and hitting the cattle, banging on the horses, but he better not try it with him. Looking around at the dark Sandhills covered with snow that worked their way north across their corner of western Nebraska up into South Dakota, where they smoothed, then disappeared into the older, broader hills, he'd known what he was going to do. "I have to bail," he'd said.

Harney had glanced at him. "Now?"

"We're shipping cattle at dawn. Let's call it a night." He used the tone that said he'd had enough.

Harney shrugged and slowed, pulling into the snowbanked road to somebody's ranch and letting the car drift to a stop. He turned out the lights, muted the tape, but left the engine running. "End of the line, chiefs," he said, watching them in the rearview mirror. The two in back didn't move, and he repeated himself in a louder voice.

The bigger Indian rubbed his pocked face and stretched his

mouth open and shut, but he didn't move. It wasn't a good sign. "A little farther," he said, "up there." He gestured toward the snow-covered hills. His buddy leaned forward as if he were collapsing and started retching, but nothing came out.

"Get the fuck out of the car!" Harney yelled and yanked his door open and jumped out. The sick Indian fumbled with the door handle and was just sticking a leg out when Harney grabbed him and threw him to the road.

"Hey—" The big one started out his door and Ty knew this was it.

There would always be Harney or someone like him, and Ty couldn't stop him. First his brother Ronnie, then the Indians, now the colt. The shame came upon him as it had before, when he'd run away from home that night. He should've gone back to stand trial, should've stood up and gone to jail. But he hadn't, and now here he was. Dakota was lucky she got away. He said it to himself, but he couldn't help wishing it weren't true. Couldn't help remembering those times they'd made love, and he'd been able to fall into the comfort of her body and find acceptance and ease as he'd never found before. It was wrong that he should lose that, he felt, but it was what he deserved.

Then one night the dreams began where Ronnie was alive again, sometimes playing happily like a little kid should, sometimes howling like that time their father beat Ty with a belt for the loss of calves in the late April blizzard, but always the dream came to the moment of his brother climbing on the tractor, the light one they used for mowing the subirrigated hay meadows, bouncing off over the hill, waving as he stood because he was too short to reach the pedals if he sat, his small body held tense and as much like the adult man he wasn't as he disappeared in a blur of red metal and hazy heat. Sometimes it was his own voice calling out after his brother, trying to stop him, that woke him up, sometimes it was the sound of the boy crying out, pinned under the tractor those hours when nobody missed him or thought to check while the weight slowly crushed his chest and spine, slowly suffocating him in his own blood. Sometimes when Ty rode up to the scene, Ronnie was still alive, and he would get to say good-bye, say how sorry he was and hold his brother's small hand. Other times, he would find his father there, yelling at the dead child, and Ty would jump off the horse and beat the older man with his fists until he woke up crying.

When he lay there in the night, soaked with sweat, his tears caught inside, he'd remember the way it really had been. The way he roped the tractor and pulled it up off his brother, because the ground was too soft to dig him out. Ronnie's face so pale, his lips blue as if he'd frozen to death in the cool moist field. And his little hand, outstretched, palm open, fingers softly curled like they did when he slept in his own bed next to Ty's. Ty had not wanted to bring him home that afternoon. Not wanted the next part. He'd sat beside him out there till supper time. A part of him waiting to see if their father came, if he even thought to wonder and worry, a part of him feeling he could have stopped Ronnie, should have. Finally, the horse had gotten restless, and as the wind died down at sunset, he had heard the cattle lowing in the next pasture as they headed to the basin they'd spend the night in, and strangely, he thought he'd heard his father calling his name, then his brother's. Although it couldn't have been so, he rose, shook the sleep out of his legs, picked up his brother's body, made the horse stand while he climbed on, and rode toward the ranch house.

Ronnie had gotten heavier, the stillness concentrating the weight until his arms hurt excruciatingly, but Ty had never relaxed them, never let his brother rest on the saddle or neck of the horse. It was his to carry, this weight, and he would and he had. All the way to the house, where his father waited on the porch, a hand on the post, shaking his head, saying "No, no," as if Ronnie were the only thing of value in his whole world.

And so it had seemed after that, for both of them. They became quiet men together. Morose. His father couldn't keep a hired hand on the place, because with Ronnie gone, there was no room for any-one else in their lives. It all led him here, he saw, and he was now as broken and alone as his father.

Chapter Twelve

The runny afternoon light pushed only partway into the living room, where Ty sat in the broken recliner, tilted back to rest on the two cement blocks he'd put there so he could sit facing the window and watch the new snow fall on the two feet that had already accumulated since a deep cold set in at the beginning of December. When the truck pulled up outside, he immediately thought it was Dakota, though he knew that wasn't reasonable. He'd gotten out of the habit of answering the door, so he stayed where he was, certain the person would go away. Only he'd forgotten to lock up last time he went out to throw corn to the deer he was feeding now that the horses were gone. The heavy feet stomping snow off in the kitchen made him pick up the .38 he kept on the little round table with the pole lamp spindled through it. The rifle was leaning against the bookcase beside the TV, close at hand, but he pulled it over next to the chair.

"What is this, the Wild West show?" Logan came in dropping snow in clumps off his jeans and jacket. His face was pink from the cold, and frost fringed his mustache. He held up a six-pack of Bud in each hand.

Ty stared at him, hoping he would get the message, but he sat down on the sofa instead, half-blocking the view of the snow out the window. "Figured it was time we talked." He popped a beer and got up and held it out in front of Ty, until he took it. Then he popped one for himself.

Watching Logan, Ty found himself wanting to taste that beer, to feel its long icy shovel down his throat. He didn't drink, he reminded himself, but what difference did it make now? He waited a moment, then put the can to his lips, tilted his head, and drank, savoring its grainy taste and draining two thirds, stopping only because he noticed Logan staring at him. He shrugged and put the pistol on the table, the barrel facing the other man.

"As a rule I don't ask a nondrinking man to drink, but I'm making an exception in your case, Ty." He took another pull off his beer, watching Ty finish his and tossing him another to open as soon as the first empty clanked against the pistol on the round table.

Ty opened the beer without thinking and gulped it half down as if he were dying of some bizarre thirst though he hadn't done a lick of work in almost two months, aside from shoveling enough snow out of the way to get in his truck to go to town for food once a week. Still, he felt this thirst the beer only increased, and sure as hell, he didn't care why Logan was trying to get him loaded. He drank the rest, and Logan got up and handed him the last three cans, hooked together in their plastic ring. He kept the other six-pack by his feet on the floor and watched the next half hour while Ty worked his way through the three beers.

The beer didn't seem to be having any effect, Ty noticed. He felt exactly the same, dead cold thirsty inside. Maybe this was the effect of what had happened, he thought. Some deal, now he could drink all he wanted. But he wanted to get drunk, suddenly, he wanted to feel his head swell and burst, he wanted to get blind drunk and get in a fight or break the shit out of something, like the bad old days. He could feel the rage coming on him, and he drank to take himself right to that place it came from, he knew where it was, he'd been there a lot in those years after he'd left the Sandhills. Fought his way out of more bars and honky-tonks than he could count. Fought the world, the work, the animals, until finally he fought himself out of a woman he was with five years ago, and she'd disappeared utterly, leaving him in the torn-up trailer on the outskirts of Austin, Texas. She didn't take anything, not even the money they'd been saving together. He'd tried to find her and give her half of it, but she was gone. That's when he'd quit drinking.

Fat lot of good it did him. Here he was. Hospital bills, no horses, no way to finish paying for the place he'd put his savings into over the years, and a stolen rig he couldn't sell. And Dakota, he reminded himself, he'd sent her away. Well, that was pretty. Real pretty. He crushed the empty in his hand and tossed it over his shoulder, irritated when all it did was clank harmlessly on the linoleum kitchen floor. Wouldn't matter, she was gone, nobody around to make him clean up anymore.

Logan was watching the snow fall now, his long legs stretched out on the sofa, leaning against the end, sipping his first beer.

"Gimme another," Ty said and although he didn't feel drunk, he could hear his words had a little slur in them. The older man ignored him.

"Give me another beer, goddamn it." Ty pulled the recliner upright and stood up, swaying. Shit, he was drunk. Didn't matter.

"Start talking, then." Logan looked at him.

"What? What do you want?" Ty sat back down on the edge of the seat to keep the recliner upright. He didn't know whether he could climb out of it again. "Nobody invited you here," he mumbled.

"Never thought you were the type to feel sorry for yourself." Logan unhooked a new beer and handed it to him.

It wasn't cold anymore, but Ty opened it and drank some anyway, ignoring the warm suds that wanted to come back up in a long burp. "Not feeling sorry for myself. Just—" He waved a hand at the pistol. "Have to be careful now."

"Blaming yourself, huh. How many were there? Sheriff said you told him four with guns. Guess you could have fought them and gotten shot, that would've been brave. You played for time and it didn't work out. Least you tried. Thought you could take your licks, Ty. Never struck me any other way. This thing you're doing now though, I can understand your wanting to hole up and nurse your wounds, get yourself back in shape, but you've turned against the people who care for you, and that's not a thing a man does, now is it?"

Ty drank some more, not liking it quite as much now. He was feeling too full and his head was hurting too. "Things change. Can't take care of things anymore. Maybe I never could. Anyway, I'm done here. Horses gone. Broke. Not much good to anybody now. Might as well crawl in a bottle—" He drained the beer and had to swallow twice to keep that damn warm suds down. Still, he held out his hand for another. Logan gave a mean little smile and handed him another. He almost choked swallowing this time. Maybe this wasn't such a great idea after he'd been hurt so recently. He drank again.

"A person could get back up on his two hind legs and go after them, I guess. You told the sheriff you didn't know them, but I think you're lying. That's why you're holed up here."

Ty squinted at him over the top of the can.

"Known for a while you had something you were holding back. You think you're keeping it in there, but it shows. Sooner or later, you're going to have to do something about it. You were always alone here, until Dakota came along. Alone for a reason, I figure. I think it's a relief for you she's gone. Not that you don't miss her, but you were afraid you'd get so close to her, one day you'd tell her or she'd ask and you'd blurt it out, and then what? She's a good woman, Ty. You made a mistake making her go, and you know it too."

Ty drained the can, fighting the nausea all the way. He couldn't remember when he last ate, maybe breakfast, but maybe the night before. Goddamn Logan. "What do you want me to say? Want to hear the whole stupid fucking shit?" He wanted to tell, he did, and he could feel it on the tip of his tongue, working loose, and he held out his hand for the next beer, knowing it would make him sick, and hoping it did, because then he might accidentally spew out the rest. He drank and heard himself talking while he stared at the fading afternoon light that made the snowflakes big, individual, and bright just before the dark slammed them down to nothing.

"Harney was the one started it, kicking the guy on the ground all curled up against the pointy-toe cowboy boots . . ."

When they'd pulled up in front of Mickey's Nook after leaving the Indians in the field, Ty had gotten out without a word and climbed into his old truck. "Have it your way," Harney called as he slid behind the wheel. "Pussy," he spit into the dirty snow-packed street, slammed the door, and spun away. Ty's truck started after whining a couple of times and he drove slowly out of town. Just past Doc's Gun Shop on the very outskirts, the shakes hit and he had to stop and throw up. On the road again, he wondered what the hell happened. Had he shot the other boy? He'd killed rattlesnakes and coyotes, done his share of hunting, but never aimed at a person before except those couple of times standing behind the old man and fantasizing. He'd never thought about Indians one way or the other. No one in his family ever went to the reservation though it was only thirty-some miles away. "I didn't lose anything up there," his father always said. In high school Ty had gone to Rosebud a couple of times with Harney to see if they could pick up girls at powwows, basketball games, rodeos.

But gradually it had come out that Harney hated Indians. The part Harney hadn't told in history class that day was how his grandfather used to take him cruising for Indians on the road to Rosebud. Chased them down in the truck, throwing stuff at them, shit like that.

Ty thought about all the blood again. "Fuck." He punched the dashboard, sending the accumulated crap jumping and a pair of pliers onto the floor near his foot. He'd have to go back there. He'd dropped the gun. Christ, maybe he *had* shot the son of a bitch. He pulled a U-turn.

He'd tried to remember what they looked like, but couldn't think of anything more than the small, delicate hand on the window, like a young boy's. Ronnie, his brother. Those Indians were drunk, he tried to argue, they deserved it. But so was he, and they had been trying to get home, they'd trusted him. He tried again to recall their faces, but all he saw was two figures dressed in worn jean jackets and rags for scarves and no gloves.

"You only remember what you want to," his father had said just that morning.

That isn't so, he'd wanted to argue. Ronnie was your fault.

The wind had died by the time he retrieved his pistol and found the Indians a quarter of a mile farther up the road, huddled there waiting for God knew what. The cold had settled bitterly and it had to be well below zero. They didn't seem to recognize him as he dragged and lifted them into the truck, leaking blood they mumbled apologies for, holding themselves as if they were broken and cut in too many places. When the taller boy Ty had fought fell against his shoulder on the curves, Ty's first impulse was to push him off, but he stopped himself. The gagging stink in the cab was more than vomit and drinking now, it was the peculiar decaying garbage stench of blood as it hit the air and sat. Ty's stomach heaved, but he didn't dare crack the window on the half-frozen men since his heater didn't work, so he tried breathing through his mouth until the smell settled into a rotten taste on his tongue. He pressed the gas pedal to the floor and prayed the deer would stay out of the road tonight.

He took them to St. Francis because that was the closest town and drove around until he saw the big, pale cream Catholic church on the old boarding school campus, and pulled up in front of the priests' residence across the road. Banging on the door, he managed to wake a young priest, who impatiently yanked the door open. "Now what—" He stopped when he saw the blood-splotched jacket in the porch light.

"There's been an—accident—" Ty cursed himself for the chicken-shit lie.

The priest looked at the slumped figures in the truck and shook his head. "There always is—can't you take them to the hospital in Babylon? It's equipped for—"

"The one's bleeding pretty bad—" The truck door opened and the smaller Indian half-climbed, half-fell out and lay groaning on the snow-packed ground. The wounded boy slipped sideways on the bench seat, his arm stretching out the open door, blood falling in dark drops off his hand into the snowbank beside the truck.

"These two again? All right, wait here—" The priest closed the door and for a moment they were left there in the special silence cold made, the only sounds the ragged breathing of the bleeding boy and the squeak of snow under Ty's boots as he shifted his weight to warm his toes.

When the door finally opened again, the priest was accompanied by a much older man, who still wore the traditional long black robe. "Come on," the young priest said.

After they'd seen to the Indian boy's wounds and called an ambulance from Babylon, the old priest treated Ty like he'd done something good and he felt his soul sicken. "You're hurt too." The old man lifted his fingers to the ear and Ty flinched automatically, hating that he had that reflex from being around his father. Recognition passed across the priest's face, but didn't linger as pity, which Ty was grateful for.

"Sit down," the priest ordered and Ty followed his instructions. He was so tired, so very, very tired. When the priest tried to help him out of his coat, the gun clunked against the chair, and he quickly pushed his arms back into the sleeves and pulled it around him despite the blood-soaked cloth.

"What's your name?" the priest asked as he cleaned the ear and began sewing it.

Ty remembered the face he'd kicked and made himself stay as still against the pain as the Indian had. He concentrated on making up a name to tell the priest, but nothing came, so he just told the truth. Harney would've laughed his ass off at him.

After bandaging the ear, the old man tilted Ty's head back in the light to clean the cut over his eye that stung like a bastard. The priest's fingernails were yellow and scaled as an old rooster's claws, and the sleeve of the heavy black wool robe smelled like mothballs when it brushed his face as the old man leaned over to set Steri-strips to close the cut.

"He'll live, the wounded boy." The old priest's cool hand rested on the back of his neck when he was through, and Ty had to fight the urge to lean into its soft strength. "They're lucky you came along." The fingers squeezed into the nerves at the base of his neck so it almost hurt, then relaxed. "That's how it happened, wasn't it, Ty Bonte?"

He nodded. He wanted to ask whether the boy had been shot but couldn't.

"Let's have a look at those knuckles, then."

"They're okay—" Ty stood and stepped around the priest, letting his eyes slide out the door of the little office to the infirmary. "Thanks—"

Walking swiftly down the black-tiled hall, he only glanced into the room where the two Indians lay. He'd done what he could, he reasoned, and shook his head as he pushed the door open and stepped out into the cold. Now he'd probably never know the truth.

Before he left the ranch for good that dawn and though he had nothing else to replace them with, Ty stuffed his bloody coat and gloves in the burn barrel, doused them with gasoline, and watched the match he'd thrown send them up in a whoosh of flame. He wrote a note for the old man saying he didn't owe him for the last ten years of backbreaking, ass-kicking work because he was taking the fifteen-year-old truck he'd put the new engine in last year. Then he called his mom at five, waking her up and telling her he was leaving and he loved her, which was met with silence. The last thing he said was how sorry he was about Ronnie. He threw his bag of clothes on the truck seat and climbed in, carefully tucking the gun beside him before he drove out the long snow-packed ranch road to the highway. He'd wanted to tell his mother about the other thing he was sorry about, but he couldn't bring that shame to light. Not yet, maybe not ever.

"There's probably still a warrant out for my arrest. When you take off like I did, it never goes away, I guess. Harney told them it was all me, of course. My mother sent me the newspaper articles."

Ty realized they had been sitting there in the dark for some time, listening to the clock in the kitchen ticking and the heat coming on with a low rumble and breathy hiss up through the registers.

"Dakota called me today," Logan said. "She's in Minneapolis staying with some guy named Eddie trying to get your horses back. She thinks he's seen them for some reason. I'm worried about her, Ty. She's talking about going out to the Sandhills to confront this Harney Rivers fellow. She's convinced he's responsible. Is he?"

Ty jerked his head up. "She'll get hurt, Logan, why didn't you stop her?"

"How was I supposed to do that, Ty?"

"I don't know—God, she's crazy! Damn it, Logan, you should've told her to call me—"

"Yeah? And what're you going to do? You can't go out to the Sandhills after him, they'll throw you in jail—"

Ty rubbed his face, hurting the bone under his eye, which was still sensitive from the break. "Aw shit," he moaned. "Shit, shit, shit." He stood up and strode to the kitchen, flipped on the light, and looked at the phone on the wall as if he could will it to ring, then came back and flipped on the other lights. He wasn't feeling so drunk now. He'd reached that little clear space in the middle, like the eye of the tornado, just before the world blew up.

"Calm down, here's the number where she's staying in Minneapolis. Now don't start a fight, for chrissakes, Ty." Logan stood and held out a scrap of paper.

"I *know* Eddie's damn number, Logan."

"Ty, just don't forget—you're not the same person you were back there in the hills. You're a grown man living a decent life. That counts for something—you could tell the authorities the truth. You could tell them how it was Harney Rivers did this to you too—"

Ty lifted the receiver but held the button down, staring at the numbers. "Yeah, I've thought about that plenty of times, Logan, but at seventeen I knew what I was doing. The difference between right and wrong. I don't have any excuses. This is just between Harney and me now." He lifted his finger and started punching in the numbers.

"Even if it means going to jail when you're done?" Logan asked.

∽ Chapter Thirteen

Since Eddie was living in a motel near the Fairgrounds in St. Paul while the Winter Horse Show was on, Dakota had convinced the barn help that it was fine for her to stay at his stable while she tried to track down the stolen horses. Initially she hadn't believed she'd find Bobby there, but yesterday in the corner of the hayloft she had found his halter with the brass name plate tucked under a heap of moldy, torn leather goods and blankets to be sorted and repaired or discarded. At first she'd taken it as a bad sign and her stomach had lurched, but then she'd noticed the missing buckle at the throat and realized it had broken. So Eddie was involved. Examining the horses in the paddocks and the few dozing in the twilight of their stalls, she thought she'd found one of the two-year-old chestnut geldings Eddie had liked, but she couldn't remember for sure, and she intended to ask Ty as soon as she could figure out a way not to get him so fired up he came charging in here. She couldn't stand to see him hurt again.

The big gray with the suitcase head she'd ridden for Eddie that day was nowhere to be seen, probably sold, she decided, not fancy enough for Eddie's stable. Of the others, she found no evidence. He'd probably scattered them across the country by now, she'd realized with a bitter clenching of her teeth. That bastard. At first, she'd wanted to go straight to the shed where he kept the Corvette and other cars "in transit," the way he described the vehicles with questionable titles that occasionally appeared and disappeared. She'd wanted to pour dirt in every gas tank, slash the tires, smash the windows, ruin them, but she'd stopped herself. She still needed to find Bobby, and Eddie would be her best bet, so she took the halter as evidence and hid it.

She had been at the Fairgrounds since early this morning, talking to old friends, picking up gossip, and watching Eddie and his people. She hadn't gone over to his stalls when he was around because she knew she'd start yelling at him about Bobby.

They were having an unusual warm spell for December and people were walking around with their jackets open or slung over their arms. The horses, body clipped and slick for showing, still wore their blankets unless they were in the ring. This was the first time they'd had a show in December at the Fairgrounds, and the sponsors had arranged to use the judging arena a half block away for the warm-up instead of the usual outdoor ring, so there was only the long, cold walk to the hippodrome to be faced in case it snowed or the temperature dropped. Usually the horses were laid up this time of year, but somebody wanted more money, and the competitors were anxious to show year round now that so many southern and western circuits picked up again in February and March.

Watching the Grand Prix Jumpers from the rail this afternoon, Dakota felt the same flutter of excitement she always did. She'd missed horse showing, she realized. But she also remembered the bad parts with Eddie and concentrated on the Grand Prix horses who moved, even at a walk on a loose rein, with a confidence and pride that seemed to overshadow the other horses, even the fancy hunters with national standing. When they trotted, it was with collection and spring, each step positive and balanced. No falling in on the shoulder in the corners or near-collisions with other horses. It was like watching professional basketball or hockey players warming up with the pony league.

Dakota counted four of Eddie's horses entered in the Grand Prix tonight, each owned by different and competing clients. Eddie would make money no matter who won because the losers could more easily be convinced to sell the poorly performing horses and spend more money on the next great promise. In the old days she used to help with the drugs, the special abrasives they painted on under the bandages so the legs stung if the horse even touched a rail, anything to make the animals perform beyond their normal ability, and the innumerable ways they had to make the animal perform at less than peak. It had finally made her feel as if a part of her were rotting inside, as if there were something pus-ridden on her breath every time she spoke. Dusty's little string of pathetic losers had seemed like a step up from working for Eddie. Then Ty—that's why she had to get at least some of his horses back if she could, so he'd take her back too. He haunted her sleep and especially now that she was around the horses, she couldn't help but think of him constantly. A couple of times, she thought she even saw him out of the corner of her eye, his long lean body in worn jeans and boots, but it always turned out to be someone else.

After a while the warm-up area started to clog with adult riders whose clumsiness sent the Grand Prix horses fleeing in self-defense. Keeping her hat pulled low to her sunglasses, Dakota sat waiting. It wasn't long before Eddie took his customary place by the oxer in the middle and began yelling at his adult riders for their warm-up jumps before they did back-to-back rounds in the big indoor hippodrome. Eddie called this group his "special ed class."

"Canter the vertical, Bill," he ordered a red-headed man in his late forties on a huge seventeen-hand chestnut that must have been twenty years old from the way he tiredly plopped each foot down at the trot and ignored Bill's conflicting hand and leg signals. Bill jumped the X set between the vertical and oxer, almost crashing into Louise, who was circling for her go.

"Bill, are you fucking blind or just fucking deaf?" Eddie yelled it loud enough so everyone in the warm-up ring could hear.

Bill smiled and bit his lip. "Which vertical?" he asked; showing made him nervous, a feeling he was unused to.

"Which vertical? Why the one with the little green stripe, the only goddamn one out here." Eddie shook his head in disgust. He really hated the adult riders. Give him a junior or a kid any day of the week. But Bill had a lot more dollars to donate, Eddie had always said.

"Okay, Bill, just relax, aim the horse and let him canter over it. Pretend you're Helen Keller and don't move."

Bill laughed and cantered around the end of the ring. Dakota knew that although it was only two foot six, it looked five feet as it rose in his path now. She'd been there. The rail looked thick as a telephone pole you'd crash if you didn't help push the horse faster and upward. It was all a rider could do sometimes to just sit there.

"Don't move, don't move, don't move." Eddie's voice took over the rider's hands and body, riveting him in position. "Release." Eddie let the word out slowly so Bill would follow in slow motion, sliding his hands up the crest of the horse's neck, freeing its head to jump and land in balance without the rider jabbing it in the mouth.

"Beautiful," Eddie crooned, "now come around and pick up the oxer, just settle around the corner and keep the pace. Remember, you bought a horse that big so he can do the work, you just relax, take a load off—that's it, don't move, don't—no, don't—Jesus Christ! What the fuck was that? Are you on drugs? You have to be— you could have put a house in that distance you took off from. Pat him, give him the registration on your Mercedes, he earned it. Saved your fucking life." Eddie shook his head. "Walk, goddamn it, walk and breathe, you must have oxygen deprivation taking off at a distance like that."

Eddie looked at Sarah standing next to him, warming up her riders over the same fences. "And he thinks he paid too much—the horse should get a Presidential Medal for life-saving." Sarah grinned and nodded.

"Louise, what are you doing? Trail riding?" Eddie looked around at another one of his adult riders. Her tidy, sixteen-hand bay was half asleep, with the rider's reins and legs flopping. "Are you in this class?"

Louise picked up her reins abruptly, hitting the bay's mouth and causing him to jerk his head up in surprise.

"Louise, what did I—" Eddie shook his head. "Giving you reins is like giving Jack the Ripper a chain saw. Okay, do the X. No, I didn't see it last time—"

She trotted down over the fence, jumping onto the horse's neck at the last minute so the animal lost its balance and lurched and fumbled over the foot-and-a-half-high rails. On the other side, she swayed, dangerously close to falling off. Of all his clients, Dakota knew, Louise was the one he hated most. She wouldn't concentrate, forgot the rules constantly, and was, worst of all, cheap. He wanted to kill her, he used to tell Dakota, but her husband was a heart surgeon and someday, just someday, they might spend some real money. In the meantime, he could always scare her into paying her bills on time.

Louise righted herself. "How was that?"

Eddie shook his head and grinned terribly while Sarah snickered behind him. He took a deep breath. "Do they trot fences in your class, Louise?"

"At home we do."

"Are we at home? No? Then canter the goddamn fence, and *sit still.* If you move, I'm going to hit you."

Dakota could see the satisfaction on Eddie's face as the bay cantered flawlessly over the fence, Louise frozen in perfect form on top.

"Can you believe it?" Eddie sighed.

"She looks good," Sarah offered.

Louise had the perfect rider's body: medium height, thin, curveless as a boy and supple, with just the right length of leg to fit neatly against the horse's sides.

"Okay, Louise, that was better. Now do it again, this time balance through the end of the ring and don't jerk his mouth after the fence. Then go around and jump the others, and don't, for chrissakes, take the oxer backwards."

With any luck, his riders would take the top ribbons in this class, and he'd have them convinced they could win at bigger shows with better, more expensive horses now that they were riding so well.

Dakota trailed along behind as the adults followed their trainer to stand and wait their turn at the in-gate. The grooms threw blankets over the haunches of each animal so the back ends wouldn't chill and stiffen up, then went around painting each hoof with oil and wiping boots, reins, bits, and martingales with rags. The adult riders mostly sat nervously staring at their hands or at the horse already in the ring, hoping not to humiliate themselves. Mostly hoping not to hear Eddie's low sarcastic voice when they came out. The children were always laughing and looking around at each other as they waited at the in-gate, while the juniors, like typical teenagers, ignored each other and stared haughtily into space. The adult amateurs who came to riding later in life were the brunt of humor on the show circuit. Though they paid their bills and spent the most money these days, they were ignorant, and their bodies and nerves showed it.

This was the kind of hierarchy Dakota hadn't missed while she was away from the horse show world. There was some of it at the track, but they were all dealing with horses first there, not the riders. And at Dusty's level, the only concern for money was having enough to buy hay and grain. At Ty's place, she'd finally gotten back to what she'd loved in the first place—being with horses every day. Without all that interference. Until those men had shown up.

She sat behind the announcer on the in-gate side across from where the grooms, owners, and trainers sat watching the show. Eddie's people did well, as always. They were too scared to do anything else, and by simply turning themselves over to him in the ring, they gained relief from having to make decisions they were too scared or confused to make accurately. Maybe that was what attracted them to someone like Eddie. They needed to be bullied through a dangerous sport they were too old to be undertaking, and he was more than happy and competent to make it happen for them.

She listened as they came out of the ring, collecting in a small group around him while the grooms took the horses.

"Can't expect much from a dick-head like him, can we?" Eddie said to one woman who slipped off her horse and stood tiredly staring at it like he was a husband caught in bed with another woman. Although she'd finished seventh in a class of thirty-five, she was ready to replace him. Seventh wasn't the same as winning. Dakota remembered when the woman, Julie, had shown up at the barn with this horse she'd raised and trained herself. A pet she lavished every attention upon. Now he was dog food for all she cared. Like Bobby. Dakota wished suddenly that she had some money to rescue this horse from the fate Eddie would plan, but maybe Julie would sell it or retire it to her farm instead. After all, unless Julie had no other money, Eddie could easily find her another horse without hurting this one. Even he preferred that, he always insisted.

"You're knocking on the door now, closer each show, huh?" He slipped an arm over the shoulders of a tiny, middle-aged brunette who was the most tentative rider of the group. Her horses required lunging and riding by someone else at every show before she could get on and steer them around courses. Recently divorced, she still had enough of her own money to earn Eddie's respect for a while longer. Unless he got tired of her for some other reason, like whining. He couldn't stand a whiner or a troublemaker. No matter how much money they had, he'd take them down for a big hit, then dump them or force them to change stables by ignoring or harassing them. Plain stupidity didn't especially bother him, since he assumed most people willing to pay money to jump over fences on horses were stupid on some level. He'd told Dakota as much.

"Titus is a little sore," he said to an older silver-haired woman, Callie, who handed her reins to the groom. "Pack his front legs good, that nerve block is wearing off," he ordered as Callie slipped a piece of sugar between the horse's lips. "Still an old campaigner, though, aren't you, buddy?" He patted the horse's neck and handed the Reserve Champion ribbon to the groom. "Make sure he gets his Ionacare too." The groom nodded tiredly, and Dakota felt the ache he must have in his shoulders and back by now, sleeping three or four hours a night during week-long shows like this.

"Louise, was that a speed class out there?" Eddie asked as she dismounted and dropped the reins into the groom's hand, taking the can of Coke he offered without thanking him.

"I placed." She turned to walk off.

"Louise!" Eddie yelled. Louise whitened and turned back. "Don't you argue with me. You lucked out because everyone else in there sucked. You got lucky! One of these days you're going to run out of the corner like that and eat the fence." He turned his back on her and clapped Bill on the shoulder.

"Good work, buddy. You tried to take it away over that last oxer, but he wouldn't let you, would he?" Bill grinned and finished running up the stirrups before loosening the girth. He hung the championship ribbon on the browband so it fluttered gold and blue and red in the breeze and patted the big chestnut, who ignored him and began to fall asleep. "You should've paid a lot more for this one," Eddie said, meaning it though no one but Dakota knew that for sure.

His adults had won the top places in their classes, but it was never enough. Now he'd be hustling from one out-of-town stable to another, working deals, trying to get a percentage of every horse bought and sold on the show grounds by putting a word here and there, or claiming to. He had all of his riders trying new horses, some on the pretense that the animals were for other clients who weren't around at that moment. It would take the rest of the day and Dakota wondered when she'd have time to get him alone. Maybe after the Grand Prix or—

"Oh no." She'd looked out across the in-gate area to the horse barn just in time to see Ty's big rig pulling up.

Slipping down the hallway and out a side door, she managed to avoid being seen by Eddie or any of his people as she ran across the intersection of streets to stop Ty. She jerked open the passenger door as he was getting ready to get out.

"Don't stop here—drive on, turn the corner!" The truck began rolling while she was still climbing in.

"Eddie's right over there—I hope he didn't see you," she panted.

Ty pulled into the shade of the cattle building and parked. "That's just who I came to see." He tucked the revolver in the waist of his jeans and buttoned his jeans jacket over it.

"You don't understand—" She reached for his arm and he pulled it away.

"Are you protecting him?" he asked quietly.

"Of course not." She looked at the new curved scar over the old one on his cheekbone, and the slight change in his nose from the break. His face was thinner, paler. He'd lost something, or maybe something else had been added. She couldn't tell whether it was good or bad, this change in him. He was different. No telling what he was planning to do.

"Well, you can't just walk over there and shoot him," she finally said.

He sighed. "Guess you're right. I thought about what you said when I called, decided he was in on it. Never called about those horses he'd put money down on. Never sent anyone for them. Meant he had them. All of them but the colt, that is."

"Was it bad, what they did to him?" she asked in a soft voice, watching the horses walking back and forth in front of them, their bright wool blankets swaying rhythmically as the long legs reached with so little effort.

"They tortured him, and they didn't have to. They had guns. I don't think—" He sucked in his lower lip and frowned at the distant figures under the stone canopy of the in-gate. The red scar on his cheek whitened as he clenched his jaw, then relaxed it. His battered eyes still slipped out of focus once in a while when he was tired, and he'd been on the road for over eleven hours. His half-healed jaw ached, but he'd made the doctor unwire him before he took off.

"Eddie's done stuff before, for insurance." She leaned against the door, scrunched down, wishing she'd told him earlier that she'd stolen the colt to save it.

"He wasn't with Harney that day, but it doesn't matter, does it? You find anything at his barn?"

"One of the chestnut babies, I think. And Bobby's halter."

He looked at her quickly, but she couldn't see his eyes behind the sunglasses. He took a deep breath. "What do you think?"

"I think he's still alive, I don't know, wishful thinking maybe. But I want to confront Eddie, maybe see if I can convince him to tell me the truth. I have to try at least. I mean—"

"I know." Ty gripped the wheel of the truck and looked at her again. "Anybody out there now? At Eddie's?"

She looked at her watch. "No, someone'll come to feed at five, but the place is deserted until then."

Ty started the engine. "Okay, let's get going. Start with the horse at Eddie's farm. Then we'll come back and settle up." Ty slipped the gun from his waist and laid it on the seat between them. "Believe me, Eddie will tell us what he knows."

⨍ Chapter Fourteen

Hefting a bale of hay for the chestnut colt they had brought back
to the Fairgrounds from Eddie's, Ty winced as if he were still hurting from the beating. Dakota put out a hand to help but he swung
the bale away and let it drop in the aisle. Pulling a knife from his
pocket, he cut the twine and tossed hay to the horse. He was moving gingerly, bending and straightening as if these were conscious
acts now. Sliding the stall door closed, he asked, "Think he'll be
safe here?"

Dakota nodded as they stood watching the horse grab hungrily at
the hay on the floor. "Eddie's too busy to wander around back here.
What now?"

Ty rubbed his stomach and looked down the dark aisle. From the
far corner of the second barn, they could hear the distant noise of
radios, horses, and voices of the occupying show stables. "Guess we
have to get a hold of Eddie."

"The Grand Prix starts in a little while, he's probably busy warming up the horses. Won't be free till later tonight. Ty—" She
touched his forearm and when he didn't pull away, she tightened her
fingers until she felt the muscles tense underneath. He turned toward
her and she wrapped her arms around him, feeling his body go rigid,
then relax against her for a moment as he put his arms around her
and hugged her hard. She felt his lips on her hair and, lifting her

face, his lips blindly seeking hers. When her lungs were bursting from no air, she twisted her mouth away gasping. With a growl, he pushed her away.

"No—" she said and reached for him again, but he stepped back, holding his hands up to stop her.

"What? What do you want, Dakota?" He folded his arms across his chest and stared at her, his eyes hidden by the dark twilight of the barn.

"I don't know—" She knew it was the wrong answer.

"I have nothing to give you now. Going to lose the farm, already lost my livelihood. There's nothing here for you, see—" He spread his arms at his sides, knocking his hands against the stall door, but not even registering the jolt. It scared her.

"It's not the end. We'll get the horses back—we can—"

"Oh yeah, sure. They're probably dog food by now. Lucky to find this one. You think Bobby's out there waiting for you? Think again. You're living in a dream."

She hated this new side of him, defeated and cynical, she wanted to smash it down. Stop its voice so much like the one in her head from her father and Eddie and her husband. The voice that never let anything dream. "My horse *is* alive out there. So just screw you. I don't need you to find him either. Go ahead, give up. Who needs you anyway. I was perfectly capable of coming up here alone, I didn't ask you along. And I'm going out there to Nebraska next, and I am going to find Harney Rivers and make him tell me what happened to our horses, damn it. And you don't have to lift a finger. You can go home and rot for all I care, sit in that stupid little house and feel sorry for yourself, if that's what you want. Because I don't give a shit!"

She started to walk away, but he grabbed her and pulled her around, holding her with his hands pinching her upper arms so she couldn't move.

"You're not going out there alone, you dumbass. You don't have a clue what you're dealing with, not a goddamn clue. This isn't some game. Harney Rivers will hurt you, he might even kill you if he feels like it. He's dangerous, Dakota, dangerous and sick. I don't care if you don't care about me, but I can't let him hurt you, understand?"

He jerked her arms and pulled her against him for a moment so their bodies met in a hard heat, then pushed her off. She stumbled backwards and rubbed her upper arms where she could still feel his fingers digging in. It made her madder. "I'm sorry you got hurt, but I'm not lying down for this. Bobby's the only thing in the world I care about, that cares about me—now"

A startled expression crossed his face and he let out a breath that ended in a sigh. Looking at the floor, he scuffed the toe of his boot on the dust-filled grooves cut in the concrete. "That's not true, Dakota. I'm not saying we aren't going to find the horses, I'm just saying you have to let me do it my own way. I can go out there without raising a fuss. My family's from there, my mom lives in town and my dad still ranches there. I can show up and hang around, and it will be more normal than a stranger coming along asking a bunch of questions. I doubt Bobby is there, anyway. Harney would put our horses as far away from himself as he could."

"Then why go there?" She wanted to be back in his arms, but she was afraid now to make the move toward him.

"I have to settle with Harney. He was the one who did all this to me." His voice was soft and he glanced at her face for a moment before his eyes slid away to stare at the dark empty stalls beyond them.

"Why did he do it?" She took a step, putting herself close enough to smell the sour sweat on him, different from before. This scent was metallic, mediciney. She took another step, so she could see the knuckles whiten on his hand when he reached out and gripped the stall bars. "Ty?"

He shook his head, looked over at the stalls, grimaced, then looked at her. "What?" His voice was low and husky.

"Ty—" She put her hand on his cheek, touching the new scar with her thumb; sliding up behind his ear and knotting her fingers in his hair, she gently pulled. His mouth caught hers again, opening to each other, not fighting as they'd done before. He lifted her and she wrapped her legs around his thighs as he pressed her back against the stall, not breaking the kiss as his fingers found the buttons on her shirt and the cool air hit her skin.

Afterwards, they stood shaking and leaning against each other, keeping their eyes closed until they could breathe again. The sounds of kids' voices coming nearer made them rush to pull their jeans up and smile as both tried to fasten her shirt. When they looked down, they laughed at the lopsided front. Then the voices faded again and they took deep breaths and held each other in the darkened barn with the munching hay, occasional snorting, and stamping hoof a kind of music they found soothing. After a while, they separated and smoothed and tucked their clothes, self-consciously awkward again, the grace of loving gone so quickly.

"Better get over there and keep an eye on Eddie," Ty said finally.

"Yeah, the coliseum will be filling up." Dakota started down the aisle ahead of him, but he caught up and slung his arm around her shoulders and hugged her against his side before letting go. Their hands and arms brushed against each other as they wove through the gathering crowds. She'd been able to con two exhibitor buttons and tickets from an old friend from an out-of-town stable, so they passed easily through the in-gate area to seats close by. The large oval arena was a maze full of jumps, ranging from three and a half feet to five feet in height, with spreads up to five feet. There was a huge brick wall lined with Christmas trees, with a life-size blown-up Santa Claus on either side; the Swedish oxer of yellow and blue rails that looked impossibly wide to jump over, followed by a Liverpool with water in a bright blue plastic inset underneath; a gaudy gold-and-black American Express panel jump off a corner sure to make the horses suck back; a long run to a triple combination of red and white rails ending in a huge oxer along the side toward the in-gate where the horses were going to be picking up speed when they needed to collect; and a very narrow vertical fence with rails curved in a soft U set in very flat cups, among others. In fact, the Grand Prix cups were always shallow, if not flat, and often a mere flick of a tail, tick, or rub of a hoof would drop a rail. Jumping at this level required horses that could do more than clear the height, they had to fold their front and back legs tightly, be able to spring off their hocks and stretch their backs, collect and extend and turn in half a stride. And there were so many possibilities of error that no single horse ever won every event.

Eddie's first horse went third and as they watched, it made it through all the elements until the final big red-and-white 3M panel jump, where it dropped a rail with a trailing hind foot and the crowd groaned. Dakota wondered if that was planned. Eddie often made agreements with other riders to help his business. She could see him shaking his head with the owner as the horse trotted out the in-gate. There were three clear rounds before the next horse of Eddie's went, a big black Hanoverian who was lumbering around the course slowly, grunting over every fence, brushing a few with a right front ankle that didn't want to fold tight, but by some miracle, all the rails were staying up. When it came to the Liverpool, however, it put on the brakes, smashing its chest against the fence and dropping the rider into the water on the other side while the rails came banging down on her. The arena was suddenly quiet as the rider lay there not moving, then the horse gave a jerk of its head and shuffled off, stepping on the reins and breaking them before it came to a halt by the next fence. Medical workers knelt by the rider, who sat up, holding her head and trying to shake the water off her soaked coat. When she stood and limped off between two men who half-carried her, followed by the captured horse, the crowd clapped and the announcer sent the next horse in.

"Not light enough on its feet," Ty said and Dakota nodded.

"Probably never saw a water jump before, knowing Eddie. He says they sometimes jump better over strange things."

There were a few horses that brought down several rails, including a big gray that jumped around with a bewildered expression on its face, looking at each jump as if this were the first time such a thing had stood in the way. The rider-owner was a man famous for buying cheap horses and turning them into overnight sensations, which often as not reverted back to being cheap horses for their new owners. It was like betting on the lottery, Eddie used to say—sometimes you actually got lucky. At the Santa Claus jump, the gray shied at the evergreen bushes and had to circle around to slaps of the crop on its butt and much spurring and yanking in front that sent its head skyward; then it caught sight of the plastic man in red and white on its left and shied hard to the right, only to find the same thing. At that point, it planted its front legs and stood rigid and shaking, unwilling to move in any direction. As the crowd began to whistle and cluck, the horse looked up at the noise, confusion and fear in its eyes. After the rider began beating it, the crowd started to boo and the announcer had to say three times that he was excused before the rider dismounted and led the horse out.

"That horse look familiar?" Ty leaned forward to follow the horse's exit.

"The gray Eddie tried?"

"No, the gray with the bowed tendon I got from Danny Bladstrom that trip to Canterbury. Looks green enough, and it sure has no business in this class. Think I'll go down and check it out. You stay here." He was through the row and down the ramp to the stairs before she could stop him.

"Be careful," she whispered.

Only one of Eddie's horses went clean, a small buckskin gelding with an odd white splash on one haunch who could jump the moon. He went in a hackamore and spun on a dime like a cow pony. Eddie probably got him cheap, trained him, and sold him for big dollars. She'd seen it before, how a five-hundred-dollar nag became a twenty-thousand-dollar beginning jumper and on from there. A Grand Prix horse could cost from thirty thousand to more than half a million, depending on where it would be competing. This horse's price would go through the roof tonight if it won. That was clearly the plan, too, she decided, as she watched Eddie in conference with Bradley, a well-known rider who occasionally branched out from training and showing to stealing saddles and fast-shuffling horses from one part of the country to another.

When she was with Eddie, the two men would sit around laughing about how they'd made money when they were starting out in the business by going through the Sunday want ads and buying all the cheap backyard horses they could find and hauling them to the killers when the price of horsemeat was still high enough for a good profit. These were kids' pets, family horses to be sold only to good homes, the ads declared, and the two men would take turns eating cookies and drinking lemonade at kitchen tables while promising the best of care as they went from farm to farm. One of their favorite tactics in the show ring when they were getting started in those days was to stand on the rail when an opponent's horse came by and squirt a syringe of sulfuric acid on the animal's hindquarters, sending it into immediate fits of bucking and bolting. The stories went on and on, and they'd helped Dakota decide to leave after their novelty wore off and she began to let the horror sink in. No doubt they had some plan tonight. Betting for or against themselves, because sometimes they won more losing than winning.

The last entry, a junior on a big Appaloosa-thoroughbred cross also went clean, and that was the field for the jump-off. Dakota didn't have to go to the warm-up area to know what was going on. Eddie would have one of his grooms keeping track of the steward, distracting her if necessary, while he quickly strung a thin wire just above the top rail of the jump he'd have the rider practicing on. Without the front boots or wraps, the horse would hit the wire, which would surprise and sting him. After a few such times, the horse would be clearing the tops of the standards to avoid the cut. Some of the riders depended on poling with a light poly pipe they lifted at the last minute to rap the horses' front or hind legs to make them jump neater and higher, but often the horses would get to know the pole and refuse to jump at all. That's why Eddie devised the wire.

"It's the gray all right, saw where the bow had been pin-fired and healed." Ty settled in the seat next to her, handing her a tray with four hot dogs while he extricated the pops from another cardboard tray. "Mustard and pickle relish okay?" He took a hot dog and bit off a third. She nodded and crammed one end in her mouth. She was starving, always forgetting to eat around this man, like it was bad manners to show she was hungry.

When they'd finished eating and the announcer began to describe the timed jump-off course, they leaned back and watched the jump crew put poles on end in front of the jumps that were excluded. "The buckskin might have a chance here. Looks like you'll need roll-backs to make some of these turns," Ty said.

"What about the gray?"

"Pick him up after the class. Thought about it, decided our friend Eddie's going to have to get him back for us."

She didn't miss the "us" and snugged her shoulder against his. He lifted his arm and put it around her, letting his fingers curl back up to play with the wisps of hair at her neck.

"I like long hair," he said, and she both wanted to tear his fingers away and make her hair suddenly waist length.

"So do I." She reached up and pulled at a curl on his shoulder. He grinned.

The first horse took a rail down on the Swedish oxer but turned in a very fast time. The next horse went clean by taking its time, but was clearly beatable. The third horse crashed the wall and was led off limping. The junior on the Appaloosa had trouble getting her horse through the in-gate and although he jumped around, he was stiff and scared at most of the fences, coming to a complete standstill and jumping straight up and dwelling over the fence. "Got trained on too hard," she said.

"Saw them back there poling it with Eddie's help." Ty lifted his arm and leaned forward, rubbing his mouth with his hands.

"Buckskin will win, I bet."

The horse ran around the corners like a barrel racer and indeed did rollbacks to cut the distance to jumps, taking off from impossibly close distances, with the crowd groaning and clapping as it landed clean to win the class. Eddie and the rider gave each other high fives as the horse stood exhausted and wild-eyed outside the gate.

"Let's go—" Ty stood and pushed his way out of the crowd, dragging Dakota by the hand behind him.

"Shouldn't we wait for people to clear out?" She bumped against him in the hallway, where they were stuck in traffic trying to get out the doors to avoid the rush.

"Now's better." He pushed on, ignoring the grumbles around him.

At over six feet, he could do that, while at five five, she was taking a lot of jabs and thumps to her body and feet, being dragged behind like a tail on a dog.

"There he is—" They were at the in-gate, where an official with a long flashlight was trying to clear the area so the horses could reenter the arena for the award ceremony. Eddie stood next to the red-headed man Dakota recognized as Bill from his adult riders, who was patting the buckskin and smiling.

"Go get him and bring him over here—" Ty ducked around the corner.

"Eddie?" she called as she slipped under the arm of the man directing traffic. Thank goodness she was wearing her exhibitor button, which gave her some authority to be in the gate area.

He frowned. "Yeah?"

She grabbed his arm and pulled. "Come here, I have to tell you something, hurry, it's important—"

He shrugged at his customer and let himself be pulled across to the doorway. "Be back in a minute," he called over his shoulder.

"No, you won't." Ty yanked his body close and stuck the gun in his side. "Let's go." He nodded toward the door people were pushing out of, keeping Eddie in front of the gun.

They walked into the dark cow barn directly across from the in-gate to the hippodrome. The acrid green smell of cow manure and alfalfa lingered in the cold, gloomy concrete wash stall in the far corner where Ty finally stopped, illuminated only by gray light seeping in through the row of high dirty windows overhead.

Eddie didn't look scared, which surprised Dakota. Ty had reverted to being cold and efficient. Suddenly, much as she'd wanted to get her horse back, she didn't want to be in the middle of this, she didn't want anyone or anything else to get hurt. And she didn't know whether she could stop Ty once he got started. For now he was just standing there, the gun drooping from his hand, staring at the other man. She wanted to tell Eddie not to be so cocky.

"I could shoot you," Ty said in a casual voice that scared her.

"Why don't you?" Eddie smiled.

The gun fired such a loud bang, Dakota jumped. As the after-echo bounced along the concrete walls and floor of the barn, the bullet ricocheted off the wall behind Eddie and tore through the side of his thigh and rattled harmlessly onto the floor. Eddie gasped, then slowly crumpled. "You hit me, you dumb shit!"

Shocked by what he'd done, Ty tucked the gun in his belt, but waved her off when she started to kneel at Eddie's side.

"Ty, do something—" she said.

A dark trickle of blood appeared on Eddie's khaki pants leg. "I'm bleeding," he remarked.

Ty and Dakota looked into the brown darkness around them. Had anyone heard? No, they were tucked away in the back of the barn, the crowds were making too much noise, horse people too tired to care about a firecracker bang. Although the burning cordite blotted the cow odors out, they were the only people in the huge empty barn.

"Man, you are lousy with a gun," Eddie said and tied his white handkerchief around his leg. "Don't quit your day job."

"Next time it'll be the knee," Ty muttered with his hand on the gun butt.

"You'll be lucky you don't shoot your dick off." Eddie grimaced and stood, leaning against the concrete wall. "Ruined a perfectly good pair of pants too."

"Stop whining. Just tell me about meeting up with Harney Rivers."

The two men silently appraised each other, Eddie being the first to look away.

"He called just like I said. After your place, I flew home, next thing I know, next morning, two goddamn loads of horses show up, including the ones I was buying. I recognized some of the others, but nobody said anything and I figured you wanted me to get rid of them or something. Tried to call, but nobody ever answered. So I did it, got rid of them. That's all, man. You don't have to go around shooting people for trying to help out." Eddie winced as he lifted the blood-soaked handkerchief to look at the hole in his leg.

Ty pulled the gun out again and waved it. "You never know where the next one will land."

"He's crazy, Dakota, stop him—"

"Ty—"

"Stay out of it." He didn't take his eyes off Eddie. "Harney wanted to kill me, and you led him to me. Figure I owe you."

"I didn't know, man, honest. Dakota, you know I wouldn't—"

"Ty, don't—" She stepped in between the two men and Ty jerked her out of the way.

The click of the gun being cocked echoed almost as loudly as the sound of it being fired a few minutes before. "What'd you do with my horses, Eddie?"

"All right." Eddie sighed and pulled the handkerchief ends tighter. "He called and told me the horses were coming, that they were free and all I had to do was keep my mouth shut. Sent some money too. I checked and found out you were in the hospital, not expected to live. The colt he'd wanted wasn't in the load. Figured he took care of it. You know the rest. Most of them are gone, man. Some I sent to the killers, sold the others, they're scattered all over the fucking place."

"What about Bobby?" Dakota whispered.

Eddie looked at her, but said nothing.

She shivered. "Where is he?"

"Tell her." Ty lifted the gun so it pointed at Eddie's face, which showed a sweaty paleness as the bloodstain spread down his leg.

"He called a week later. I was hanging onto the horse because I figured she'd come looking for it or I could sneak it back to her somehow. I'm not a complete bastard, you know. Anyway, he wanted the horse for some reason. Said he was sending a truck for it. I argued, tried to tell him the horse was gone, but he just repeated what he said. Sending a truck. Have it ready. He took it, Dakota. That's all I know. I tried—"

"I found the broken halter at your place." She stepped in front of him, trying to tell if he was lying or not.

"Darn horse broke loose as we were trying to load him. You know what an easy loader he is, he must've known something was wrong because he raised pure hell, could've pulled Christ off the cross the way he yanked on that lead rope. Took us an hour to catch him again, by then he was his old self. Go figure. It was a nice rig, first class. Don't know what it was, but old Bobby wanted no part of that trip." Eddie shook his head.

Ty pointed the gun at Eddie's other leg. "I said, tell her *the truth*—" Eddie's eyes shifted to the blood-soaked pant leg.

"Rivers called, like I said. Told me to get rid of Bobby—killers, whatever—"

Dakota sobbed.

"I tried to argue—" Eddie glanced at her, but focused on Ty. "You know what a stiff dick he is—asked how good my fire insurance was—" His voice pleaded—"I couldn't—"

"You finished him, then?"

Eddie nodded. "It was painless, an injection. He just sort of fell asleep—he never suffered, Dakota, I swear—"

Ty reached out and slapped Eddie so hard the smaller man staggered back against the wall and stayed there, out of range of Ty's hands.

"I buried him in the pasture," Eddie offered, "so you could—"

"No—" Dakota wailed.

"Just shut up, Eddie."

As Dakota turned away, Ty reached out and caught her against him. She buried her head in his jacket for a moment, holding back the tears.

"I ought to shoot your hands off," Ty said. "What about the chestnut baby?"

"You found him, huh?"

"Greedy little prick. He's mine now, and I want the gray your buddy was beating on tonight—we're going to go get him and put him in my rig. Walk."

"I can't—" Eddie protested.

"Then crawl."

"Dakota—" Eddie whined.

She couldn't move. The images of Ty beaten and stabbed, the horses killed, and now her own horse crowded Eddie out.

"Here." Ty grabbed Eddie's upper arm and hauled him limping toward the exit to the street. "Lucky I didn't give the gun to her, she'd have shot your balls off just now."

III

The Smoke of Mean Houses

∽ Chapter Fifteen

At 4 A.M. they pulled into a rest stop just before Sioux Falls, South Dakota, hiding the rig among the other trucks while they slept. The horses had plenty of hay and they'd been watered too. It was colder out on the high plains, with snow moving in by noon, the radio warned, but they were both too tired to continue. They curled into each other in the little sleeping loft bed behind the cab, their clothes on, too exhausted to do more.

Ty woke three hours later, with the flat gray light of the snow-heavy sky staring back at him through the windshield. Dakota was sleeping with a piece of his shirt clutched tightly in her hand like a little kid. There was an awful lot they had to tell each other, but he knew why he'd held back and it made him wonder what she wanted to hide.

This next deal—what was he going to do with Dakota? He was driving right into the county that held the warrant on him. Would he make it as far as the ranch? Could he take her out there? His own mother couldn't stand it, how could a woman who wasn't even related to the old man? Loosening Dakota's fingers from his shirt, Ty lifted one leg over the edge of the sleeper, then the other, slid down, and went out to pee and check the horses. After walking each one around for a few minutes to stretch their legs, he gave them fresh hay, watered them again, and started up.

When he stopped for gas at Mitchell, she woke. It was just

beginning to snow lightly and the wind was picking up. Still, when she asked about all the signs for the Corn Palace, he maneuvered the rig through town and stopped in front of the building covered with field corn, barley, milo, and wheat, set in elaborate designs depicting scenes from the state. It was a bizarre apparition in the middle of the otherwise sedate South Dakota farm town. Dakota looked at it in a kind of stunned silence. "We can pick up souvenirs another time," he offered as he shifted gears and inched forward into the dusting snow.

"Weird." She craned her neck to watch it recede. Even in the gray December cold, tour buses and RV's full of retirees were pulling up to park and unload.

At Chamberlain, the ridges on the other side of the Missouri River were almost black in the gray morning light, and the water that was often the deepest turquoise blue was slate color with a growing chop to it. "Where the West begins," he said as they left the flat prairie behind and entered the hills on the other side. From there, the land rolled and humped like a great rumpled hide. Black dots of cattle feeding off in the distance relieved the austere hills, and once in a while a town on a flat area, with buildings clustered together and silos that rose like church steeples high into the blank sky. The grasslands were relieved only by half-frozen ponds with rinds of silver-blue ice and an occasional lone tree. Ty didn't mind at all. Trees got in the way of seeing. Good for shade once in a while, but really, he could never live in Minnesota or eastern Nebraska with all those trees. They made him feel trapped, panicked that he couldn't get past or over them to the sky.

"Horses are riding good." He glanced over at Dakota, but she was staring out the window, her fingertips at her mouth. Probably thinking about her horse. He'd had to argue her onto the truck at the Fairgrounds. She'd wanted to go back to Eddie's and find her horse's grave.

Finally, when he pulled off at Murdo for gas and sandwiches to go, she looked at the signs for the Badlands and Mount Rushmore and asked him what had clearly been on her mind for a while. "Do you have a plan, or are we just wandering around out here?"

He slowed and stopped at the gas pumps. "I thought you wanted to come out here—"

"We have to have a plan, Ty, we can't just—" She stopped as he opened the door and got out, his gimme hat immediately lifted by the gusting wind he'd been fighting but not really registering for the past forty miles.

He pulled some dollars out of his pocket and tossed them on the seat. "Get some sandwiches and coffee to go—"

She looked at him, then ignoring the money climbed out, slammed the door, and ran to the restaurant inside the station. He quickly checked on the horses, refilling the hay net for the chestnut colt, and patting the gray, who seemed to remember him in a kindly way despite his recent bad experiences. He couldn't imagine being able to sell it to anyone out in the Sandhills, but the chestnut colt he might palm off for a few bucks as a kid horse, maybe a barrel racer, although he was a little big at sixteen hands. He needed money one way or the other, so he'd have to sell the horses for what he could get. No time to take them to a real market, and December was usually real slow.

Maybe he could dump the rig for cheap. He had the papers on him, much good as they'd do, but someone in the Sandhills might not mind a deal like that at the right price. Not likely anybody'd be able to find the rig on one of those ranches anyway. If he could get enough for a used truck, work some, *and* stay out of jail, he could start tracking down—what? He had no hope for the other horses. They were long gone, lucky to find the two he had. No, what he wanted was to take care of Harney Rivers. That's what he was doing out here.

Leaving Murdo, they turned south down 83, which would lead them across Rosebud Reservation and on into Nebraska and the Sandhills to the ranch. The rising wind buffeted the rig sideways, punching at it hard enough that he had to keep both hands on the wheel. He could feel the extra sway of the trailer and hear, on the intercom, the horses shifting uncomfortably. As the clouds moved closer, the sky darkened and an icy rain began to fall in between gusts of sleet and snow. The wipers and heater made little headway against the ice sheeting up the windshield, and a couple of times he had to stop, get out, and hand scrape a hole big enough to see out of. The two-lane blacktop was starting to ice over too, and he slowed to twenty-five, which was better anyway for the wind blowing straight across, tossing tumbleweeds and debris that made them have to resist ducking the objects charging the truck. He dropped into four-wheel, knowing it wasn't going to be that much better on ice. Twice on the big hills to White River, he considered stopping to see if the storm would blow over, but he kept going. Dakota sat tense and still beside him, one hand gripping the door rest, the other in a fist on the seat beside her.

At White River, they pulled into a gas station and Ty tried to clear the windshield while Dakota ran to the bathroom. The cedar boughs draping the posts of powwow grounds across the street flapped up and down in the wind, and beyond there was a solid wall of dark, almost black clouds broken only by the deep bellies of heavy gray clouds dropping a curtain of obscuring snow. The streets were empty, even the dogs were missing, holed up, like they should be. He wasn't sure if they'd make it all the way down to Nebraska, but there was really no place to stop now, and he wanted to hit the ranch before dark. While the old man was still conscious enough to talk if he was drinking, and not in the awful piss-poor mood the evening brought on if he wasn't.

"They said the sanding truck is out between here and Mission. Are we going to Mission?" Dakota asked, leaning forward and shaking bits of ice out of her hair.

He nodded. "You should have a hat on."

"For this little bit of stuff?" She ruffled her hair and it sprang into waves.

"We go off the road, you'll wish you had a hat. This is different country out here, need to be prepared—"

"What if I don't have a hat?" she asked.

"Gloves? Scarf? Boots?" When she shook her head at everything, he stared at her. "Where the hell'd you think you were going, Disneyland?"

"We left in kind of a hurry, you know. My clothes are still at Eddie's."

"We'll pick up some stuff in Babylon." He started the truck and pulled onto the empty highway. "Or maybe my mom has some things you could use," he added when he remembered the money problem. He was probably going to have to borrow from his mother as it was. She was going to love that. He had about a hundred more bucks on him, and he didn't know what Dakota was carrying, probably not a lot. She'd paid for the food he hadn't been able to eat yet. Coffee'd be cold by now.

"I have money," she said, "we don't have to go around borrowing clothes."

"Better save your money." He had to hold the truck steady against the wind as they started down the hill. The ice had melted on his hair and water was dripping down his cheeks, but he didn't dare let go of the wheel.

"Here." She took a Kleenex and wiped his face, then unwrapped his sandwich and put it to his lips.

"Mayonnaise," he muttered through the bite of ham and cheese.

"What do you like?"

"Mustard." He swallowed dryly and gestured toward the coffee, which, cold or not, he needed.

"We always put mayonnaise on ham and cheese at home," she insisted, holding the lukewarm coffee up.

"Yech, cream and sugar?" It tasted like ice cream.

"Watch where you're going—" She braced herself as the truck wiggled and began to turn sideways in a slide down the hill.

He fought the wheel and managed to straighten the truck as the rig slowed itself at the bottom and they started up. The sanding truck appeared over the crest of the hill, spraying sand in both lanes.

"Thank God," she breathed.

A few miles farther, a wild turkey sprinted into the road, stalled in the middle, then ran on with a wild-eyed look, its wet feathers clamped to its body.

"Poor thing," Dakota said.

"You want to feel sorry for something, look out there to the west. We'll be going into snow by the time we get there."

Main Street in Babylon was empty except for a few trucks pulled in front of the western outfitters store, open on Sunday for holiday shopping. Ty was thankful that there was no one around, especially the sheriff, and that except for the fanciness of the rig, he looked like any other hauler. He pulled the cap down and raised the collar of his jacket. With the storm moving in, most people were at home getting ready. Out of the corner of his eye he saw the Sweetheart Garden attached to the bar and restaurant, where he used to hang out with Harney. Although the restaurant was dark, there was an older Native American man standing in front with a white woman who was jiggling back and forth on her feet and holding her mittens against her ears. Something about her face looked familiar, but Ty dismissed it. Everyone in this town was familiar. There just weren't that many people in the Sandhills.

He pulled around and parked in front of his mother's little house on the side street two blocks from the public school complex Charla and Ronnie had gone to. Ty'd started at a one-room schoolhouse in the hills, and eventually ended up going those three years to the high school here in town before he quit. Somehow, he'd never gotten along well enough with his mother to move into town during the school year like other ranch kids did. Or maybe it was that he was needed out there with his father on the ranch. He never knew, just that he was the oldest, and when the others had come along, he naturally moved out of the way. When he'd called over the years to report in, he'd thought of it that way, reporting in to her. It was a thing a son should do, but it didn't make them any closer. After the assault warrant was issued, she'd showed more concern for him, in an awful, long-suffering kind of way. He parked, looking around to make sure he wasn't going to be recognized by someone on the street before he got out. He didn't know what his mother thought, he realized again as he banged on the door and she answered it with not even a hint of surprise on her face.

They hugged stiffly, and she stepped aside so they could come in out of the weather. The house had the same smell of furniture polish and lilac room deodorizer. There were no pets, of course, she was allergic to animal fur. Her skin broke out in angry, red itchy patches and she wheezed herself into bronchitis every time she was near fur of any sort. That's why she stayed away from the ranch, she'd taken to saying these past twenty years. As if the whole world didn't know the truth, he thought as he watched her raise her thin eyebrows at him and glance at Dakota.

He introduced the two women, and smiled when Dakota put her hand out. His mother wasn't used to that, he could tell by the way she hesitated.

"Well," she said and looked toward the kitchen. "Would you like something hot to drink?"

"Yes ma'm, please," he said.

"Thank you, Mrs. Bonte," Dakota said and unbuttoned her light coat.

As they sat uncomfortably around the oak pedestal table in her dining room, self-conscious of the stink on their clothes, Ty remembered to ask his mother about his sister.

With a sideways look at Dakota, she said that his sister wasn't very happy these days and was talking about going back to school for something or another. "I don't know why she doesn't settle down and have children." She looked quickly at him, and Ty felt certain she could read the same quick stab of blame for Ronnie he'd always felt from her. She'd told him to look after his brother that summer, not to let him—

"What do you do, dear?" His mother turned to Dakota, who quickly swallowed her bite of store-bought ginger cookie.

"I'm—" She blushed and picked up the good china cup of weak tea.

"She's with me, in the horse business," Ty said and tried to smile though he wasn't feeling one bit like it. "We're picking up some horses. Stopping at the ranch. She's never seen the Sandhills, so I told her to come along. But she forgot to bring her winter stuff, you have anything extra she can borrow?" He felt proud of himself for stepping in so smoothly until he noticed his mother's sharp expression. He could never fool her, never in a million years.

While his mother was gone, the two of them sat in the silence, so still they could hear the flick of ice against the windows and the grandfather clock, stripped and polished to the same bright yellow oak as the rest of the heavy furniture. She'd had the floors redone too, and shellacked to a high, show room gloss. The braided rugs she made herself sat tentatively on the floor, as if they expected to be yanked up any day because of their dullness. Ty looked at the pink-and-gray flowered wallpaper and ruffled curtains. Like a damn dollhouse, his father had said the one time he came inside for Ronnie's funeral. After that, his mother had trimmed the outside of the house with gingerbread moldings and painted it gray and pink too.

"What a pretty rug." Dakota got up and went to the living room, where she knelt on the floor in front of the fireplace. Ronnie's rug. His mother had insisted on saving her son's clothes, and one day Ty had come to town to find her right there in front of the fireplace with a fire going in the middle of July the summer after Ronnie's death, weeping and tearing the clothes into strips for the rug, and burning the rest. They'd never spoken of it, but he found himself unable to look at the rug, let alone step on it. He wished Dakota would get up before his mother came back.

"We'd better get going." He stood, bumping the table and slopping some of the tea he couldn't drink into the saucer and onto the ruffled place mat. Dakota came back to finish her cookie and tea.

"Here we are, try these, dear." His mother held out a cardboard box to Dakota. "Some of your sister's things—" She glanced at Ty and the spilled tea.

While Dakota tried the hats on for the one that fit best, then gloves and boots, his mother brought a couple of coats from the front closet. "Your friend up at St. Francis called last week."

They looked at each other, almost the same height and with the same slender build. She never asked, and he never told her the rest of the story. "The old priest?"

She nodded, one eyebrow arching.

"And?"

"He said to tell you that that Indian is dead. Hit by a car on the road to Cody."

"Oh." He looked at Dakota sitting on the floor trying on lined winter boots.

His mother wanted to ask him about it, he knew, but she wouldn't. She never asked, not even when Ronnie died. That was how he knew he'd let her down again. Now he couldn't ask her for money either. It was just as well. They had nothing to offer each other. Better to keep it that way. She gave him the usual little peck on the cheek when they left and he gave her the usual quick hug that left him feeling worse.

"Your father know you're coming?" she asked as she held the door open for them. He shook his head.

"He's not doing very well," she said. "I'd go out there, but I've been busy getting ready for Christmas at the church, and now I have this place to do alone too." She closed the storm door.

He looked around at the little neighborhood of modest one-story houses, most of them frame but a couple with brick fronts. The small front yards still held a tinge of green, but there was a lifelessness about the street despite the Christmas trees blinking their color from the front picture windows. He'd forgotten about Christmas. Was his mother expecting him to stay? No, she hadn't even asked, not for years now. His sister and her husband would probably come down from Pierre, maybe his aunt from Scottsbluff.

He paused at the truck and looked back at the house before he got in and drove slowly down the street. Well, this wasn't his finest moment, he had to admit. He wondered what his mother had meant about the old man though. Was his drinking worse? They never talked about it. Ty had tried when he was thirteen to discuss it with her, but she'd brushed him off, saying there was nothing she could do. In sixth-grade science, they'd studied alcoholism and the genetic predisposition his father's few drops of Native American blood could be giving him. Another thing they never spoke of in the family. Ty didn't even know who or what the hell he was. A splash of Injun, nothing to write home about, was all the old man would say. His mother was German and Irish. That much he knew.

He glanced at Dakota, who was staring out her window, quiet.

"You need to stop for anything?" He drove slowly by the western store.

She shook her head.

"We'll be there in an hour. Down 20, then turn into the hills. Slowest stretch is the twelve miles into the ranch. Two tire tracks most of the time. Lucky if the rig doesn't get stuck."

"Your mother doesn't like me," she said and brushed the red wool mittens against each other. There was a moth hole in the center of the right thumb.

"Yeah, well, she doesn't like me much either." Ty felt his stomach sink a little. He'd never said it out loud before. Wait till you meet my father, he wanted to say.

The wind picked up and it began to snow fat, heavy flakes that covered the icy road and made them creep along. Two hours later, in the dark, they finally saw the ranch yard lights.

"You sure took your goddamn sweet time," his father's voice called from the porch as Ty opened the truck door.

"I'll just put the horses in the barn," Ty hollered and quickly closed the door against the snow swirling into the cab. He was careful not to look at Dakota as he swung around the ranch yard and pulled in front of the barn so they could lower the ramp and unload directly through the big door.

The ammonia stench of old manure made Ty cough as he felt along the wall for the light switches. "Son of a bitch," he cursed when the lights came on, revealing an aisle clogged with trash and equipment. A quick inspection proved him right in the assumption that the chaos extended to the stalls, two feet deep with old manure. He was too tired to deal with this tonight, he decided, and pulled down a couple of bales of old hay, bedding the stalls the way they were. He brought in the fresh hay and grain he'd taken from Eddie. Dakota had the unloading under control and the horses were quickly deposited for the night. As he followed her out again, she kicked at a ripped garbage bag spewing debris, but she didn't say anything. He pulled the rig around and parked it angling out where he could pull it with the tractor if the snow got too deep. The run to the house wasn't long, but the wind had picked up and the thick, wet snow was sticking to everything.

By the time they were on the porch, they were plastered with snow they tried to stamp and shake off onto the mounds of papers and trash bags. Even in the cold, Ty noticed the smell of rotting garbage and hoped it wasn't that bad inside. He wanted to apologize to Dakota, but he was too embarrassed.

"You staying out there all night or you wanna come in?" His father opened the door a couple of inches.

"We're coming." Ty kept his voice neutral, slipping into the old habit till he could figure out the lay of the land again. "We can hang our coats inside," he said to Dakota.

The kitchen wasn't so bad, at least the trash was out of sight and the place smelled like it always did, behind the odor of coffee and some kind of meat roasting in the oven, a back smell of wet, musty newspapers and old clothes and things collecting dust like in an attic. That's what the room he slept in always smelled like, dust. And the front room they rarely went into. At least the whiskey his father favored was absent. Maybe that was good, maybe not, he thought, have to wait and see.

"Gone twenty-some years and he stands there like an old dog sniffing the wind." His father's harsh laugh had no humor in it. Never had. "Sit down." He gestured toward the round table with the painted top, black over green that was showing through the scratches. "Your mother called, said you were coming."

Ty glanced quickly at Dakota, who was taking off her coat and mittens. He reached for her things and draped them in the corner on a hook over an old jacket of his that looked like it hadn't moved since he hung it there last. He hung his own things up and slipped off his soaked cowboy boots and looked at his sopping wet socks. Then he pulled them off too, and the rush of cold along the old linoleum floor iced his feet.

"You'll find some socks in your old room. Hate to see a grown man with his feet hanging out in the house." His father went to the stove and lifted a lid and stirred something and banged the lid back on. "Go on now, supper's ready."

"Dakota?" Ty didn't know what he wanted her to do, but he looked at her. She tried a small smile and shrugged. He went through the kitchen into the dining room, whose table was stacked high with mail, and on around the corner to the stairs just between the dark living room and study. Study? No one ever studied there, not unless that's what a person called his father's long evenings propped in a chair drinking and staring out the window or sometimes reading until he passed out.

Upstairs he passed his father's big room, then his sister's, until he came to the one he'd shared with his brother. The door was closed and he wondered if it had been closed since he left. He opened the door and turned on the overhead light. The two narrow beds with the old mattresses sunk in the middle were still on opposite walls, with a small table and lamp between them directly in front of the single window looking out the back of the house toward the hills. His bed was made with the cotton cowboy on a bucking horse spread, just as he'd left it. Probably hadn't been touched since he'd made it that last morning. The other bed, covered in a matching spread his mother had bought to please Ronnie, was dented on top, as if a body had lain on it. He didn't even want to think about that, he decided, and turned toward the dresser against the wall at the opposite end of the small room. Sure enough, in the top drawer, the mess of mismatched boot socks he'd left along with three .22 shells, a pack of matches, and a condom. Wishful teenage thinking. He stirred the socks with his fingers and a small black-and-white picture surfaced. It was a group of grade school kids—Ronnie in first grade, in the front row because he was so small, arms folded over his chest, with big ears and a scowl as if even then he was trying to be a big man. Ty smiled at his brother, started to put the picture back in the drawer, then slipped it in his shirt pocket instead. Maybe he'd go through the rest of the drawers tomorrow.

With the dry socks on, his feet started getting some feeling back as he hurried back downstairs. He could hear voices from the kitchen as he came through the living room and hoped his father wasn't haranguing Dakota with some of his crackpot political notions. The table was set and his father was putting a roast beef in the center as he walked in. They stared at each other for a moment, and Ty could feel himself tighten up, but his father turned back to the stove without a comment.

They ate quickly and silently, the men ignoring Dakota's attempts at small talk. Although Ty felt sorry for her, she didn't understand what was at stake here. He watched his father carefully, however, looking for any telltale signs. There was a lot more wear and tear on him than Ty would've expected. His mother had looked about the same as ever, though he suspected she was dyeing her hair to get that even dark brown that made her look like a younger sister next to her husband. Her face had a few more wrinkles maybe, but she'd never looked any age at all to him. She was just his mother, a name. His father's body was collapsing though, as if he had to age for the two of them. His fingers were bent and swollen and clumsy, the nails thick and horny with ridges like the hooves of a foundered horse. His thick, shaggy hair that had once been dark brown was streaked dirty gray and yellow-white. His long face was mottled and red from more than the weather, it seemed, and there were deep pouches under his eyes and swollen puffs on his cheekbones. The whites of his eyes were yellowish, as if some disease were working its way up his body. White whiskers sprouted unevenly on his jaw. He wheezed as he ate, and it seemed that there was a race between the food and the air trying to get into him.

"Ready for dessert?" His father dropped his fork with a clang on the empty plate and looked at the two of them expectantly.

"We're not done yet," Ty said, conscious of Dakota's surprised expression.

"I'm getting dessert." When his father climbed to his feet, Ty noticed how it seemed like such an effort. His shoulders were humped too, as if his back hurt him more than usual. Ty remembered how when he was a small boy, his mother would have to rub his father's back every night while he lay on the floor. Later, after his mother left, there were times when the back hurt so bad his father would ask him to use the rolling pin up and down his spine, smoothing out the muscles and helping the bones click back into place. But he had to really hurt to ask anything of his son, Ty knew, and after a while he despised his father's weakness, but longed for it too.

"Drove to town for groceries today." His father set down the lemon meringue pie encased in a plastic hood. The yellow was that too-good-to-be-true shade, and the meringue had started to melt in a slick line along the crust.

It had been a long time since Ty had eaten one of their good, ranch-raised roast beefs, and he helped himself to seconds and thirds, being careful to take the most-done pieces. Nobody who raised cattle wanted a rare piece of meat, his father had once told him. Dakota reached for the pinkest slices.

His father ate the pie noisily, his mouth open as he simultaneously chewed and gulped air. Ty noticed that Dakota kept her eyes on her plate or looked around at the once white kitchen walls stained and streaked with yellow-brown grease. The big electric stove was spattered with old grease too, and the counters were cluttered with every knickknack his mother had left, along with three coffee cans of bacon grease, the old toaster and mixer, and dishes they used to keep in cupboards. What could be left in the cupboards?

After they were done eating, Ty waited for his father to light up his usual cigarette, but the old man just smiled at him. "Quit five years ago."

Ty nodded.

"You ever smoke?" he asked Dakota, who was licking the last of the meringue stuck to the back of her fork. She shook her head.

"Neither did this one. Too good for it." He waved at Ty in a gesture that was so familiar it made his stomach jerk.

"So what'd you come back for?" He moved his chair sideways so he could look out the window at the storm blowing outside while he propped his head tiredly with his hand.

Ty picked up his fork and set it down again. He'd been dreading this moment because he couldn't tell his father the truth. In fact, he hadn't come up with a single story yet to cover why he was back, and nothing was arriving now either. He just prayed his father would keep quiet about the warrant. No chance in hell he would've forgotten.

"I asked him to bring me." Dakota stood and began collecting the plates.

"Leave 'em," his father said.

She kept moving though, ignoring his frown as she went to the sink and started running the hot water and looking for dishwashing soap.

"Use that bar there—" His father pointed at the thick yellow bar of cheap soap Ty remembered was used for everything from hair shampoo to scrubbing clothes, a habit left over from his father's upbringing. "Got some powdered cleanser and steel wool there for the pans, see it there beside the soap?" He turned toward Ty. "What'd you say her name was?"

"Dakota Carlisle."

"Knew a Carlisle once, from Wyoming." He rubbed his jaw.

"You can call me Ryder," he said in a loud voice to her back. She turned and said, "You can call me Dakota then."

He grinned with one side of his mouth and seemed to perk up. Ty had forgotten this side of his father, around women he wasn't related to.

"Ty here used to call me Ryder to get me riled. Now he don't call me nothing, I notice." He tilted his head toward the counter behind him. "Get me a toothpick there."

Ty got up and brought the sticky red cup to the table and set it in front of his father. "Here you go, Ryder." Let the games begin, he decided, as he finished clearing the table and brought the dishes to the sink, where Dakota was struggling to create suds with a shredded rag and the bar soap.

"Here—" He pushed up his shirtsleeves and stuck his hands in the water. "Find a clean towel and dry." He'd had this chore for too many years not to remember how to make it work.

"Not a hello or howdy-do in twenty years and his mother calls this afternoon to say he's back. Too bad we got nothing to toast with—" Ryder's eyes were watching for his reaction as Ty turned around.

"Yeah," Ty said and scrubbed at one of the sticky glasses lined up on the counter. Not a dish he touched wasn't coated with old grease or food. Man needed glasses he couldn't see the dirt any better than that.

Dakota dried some plates and opened the nearest cabinet to put them away.

"Might as well leave 'em out there on the counter," his father said. "Easier for me to get at 'em. That is, unless you're staying."

Dakota put them on the shelf. "We're staying," she said and pushed her elbow into Ty's side as she picked up a bowl to dry.

"That right, boy?" his father asked.

"For a bit." He felt the elbow in his side again.

" 'Bout time. Last man I hired quit on me first of September. Took a damn saddle with him too. Figured on having him bring the cattle in to winter pasture, get the horses up and the feed ready. Son of a bitch never even finished the haying. That south field is cured on the stem, only way we're going to get it to the cattle now is turn 'em loose on it. Almost called the sheriff about that saddle, it being that last one I won at Bennett's fall round-up when old man Heywood was still alive, but then I figured, what the hell. Leather was getting brittle and chewed on from sitting out in that barn, maybe some-body'd get some use out of it. Soon as this here snow stops, you can get started on those cattle."

The muscles in Ty's neck stiffened and sent an ache all the way down his arms. Another old feeling, and the only thing that seemed to loosen them again was punching something. He looked at the glass in his hand. Milk stuck in the bottom. He crammed the dishrag in and pushed until the glass cracked and split in his hands, cutting two of his fingers. He let the blood bubble and drip onto the surface of the gray scummed dishwater before Dakota grabbed his hand and wrapped it in the dish towel and shoved him out of the way.

"Act your age," she angrily whispered.

"Band-Aids?" he asked Ryder, who tipped his head at the cup-board nearest the back door where they'd always kept the first-aid kit.

"You're a clumsy so-and-so," his father said. "What happened to your face? Looks like somebody tried to stomp a new shape on it."

Ty ignored him and bandaged his fingers while Dakota finished washing the dishes in the sink.

"Too damn skinny too. You don't have one of those diseases, do you?" his father asked, shoving the toothpick cup to the center of the table.

"What do you think?" The anger was coming, Ty could feel it the way he'd felt it in the deserted cow barn at the Fairgrounds when he'd shot Eddie. He grabbed the back of the chair next to his father's.

"Think you oughta take a load off. Tomorrow's a busy day. Got the satellite dish coming if the snow lets up, and the television. Doc told me I better figure on sitting around a lot from now on. Some of those new dishes are only a foot or two across, too. Nothing to 'em. But I ordered the big size, get more bang for your buck. And the biggest damn television in the world too—thirty-five-inch screen and one of them VCR's for movies. You came back just in time, boy." Then he coughed so long and hard Ty wondered if a piece of lung was coming up. When he stopped, Ryder stood up, more hunched over than before, and headed out of the kitchen. "Get some sleep," he rasped.

"He's really sick," Dakota said, letting the water out and wiping her hands on another towel. "No wonder this place is such a mess." Her tone and her face were accusing.

"He's fine," Ty said, not wanting to admit the truth. Hell, he didn't want to stay here and take care of this hateful old man.

"Your nasty attitude doesn't help either." She shook her head and spread the towel to dry on the edge of the sink.

"Don't worry, there's two rooms upstairs," he muttered and looked out the window at the snowstorm.

"Don't be such a brat. You going to bring in our stuff?"

He looked at the truck parked out by the barn, now a white hump, and sighed. So the Indian was dead after all that. A hit-and-run wasn't Harney's style though; he liked it up close and personal. Ty touched the bone under his eye that ached in the cold now.

⚭ Chapter Sixteen

"Maybe Mr. Ty Bonte's been sneaking home all along, and I just missed him." Joseph Starr rested his hand on the dashboard as the truck slowly whooshed through the slushy snow.

Latta Jaboy shook her head. "No, someone would've said something with that outstanding warrant."

"He's cocky enough—driving right through town yesterday. Lucky you recognized him."

Latta nodded. "Surprised me too. From that rig he was driving, it looks like he's done well for himself."

"His kind usually does just fine. Now slow down, woman, you want to kill us?" Joseph spoke ironically, watching the few landmarks of an occasional tree or a hay field with the bales left down inch leisurely past the truck window.

Latta pressed cautiously on the gas, waiting for the slightest waver of the rear end on the slushy road. "Thought you said the Rosebud Court never starts on time."

"If the crabby judge is there, she likes to make sure you're checked in on time, no matter when she starts. Nobody else much cares. Turn here and we'll take the back route—"

Latta slowed and eased through the turn onto an unpaved road packed with snow.

"We're too macho to need our snow plowed up here on the res.

That's for you soft white people," Joseph said, trying to keep the smile off his lips as Latta struggled with the wheel.

"In that case," she said, "I'm sure you old chiefs won't mind pushing us out of a ditch." The truck squiggled as she pressed on the gas harder. "Besides, I'm half Indian and I *do* believe in good roads, unless you plan on walking—"

"Done my share of that in Nam, Latta. Gimme a truck any day of the week."

They passed a man and a woman bundled against the cold wind, walking single file with their heads down, going the other way toward Mission.

"Done my share of that too," Joseph said. "Only I was heading for the bars then."

Latta glanced quickly at Joseph. He was medium build, around fifty-five or sixty with deep creases in his face from earlier years of hard drinking, but his eyes were clear and thoughtful and his mouth was kind. These days he wore his graying hair in two long braids that the whites down in Babylon mocked him for and his own people stared at because it reminded them of the old ways. Joseph had come down a long road in the past few years and was slowly reclaiming his name and building a life for himself. Occasionally now he was called to conduct a healing ceremony or give advice about problems a family was having. Despite his age, he had sundanced last August, and it was a good one, with the spirits of the old ones in abundance around the circle, lounging in the shade of the cedar boughs with their descendants. When Joseph had completed his piercing and torn the sticks through his skin, a breath of wind had rushed in through the eastern gate and cooled everyone in a sign of approval that was well noted.

"Here we are—" Joseph pointed to the long yellow cement block building that housed both the Rosebud Tribal Police and the Rosebud Tribal Court. Across the highway was the Rosebud Utilities building, but around them the land stood empty, stretching to the horizon all around in dazzling, almost hurtful white. The snow in the parking lot had been pushed into large mounds, as if the people inside the building were under siege. Pulling in beside a dirty brown-and-bronze seventies Chevy two women and three children were climbing out of, Joseph looked around.

"At least they made it." He sighed and nodded toward the Ford Taurus his brother had salvaged from a wreck in front of the Rose-bud Casino last year. The front end was silver-gray, and the body black, which gave the car a racy, almost official appearance and seemed to please his brother, who was in his perennial drive for po-litical office.

On the double row of chairs down the hallway to the left of the entrance sat women with small children, two battered-looking men who ignored everyone, and two sullen teenagers. Another pair, Joseph's nephews, stood by the door, as if monitoring the parking lot. He nodded to them as he entered, and they mumbled hello, not looking particularly pleased at his arrival. The low counter opposite the front door was posted with signs asking people to check in and insisting they go no farther. Beyond it, the area was crowded with desks, computers, and file cabinets, next to which one and some-times two people dressed in jeans sat and worked while others shut-tled back and forth to the L that held the judges' offices and rear entrances to the small courtrooms.

"That's the defender's office—" Joseph nodded toward the open door to the far left of the counter. Latta could see a large color photo of a powwow dancer on the wall and lots of books.

"He's helping the boys—I hope. Last defender wasn't even a lawyer." Joseph was on the verge of asking his nephews where his brother was when the man came out of the restroom at the end of the hallway waiting area. They lifted their chins at each other and his brother took up a seat next to a white woman with fuzzy brown hair she wore pulled back in a single braid. They began to chat and he handed her a card. Joseph and Latta sat in the two chairs closest the door.

"Be better if he kept his attention on the two boys," Joseph whis-pered. "That woman could get him in real trouble. She's Johnny Drum's old lady. Gets booze for her kids, lets 'em walk all over the neighbors. When the last one was little, woman next door caught her kissing his privates. Guess she loved him a little too much."

Latta forced herself to stop staring. "Really? You think that's true?"

Joseph shrugged. "The kid's hell on wheels now. Some of the Indian women avoid her." As they watched, the woman laughed and her son, sitting in the next chair, slouched deeper and folded his arms across his chest like a gang-banger in a rap video. Although his hair was shaved up the sides, his arms were decorated with clumsy drawings, and his jeans hung so far below his waist his underpants showed, he had a sweet, clear-featured face that kept trying to break into a smile despite all his efforts to look bad.

"He's the one supposed to have broken the neighbor's windows—the neighbor who caught Mama kissing her baby's peepee. He's been a problem since he started school—put paint in the teacher's coke can at five, set a fire in the bathroom the next year. He's been sniffing glue and anything else he can lay his hands on since he was seven. Dopey look on his face is not from any overabundance of brain cells. He'll end up in the pen or dead in a ditch."

"He's just a child," Latta protested.

Joseph glanced at his nephews out of the corner of his eye. They were still standing by the glass door giggling about something, then they pulled it open and disappeared around the corner of the building. "Now where are those two going? They better not be getting high." He looked at his brother, caught his eye, and tipped his head. His brother shrugged and continued to talk to the woman.

"That's the problem. Attitude on the res is let 'em be little warriors. They're not hurting anybody." Joseph and Latta looked up at the poster on the wall facing them, with the school picture of the plump, smiling young girl in the middle, offering $20,000 for information leading to the arrest and conviction of the person or persons responsible for her murder. It was signed by the Rosebud Police and the FBI. She'd been found in a ditch, naked, strangled.

"Gang-banger wannabees," Joseph said. "Drugs and booze. These mothers would tell you it's some white man did it. And the fathers?

Look at those two men sitting there—they're either working too hard to have time for this crap or they're too out of it to know what day it is."

Latta looked at the men, who were so skinny their knees poked the material of their jeans in two sharp points. The arms and necks of both bore jailhouse tattoos, and their faces were bloated and scarred with despair. They didn't look at anyone in the hallway, simply leaned forward, elbows parked on their thighs and gimme caps riding low on their foreheads, and studied the brown linoleum tile floor. An elderly man whose cheeks were sunken from missing teeth came in and sat down in the last remaining chair. His flannel shirt was clean, but the elbows were busted out and the fleece-lined jeans jacket he placed carefully over his lap was washed pale and ragged. The knuckles on both hands he set on the coat were humped painfully from arthritis. But his narrow, weathered red-brown face was stoical, and his dark eyes liquid with alertness as they looked down the opposite row of chairs. Joseph nodded slightly and the man's lips stretched into a brief smile.

"They're still just kids—" Latta continued the argument, thinking of her own daughter, who at five was becoming much too independent.

"Like Ty Bonte, I s'pose." Joseph turned his hands over and folded his fingers for a lengthy examination of the nails.

"He *was* a boy when that happened, and you know it." Latta's voice rose, causing the woman next to her to look up curiously.

"Come to watch the kangaroo court today?" The woman's voice was unexpectedly loud and shrill, which made people along the two rows of chairs laugh. "This here's a joke, you know—kangaroo court—" She ran her hand along the side of her hair, clamped in a tie at the back of her neck, and enjoyed the response she'd created. Her two young daughters and little boy squirmed and kicked their legs as if in agreement.

"You should've seen my cousin, Latta. Those two meant to kill him," Joseph insisted.

"Ty had a terrible life with his father out there alone on the ranch, Joseph. He was drinking and using drugs—"

"No excuse for murder. I've been in drunken brawls too. This here was different. Vicious. Really cold. No, Mr. Ty Bonte made a mistake coming back here, thinking we poor dumb redskins would forget a thing like this."

Latta looked at the stern set of his jaw where the muscle worked. "What're you going to do?"

"I'm thinking—I'll let you know when I decide, but he's not walking out of this again. And now that my cousin is gone—it's not right to his memory to let this man go free."

"What about Harney Rivers? I always thought he shifted the blame to Ty because it was easy. He's been back in town for two years and you haven't done anything about him—"

Joseph pushed at the wide wood splinter that was working its way out from under his thumbnail. "He'll have his day in court too."

"What do you mean?"

"Something I'm thinking about. The feds and locals were nervous about AIM and Wounded Knee when the assault occurred. They didn't want a bunch of trouble starting on this reservation too. That's why they squashed the investigation on Harney. Issued the warrant for Ty after he was long gone. Basically let those little white shits go. But—oh, here comes the defender, I'll get the boys—"

The courtroom door opened and a slim white man with a shaved head and intense dark brown eyes looked quickly around at the seated people. When his eyes recognized Joseph's brother, he crooked his finger at him to follow him into his office. The door closed behind them just as Joseph pushed the two boys ahead of him into the building. They had pink eyes and red noses and despite their attempts at seriousness, they were suppressing giggles. A burning-leaves smell drifted off their clothes. The other two boys gave them a sign with their hands.

The defender's door opened again and he reappeared, beckoning the boys into his office.

"Let's go watch some of the civil court. I want to see how Lame Horse does—" Joseph stood to follow the older man into the courtroom.

It was a small, crowded room with honey-colored oak pews for spectators and two blond tables and chairs for both sides of a case. A row of orange plastic chairs lined the wall across from the judge's high wooden bench and the clerk's lower one, wich rested next to it like a set of stairs. The formality of the judge's bench was breached by three thick black computer and microphone cords sprawling across the floor and snaking their way up the bench. The lighting was dim, almost soothing, and on the wall to the left hung a large satin star quilt, while on the wall to the right hung a huge portrait of a native elder, painted on deer hide mounted on wood.

At the prosecutor's table sat a young white man in a dark gray suit, white shirt, and yellow tie. His brown hair was clipped short and he wore horn-rim glasses and a benign expression. The old man sat alone at the defendant's table, his hands resting on the top as if he expected them to be encased in cuffs or his fingers cut off.

"Mr. Rose, is Norwest Bank ready?" The judge, a tidy, balding white man in wire-rim glasses, leaned forward and spoke into the microphone, then inched it toward himself.

"Yes, Your Honor. In the matter of the $276.47 owed by Mr. George Lame Horse on his Visa credit card, we have come to a payment agreement. He will pay us ten dollars a week until the amount is repaid and we will cease interest." The young man read his statement in a monotone that implied no ill will or judgment. He was simply doing a job.

"Mr. Lame Horse, do you agree to these terms?" the judge asked in a kind voice.

He mumbled a muffled yes that could barely be heard and pulled his hands off the table, as if they had received the blow they had anticipated.

"That's probably half his food allotment for the month," Joseph whispered to Latta when Lame Horse rose and shuffled out.

The credit and loan cases with Norwest continued, one after another, with the same small dance of deficit and failure and redemption. It had a grim impersonality that bothered Latta after Joseph had disclosed the financial ruin facing the elderly man because of $10 less a week. Each case seemed a rehearsal of absurdity in light of the promise to pay despite the lack of income. She wondered if the young man from Sioux Falls came up for the day only, or if he spent the month going from one reservation to the next, extracting promises. She tried to imagine her Lakota mother in court with the bank but couldn't. Her mother had made certain that theirs was a well-organized life, without the possibility of the kind of chaos reservation life often brought. She would have been horrified to see her daughter here today.

When civil court was done, and the judge and clerk left, the public defender entered, followed by the boys and Joseph's brother and the criminal court prosecutor. Below his expensive navy blue suit jacket, white shirt, and tie, the public defender wore almost new jeans, ironed with a sharp crease, and black cowboy boots. Joseph and Latta moved up and sat behind the railing directly in back of the two boys and lawyer. At the prosecutor's table, a Native woman with her hair cropped short, in a navy blue suit and plain white blouse, was lifting and sorting papers and manilla file folders.

"That one's fresh out of law school—" Joseph tipped his head toward the prosecutor. Nodding toward the judge, he added, "But she's pretty good."

They got under way with a reading of the charges, and the judge, a slight, pretty Native woman in her thirties, wearing thick-black framed glasses, shuffled her papers. The boys had thrown a rock through the windshield of a tribal police car while it was parked in front of a white woman's house, after her son had smashed the neighbors' windows as part of the long-standing feud between the two families.

"At first they didn't want to come forward, your Honor," the defender said, "but you can see now that they've had time to rethink their actions and be repentant."

The boys were so slumped in their chairs that Joseph used the point of his boot toe to poke them hard in the back. They quickly straightened, with a scowl over their shoulders at him.

The judge scanned the two pages in her hand and pulled her glasses down her nose. "They have a long list of complaints against them. Henry, David—I'm wondering just how dumb you two have to be to do something this stupid. Looking at this list, I see the road out of here—straight to prison. You think your family's going to be proud of you then? Think you'll be big men in jail, get some more tattoos, some more battle scars, come home the big-time warriors?" She paused and put down the papers. "No, I see you two again, you're going next door to do some time in jail." She looked at the boy's father, who sat with shoulders stiff and straight, watching her with stern respect. "These boys are on curfew for the next four months. They aren't to leave your house except to go to school. You have to promise me that you'll make them obey." He nodded. "No hanging out with their friends, no going to town unless you're with them, understand? If they're seen, off to jail. No driving. The police catch you, off to jail. And especially no drinking or drugs. I'm going to arrange for weekly testing. If you have illegal substances, any-thing, in your urine, off to jail." Their father nodded again and the boys nudged each other with their elbows.

"Yeah, they know they got away with it. Police aren't going to be checking up on those two. Nobody cares that much," Joseph said.

As the boys tried to push out ahead of the adults, Joseph rose and grabbed their arms. "They're riding with us," he said over his shoul-der to his brother. At the truck, Joseph shoved the two boys toward the back and made them climb over the tailgate and squat in the snow. "You want to be warriors? Gang-bangers? Let's see how tough you are—" He climbed in the cab and waved at Latta to start the en-gine.

"If I don't do something pretty soon, they're going to end up like my cousin because some white asshole like Ty Bonte feels like kick-ing the shit out of a drunk Indian. They get these little slaps on the wrist, then they're shocked the day the feds yank 'em out of tribal jail and haul 'em up to Rapid City to stand trial for something really serious they've done. Or they move to the city and get busted first time they pull their shit and they're crying injustice all the way to jail. They get out, they drink and drug themselves to death. No, I'm not losing these two—we're going down fighting—" He slid the window open to the back. "You boys comfy there?"

"I hope you know what you're doing," Latta muttered as she backed up and turned toward the highway.

"Straightened your husband out, didn't I?" Joseph braced himself as they bounced through a deep hole in the drive.

"Maybe it's time to do it again," she said and squinted down the road, checking for traffic. "He hasn't been home in two days. I had to leave the baby with Juanita when you called for the ride up here. He probably won't bother coming home tonight either."

"But he's with his sister—Kya's been trying to get someone to drive to Omaha with her." Joseph checked the side mirror to see if the boys were leaning out of the back, considering jumping.

"He usually tells me first or calls when he's with her." Latta sucked in her stomach and tried to push the worry up her chest. She hadn't meant to tell him. She'd been keeping the crisis in her marriage quiet for several months now, but somehow seeing those boys in court and Ty yesterday reminded her of the bad old days with her first husband, Jaboy, and the years alone afterwards—until her marriage to Cody Kidwell. Maybe he was too young and too wild, maybe he couldn't stand the stability and quiet of marriage and fatherhood. She clenched the wheel at the thought of Caddy, their daughter, who was showing every sign of the fierce individuality and independence of her father and his mother, crazy Caroline. And his half sister, Kya. She glanced at Joseph, who was watching the side mirror. Kya and Joseph lived together on and off when she wasn't running around organizing political protests or causing trouble, sometimes it was difficult to tell which. She had way too much energy for her own good, Cody always said as a way of excusing her. It was a bad family trait, as far as Latta could see.

"Is he drinking?" Joseph asked.

She shrugged. "I don't know. I don't think so—I think—" Her eyes filled with tears and she sniffed and swallowed. "I think maybe there's someone else."

Joseph turned sharply. "Why?"

She shook her head. "It's just a feeling, and—little things that—"

"You're sure he's not drinking?"

"I'm pretty sure. There's no smell—he looks all right except for being a little more tired than usual. He's gone all the time, comes home late when he says he's been at Bennett's ranch or town doing something or other. He goes to auction and doesn't come home for an extra day. I don't know what's going on. I wasn't going to trouble you, you've got your own family to take care of, I just—" She pressed the sleeve of her coat against her wet eyes.

"I'll see if I can find out what's going on." He turned around and saw the boys hunkered tight against the cab of the truck, their heads buried in their coats, their arms clutching their bodies. "You can do me a favor too—"

"Of course."

"See if you can get someone in Babylon to hire my nephews. They need a job off the reservation. They need to see what working is like for a change, working that means you have to be there on time and put in real effort. And get paid for it too. I think it's the only way I'm going to get their attention. They're like spoiled horses, these two—their heads are so full of themselves, they need to get stung. I don't want to see their faces on posters like that one back there."

The image of the dead girl floated into the truck, her happy eyes pleading with them to bring her back, not to let her go so easily and completely, but all the way to his brother's house to drop his nephews in the safety of their confinement, the girl's body, abused and reviled, lay in a sea of deep ditch grass, unrecovered from an act unclaimed. A *wanagi*, a ghost the people could not please or escape.

Maybe some dreams were too terrible to ever end, Joseph realized. They were the ones that had to be fought off with ingenuity and cunning before they devoured the world. In the old days, people believed in Bad Gods such as *Iyo*, the chief evil, who could appear as a giant or a cyclone, and *Anog Ite*—Double Face, and there were gods and spirits who lived in water and trees and roamed the earth looking for bad things to do to people. *Gnaskinyan* was the most feared, because he could appear in the form of the good Buffalo God and persuade people to do evil. His *Hmugma Wicasa*—wizards—helped by doing his ceremonies. Joseph had to wonder if *Gnaskinyan* was the influence here, bringing Ty Bonte back, urging his nephews to wrongdoing, sending Cody away. Joseph despaired that he'd ever figure out which god was the one he needed and that he'd learn the ceremony of appeal. With the little he knew, he could bring all hell loose on his own head if he wasn't careful.

Looking at the side mirror, he glimpsed a coyote trotting across the top of the new, wet snow along the side of the road without wetting its paws. When their eyes met in the mirror, he felt a chill. Maybe *Iktomi* was loose with his tricks. He could ride a coyote. In the old days, the people had had to learn to recognize him by his actions, since he could make himself appear as an old man or be invisible if he chose. He played tricks on animals, as well, and he could talk with everything that lived, including trees and stones. Early on, he persuaded the Lakota to scatter and live alone, so they were vulnerable to their enemies until the Wise One came and told them the truth. Joseph looked at the small house surrounded by an acre-wide apron of junked cars, appliances, and trash sprawled across the bottom of the next hill. Above it perched a plain white frame church with a tall steeple that could be seen for miles. Maybe *Iktomi* lived there, where he could watch his evil tricks at work. That was a thought he wasn't going to be sharing with the old priest in St. Francis this afternoon when he was going to propose hiring that new public defender he met in court today. The man mantained a private practice along with the work for the tribe, he'd found out. They'd be ready to make the move against Mr. Ty Bonte by late winter.

↶ Chapter Seventeen

The snow had stopped sometime in the middle of the night, and by morning the sun was glaring off the hard, white surfaces, bouncing the light against the windows and out across the hills. Although Ty was dressed and downstairs by daybreak, his father was already sitting at the kitchen table, drinking fresh coffee.

"There's a ten-year-old buckskin gelding will work cattle. Keep him in that little run off the barn. Have to rope him though, likes to get into it 'fore he settles down to work. The bay mare is a granddaughter to that King mare I had back when. She broke a leg in a damn gopher hole year after you took off. Spent too much time in my life fighting them dang things. Ruint the best roping mare I ever had. The bay is too particular for my blood, doesn't like getting her toes wet, but you might like her. Or Dakota can ride her. Aside from those two horses and a couple of cripples, there's some half-broke babies I had to quit on. Tried teaching that hired man how to work them horses, but he was 'bout as useful as a dead rooster in a hen house. He pawned that saddle, I expect."

It was just like always. Ty silent, standing at the sink and looking out the window with his back to the old man, taking instructions for the work, drinking his coffee, sometimes the only thing he'd have in his stomach till dark. "Still have a tractor for the plow blade?"

"Same old John Deere. Think you need it? Got me a new lightweight Case—'less that hired man ruint that too."

They waited in the silence for the image of Ronnie under the old red tractor to wash through the room and flow on out.

"Don't 'spose he drained the fluids for winter," Ty said after a while.

"No, don't 'spose he did."

"You up to getting on a horse to help with the cattle?" Ty turned and looked at Ryder in time to notice a brief flicker of pain, replaced by irritation on the face.

"What's it look like to you?" He started to climb slowly to his feet, wheezing louder than he had the night before as he reached toward the coffeepot on the stove.

"Here—" Ty picked it up and poured the fresh cup while the old man settled in his chair.

"Soon as that gal wakes up, I'll send her out to help. She can ride, can't she?" He pursed his lips at the edge of the coffee mug and looked at Ty, a challenge in his eyes.

"I'll plow the road and shovel first. Give it a chance to warm up out there. Where're the cattle now?"

"Drove the pickup over hell's half acre looking for 'em the other day. They're in that pasture joins up with Jaboy-Kidwell over west of here."

"Kidwell?"

"Yeah, that Latta Jaboy hooked herself some young stray and taken up light housekeeping over there." Ryder shifted his legs slowly under the table and grimaced.

"They're not married?"

"Oh, I don't know—whyn't you ride over and ask 'em? I got this whole damn place falling down around my ears and you're asking me for gossip. Call that mother of yours, she keeps track of all sorts of nonsense. And why don't you make yourself some breakfast—man can't do a real day's work without food in his belly—"

"Better feed the horses first—" As Ty said it, the old man's shoulders let go an inch or two, but he ignored it, quickly going outside.

He tossed hay and corn to all the horses, hooked up the plow to the big John Deere, which started after a few tentative sputters, and noticed in the very back of the machine shed the abandoned dirt-coated red tractor. That surprised him. Although they'd kept using it after Ronnie, Ty had always hated the machine and assumed his father would trade it when he bought the next one, like he usually did. The new yellow tractor that looked like a toy next to the John Deere sat stranded in a snowdrift by the barn.

After he'd plowed the barnyard into big wet piles where nobody was likely to need to go, he stopped the tractor by the yard fence and went inside to look for some insulated boots. Dakota was just setting a plate of scrambled eggs and toast in front of the old man as he came through the door. "You want some?" she asked.

He was hungry, but arguing with pride as the old man smiled and picked up a forkful. So that was what he wanted, someone to cook for him.

When he hesitated, Dakota smiled sleepily and said, "Come on and eat something, Ty."

It did taste good, although he ate so quickly it was a wonder he got any flavor at all. He kept his eyes on his plate, not wanting to see the gloating in Ryder's eyes.

"Weather people say there's a warm front moving in middle of the week," his father said.

"You want me to stop plowing?" Ty leaned back and sipped some more coffee.

"No, them satellite people need to get in here today."

Dakota was picking at the toast crusts on her plate, dragging them through the raspberry jam and making red swirls on her plate.

"You can't wait a couple more days?"

"Just plow the goddamn road." Ryder set his arms on the table so heavily the dishes shivered.

"Saw the red tractor in the shed—" He locked his eyes on the old man's face.

His father stared back with the same brown-black eyes Ty saw in the mirror when he shaved. He wanted to look away, but couldn't until his father said, "Left it for you, Ty."

"Coulda saved yourself the trouble." Ty pushed back his chair and stood. "Soon's I finish plowing the road, I'm going out to get the cattle, Dakota. Think you can help?"

She nodded with a quick glance at his father, who was scraping at some old food caught on the sleeve of the red-and-black flannel shirt he was wearing.

"Dress warm," Ty said. "Got any boots I can use?" he asked his father.

"Closet there off the front door. Keep an eye out for coyotes, son. Thought I saw one sniffing around the hay yard the other day."

He met the satellite truck at the end of the twelve-mile road, turned around, and followed it back, finishing the other side. Although the wind was cold, there was an occasional gust with a warm edge to it that promised the midweek melt. In the Sandhills the water sank away quickly, so there wouldn't be a problem of mud except on the gumbo flats or the ranch road. When he was a kid, they'd brought in dirt to cover the sand and blacktopped a narrow strip all the way to the house, but erosion quickly took its toll, so now there were only broken chunks and pits left. Come spring, he'd tell his father, he should hire someone to come out and scrape up what was left and haul it away to one of the blowouts.

Dakota was already in the barn, trying to organize the trash—stuffing new garbage bags and clearing the saddling area. She's worked up a sweat that worried Ty. Out in the hills on a horse, that could freeze and chill her body so much she'd be in real trouble. Maybe he should go alone. He collected a rope from the tack room and went to settle things with the buckskin. But by the time he got back, she was waiting for him with two western saddles and bridles hanging on the side of a stall.

"I'll take the buckskin, you ride the mare," he said. She nodded and handed him a brush and they quickly went over the horses' bodies. When he picked the feet, he noticed the gelding's shoes were long overdue. Wasn't the old man taking care of anything? A glance at the mare's feet proved the same thing, and her shoes were loose. He wondered if he should pull them or let them fall off. But he de-

cided he didn't want to get in a war with the touchy mare over
hooves right now.

He slung the blanket on the mare, then the saddle Dakota
handed him. But when he reached to wipe the dust off the seat, he
realized it was Ronnie's saddle. Too big for the kid, but it had been
Ty's at one time, so Ronnie had insisted. Ty put a hand on the horn
to pull it off, but stopped. What the hell. He began to tighten the
cinch, putting a knee into the mare's stomach when she started to
hold her breath. The mare grunted as if he'd hurt her. "Good acting,"
he muttered and finished it off, giving her a slap on the neck to show
there were no hard feelings. The mare looked around at him. She
had a pretty head, nice and clean with a white blaze like that of her
grandmother, whom he'd pulled out of the marsh all those years ago.
Clean-legged too. Probably hadn't seen much use from the look of
things around the ranch. He let Dakota bridle her while he saddled
his horse.

The saddle she'd chosen for him was the only one he'd ever won
for riding saddle broncs, and he'd almost ridden it to death he was so
proud of himself. But when he'd driven away that morning, he'd
taken the old roping saddle he'd inherited from his father. He knew
why too, but he didn't want to think about it. He saddled the buckskin and led the way out to mount up.

Spiky brown soapweed stalks pierced up through the snow in
deeper places, and on the tops of the hills, where the snow had
already started to disappear, their thick green leaves were bright
against the tan and white. On the flats, clumps of reddish brown
bunchgrass punctured the snow. As far as they could see, the hills
unrolled before them, uninterrupted by houses, utility poles, or
trees. Much starker than the Kansas Flint Hills. Occasionally there
was a windmill and a stock tank, but not enough to dispel the sense
of distance and space that told how a person could get lost out here
and never be heard from again. The higher hills were striped around
with corduroy ridges from the wind, and the lower ones blown
ragged as if they'd just been constructed a day or two ago, making
the land appear raw, half-formed. He'd really missed it these past

years, and now it could be taken away in a heartbeat again if someone decided to talk to the sheriff about him. After he settled with
Harney, of course, he'd be on the run again. Or in jail. He glanced at
Dakota, who was looking around with a little smile on her face. He
was going to hate being away from her.

They rode west, passing the fenced-in subirrigated hay meadows
and marshes, where the aquifer ran close to the surface and thou-
sands of geese, ducks, and pelicans, among others, would migrate or
nest in the spring. Now there was a deep and utter silence, broken
only by an occasional cry of a hawk hunting and the steady squeak
of the saddles that needed a good soaping and oiling.

Then the mare started chewing and clanking the bit restlessly
against her teeth, and they let the horses pick up a trot. "It's so big—"
Dakota said, spreading her arm at the hills. "I didn't think it'd be so
big and empty."

"That's what I like about it," Ty said and nudged the buckskin
into a lope down a small rise, along the base of a large hill, and up to
the fence leading to the pasture the cattle would be waiting in. He
got down and opened the fence, carefully laying the barbed-wire
gate all the way back so the cattle could be pushed through without
trouble. In the old days, they'd taken the cattle down the road, but it
took at least three, usually four riders to manage that. If he'd thought
about it, he might have convinced the old man to help out in the
pickup. Maybe Ryder was finally getting old and lazy.

When they got to the cattle, they were bunched around the stock
tank, so clogged with tumbleweeds it was hard for more than two
animals to drink at once. "Lucky it snowed," he said and began working his way around the herd. The cattle didn't look in bad shape
though. Another testimony to the Sandhills grass. "You take that
side and we'll check the rest of the pasture for the others, then
bunch 'em and push toward the gate."

Dakota nodded but looked doubtful. "What if I get lost?" Her
face was burned red by the cold, and she bit her lip.

He leaned over and kissed her cold lips. "Just holler, I'll find
you—"

She laughed and turned her horse toward the next hill.

Riding off, he turned back once to watch her follow a cattle trail up and around the hill, then disappear on the other side.

He found another bunch of fifty a quarter of a mile away and started them moving toward the tank. By the time he had them close enough, he rode south, planning to circle around as far as Jaboy's fence to the west. He'd probably pick up Dakota along the way. It worried him that he wasn't finding the biggest bunch of cattle. Should be more. Unless the old man had cut way back. Hadn't said anything though. Stuff he'd found so far looked like it hadn't been culled in a while. Yearlings, two-year-old steers, and dry cows mixed in with the pregnant cows and this year's crop of calves. He must not have shipped last fall, or spring either. Cattle prices were way down in the spring and had come up only a few cents this fall, but a year ago— Ty had never been able to stop himself from listening to the livestock reports on the radio first thing in the morning.

What about the bulls? He'd just assumed they were taken care of. Where the hell had he stashed them? They weren't near the house either. "Shit"—he'd have to come back out tomorrow and bring the bulls in. The buckskin would be dead on its feet after today.

It was early afternoon before he found another sizable bunch and began moving them along the fence line to the west. He was beginning to really worry about Dakota too, no sign of her tracks even. When he came to the break in the fence though, he found where she'd gone through. From the drifts over the wire, the break was done before the snow, but he could still see some of the pocks the cattle hooves made in the soft ground. He cursed and sat there. Should he take the cattle on or go after her and risk them scattering again? She could wander around Jaboy's land till tomorrow before he'd find her.

The buckskin's ears twitched back and forth, and he lifted his head looking across Jaboy's land and snorted. Ty shaded his eyes with his hand and tried to see into the snow glare. The buckskin stamped a front leg and nickered in a high, questioning tone. Then the first of the cattle appeared over the hill headed for the fence line. Ty jumped down and quickly clipped the opening bigger with the wire cutters he always carried working cattle. By the time he had cleared the opening and remounted, the cattle were spilling into their pasture, trotting eagerly up to the others waiting a little ways off.

And Dakota wasn't alone. As the other rider stopped and tied his rope back on his saddle, Dakota came through the fence, smiling. "I found them—Cody was already driving them back for us."

The cowboy rode through the opening and touched the brim of his hat, tied on as Ty's was with a scarf. He was younger than he was, Ty suddenly thought, early thirties.

"Thanks. I'm Ty Bonte—"

"Cody Kidwell—" He dipped his head and looked away, not really meeting Ty's eyes.

Maybe the kid knew about the assault warrant, Ty thought. He'd have to tell Dakota before someone said something.

"I'm ranching next door," Cody said in a quiet voice. "Married to Latta Jaboy." It was a still face, Ty noticed, unsmiling but not hostile. A face that waited for what you were going to do before it decided anything. Well, at least that was settled, he'd tell the old man they were married. But then he probably already knew that.

"Cattle broke through sometime last week. I was in Omaha, and Latta couldn't push them back by herself. Then I saw Dakota here and figured the two of us could do it."

"I appreciate it. My father's hand took off and he's laid up right now."

"Yeah well, same thing happened last spring? Only it was our cattle. Ryder charged us fifty cents a head a day for five days' grazing." Cody set his lips and looked out across the hills to the south of them.

"Son of a bitch," Ty cursed under his breath. What could he say, the old man didn't mean it? He sure didn't want to get in the middle of some feud his father was having with the neighbors, but he couldn't poor-mouth him to a stranger either.

"Send the bill, I'll make sure it gets paid." He reined his horse around and looked at Dakota. "Let's go—"

"Ty—" She shook her head and trotted back through the opening. "Just a minute, I better thank him—"

"Fine," he muttered and reined the buckskin around to push the cows toward home.

"Why're you being such a jerk, Ty?" Dakota trotted up next to him and slowed to the plodding walk required for herding.

"I don't know—being put in the middle of some hassle my father's cooked up with the neighbors, I guess. Sorry." He put a hand on her leg and squeezed her thigh hard. When she yelped and batted at him, they both laughed.

It was dark by the time they finished pushing the last of the cattle into the big hay meadows on the flats by the house, and Dakota got off near the porch while Ty took the horses to the barn. He stepped out of the saddle stiff and cold, his fingers barely able to unfasten the buckles and tear the strings off the bales of hay for the horses. Not only that, Ty remembered, he'd have to bring the bulls in tomorrow first thing, then start cleaning up the barn and organizing the winter feed. See if the deer were nesting in the hay yard, their pee ruining the hay. Check to see if they had enough corn and supplement. Had the old man put the storm windows on? He'd have to look. Set up the snow fences too, stop the road from drifting shut. Make sure the water tanks in the hay meadows were clear, repair the fences. Jesus Christ on a cross, he'd be done sometime around March at this rate, then the calving would start. He had to get away from here, sooner the better. He hadn't even had a moment to think about the best way to get at Harney either.

Turning out the barn lights and pausing in the doorway, he looked across at the house, where Dakota's figure was passing to and fro in front of the kitchen window. He wondered what it was like inside Harney's head when he stabbed the Indian and put a pitchfork in him. What made a person think he could go that far? Sure, he'd said he'd like to kill so-and-so, but he'd never meant it. Not until Harney. The only thing that made sense was that it was necessary, like a driver's license or oil in an engine. It had to be done or nothing would ever work again in his life. The mere thought of watching Harney Rivers die lifted him a little as he started across the snow-

packed barnyard. Maybe, he realized, maybe he wasn't so damn different from Harney after all.

"You owe Latta Jaboy and that Cody kid some grazing money,"
he announced as he pried himself out of his stiff winter coat and
stomped the snow off the boots.

"You pay 'em, you're so worried about it." Ryder waved him off
with a deep, choking cough.

"Ty, shut up," Dakota ordered.

He stood there watching them. Dakota was busy setting the table
for supper, moving awkwardly around the four-foot silver cylinder
marked OXYGEN sitting on the chair next to his father. That thing
must have arrived today while they were gone. The old man
coughed some more, then picked up a circle of plastic tubing and
slipped it over his head, positioning the plastic clips at his nose and
drawing short breaths.

Dakota paused and brushed the old man's gray hair off his forehead, looking down at the shaking hand holding the tube under his
nose. Without glancing at Ty, she turned back to dish up the food.

Looking at his father's helplessness, Ty's stomach sank and
churned. There wasn't any way he was going to eat with that going
on, he decided, and headed out of the kitchen for the stairs. He
wasn't hungry anyway. He didn't want to start caring about this goddamn place and he didn't want to start caring about that goddamn
old man down there. Tomorrow he was going to town and find that
prick and kill him, he decided, falling into the sunken mattress his
back protested against as he dropped into a groggy half sleep.

"Ty, come on—" He thought he was dreaming of someone rubbing
his chest and brushing his cheek. "You have to eat something; come
on." It was Dakota. He didn't open his eyes, but parted his lips and
felt hers meet them. He put his arms around her and pulled her on
top of him, making the springs squeal. He pushed his right hand up
under her shirt and felt her shiver as he stroked her back, lingering
along the hooks of her bra. He kissed her deeper and slipped his left
hand up the front of her shirt, touching her breasts while the nipples

hardened. She groaned and her body grew heavier. He struggled to turn them onto their sides, catching her lower lip with his teeth to hold her. The bed was so narrow there was barely room for him to lower his head to her breasts as he undid the buttons. "No," she whispered, "he's waiting for us down there—"

He unsnapped the bra and lifted it up, found the nipple, and began to tease and suck. She pushed onto him and he sucked harder, getting a hollow low in his stomach as she used both hands to cradle his head against her while she moaned. He found the other nipple with his fingers and gently rubbed and squeezed it till she pushed his mouth to it. He could feel how hard and urgent her body was against him, locking her hands around his neck. He put his hand between her legs and began to rub and press. "Harder—" she whispered and he let his teeth graze the nipple, wanting to take her where it was she was going. "Oh yes—" she crooned and arched and cupped while their moans became indistinguishable. Suddenly she fumbled at his belt—"Hurry—" and they undid their jeans and yanked them down, and he found her and mounted hard, stabbing hard with the waves that bucked her hips at him until he caught her and plunged up, then down deep toward darkness.

"You hungry?" he murmured, repositioning his arm, which was falling asleep under the weight of her head.

"It's on the table," she whispered in a sleepy voice. "Probably cold by now."

"What's he doing, watching that TV of his? Or waiting for me so he can have live entertainment?"

"You don't know what's going on, do you? Bet you haven't even looked in the study." She brushed his hair off his cheek and kissed it.

He tightened his arm around her neck until she pushed her fist into his side, against the barely mended ribs, and he stopped.

"He's sleeping in there. In this recliner. Afraid to lay down in a bed. Afraid he won't wake up if he goes to sleep prone, because of his breathing. He's terrified."

"What—he's got bronchitis, pneumonia, or something?"

"Emphysema. He's dying, can't you see that?"

"No, he's playing your sympathy to get me mad. One of his games, that's all it is." Ty wondered though, maybe he was wrong.

"I talked to the doctor on the phone just a little bit ago. He sent the oxygen tanks and some special breathing treatments out today while we were gone. He's been calling every day to check on your dad because he's all alone. Ryder can't even climb the stairs here— the doctor's trying to find a hospital bed for him, and sending a home-care person to stop in daily as soon as he can arrange it. He said the deterioration has really accelerated this past month." Her words got hurried, as if she could feel the resistance rising in the body next to her.

"No—" It couldn't be, he wanted to say, that would be just too goddamn unfair, the old man reaching out at him again, making him stay and take care of him now when they hadn't spoken to each other in so many years and he had this other thing to do.

"It's true. You have to stop fighting with him, it makes his breathing go crazy. He could die right there at the kitchen table, would that make you happy?"

Ryder dead. Well, in his mind he'd always waited for it, for the relief it would bring, he guessed, but this deal, no, this wasn't what he'd imagined.

"It's a terrible death. I watched my grandfather die that way. Drowning in the fluid that fills the lungs. Or his heart could go, too much strain trying to breathe. And the steroid medications he's taking are making his bones brittle. Ty, when he was in town the other day, they took X rays of his back—there's three hairline fractures already. The pain he must be in—"

Ty felt the wrong like a club on the top of his head. It was all wrong, he was sorry and not, he cared and didn't, he couldn't sort any of it out. What the hell was he supposed to do now? The old man hadn't asked him back to help, had he? Yet here he was, being expected to pitch in. Well, screw him, just screw him. Oh shit, he thought, that wasn't right either.

"Christmas is in ten days. We should stay and see him through that, don't you think? Ty?" She pushed his sore ribs again, and he pulled his arm from under her head.

"Sure, why not. Fine. Just perfect." They lay there silent. "Where is he now?"

"He's watching his new TV. Only thing he can do now, he says, reading's too hard. His eyes are bothering him and he can't concentrate long enough."

Ty sat up. Why'd the old man have to pull this now, when Ty had something else he needed to do? It was just like him. Not like he didn't deserve dying this way. Man had ruined his own health. Not like he hadn't been warned by plenty of doctors over the years too. Ty thought of his mother and wondered what she felt about all this. She knew. She'd tried to warn him. Well, why the hell hadn't she said it outright? Why the hell were those two always putting him in the middle like this? And what the hell was she going to give her husband this year for Christmas? Another fucking robe? He could probably use it for a change. Ty pulled his jeans up and stood, fastening the buckle without tucking his shirt in.

"Come on," he said with his back to her. "Let's go see what kind of trouble he's making down there by himself. He's always fighting with the neighbors, you know. Pissed off every single person in a hundred miles of him. That's why he's alone out here and nobody gives a damn."

"That doesn't matter anymore, Ty." She pulled up her jeans and refastened her bra and stood.

"It will if we don't settle up with Harney for your horse because of it." He knew instantly that he'd made a mistake, but it was that damn perversity in him, just like his old man, he thought grimly as he went down the stairs ahead of her hurt silence.

∞ Chapter Eighteen

Thursday the warm front moved in, raising the temperatures into the fifties and melting most of the snow off until water stood in shiny puddles as Ty looked across the hay meadows and hills the next morning. They'd be gone in another day or two, soaked up, but for now sparrows were hopping in and out of the puddles in the barnyard, and the horses were enjoying muddy rolls in their pens. He'd move them into the larger field next to the bulls today, he decided. Ryder had been keeping his horses close because he couldn't walk too far to feed them. Although the two Ty had brought with him needed work, he didn't have time. But what was he going to do for money if he couldn't sell the horses? The winter sky was a pale blue that sat too high above the hills to give him any answers.

Ryder wanted him to go to town today to pick up some more banana-strawberry Jell-O, for chrissakes, one of the few things he was finding easy to eat. Ty figured he should make a list of things he'd need for immediate repairs around the place and see if he could get someone out to help spell Dakota in the house. He'd stop by and see his mother too. Maybe she'd come up with one of her Christian buddies. And he'd run into Harney Rivers. Maybe today was the day. The thought gave him a little lift as he walked back to the house until he remembered that being in town meant the sheriff could just as easily cart him off to jail.

Inside, Dakota was finishing the oatmeal she'd made for breakfast and talking to the old man, who insisted on carting that oxygen everywhere he went, though Ty couldn't see the point. Ryder was breathing okay, about the same as before, as far as he could tell. When he entered the kitchen, his father's expression made him feel like an intruder. He poured himself a cup of coffee and sat down at the table anyway. Screw you, old man, he thought. Dakota looked at him quickly over a spoon of oatmeal, then looked away. They were sleeping together, or trying to in his narrow little bed. But when he'd woken up at dawn this morning and found her in Ronnie's bed, he had picked her up and taken her to his sister's room. He couldn't fall back to sleep after that, so he'd gotten up and done chores early, making sure the coffee was ready before the old man showed up in the kitchen. It made him feel good in a small, mean way to beat his father up in the morning. Like it put him more in charge or something.

"I need to pick up some things at the hardware and feed mill. Looks like nothing's been done around here in a long time. Least I can fix some fences and work on the machinery and barns. I'll do the outside work while the weather holds. How's this roof?"

His father shrugged and reached for the pencil he was always using to write stuff on the long yellow legal pad. "That valley by the dormer over the big bedroom's leaking again." Ryder had started referring to his bedroom that way after it became obvious his wife wasn't coming home again. Before that it had been "our room."

Ty nodded. "I'll get up there soon's I get back from town. The ladder in the shed?"

"Should be. Try tar this time."

Ty stared at him. "How am I supposed to get tar to stick in this weather?"

Ryder shook his head. "You never were much good on a roof."

"You wanna give it a try?"

Dakota dropped her spoon in her oatmeal and pushed her chair back with a flourish. "I made a list of groceries and cleaning stuff—"

"You still running charges in town?" Ty stood, trying not to let his father see that asking this was costing him.

Ryder lifted his hand. "Fetch the checkbook from the dining table—"

"They're not going to take your checks from me—they don't know who the hell I am."

"They'll know from looking at you. Those that don't, they're used to the hired man coming in with checks. Closed all those charge accounts to stop the son of a bitch two years ago from charging up his family goods on me. Gave the man a place to live, that trailer the other side of the barn, he brings in some woman with three kids aren't even his, and he expects me to pay for them. Booted his behind, let me tell you, soon's I got that two-hundred-dollar grocery bill. Never spent two hundred dollars on food in a month in my life—" His face flushed as he struggled for breath.

"Believe that," Ty muttered and pushed the stacks of papers on the dining table around, looking for the checkbook. What was all this shit? Several of the bills on top had OVERDUE! stamped in red ink across them. Pulling out the large bound checkbook, he quickly thumbed the pages until he found the latest balance and last checks written. Only a thousand dollars left? He should have a lot more in there than that. For the first time, Ty felt worried.

"What is all that in there? Aren't you paying bills anymore?" He slapped the checkbook down on the table.

"That's none of your damn business." He tried to sound angry, but his voice was muffled. What the hell was he hiding?

"Did you ship anything at all last year?"

The head bent over the checkbook shook once. The shaking hand picked up the pencil.

"Here—" Dakota handed him a pen to write with and frowned at Ty.

"You have no money left, do you?"

The hand paused over the amount of the check. His father looked up. "In savings."

"Anything invested?"

Ryder shrugged.

"We have to ship next week. I'll have to find help and we'll cull

234   ∞   JONIS AGEE

and ship. You have to have operating money, Ryder. You're in the cattle business, you can't just keep the cows." Ty stuck his hands in his jeans back pockets and looked at Dakota. "How much do you owe?"

The old man shook his head again.

"How'd you get that satellite and TV, then?"

"Credit cards. They keep sending 'em to me, figured what the hell, I'm dying anyways, why not use 'em." Ryder signed his name, leaving the amount blank on four checks, and tore them out.

"You never used credit cards in your life." Ty couldn't keep the bitterness from his tone, remembering the things they'd done without because his father wouldn't buy on credit.

"Had your mother to take care of, Ty. And you kids. Couldn't afford a lot of debt piling up against me." He pushed his hand through his thick hair, not so yellow now that Dakota had helped him clean up at the kitchen sink. "She hasn't asked for it, but I owe her. She came to this marriage with nothing, but I'm not going to let her out without something. A man doesn't do that to a woman."

"So you're still giving her money?" Hopelessness was making his arms and legs weak. His father had dug a pit and dropped his entire life in it.

"I signed things over to her a couple of years ago so she'd be taken care of without having to come to me all the time. Lucky I did too." He closed the checkbook and flattened his big hand on it, the knuckles swollen and humped with arthritis, the long horny fingernails coming to points.

"Fine. You're going to lose this place if you don't do something, you know." Ty picked up the checks, folded them, and put them in his shirt pocket.

"And what does that have to do with you?" Ryder's voice was a stone that dropped through the conversation.

Ty wanted to say that he didn't care, he didn't give a good goddamn. But he couldn't, any more than he could explain that it was all those years of his life working there, keeping the place going, and that he couldn't just see it go away now, and take that time away with it. What did anything mean if that could happen so easily.

"Ronnie died here. Hell, he died because of this place. So you're not going to throw it away now. I won't let you. We're shipping cattle. Period. And tonight, we're going through every goddamn piece of paper in there to figure out what you owe and what it will take to keep going. You're not going to sit in front of that TV and die until every last goddamn thing is done." Ty grabbed his coat and hat and yanked the door open before anyone could say anything else. He was in the truck starting the engine when Dakota knocked on the window with the list he'd forgotten.

"You're killing him, Ty, you've got to stop," she said. "Please?"

"Leave me alone, will you?" He picked up the sunglasses on the seat next to him and put them on.

"I can't stand to see you this way—" She hugged her arms around her chest and looked across the truck hood at the house.

"Nobody's asking you to stand anything. But he's my father, and I'll handle him. You don't know what a real bastard he is, and now this self-indulgent shit he's pulling with the money and ranch—I put my whole life into this place. Ronnie too, and he's flushing it down the toilet like it was pure crap—" He paused and gripped the steering wheel so hard it creaked as if it were about to snap. "I don't mean to put you in the middle. I know you're just trying to help out—"

She put her hand on his arm, and leaned in and kissed his cheek. "Just be careful in town."

He shifted and stepped on the gas, accidentally spraying muddy water on her jeans as he drove off, stopped, and backed up. "Nice—" She smiled ruefully and brushed at the water. He laughed and spun out again; this time the water sprayed higher.

Dakota was brushing Ty's big gray horse when the home-nursing car pulled up in the yard. Together they went in the house and found Ryder dozing in his recliner while Winston Cup cars raced silently around a track and scores from all the games the night before ran in blue and white along the bottom of the screen.

"He'll wake up in a minute," Dakota whispered. "Let's get some coffee."

"Doctor Wilkes said you were taking care of him, and I should show you how to do everything," the woman announced. She was a short, round woman with a small, pretty face that made the extra flesh seem sweet, succulent, rather than gross. With delicate hands and feet, she was the surprising kind of woman people stared at and ended up smiling with when she looked at them.

"Verna Stromme." The woman held out her hand and they shook awkwardly over the cups. "Well, this sure is a pretty place." She glanced around at the kitchen walls streaked with grease.

"Isolated," Dakota said.

"I'll say. My brother-in-law ranches right on the Niobrara outside Babylon. His place isn't so far away. I could see that distance maybe, I tell my husband. He wants to rent a place. But I have my career, I have to be close to town—"

They both looked out the window at the gray Plymouth with its white magnetic plastic sign whose bold black letters advertising HOME CARE, INC., attached to the driver's door.

"You and that Ty engaged, then?" she asked, looking out of the corner of her eyes at Dakota.

"I'm just visiting."

"Oh sure, well, Dr. Wilkes said this wasn't going to be a very long job. I mean—" She blushed and sipped at the edge of her coffee mug like it was a fine porcelain cup.

"It's all right. Do you know Mrs. Bonte or the daughter, what's her name?" Dakota figured this gossip business could go both ways.

"Well sure, I went to school with Charla, and Mrs. Bonte lives two doors down from my mother. Ty, well, I only saw him once in a while before he got in trouble. He stayed out here with his father and that poor little boy who died, Ronnie. Everyone blames those two—either the dad or the older brother for what happened. It was a real shame. I don't think Mrs. Bonte ever came out here after that. I'd see Ty in town once in a while, and later when he started hanging out with that Harney Rivers. Well, that is a story." Her little blue eyes sparked as her words tumbled out.

Dakota felt a straight pin catch in her throat at the mention of Harney Rivers. "What story is that?"

Verna looked quickly at the doorway to the kitchen. "I shouldn't really be saying this—but Harney Rivers said that Ty got drunk and stabbed an Indian. Ty ran away that same night. Only seventeen years old." Verna looked at the table, her cheeks flushed pink.

"Did the Indian die?"

"Oh, he's dead now. On the Reservation. Took him long enough. Used to stagger around the streets all hours of the day and night, drunk as a skunk. Stinking to high heaven too. Half the time I had to cross the street to avoid him. No loss there, let me tell you. But they never proved Harney did anything, and he said Ty was the one with the knife. That girl, Donna Allen, testified, but she didn't see anything but a pool of blood in the snow, and the knife she claimed Harney gave her never showed up. I were Donna, I would've left town a long time ago, the way people feel around here. But she stayed. I don't know. Ty ran away and they issued a warrant for his arrest. Now he's back. He must've worked something out with the sheriff now that the Indian is dead. Harney left right after Ty, of course. Then his poor father died, owned the bank? Now Harney's back, running the bank and taking care of his mother and two sisters. Bought himself a ranch west of town, bid against that Ted Turner and Jane Fonda for it. They'd just put more buffalo on it, knowing them. They already own two huge chunks of the Sandhills full of buffalo. Buffalo, can you imagine? What for? I ask my husband. You see the kind of diseases they spread out in Yellowstone, making cows abort. It would wreck this economy if those buffalo ever got loose, I tell my husband. Someone should do something."

Dakota shook her head.

"Where's that Ty been all these years?" Verna reached for the plate of oatmeal cookies Dakota had baked.

"Kansas. He trains and sells horses on a place he owns down there." She was making it sound better than it was, but figured Ty could probably use the PR. God knows he could use something these days.

"Is that how you met?" Verna smiled and chewed, her pink bowed lips carefully pressed together.

"I train and show horses too." Dakota liked the sound of it even if it wasn't exactly true. She wasn't going to let Verna tell the world that Ty Bonte was shacked up with a homeless woman who mucked stalls for a living.

"I'm not paying for the gossip too, am I?" Ryder's voice jerked both their heads toward the doorway as he came shuffling through. Dakota wondered how long he'd been standing there.

"Mr. Bonte, I'm—" Verna stood and held out her small pink hand.

"I know who you are. Knew your mother before you were born. How's that husband of yours doing? Still looking for a place to rent?" Ryder eased himself into a chair and patted his chest as if to encourage it.

"Gene's fine. He'd like to move out, but it's so far—"

"Tried to give him a job here couple a times, but he's working too hard pleasing you, Verna. Now what's this visit all about?"

For the next hour, Verna instructed them both on the various medications they would be using, the breathing treatments with the special wide tube that would administer the drug into the mouth, the schedule and billing information for Medicare.

After Verna left, Ryder pushed the forms away. "Not going on the dole."

"It's not welfare." Dakota picked up the papers and stacked them carefully. If Ty was good to his word, they'd need them tonight.

"Man should be able to pay for his dying, same as his living." He got up and went back to the study.

She sat at the kitchen table, eating a cookie and trying to figure out what she was going to do here. Eddie had told them that Harney had ordered her horse to be killed, but things had been in such a crisis since they'd gotten here she hadn't had time or energy to sit down with Ty and make a plan. Every day that passed seem to push them deeper into these silent, lonely hills. Ryder would be in real trouble if she left. God, she missed Bobby so much. That terrible, helpless feeling made her head feel disconnected from her body, and for a moment she didn't know whether she'd be able to command her arm to lift again, her legs to move. This must be what it feels like to be paralyzed—you think something, but it doesn't result in anything happening. For the first time she admitted that her horse was really dead. It sealed her breath shut for a moment, and her chest jerked from the hammer blow of grief. After letting the tears silently slide out for a while, she got up, washed her face, and sat down with the dish towel in her fists.

Harney Rivers. The man who tried to kill Ty had tried murder before. Either he was an incredible fuck-up or he had bad luck. *Disorganized thinking*, her mother called it, what made criminals screw up their crimes. But maybe Harney had been successful other times nobody knew about. And he'd called to make sure her horse was gone after he found out Ty was alive. He knew they'd be coming out here then. As soon as Harney found out Ty was out here, he'd have to try again, wouldn't he? They were so dumb, of course he would.

Ryder laughed for the first time in days when she asked him about the guns. "That Verna set you off?" he asked and flipped the remote to the home shopping channel. "Christmas shopping," he said.

Dakota didn't have the nerve to tell him not to use his credit cards again or Ty would go through the ceiling.

"Rifles I keep there in the cabinet, loaded. When the kids were young, I kept them unloaded, but after they all left, figured what the hell, only accidental shooting there'll be is myself or some trespasser. Pistol though—where'd that thing get to?" He looked around the room, paneled in old knotty pine turned maple syrup golden brown with age. One wall held a large bookcase reaching almost to the ceiling, and along the others were the gun cabinets and pictures of men with dead animals, and children.

Her eye caught on a framed newspaper clipping. Ryder's eyes followed hers. "Bring that over here."

It sat between two photos of the boys, one where they were dressed in their best clothes, scowling in stiff poses side by side against the house. From the budding bush next to them, she guessed it was their Easter Sunday outfits. The other photo was the boys in swimming trunks, cowboy boots, and hats, laughing and pointing at something behind the picture taker. Ty was already pole lean and wide-shouldered at thirteen or fourteen and his brother was the opposite, small, tiny really. And they both looked so happy, she thought as she examined the picture. Both had those chins and cheekbones, and wide mouths, big dark eyes. Rugged good looks. But Ronnie had lighter skin and hair, as if he were a paler, diminished version of his older brother. She could tell that in the next minute the younger boy, with admiration in his eyes, would look over at his brother, having to cant his head slightly up and back. And Ty would do something a brother would do—tousle Ronnie's hair or throw an arm around his neck. What broke her heart, though, was the openness in Ty's eyes, the pure future that lay before him at that moment, about to disappear forever. Maybe he'd never see the world that way again, she had to admit. Maybe none of them would.

She took down the framed clipping and handed it to Ryder.

He looked at the grainy picture of the figure on the bucking horse for a few minutes before he spoke. "I told Ty not to enter that saddle bronc competition. Cherry County Rodeo was drawing some big names. Stock contractor had brought in some real rough horses. He was only a kid, what fourteen, fifteen years old, and I couldn't afford to have him laid up. So I told him no and didn't think a thing more about it. Not till he turned up missing at evening chores. Rode his horse twelve miles to the highway and hitched into town. Third time he'd done it too. I was—well, I was drinking some then, so I didn't miss him till the third day. Guess he got a ride back every night and up in time for chores. He was a tough son of a gun. But I figured it out and drove on into town myself. Sober enough to track him down and give him a whaling right there behind the barns. Figured that was that, and went on into the Buckboard. Damn if he didn't go right back and enter hisself and win the day money and that danged saddle. Don't know how he sat that bronc after the whipping I gave him. I was not an easy man in my drinking days, I have to admit. But he had his cry and went out and showed me. Rode that saddle around here like a lord. Wouldn't speak to me for a month neither. Then left it when he took off that last time. Showed me all right."

Staring hard at the TV, Ryder's eyes filled and his breathing came in short gasps. But he waved her off when she put a hand on his shoulder.

"He's forgiven you by now," she whispered.

"No ma'am, he has not. He's stubborn as they come. I should know. Tried to beat it out of him too, but he's just like me. He never forgets and he never forgives. And it'll kill him sure as it's killing me."

Dakota stood there for a minute, unclear what she should do or say. Then he waved his hand at the doorway and she left. She wanted to ask him about Harney Rivers, about the warrant and assault. Why hadn't Ty told her that coming back here meant he could end up in jail? She had to find the pistol. Maybe in the cabinets under the rifles. She'd look next time she could. Maybe upstairs in his old bedroom. She had already been in there a few times getting clean clothes and bedding for Ryder. She and Ty should move that spare single bed from his room downstairs.

Meanwhile, she had to get out of this crazy house for a while. No wonder Mrs. Bonte stayed away. These men would drive *her* to drink. She'd go out and ride the gray around. He was sensible enough to take down the road and back even on a warm winter day when every rabbit and bird in the state would be out figuring ways to get her dumped off. She grabbed her coat and stopped. Should she tell Ryder where she was going? She wasn't really his nurse or keeper, and he was certainly used to being alone. Like Ty. She had to wonder about those two, living a state away, both of them isolated in the middle of nowhere. What terrible things happen to people to make them like this? She always liked being with another person, even Ty and Ryder were a relief from having no one to talk to. Her mother too. That's why Dakota would sit there beside her, both of them reading a whole evening away, just to have another heart beat near, just to share the air they were breathing. You were alone so much in yourself anyway, you sure didn't need to make that space around yourself any bigger than it already was.

Chapter Nineteen

She was almost to the place where the cows had broken through the fence when she saw three riders coming toward her. As they approached, she recognized Cody Kidwell carrying a rifle across his saddle. The other two riders were a forty-something woman on a big, heavy brown horse and an older man who looked Native American, with two gray braids hanging down his chest. On the saddle in front of him rode a small, dark-haired girl with that same beautifully shaped mouth she'd noticed on Cody the other day.

"You must be Dakota, Ty's friend; I'm Latta Jaboy." The woman smiled and nodded toward the older man and child. "That's Caddy, our little girl, and Joseph Starr, her godfather."

"Seen any deer or coyotes?" Cody asked, and Dakota again noticed those light changing eyes that made her feel like they were asking her closer, but she'd better be careful, they didn't know everything they could do to her.

She shook her head. He *was* pretty. She glanced at Latta, who was chattering and waving to her daughter. Best keep this one on short feed, she wanted to advise, but then Cody looked at his daughter and wife, and those lips widened into a smile and she could see he was definitely safely in love. She wondered if people saw the same expression on her face or Ty's.

"We're following a yearling deer with a broken leg we saw feeding with a herd at dusk over at our place," Cody explained.

His neat paint horse snorted and stamped a white front foot impatiently. Cody lifted the reins and resettled them on the horse's neck.

"You're welcome to look here. This pasture's empty now we moved the cattle down by the house. But Ryder—Mr. Bonte—told Ty there was a coyote hanging around the stack yard."

"How's Ryder? Doc Wilkes told us he's pretty bad off when we had Caddy in for a sore throat the first of the week," Latta asked.

Dakota nudged the gray away from Cody, closer to the older man and child. "He's not doing too well. Going downhill pretty fast. Emphysema." She wiggled her fingers at the little girl, who smiled shyly and ducked her head under the older man's arm. He hugged her against his chest and looked at her quickly, then away.

"Anything we can do?" Latta asked. "I told Cody we weren't going to send the bill for grazing on those cattle busted the fence." She looked over Dakota's head at her husband. "Ryder Bonte's been a hard man all his life, but I don't want to fight him down to his last breath." She looked back at Dakota. "How's Ty taking it?"

Dakota wanted to say that he was as bad as his father these days. "He's trying to get the ranch back on its feet."

An odd expression flickered across Latta's face. "I thought things had to be going poorly this fall when he hadn't shipped anything in over a year. Ty need any help?"

Dakota shrugged—of course he did, but would he take it? "You should ask him. I'm trying not to—well, he's running that end of things. I'm just—visiting—"

Cody's horse swung his haunches and tried to turn toward home but stopped sideways, facing Dakota's gray.

"What kind of horse is that?" Joseph Starr spoke for the first time and the little girl pulled her head out.

"Thoroughbred off the track. He's a nice old guy, aren't you?" She patted his neck and the ears flicked back and forth. "Belongs to Ty. He trains and sells horses."

Latta raised her eyebrows. "Ty should come and look at some of my horses, then. I have an imported Irish stallion. This is one of his daughters I'm riding. Cross-bred."

"Yeah? I love Irish horses. They make great jumpers." Dakota felt a twinge of jealousy.

Cody's horse inched forward to nose her gray's neck. The gray snorted and reached around with his ears flat. She pushed at the paint with her hand while Cody just watched.

Latta asked, "When do you want to come?"

"I'll have to ask Ty. When would be good?"

"The weekend maybe. I'll call—we'll have lunch if you're not too busy. Joseph's here for the holidays. And Cody's sister might be coming in too. Never know with her though—" She glanced over at her husband again. "You'll be home, won't you, Cody?"

He shrugged and dropped his gaze to the rifle, then legged the paint away.

"Sounds great. Just call us—" She hoped she didn't seem too hungry; Joseph Starr was watching her closely, although he was pretending he wasn't. He should try being locked up with those two Bonte men for days on end.

"You're welcome to ride along with us now if you want—that way if Cody gets a shot, you'll be in safe range." Latta moved her horse forward and when Dakota turned to follow, the gray sniffed the paint's tail and tried to rest his chin on its haunches. The paint squealed and gave a half-hearted kick.

"Cody's going to need all the room he can get too." Joseph smiled at the other man. "Packs an extra box of shells to kill a rabbit these days."

Cody shook his head and started searching the ground for tracks.

"Can't get anyone to help with the cattle till after the new year. Nobody's interested in shipping till then either. We're stuck for now, I guess." Ty kicked another bale off the back of the truck while Dakota cut the strings and spread the flakes in a long line for the pastured horses. It was almost dark and the animals moved up slowly like big purple-brown shadows in the cold. She scooped coffee cans of corn out of the burlap bag and spilled them out beside each pile of hay. Her fingers were cold from holding the metal, and the knobs of corn rattled like pieces of ice. She wondered if it bothered the horses picking corn in the manure-strewn field. They're lucky to get grain, Ty had told her when she'd wanted to stall the horses in shifts for feeding. The gray was at the bottom of the pecking order though, below even the youngest horses, so she tried to separate his pile several yards away from the others. At least he'd get a chance to grab a few mouthfuls before someone came over and drove him off. She'd have to start feeding him secretly in the barn. The old Ty would've recognized the problem and taken care of it, but he was too preoccupied with the ranch now.

"Went to the bank today—" he said when she climbed in the pickup beside him to warm her hands in the hot blowing air of the vents. He stared out the windshield at the headlights cutting two dim trails into the dark.

"They turned us down for a loan against the cattle. I went in, talked to them, ran some errands, and came back thinking they'd have it all ready. Turned us down flat after all those years of doing business. Makes me wonder what Ryder's been up to that nobody wants to help him." Ty lifted his gimme cap and rubbed the back of his head. When he resettled the cap, a piece of hair was sticking out the hole in back. Dakota was tempted to tuck it back under for him.

"Harney's taken over running the bank."

He turned sharply toward her. "What?"

"The home-care woman, Verna Stromme? She told me this afternoon that Harney's dad died and he's running the bank now. That's why you couldn't get a loan. Ty, what's going on with you two? Verna said some things—"

Ty looked out his window into the dark, but she could see a dim reflection of his worried face in the glass. "Like what?"

"Something about Harney being arrested for stabbing an Indian, and a girl named Donna testifying against him but everyone around here sounds like they believed him, not her. He said you did it. You didn't—"

Ty shook his head slowly. "Harney and I just don't get along. Never did unless we were getting high."

"Verna said there's an outstanding warrant for your arrest."

"What does that old bag know? You stay here long enough, you're going to hear a bunch of crap about everyone—you just need to mind your own business."

"Okay, sure—that's what I'll do. And let me tell you something else, it won't be you anymore!" She opened the truck door and slammed it as hard as she could. She was sick of being told to back off anything personal with him. Going back down the line of horses, she found the gray trying to nibble a few pieces of hay away from the pile she'd left for him, which was now being guarded by the buckskin Ty worked cattle with.

"Go on, git—" She waved her arms at the buckskin, who lifted his head, stared at her, and dropped his head again. "All right." She went to the gray, pulled her scarf through his halter for a lead, and started for the gate.

Ty had stopped the truck just on the other side and was getting out to close the fence. "What are you doing now?"

"Just stay out of my way." She led the gray through.

"That's my horse." He fastened the gate while she stood thinking about it.

"You don't deserve a horse this nice. You're being such a complete asshole you don't even care what happens to him or me or anyone but yourself anymore. If you want to know, he's starving out there. He's not tough enough to get food from those others. In the old days, you would've paid attention to him. Now you're being a hardass just like that old man you hate—and frankly, I don't see any difference between the two of you." She started the horse toward the distant blurry lights of the barn. What was she doing out here? Nobody wanted her around. She stopped and leaned her head against the horse's warm neck while the tears started down her face. The horse bent his head around and cupped her body with his neck, nuzzling her back.

The sound of the truck rumbled past and disappeared, the silence in its wake broken only by the sound of the horses chewing behind her. She felt safe in the warm, musty horsehair, maybe as safe as she'd ever felt with horses. They didn't fill the longing she had to be wrapped up in another person's heart, but they were the next thing to it. They let her put her arms around something living, reach out beyond herself. And the ones she'd loved had loved her back. Hardly ever disappointed her. Suddenly she didn't want to go back there, she didn't want to go anywhere. If she could, she'd stand here with this horse until the temperature dropped and she froze to death. Maybe that'd be okay, because she didn't want to go back to that house, to that fighting and loneliness she'd felt her whole life, the same loneliness that drove her to men who were alone too. It could never work, she could see that now. People were always alone for a reason, and while she could see it in other people's lives, she didn't have a clue about her own. She'd figured leaving Divinity she'd naturally find the answer. Now she saw the truth: There wasn't one. She ended up here on this ranch in the middle of this grassy desert for a reason. She was doomed just like these people. The idea made her sob harder, while the horse reached down to nose at a clump of grass poking up through a patch of snow.

She didn't hear Ty walking back until he put his hand on the back of her neck and pulled her into his arms. She cried harder against the heavy canvas of his coat, which refused to let the tears soak in, sent them instead trickling off her chin into the open neck of her shirt and down her wrists.

"You're right," he murmured, "I'm sorry. I've been a bastard, please don't cry—please?" He rubbed her back and pressed her tightly against him, and she felt small and broken in his hands, but unsure that he could put her back together.

In a few minutes, she pulled away from him and wiped her face on her coat sleeve. But she couldn't look at his face.

He wiped a wet spot on her cheek with his thumb, and as he rested a hand on her shoulder, she could feel him trying to get her to raise her eyes. "Dakota? Just hit me or something if it'd make things better—"

"I'm not your father." She heard the harsh truth of the words the minute she'd said them, but it was too late.

He dropped his hand and sighed. "I know that."

There was such a weight of sadness in his voice she put a hand on his arm, remembering the story Ryder had told her earlier. She couldn't explain to either man how they were hurting each other, how they were defeating each other.

"If you want me to leave—"

"I couldn't stand that, couldn't stay here without you. I know how awful it is, but please don't go. I'll try harder, I will. I won't let him get to me. I'll be more like—I don't know, whoever I was before—" He put his hand over hers and hugged his arm against his body.

"Just stop taking it out on me, that's all I want. I know things were bad, maybe terrible, in the past with your father. He's even told me some of it—but he's in real trouble, Ty, and he's still your father. It makes you less to treat him badly, don't you see?"

"What did he say?" He took a deep breath and let it out. "Never mind. Just don't leave. Whatever I have to do, tell me, but don't leave, okay?" He shivered and pulled her close and kissed the top of her head.

She put her arms around him, rocking with him until the horse gave a tug on the scarf, trying to reach for another clump of grass.

That night they went through the stacks of paper on the dining-room table while the old man sat in his recliner, turning the TV up louder and louder to cover the groans and curses from his son. Dakota sat in front of the calculator, running the figures and cringing at the news she was giving Ty.

At eleven they gathered the papers into piles, consulted the tablet with the final numbers, and went to present them to Ryder. At first there was denial, then silence.

"Giving Mother the money meant mortgaging the ranch, which meant you had very tight margins on the cattle and absolutely had to meet the yearly production estimates. You haven't. Plus the drop in cattle prices means you're in the hole, and it's only getting deeper." Ty paused and drank some coffee while Ryder stared at the TV with narrowed eyes and lips, jaw muscles working against themselves. Dakota was scared he was going to start having one of those breathing attacks Verna had described and wanted to go fix the medication, but didn't dare leave these two alone. Ty was trying to keep his voice neutral and calm, she had to give him that.

"We have to think bankruptcy, or at least restructuring the debt and refinancing the whole operation. You're only a couple of months from bottom. I stopped at the bank today to see about borrowing against the cattle. They turned us down. I—"

"What gave you the right to do that?" Ryder said bitterly.

Ty sighed. "We're not getting into that again."

"I had a perfectly good relationship with that bank for over forty years. You go in there and suddenly I got no credit?" The old man's voice broke into a hoarse whisper as he gasped for air and pulled the oxygen tube dangling from the tank next to the chair up to his nose.

"Harney's running the bank now, Ryder. Things have changed." Ty picked up the stack of papers off the floor beside the chair.

"Thought he was your friend, your big drinking buddy." Ryder's voice had a mean, icy edge that made Dakota remember what Ty had been saying about his father.

"No, not after—look, we could try a North Platte bank, or one in Ainsworth maybe, but I think the answer's going to be the same. You have to face facts. We're out of money and could lose the ranch." Ty stood.

"We? Since when did you ever—"

"I'm going to see the lawyer tomorrow, Ryder. We're bleeding to death here, and I'm going to stop it." He walked carefully around the big oxygen tank standing guard by the chair, and left the room.

"You're not doing anything without my say-so—" Ryder half-rose in his chair, yelling at his son's retreating back.

"Get away from me—" The old man struck out at Dakota's hands trying to soothe him.

Later upstairs in bed, they lay on their sides in each other's arms as if they were waiting for something. When she told him about meeting Cody and Latta and the invitation, she couldn't remember the Indian's name, so she just called him some "old guy."

"Can we go?" She ran her hand down the curves of his biceps, and tried to encase his wrist with her hand, but it was too wide. She loved his arms, she decided, and brushed her hand back up to his shoulder, feeling the scarred bumps from the pitchfork that reminded her of how brave he'd been. She could never not love this man.

"You wanna see Cody again?" He put his hand on her throat.

"Sure, why not? He's pretty cute."

"Latta would have something to say about it, I expect." He closed his fingers so she felt a little constriction swallowing.

"What about you?" She reached down for him.

"I'd probably have to kill you. But first, I'd do some other things—" He pressed his fingers into her neck and moved on top of her.

"You trust me?" he asked.

"Yes," she whispered and he kissed her until they were a tangle she wrapped herself in.

Afterwards, listening to TV sounds drifting around the house, up the stairs, and through the floors like gravelly smoke, she asked, hoping he was still awake, "You see your mother today?"

"For a minute. She was on her way to the grade school, where she's an aide. After that she had to go to the group home, where she works nights. Residence for mentally—what's it—handicapped or disabled, what they used to call retarded, I guess. High-functioning. They hold jobs. She's having fits with some kid works there, she told me. Didn't sound so bad to me, but what do I know."

"You talk to her about your father?"

"Yeah." He put his arm over his eyes. "She's been in touch with the doctor. It's not good, this sudden downswing. Nobody can figure out how he's survived this long with the lung capacity where it is. Too damn stubborn to die, I guess."

She counted to ten before she asked the next question. "She say anything more about that Indian who died?"

He was quiet for a few minutes, then he said, "What about him?"

"You know, the Indian she told you about the day we stopped there—"

"What're you getting at?"

"I don't know—you tell me—"

His breathing slowed and his voice got soft when he said, "I got involved in something I shouldn't have a long time ago. There's an assault warrant outstanding on it." He sighed and she waited in its silence. "Let's go to sleep. We have a lot of work to do tomorrow—maybe we can sit down and talk about it then."

"Nothing more? What about this warrant? And what we're going to do about Harney? If it's an insurance scam, we can—" He pulled her next to him, with her face pressed into his damp skin so she could hardly breathe.

She was quiet for a few minutes before she spoke again. "Verna asked me if we were, you know, engaged—"

She thought he'd fallen to sleep, but finally he said, "What'd you say?"

"That I was just visiting. Then she asked me what I did—how we met—so I told her I trained and showed horses too."

"Good answer." His voice was muffled in the pillow.

"Is it?"

He rolled on his back, almost dropping her off the narrow bed. "Dakota—"

She could hear the apology and explanation that was going to make her feel like shit, so she changed the subject. "We need to move this other bed downstairs for Ryder. His back is getting worse from sitting."

"That would be something—"

"What'd you mean?"

"That's Ronnie's bed—think he'd sleep good in that?" Ty's laugh didn't sound funny. She looked at his face with only the yard light giving outline to the room, but she couldn't tell his expression in the shadows.

"Is that why you moved me this morning?"

"We'll figure something out. Maybe Charla's bed can be taken apart. It's newer anyway. These beds came from Ryder's room when he was a boy. Mattresses must be fifty, sixty years old. Feel it?" He bounced and the springs squeaked.

"Is all this between you two about Ronnie, then?"

"I have to get some sleep, Dakota, and you should too. He'll run you ragged you're not careful."

"Like father, like son, huh?" She kissed his mouth and his arms went around her again.

Chapter Twenty

"No, I'm taking the gray." Dakota opened the stall door and led the horse out.

"We still have to sell him to raise some money, you know," Ty muttered and walked out the back of the barn with his rope and a bucket of corn to bring the horses up.

"We'll see about that," she crooned and gave the gray an apple she'd snuck out of the kitchen. The horse crunched happily and nudged the pocket of her coat for more when he was done. She laughed. "Smart one, huh?" He lifted his head and curled his lips. "Think I'll name you Noah. You're definitely a survivor."

They took the back way across the pastures to get to Jaboy's land, where the wire was still down and would be until spring, when they'd start mending fences and getting ready for the herds again. It was a lot faster to go that way than drive, Cody had explained. On the other side of the huge Jaboy spread was the even larger Bennett ranch, left in equal parts to the three siblings, Arthur, Cody, and Kya. There'd been a real stink about that, according to Ryder at breakfast, when old Heywood had left his two bastard children equal shares.

"Not so bad with Kya who was pretty much raised with Arthur. But that Cody, he was a secret weapon Heywood kept to himself until the kid got in so much trouble his crazy mother couldn't handle him anymore and he had to be brought to the ranch to earn his keep. Wasn't until after the old man died anyone found out the real truth. Old Heywood had himself a batch of wives and youngsters. Indians and white women, he wasn't discriminating in that department. Man liked women. That young whelp Cody has his daddy's taste for it too. Latta Jaboy'll be lucky he stays to see that youngster of theirs grow up without he's added to the family on the side or worse."

Ryder had had a coughing, choking spell then that required a breathing treatment half an hour earlier than planned, which left him exhausted and gray afterwards. It was with some reluctance that Dakota had ridden off and left him midmorning, but Verna Stromme, the nurse, was due back sometime in the early afternoon, and he'd insisted he was fine.

She pushed the gray into a trot to catch up with the long legged chestnut colt Ty was riding. The colt shied as they came alongside and humped its back like it might consider bucking. Ty thumped its sides and gave a little tug on the reins to keep the head up. The colt arched its neck and jigged into a slow prancy trot. "Got a bug up his butt today," Ty said.

"Feels good, all this space on a nice sunny day. Noah does too." She had to nudge the gray to make him keep up. His inclination in life was to slow down and take in the scenery.

"Named him, I see." Ty glanced at the gray. "S'pose we should name Red here."

"What? Red? Or maybe Ruddy?"

He smiled and the horse's ears flicked back and forth.

"Weather could turn before we make it back. Look over there—" He pointed west to the low heads of clouds collecting along the line of purple-blue horizon like cauliflowers on a table.

She took a deep breath. "Ty, your dad didn't look good this morning. I don't think he's sleeping at all."

He looked south across the hills, and she wondered for a moment if she should repeat herself, but finally he said, "No reason he should sleep. He's got plenty to think about." Ty let the chestnut out into a jarring, ground eating lope, and she followed appreciating Noah's easy rocking chair canter that didn't cover as much, but was comfortable to ride. The chestnut went up a notch into a gallop, and she could see how Ty's hips picked up the motion while his torso and legs stayed still, the fringe on his worn tan chaps rhythmically rising and falling.

After the snow melt, the scattered grasses had tinges of green and mauve and pale yellow, and the soapweed pods shook on their tall stalks like small angry fists. On the way home, she'd collect some dried weeds and the pods for an arrangement. She'd always liked the skeletal forms of winter, the way everything was revealed in some truer essence after all the noisy clutter of summer. The light was purer now, the air too. She took some deep breaths and Noah snorted as if he agreed. She patted his neck, and with a sour rush in her stomach missed Bobby again.

Ty stopped the chestnut who was blowing from its run, foam dripping from the bit, sides heaving as she pulled alongside. "There's something else you don't understand here, Dakota. You're trying to deal with Ryder, with the two of us, as if we're like other people, but we're not. Believe me, Ryder has only one thing on his mind: Ryder. He's a selfish prick. Drank himself half to death a dozen times, drove his wife and kids away and it didn't faze him in the least. Used to claim there was no such thing as alcoholism. Didn't believe in it, he'd say, like we were talking about life on Mars or something. Best thing a person can do around Ryder Bonte is try not to let yourself get too close to him." Ty patted the chestnut whose breathing was slowing. "He's not just a hard man, he's a mean one."

It was on the tip of her tongue to ask about Ronnie. She knew that was the biggest thing between them. The sister, Charla, and the mother, they didn't seem particular points of pain and resentment, well, maybe the mother, but that was another whole issue. The little brother Ronnie, that was the point, and she had no idea how to get to it with either man.

"All right, I'll be careful around your father. Try not to take sides again. But what are we going to do, Ty? We have to do something about Harney pretty soon. If we wait too long, he'll have his tracks covered."

He glanced at her quickly, lifted his cowboy hat and resettled it.

His ears in the cold were bright red, but she knew he didn't want to hear about it. "I'm on borrowed time here. Soon as the sheriff gets around to it, I'm probably going to jail on that old warrant. I don't know why he's held off as long as he has. If I could get one day away from this business with the ranch and my father, I'd—"

She felt panic squeeze her chest in its tight fist. "No, come on— we have to get out of here then. It's not worth it—let him go. God, I don't want you to go to jail. Can't we just go back to your place in Kansas, go back to the way it was before or something?" She pressed Noah closer and put her hand on his arm. He tensed the muscle in response.

"It's gone too far, you know that. And what about your horse?"

The breeze blew warm from the south, but there was cold blurring its edge. "I don't know—" She said it quickly because she didn't want to hear the choice between the two things she loved said out loud. "And what about Ryder, can't just leave him and go to jail— you have to ship cattle after the first like you said or he'll—"

He looked at her, narrowing his dark eyes, raising his eyebrows and setting his jaw. "My whole life he told me to leave him alone, it was none of my business what he was doing. I don't see any reason to change that now. He's always been killing himself with liquor and hard living, it's just happening faster now. He'll tell you himself, Dakota, what he always told me: 'you live by the sword, you die by the sword.' Believe me, he doesn't want me here pitying him any-more than I want to be here." He looked around at the ragged hills, as if seeing them for the last time.

There was a final note in his words that made her feel like this was hopeless, and she hated the way that settled down on her, gray-ing the day a little. Wasn't anybody happy in their lives? She'd run away from Divinity, Iowa, to find something, maybe a world where there was less of this damn depressing shit. Where people loved each other without all this tangle of gooey strings as if they were caught in multiple spider webs. That's what she'd dreamed last night in Ty's arms, that she had walked into an old roofless barn that was really just rafters and posts and broken gray boards and before she knew it, she was fighting her way through a maze of webs with big spiders the size of fifty-cent pieces rushing toward her. It wasn't so much their biting she was afraid of, she didn't want them on her and she could already feel them skittering up her arms. She shivered at the memory, how she'd yelled for help but nobody came.

"You grew up." Latta laughed when Ty dismounted. He smiled awkwardly like a kid for a moment until she reached out and shook his hand.

"So did you," he mumbled.

Cody stood back a little and nodded at them. Dakota noticed that again he seemed distracted, only half-willing to be a part of the scene while Latta chattered away at Ty. As Latta showed them around, Dakota noticed the enormous differences between the two ranches. The stable was neat enough to meet even Eddie's standards for show horses; the metal pole fencing of the paddocks wore fresh white paint. The Irish stud's offspring were sometimes a little heavy in the body and had thick legs, but seemed to move nicely, she noticed. And there were a couple of three year olds that really took the eye, tall, almost regal, with good bone and slope to the shoulder and when Cody waved his arms and clapped his hands, the two horses lifted into big floaty, daisy-cutting trots that would win any hunter hack class.

When Ty remarked on them, Cody's eyes lifted to look at him with new interest. Latta laughed and glanced out of the corner of her eye at Cody, but neither said anything as he quickly looked in her direction and frowned.

"Thoroughbred cross?" Dakota asked to dispel the tension between the couple.

"Not exactly—" Latta said. "A couple of mares Cody found, actually. We have a running argument about my stallion. We're thinking of branching out into another line. Course, with cattle prices down, we might have to wait a bit." She glanced again at Cody, who shook his head slightly and shifted away from her.

Dakota looked around at the rambling house, the neat white fences, and the nearly new pickup trucks and wondered what money problems they could possibly have. The two of them weren't dressed extravagantly though, they wore the same stained canvas, wool lined coats and lined rubber boots the Bonte men did. A lot different from the horse people she'd known in Minneapolis on the show circuit who dressed in designer clothes if they could afford it. The women even rode in their diamond earrings and necklaces. She glanced at Latta's rough, red hands. A thin gold band and chewed nails. No makeup either. The women she'd known would never think of showing up at the barn even for a lesson without makeup and their hair sprayed in place. Latta reminded her of an Iowa farm woman. And today Cody kept glancing away from his wife like he was holding a grudge. She thought of what Ryder had said at breakfast. She hated being in the middle of domestic silences like this.

"I better check on the horses." She turned for the stable.

"They're all right," Ty said.

"I'll go with her," she heard Cody say.

Great, she hadn't intended this. She walked quickly to the door and his hand reached for the knob as hers did. His fingers lingered for a moment. Was that intentional? They both dropped their hands, then grabbed for the knob again. This time she quickly let go and he opened the door. She felt the heat of his body outlining hers as they entered the dusky barn. Unlike Ty's place or his father's, this stable was built with horses in mind, and had a clean oaty smell. The venting fans in the roof kept the air sweet and fresh, and each stall was lighted by a barred window. The outside walls of the stalls were paneled in varnished knotty pine, and the aisle floor was brick laid in a herringbone pattern.

Cody scuffed his boot across the brick. "Pain in the neck, but Latta saw it in a magazine." He touched her shoulder and pointed to the smoke alarms and sprinkler system overhead. "These horses live better than most people."

Dakota thought there was resentment in his tone so she kept her mouth shut.

They walked down the long aisle, occasionally brushing arms, and she couldn't tell if that was intentional either. Unlike the Bonte's barn, this one was free of cobwebs and dust. Each stall was equipped with an automatic waterer and scrubbed feed bucket and was bedded with clean straw. Noah was lying down on his side, all four legs stretched out when they came to his stall, and he glanced up at them through half-closed lids as if to say leave me alone. The chestnut, right next to him, was down with legs folded under him like a camel. He ignored them for the space he was staring into.

"This one isn't bad-looking—" Cody offered.

"They're both hunter-jumper prospects. We look for a different conformation than you guys do—" She was defending the manure-stained gray she knew nobody thought much of. "The gray's okay when he gets cleaned up. There isn't much we can do about that over at Mr. Bonte's—"

Cody rested his hand next to hers so their little fingers were almost touching. She lifted her hand and put it in her pocket.

"That why Ty came back—the old man?" His voice was too quiet, and she wondered what he wanted.

"No, actually, he came back—" She couldn't help herself, she ran out of breath. "He came back to show me the Sandhills."

"Oh?" He didn't sound convinced.

"You know how Kansas is—" Lame, lame, lame, she thought.

"How long are you staying?" His voice was muffled as if he were speaking through layers of earth and rock.

"How long?" She shrugged and almost said until Ty could kill Harney Rivers; she didn't know where that came from. They always talked in terms of just confronting him.

"You ever get to town?"

"Why?"

"I could tell you some things about him."

"It's Harney Rivers I want to know about—"

"Sure, him too. Monday?"

It was two days away. She'd have time to plan.

"Buyers City parking lot. There's an empty store front on the far end, I'll be in a red pickup there. Noon."

She nodded. Maybe she could find a way to put Harney in jail, get revenge for Bobby, and stop Ty from going to jail all in one fell swoop. The idea lifted her, and she felt a surge of luck coming toward them. She was always better doing something than sitting around stewing about it. She could just imagine Ty's surprise when Harney was arrested.

The house was peculiar in that the outside wall of the well-used kitchen had a big bay window cut into it, while the other rooms seemed fairly dark and were filled with dark, expensive furniture. There were a lot of toys around for Caddy, who was playing in the small family room with a Mexican woman old enough to be her grandmother. Cody lifted the child and kissed her on the lips and spun her around to delighted laughter until Latta told him he was going to make her sick. He put the child down and frowned, but didn't say anything as he went back into the kitchen.

The lunch was good, hot chili and cornbread with salad and rice pudding, but unlike the day she'd met them in the pasture, there remained some kind of strain in the air between Cody and Latta. They spoke to each other only in formal, polite terms, and once they outright glared at each other. At least that was what Dakota interpreted it as, but she couldn't be certain. She hoped she could go meet him and find out enough to help her plan. Cody and Ty didn't even look at each other, let alone talk, she noticed. It was all Latta and Ty going on about something or another that happened way back when. By the time the pudding was served, they were down to small talk that dribbled into an awkward silence. When they heard a truck slamming to a stop outside the backyard gate, followed by thumping steps and loud voices as the door opened, all eyes jerked toward the kitchen.

The little girl jumped down from her chair and ran to meet the older man in gray braids Dakota had met the other day, and a tall woman looking something like Cody who finally smiled when he saw her.

While he was trying to stand, the woman grabbed Cody in a bear hug and lifted him off the floor. Latta's face flicked with annoyance she quickly replaced with a smile. The woman glanced around the table at the two guests and nodded, but her eyes were more guarded. "This is Kya Bennett, Cody's sister, and Joseph Starr," Latta said. "Ty Bonte and his friend Dakota—Carter?"

"Carlisle," Ty said and reached under the table for Dakota's hand. Kya looked Ty over carefully. "I know who you are."

Ty's face flushed and Dakota squeezed his hand.

Stooping to her niece, Kya swept her long brown-black hair off her face and lifted her. Dakota felt the old man's eyes studying her. What was wrong with him? She smiled at him and he nodded but didn't look away, so she had to, and found her eyes back on Kya. She was as tall as the two men, and like them, dressed in worn jeans and scuffed brown cowboy boots. Her body was strong and muscular with flesh. Her size made Dakota feel like a troll. She looked at Latta, but her face was set without an expression at all, except to warm slightly as Kya and the little girl exchanged multiple kisses on the lips. The two of them looked more alike than anyone in the room, and Dakota felt a tinge of pity for Latta, but she didn't know why. Maybe that was making a difference between Cody and Latta, or maybe it was something else. She saw Cody stiffen his body against his wife's hand touching his shoulder. Latta dropped her hand and began clearing the dishes. Dakota stacked some bowls and turned to follow her.

"Who are you?" Kya straightened with Caddy in her arms, blocking the doorway to the kitchen. The woman's hazel green eyes were disconcerting in their direct rudeness.

"Ty's friend." Really, she didn't give a shit about this woman, she decided as she stepped around her.

Latta was standing at the sink, her hands under the faucet, rinsing them over and over.

What was it with these people? Dakota wondered. Was everyone out here tense or crazy? She looked out the big window that allowed a panoramic view of the entire place. The sky was starting to cloud over, and a wind was picking up the tatters of leaves left on the small, newly planted apple trees flanking the gate. The branches on the huge pine trees to the side of the house were beginning to sway and jiggle and for some reason it looked colder out there now.

Ty was standing at the double windows in the living room, away from the noise of the family gathering, watching the storm moving in across the hills to the west. They should get going. Although it was only supposed to produce snow squalls, that could mean anything from a few flakes to a blizzard, depending on the capriciousness of the wind and the hills. As he watched, the clouds seemed to lower and squat on top of the distant hills, which vanished in a gray-white mist. He was turning to get Dakota and say good-bye so they could ride back when Joseph Starr, who had apparently been standing behind him for a while, stepped up next to him.

"Storm's coming—" Ty said.

The other man nodded and folded his arms across his chest. "Drove through some of it on the Res coming down."

"Was it bad?"

"Little wind and snow, nothing much." Joseph kept looking out the window.

Ty had a feeling he wanted to say something more. "Yeah well, we rode over on our horses—guess we better—"

"We just came from the memorial service for my cousin, you know—"

Ty shook his head. Had this Joseph confused him with someone else? "No, I don't think I do."

"Father Christopher said you knew him. Thought I'd see you there."

Ty's face flushed as he shook his head again. That old priest was never going to give it a rest.

"Thought that's why you came back—say good-bye to him." The old man's voice was so insistent, so sure of itself.

"No."

Ty had to keep himself from shoving the man down and running out of the house. He was in deep, deep trouble here. He tried to keep his breathing even, but kept running out of air. God knows, he didn't want to look at this man, no, he kept watching the clouds moving closer and closer, obliterating everything in their path, darkening the land just in front of them. They had to leave, they had to get out of here while they still could. They'd get stuck here—Christ almighty—

"I have to go."

The old man's hand resting on his arm stopped him as if it were a log across a road. "That warrant on you is still alive—"

Joseph's voice reflected the disgust Ty felt churning his stomach. He was going to throw up, he thought, all that blood, the knife going in and slashing, the nose crunching under his boot, the gun going off so loud it made his ears ring the rest of the night—

"My cousin died that night. He was never the same."

Ty shook his head and pulled his arm away. "I don't know anything about your cousin."

But the old man was shaking his head sadly. "I talked to Sheriff Moon today. He came up for the service. Didn't know you were back in town."

Ty turned to go again, but Joseph caught his shoulder, digging his fingers into the nerve the way Ryder used to that made him furious. When he tried to jerk away from the grip, the old man hung on viciously. "Pretty soon you're going to tell the truth—" He whispered and let him go.

Ty staggered back, rubbing his shoulder and glaring back at him.

Twisting away from the old Indian, Ty saw Cody and Kya staring at him as if he were drenched in blood, and the mangled flesh of his kill were lying at his feet, draining into the Oriental carpet. He pushed past them, ready to fight if they tried to stop him, nodded at Latta in the kitchen, grabbed his coat and went out into the darkening afternoon. He wasn't even thinking about Dakota until he heard her saddling the gray in the stall next to the chestnut's. He was fucked, he was most definitely fucked. Harney fucking Rivers. He hadn't wanted to hurt them, yes he had, but he hadn't. He was a kid, he didn't know, he didn't know—but the old Indian's words were in him, like a knife point at the front of his skull. Poisoning him, he was dying, he was going to die, yes, he could feel it, that was true. He was going to die. A grim calm came over him. Okay, he could face that. He'd faced everything else. The day he rode with his back torn and bleeding from his father's belt buckle, dug his spurs in and raked the horse's shoulders bloody to win. The day he waited with Ronnie dying and then dead and then waited on to dark so he wouldn't be able to look down and see the dirty tear-streaked face nestled in his arms as he rode home. The days after Harney beat and stabbed him and he'd made himself live despite the jagged mind numbing pain the drugs only ate the edges off so he could come back here and finish it. Harney had taken more than blood with his knife, he'd taken all their lives.

He pushed the horse hard, ignoring its labored breathing he could hear even over the wind rising at his back, blowing stinging bits of icy snow at his neck and face. At the fence line between the two ranches, Dakota turned her horse in front of his and they knocked into each other, but the horses stayed on their feet.

"Get out of the way!" he yelled.

"What's wrong—what happened back there?" She gasped into the wind, drawing her knee up and rubbing it from the collision.

"Nothing—" The word was almost swept away by the wind.

She grabbed his rein and shouted, "I'm not letting go until you tell me!" She pulled the rein and the chestnut crowded into the gray, who threw his head up and glared.

Ty tried to pull away, but succeeded only in yanking on his horse's mouth as she pulled back. Then the chestnut reared and she let go of the rein as it started over backwards. Ty just had time to kick his feet loose and start away from the saddle as the horse came down. He rolled, saving himself from the nine hundred pounds colliding with the ground so close to him that sand woofed up in his face. The horse grunted and lay still, stunned. Ty jumped up, grabbed a rein, and tried to lift the horse's head, but the chestnut was scared it was hurt and wouldn't move. Ty knelt down and rubbed its face and neck, running his hands over the shoulder and down the belly. "Come on, you're okay, buddy, come on now, be brave," he crooned, and the horse groaned and propped his forelegs up. "Good, now up you go." Ty patted the neck with his palm hollow to produce loud reassurance, and the horse gathered his hind legs under him and stood, shaking himself off like a wet dog, a relieved look on his face to discover he wasn't hurt.

Ty rubbed his nose. "That was a goddamn dumb thing to do," he said to Dakota. He remounted and tried to ride past into his own field.

This time she grabbed both of the reins out of his hands. "Not until you tell me what's going on—" She took a turn around the saddle horn with his reins.

"Aw shit," he groaned as the chestnut shifted nervously under him. The snow was changing to fat downy flakes that blew around them in soft swirls, but she ignored it. Ty knew they could easily be in a whiteout in minutes, unable to find their way back. He doubted these thoroughbreds would have the sense to find the barn on their own. Well, he didn't care—not for himself anyway—Dakota was another matter though. He couldn't, he just couldn't take another person down with him. Not now. "All right, okay, can we at least try to ride toward the ranch before we really do get caught out here and die?"

She unwound the reins and handed them to him. "You talk while we ride though—"

They trotted just ahead of the main storm while he told her enough of the story so she'd get the idea of how Harney was involved in the version he'd told the priest that night. He couldn't bring himself to tell her he'd help beat up the men. With any luck she'd believe him.

But back at the barn, as they rubbed down the horses, she asked him, "Why did he try to kill you, then?"

"That had to do with the colt, his insurance deal, not this—"

"There's more to it than that. Just tell me the truth. Why is there a warrant out if you didn't do anything?"

He sighed and ran a hand down the near front leg, stopping at what felt like a small hard lump he hadn't noticed before on the cannon bone. "I think he popped a splint."

"Ty?"

"I was with Harney that night."

After a long silence, she asked, "So what does Joseph Starr want?"

"To blame me." He couldn't tell whether she believed him or not, and he needed someone to talk to now, someone he could trust who knew him, knew the kind of man he was. The only person he could think of was Logan, back in Kansas. He'd call him later, when Ryder and Dakota were watching TV or asleep.

When they finished rubbing the horses, Dakota went to fill the water buckets from the pump and Ty pulled a bale of hay off the stack. He took the knife from his boot and was getting ready to cut the twine when he heard her set the buckets down so hard the water slopped over the edges. The knife blade glinted in the dim light as he paused and looked up at her face, suddenly filled with suspicion and maybe even fear.

The twine snapped under the blade and the sound made them both jump. The hay fell apart in grassy leaves. He put the knife back in his boot and straightened. She took a half step back. He thought about her seeing him accidentally shoot Eddie. Her gloved hand was covering her mouth and he wanted to pull it away, but he didn't move for fear it would send her flying out of the barn. "I didn't do it—"

"Oh, Ty—"

He couldn't look at her anymore, so he bent to pick up three leaves of hay for each horse. She'd wanted the truth—he thought bitterly as he threw the hay into the stalls and watched the horses flatten their ears and grab at it with their teeth, slashing their heads to either side as if they were defending their piles from marauders.

She was still standing there with her arms wrapped around herself when he went to the big garbage can for corn. The grain hitting the buckets rattled loudly in the silence of the barn. Outside the wind shifted its attack, blowing hard against one side and then another like a relative locked out of the house.

He put the coffee can on top of the garbage can and kicked the hay to the side of the aisle before stopping a few feet to the side of her. "I'm—"

"It's okay. I know you didn't do it," she whispered. "I just wanted you to tell me the truth."

They held on to each other until the horses had finished their grain and had moved back to the hay. Then Dakota leaned back and asked, "So what *are* we going to do?"

Ty wanted to tell her how simple it really was now, but he didn't want to scare her. He shrugged. "Figure something out, I guess."

Verna Stromme's Home Care car was parked by the house, and they didn't think anything about it until she rushed into the kitchen as they were taking off their coats.

"Oh, I'm so glad you're back. I was just watching TV and getting ready to go home, I have to be back for supper, you know, but I wanted to wait and tell you myself—" She stopped, folded her hands in front of her wide stomach, her small eyes challenging them.

Ty stared, his hands stopped in midair holding both ends of the scarf around his neck. Dakota said, "What? What's happened?"

"Mr. Bonte had him an attack. A real bad one right before I got here, and I had to call the county ambulance. They took him into town to stabilize his breathing. I wasn't equipped with all the drugs and equipment they have, you see—I'm just a home-care person, not a doctor—" She looked both defiant and ready to cry.

"How bad is he?" Dakota asked.

"Oh, he's fine now. They called to say they were keeping him overnight, but he can come home tomorrow if this snow lets up. Otherwise, Monday. Doctor Wilkes said not to worry, no need to come in with the roads the way they'll be by dark. I better go now though." She looked out the window at the blowing snow, which seemed to be tapering off.

"You want me to drive you?" Ty asked.

"I got my front-wheel and a safety kit. My husband made me take the CB too." She seemed pleased with herself in this adventure, and began to put on the coat and hat she'd draped over the kitchen chair. "He was real sweet the whole time, you would've been proud of him. He's a real nice old man." She tied the scarf around her neck so only her small, alert eyes peeked out. "I had me another one of those oatmeal cookies, hope you don't mind—I'll get the recipe from you next week, if that's okay. My husband loves them oatmeal cookies."

The snow was only swirling lightly around the barnyard as she drove off. "Storm's passed over us," Ty said. "I gotta finish chores. Why don't you take it easy—" He was relieved when she nodded sleepily and let him go.

Chapter Twenty-one

When Ty checked after chores, Dakota was sleeping in Charla's old room with the lights off. It was just as well. He needed some time to think. He went downstairs to the kitchen and put on some fresh coffee while he dialed Logan's number.

"How's it going?" Marlys asked before she handed the phone over to her husband.

"Fine," he said like always and felt stupid. She'd hear the truth when they got done and know he'd lied. Maybe it was never going to end. He poured some coffee while he waited for Logan, and looked in the fridge for something to eat. There was some leftover meatloaf from last night, made the way Ryder liked it, topped with ketchup and strips of bacon. He was teaching Dakota all his favorite recipes from his childhood and early years of marriage, a fact that Ty was more than irritated by for some reason. He pulled out the meatloaf and some wheat bread Dakota liked, although Ryder wouldn't touch anything but store-bought white bread. Ty ate what was handy as a rule. He coated the bread with ketchup and piled two thick slices of meatloaf in between. He had taken the first big bite when Logan came on the line.

"Ty?"

"Hmmmm—" He tried to swallow quickly and had to put his mouth under the faucet to wash down the lump before he could talk.

"You there?"

He told Logan about hooking up with Dakota, the horses he'd recovered in St. Paul, and what was going on with his father and listened to the usual condolences he didn't want to hear, and then there was a pause. He thought he heard a click on the wire at that moment, but the lines out in the hills always picked up a lot of static and noise during storms and extreme cold.

"You seen Harney Rivers?" Logan kept his voice casual.

"Haven't run into him yet, but I will. He's trying to take the ranch, I guess. At least he turned down a bridge loan we need until we ship cattle—but I'm still planning on taking care of him. That's not the problem though. Not exactly."

"What's going on, Ty?"

He couldn't tell Logan how lonely and scared he was after Joseph Starr had confronted him, but he did describe the scene. "I don't know what to do—I can't—I mean, Dakota's after me about it now too. People are talking to her. That's all my life comes down to, I guess." He pushed the sandwich away, suddenly sickened by the pink stain soaking through the bread.

Logan took a deep breath. "I don't think you can say that, Ty. It was a bad thing to do. But it doesn't wipe out the rest of your life. You got the place here you put a lot of years and sweat into—and yes, I've been keeping an eye on it—"

Ty shook his head, catching his reflection in the window, the dark hollows for eyes and mouth. "I think maybe it does, Logan. It's no good trying to pretend I'm any better than Harney." He paused and took a deep breath. "That wasn't the first time we got in drunken brawls." He drank some coffee, but it tasted so watered down, even as strong and black as he could make it, it needed a punch, more—something to answer what was making his muscles tingle and ache, his hands on the counter clench and unclench.

"Everybody who drinks a lot gets into those sooner or later, Ty. What Rivers did to you was a different sort of deal."

He didn't want to think about the screaming horse or the way his face bones cracked under the fists. He squeezed his eyes tight, rubbed his face, being careful along the eye bone, and shook the images loose.

"This isn't working out. I have to go after him, that's all."

"Now listen." The other man paused. "You need to take it easy. Take a little time to figure this all out. Maybe you can—"

"What? There's nothing can change what happened, and now on top of it all this old guy's cousin is dead and he blames me for ruining the guy's life. You know what? He has a point. I fucked up and now I am fucked. Just fucked."

"Sounds like you're feeling sorry for yourself."

"I'm facing facts. Facts is all there is anymore. And the fact is I owe Harney and he owes me."

"What about Dakota? You love her, don't you? What happens to her when you and Harney—"

"I can't talk about that. I do love her, but what have I got to offer her? My business was stolen by Harney. My old man's ranch is about to go bust. There's a warrant out for my arrest . . ." He pressed his thumb and forefinger against his eyes so hard he saw stars, then released them, but the kitchen walls were still dingy with old smoke and grease.

"Promise you won't do anything until I get there. *Don't* go see Harney. Stay away from town. Send Dakota—from what I know about the Sandhills, the last thing that sheriff is likely to do is drive out there and try to serve that twenty-year-old warrant. *Stay put.* You hear me? I'll come up there as soon as I can so we can talk to the authorities and that old man together, but it won't be until after the holidays, I promised Marlys—"

Ty squatted down and opened the dirt-smudged maple cabinet doors one after another along the wall. Ryder used to keep liquor stashed among the pans and canned goods, sometimes going to the lengths of pouring it in syrup bottles or plastic storage jugs.

"Ty? You there?"

He reached in and felt along the very back of the shelves next to the wall.

"Let me talk to Dakota—"

His fingers touched the cold glass and he knew he'd found it. "She's sleeping—" He pulled the pint of whiskey out. Jim Beam.

"Look, you don't have to come up here, Logan. There's nothing you can do. These people have known me since I was born. Nothing an outsider can say will change that. Thanks for listening though." He lifted the bottle to his lips, paused to smell the woody brown liquid as it slid up the neck, and then drank.

"Just take it easy, and don't forget about Dakota in all this. Maybe you should see about getting a lawyer. What about the other Indian from that night?"

The liquor swirled heat into his blood, rushing up the back of his neck and spilling into his head. He took another drink. "I don't know anything about him—"

"You could try that priest on the Reservation."

Setting the bottle down, he poured some of the coffee out of his cup and laced the rest with the whiskey. "I don't know—" He couldn't imagine facing the old priest again after all these years. If Joseph Starr had seen the truth so easily, a priest wouldn't have much trouble. Hell, he was a walking billboard these days.

"Go see him, talk to him. Do something constructive, for a change—take Dakota. She's believable."

"I can't get her more involved. Look, I gotta go. I'll call you in a few days." He hung up the phone to Logan's tinny good-bye dissolving into static. "Saved by the bell." He saluted the image in the window and drank, letting the alcohol bring him to a new alertness.

Upstairs, Dakota hung the phone up as soon as she was sure the line was dead, and sat back against the pillows on the big bed in Ryder's room. She had woken up when Ty came in the other room to check on her, and had wondered about his tiptoeing away. She'd followed him downstairs and watched while he made the sandwich and started to dial the phone. The call had scared her. Ty had sounded like he was going to go after Harney alone and worse. Maybe she should go the sheriff, but why? She couldn't prove the horse had been killed for insurance or that Harney had done it. Eddie would never testify.

Maybe Ty was just doing what everybody out here did. Sandhills justice. Harney had beaten him nearly to death. She pulled the bedspread up around her legs. How could a person tell for certain who another person really was? What they were capable of, what they'd

done before you met them? Maybe she'd just been lucky over the
years bumming from one place and situation to another. Nobody
had hurt her or stolen anything from her. She'd never run into any of
those men you were always reading about who had no conscience,
no soul, the ones who left women stranded on lonely highways. She
pulled the bedspread up to her chin and smelled the stale must of
Ryder's old cigarette smoke and sweat. Well, at least she thought she
knew who Ryder was. Regardless of what Ty said, the father was
much more readable than the son. She wished she could ask Ryder
for advice about how to help Ty, but she knew deep down that that
was useless.

"I know what you said last time—" Joseph tried to keep the angry
edge out of his voice while Sheriff Moon, a former high school
coach, studied the two people in his office as if he might have to discipline them.

Finally, Moon rubbed his cheeks with both hands, tipping his
glasses askew, and said, "Do me a favor. Go home, enjoy the holidays, and let this thing work itself out. I guarantee things will look
different come spring." He lifted a file folder on his desk and let it
drop again.

"You have the warrant right there. Just serve it, that's all I'm asking." Joseph kept his voice quiet. He was several years older than
Moon but had grown up in Mission with him. Both had played basketball and left the Reservation after high school—Joseph to Viet-
nam and Moon to college.

"I agree with you, sheriff." Latta surprised them both. She leaned
forward, resting her folded hands on the edge of the sheriff's desk.
"I've known Ty since he was a boy, and I think he's turned into a fine
man. To punish him for something that happened so long ago—"

"What if it were Cody or a relative who was assaulted, would you
feel the same way?" With a quick flick of the wrist, Joseph pushed
one of his braids over his shoulder. They'd been arguing about Ty
since the lunch yesterday, and Latta had insisted she come to the
sheriff with him this morning. He wanted to say that she was always

sympathetic to these young men, look at who she married, but he knew that would just muddy the waters.

Moon opened the folder, then closed it again. "Okay, let's say this—we have a difference of opinion here. Even if I serve the warrant, chances are good the prosecutor or judge will throw it out. Harney Rivers is too big now, and Ty's family is respectable. Even if old man Bonte is a bastard, he's dying and that counts in people's minds. Mrs. Bonte is a devout Christian who carries a lot of the sympathy vote here. Put their son in jail over the Christmas holidays? Uh-unh. You know how these hills people are. Now think about it—what do you want out of this?"

The phone rang, and the sheriff picked it up and told the person he'd call back. Then he punched in a number and told the receptionist to hold his calls and bring some more coffee. The office door opened almost immediately and a Native American in his teens appeared with the coffeepot in hand. He had a large head squared off by a crewcut and a football player body that would run to sagging flesh in later years, but for now, he was powerful-looking. Carefully filling the cups, he lifted his eyes in his large round face only when Joseph thanked him.

"Internship program I worked out with the high school in Mission," Moon explained as soon as the door closed again. "He's a good kid—works hard. We're trying to get one of the small midwestern colleges with an athletic program interested in giving him a scholarship. Kid can run like the wind, he's got good hands and feet, handles himself pretty well. There's an awful lot of 'em like him too—"

Joseph nodded and waited. What Moon was suggesting was that they put their energies into saving the kids on Rosebud and forget about revenge and honor and justice for a dead man. Just this morning Latta had tried to make the same argument, and Joseph had declared that Indians prayed to the patron saint of lost causes, she should know that. Cody had taken off in the middle of the discussion and Kya had left right after him.

"Okay, okay—" Moon held up his hands. "I'll tell you something—maybe you can use it, maybe not, but I think there's a lever here. Rivers has the most to lose. At his trial, he swore he wasn't even there despite the girl's testimony against him. Said it was Ty did the knifing and bragged about it afterwards. Ty ran off too, which made him seem more guilty. No question he beat your cousin. Big issue is—does he get away with it. Rivers too."

"So you think Ty's innocent?" Latta leaned forward again, resting the coffee cup on his desk.

"Not exactly—but Harney did pull the wool over people's eyes. Here's the deal—Harney wants to buy into the Rosebud Casino. He's talking to the owners as we speak. He's contacted interests in Omaha and Kansas City about investing—and expanding the facility to include more live entertainment, add more slots and games, set up better shuttle service for weekends, and so on. This case comes up again, stirring up questions about his past, Res would turn against him. Remember, he can't be charged here in Babylon because he's already been declared innocent, but he could be brought to Rosebud Tribal Court."

"On what grounds?" Joseph asked.

"A civil suit suing him for assault and wrongful death, maybe. You'd have to talk to a lawyer. Hell, sue both of them. Link them up again. That should be enough to get things going. Sooner or later, the truth'll come out. You could get the case in the tribal paper, spread it around the Res. They won't tolerate Harney's involvement in the casino after that. Nobody'd work for him." Moon leaned back in his chair, sipped from his coffee mug, and smiled for the first time.

"This hurts Harney more than Ty then," Joseph said, his eyes searching the other man's face for the first time. Usually they avoided staring in each other's eyes out of respect.

"Well, Mr. Bonte will be served too. And of course, with a few nudges, the feds can be looking into the case at the same time. Once we get those two up there, the feds can just show up and whisk them off to Rapid City and recharge them in federal court for conspiracy. They can *always* think of something, if that's what you want. Happens to our people all the time."

Latta nodded slowly. "But not Ty. We can't let that happen."

"They can just ignore the suit—they're white men, they don't have to answer it." Joseph kept his hands folded in his lap, but the knuckles were light from pressure.

"Harney would have to show up if he wants into the casino. And you'd probably have to convince Ty it was in his interest to get this out of the way once and for all. I'll see what I can do about getting the old charges dropped here, then leak the information to the tribal papers. That should get the Res going—white justice and all that crap." The two men smiled at each other.

"But Ty won't end up in jail, right? It's Harney we're after now?" Latta asked.

The sheriff shrugged and looked out the windows to the street, where the icy wind was lifting dry snow and dusting the sidewalk and truck windows. Occasionally the wind gusted hard against the side of the building, rattling the glass.

Waziya, the north wind, the cruel bully. Great, Joseph thought, he had promised to do a sweat lodge tonight with a family that was having problems with its two boys. They had time to outline the shape of a cross with Christmas lights on the side of the house, but he'd had to talk pretty long and hard to convince them to try a ceremony. Finally all the males agreed to participate. He could imagine how much it would take to drive over and convince them to leave the cozy warmth of their house now. It would certainly be hot in the lodge, but the coming and going would be pretty damn cold. Unplug the TV, he wanted to tell the parents. Make 'em read books, don't let 'em go out at night, keep 'em away from alcohol. Easy for him to say, he'd never had kids of his own.

He thought of what it would take to get his two nephews on the right path. Although Latta had convinced the owner of the Buckboard to hire them to wash dishes, and they were making it to work and taking home some money, they still wore their baggy jeans hanging low on their butts and dragged around looking half-stoned. His brother wasn't keeping track of them. The tribal police didn't bother. They figured with all those bare miles to run around in, the boys wouldn't get in that much trouble. Next time a police cruiser was missing windows, they'd show up for his nephews though.

"I have to run up to Rosebud." Joseph stood and looked at Latta.

"You're sure about this?" She stayed seated, looking at them.

Moon stood too and put his coffee cup down on the folder bearing Ty's name. "Looks like the way to go for now, Mrs. Jaboy." She hadn't changed her name to Kidwell when she married Cody, so people still called her by her first husband's name.

"I hope you're right—siccing the whole Reservation on them seems pretty dangerous to me."

"It's only the guilty who have to worry, Latta." Joseph opened the door and held it against the wind trying to snatch it away.

"I'm not so sure that's true," she said.

The red pickup was parked right where Cody had said it would be, but she paused at the far end of the Buyer's City lot, pulling in among the other vehicles by the supermarket. She wasn't sure she should go through with this. Even though she needed to get something she could use to help Ty, and Cody seemed to be the only person she could ask aside from Joseph Starr, she still wondered if this was going to work. Ty had been awfully quiet this morning. Didn't do more than nod when she offered to go to town to pick up some special food items Ryder asked for after his wife drove him home yesterday. That had been weird. Real weird. First time Mrs. Bonte had been in the house in over twenty years, apparently. Mrs. Bonte had sat briefly at the kitchen table and let herself be served cookies and tea with her own dishes. And while the men had sat in awkward silence like two shamed dogs, she let her eyes roam the grease-splattered appliances and streaked walls, barely able to keep the disgust from curling her lip. She left almost immediately, to the visible relief of all of them.

The only sad part was Ryder commenting that that would probably be the next to last time his wife saw the house. Then he added, "The last time will be after my funeral, you know. Probably burn the place down." He'd seemed older and tireder than before the attack, and hadn't wanted to change out of his pajamas. He stared at the TV with nothing close to concentration or even comprehension at times, and mostly seemed only to want to talk, to tell her stories in pieces cut out of their natural place in his life, blown up, and given new color. She had the feeling it was the new drugs that made him so talkative, and once or twice he confessed to thinking that too, but didn't stop. She had to admit though, that one of the reasons she was listening closely was to gather information about Ty, what he did as a child, how he got along with his brother and sister and mother, how he became what he was now, and most important, how he could have done what he had done to that man. One thing was certain, and she intended to tell Cody this, Ty was nowhere near that Indian the night he was killed by the hit-and-run driver.

She glanced at the red truck in the corner of the lot again. Shifting, she backed and drove across the lot to where Cody's truck sat conspicuously alone. He wasn't very good at sneaking around, if that was his agenda, she decided as she parked next to him and looked over. He was leaning back, his hat propped over his eyes as if he were asleep. She thought about driving away, but before she could, he thumbed the hat up and looked over and tilted his head for her to move to his truck.

He leaned across the seat, unlatched the door, took her hand to pull her up into the truck, and then just stared at her.

"So what's going on?" she asked.

"We need to go someplace." He started the truck, circled around back of the lot, and drove along a side road until they caught the highway headed west. At Crookston, he pulled off and headed up a hill lined with ramshackle houses, finally coming to a stop beside one that seemed a little more destroyed than the others. The garage door hung by a hinge; the dead tree in the front yard was peeling bark in big dark brown scabs that littered the sparse brown grass and snow around it; the front yard was rutted with tire tracks; the storm door glass was cracked; and the front door was a cheap hollow core bearing dents and footprints. Inside someone had taken down most of the interior walls and erected a wood stove sitting on paving bricks in the middle of the room. The remaining walls bore half-hearted attempts at renovation in the form of slashed and peeled wallpaper, splashes of various colors of paint, and a couple of race car and rock band posters. They stopped and looked around, then he led her to the one other room, where a stained mattress piled with ragged quilts and blankets filled most of the space. When Cody sat down on the mattress, a faint odor of urine and dust rolled up, and she tried to breathe through her mouth.

"What *is* this?" She turned her head back to the other room, worried that maybe she was in real trouble here. "I gotta go."

"Sit down." He patted the mattress beside him and she backed into the door frame, letting the wood brace up her legs as she shook her head.

"It's okay," he murmured and in the twilight of the dusty room his voice had a kind of honey hypnosis.

"Do you have something to tell me or not?" Ty's name and face waited in the back of her mind.

"Bob One Pony brought me here one time when I was doing some pretty serious drinking. Well, more than once. He used to live here on and off. Sometimes a couple of white guys two doors down would drive him away. He was a good guy though, even when he was drinking."

Cody pushed the pile of blankets aside and lay down.

"Bob is—?"

"The man Ty knifed who died last weekend." Cody let his eyes follow the contours of the walls and settle on the ceiling. The light coming through the broken, torn shade and single, cheap yellow gauzy curtain hanging at the window was itself thin and poor in a way that made the silence of the house grow more chilled.

Dakota shivered and tried to think of a way out of here. If she just walked out the front door, would he follow and drive her back to Babylon?

The wind knocked something against the wall behind his head and they both jumped.

"Lakota say there's a ghost that lingers after death in the place it lived. More of a shade than a spirit, I guess." He ran a finger over his lower lip and looked around again. "You're supposed to set out belongings for it to take with it. Presents, I guess. Maybe just their own stuff. Think Bob wants anything here?"

They listened as the wind hissed and blew around the house,

pushing the bushes against the windows and rattling the dead tree in front until another small limb cracked loose with a sound like a gun going off. The cold began to creep into the soles of her boots, numbing her toes and inching up her legs to make a band around her thighs, which would take hours to warm again. She shivered and found she couldn't stop herself.

"He probably wants one of those stupid posters out there and that dirty mattress. What the hell is this? I'm freezing, let's go."

"Bob told me about it after Rivers's trial. Laughed at how easy it was to corrupt the law here. His family kept after him to have a ceremony. Got some Bear healer from Turtle Lake they'd met at a pow-wow in Minneapolis to come over, but Bob didn't mind the way things were."

Cody pulled a tattered and stained crazy quilt from the pile and smoothed it over his chest. "This was my mother's. I gave it to Bob last summer when he had pneumonia. He only got sick in the summertime." He pushed the quilt down over his thighs and she could see the heart and bag of money embroidered in dirty gold threads on it.

"Said he was probably *Heyoka*, doomed to do everything opposite. Sometimes he worried he was a *Wakinyan* Dreamer, though, and would have to commit murders eventually. He was mixed up in the head. Only drinking made him happy and clear, he said."

"So what am I doing here?" Dakota rubbed her arms, trying to keep the cold from fingering her back. She flexed her hands, which were going numb inside the gloves. Cody had his wool jacket open, the shirt unbuttoned at the throat. He wasn't even wearing gloves, and she felt like they were in a damn walk-in meat freezer. He closed his eyes, and she waited for him to open them. Under the urine and dust there was a faint sweet meaty odor of an animal recently dead. She flashed on the colt dead in the stall, on Ty hanging there with his face a mask of blood, then her mother's pictures of the Civil War, the bodies in a line that looked like rumpled dirty clothes being sorted on laundry day. She'd kept her eyes on their boy smooth faces, dreamy and sleep-filled, hair matted and uncombed. Hardly anyone wore a look of tension, pain, or agony. It was as if they had spread their arms and flung themselves into the wide brown waters of sleep and been welcomed.

"I wanted you to be with me when I came back." His words made her realize she'd been almost dozing standing up there. The sun seemed to have shifted around so the light was coming through the window at a different angle, as if it were trying to figure out a way through the house. What time was it? She'd have to get back—

"In case Bob's around—"

She lightly stomped one foot, then the other, but stopped when the sound echoed loudly back. "Can we just go?"

He looked at her and patted the mattress beside him again. "Why don't you come here and sit down and wait with me?"

She shook her head. "I'm going—" Turning, she was startled by the glimpse of a large dog out the window, trotting around the corner of the house as if it were following her motion. At the front door, she hesitated for a moment. What if it was a vicious dog and it was waiting for her out there on the porch? That scene in the bedroom had scared her in some unaccountable way. She couldn't stop shivering and her shaking hand seemed to lack the strength to turn the door knob. Her legs wobbled and she leaned against the wall.

"Are you all right?" Cody put a hand on her shoulder that seemed to push down on her body. She made her hand turn the knob and dipped out from under his hand as she went outside, not wanting to think about how not all right she was. The dog was nowhere to be seen, but the afternoon had unaccountably disappeared.

Back at the parking lot, they sat in the growing dark, the headlights two angry yellow eyes staring back at them from the vacant black glass of the empty store, until finally she asked, "Don't you have anything to tell me about Ty?"

He waited so long she thought he'd gone to sleep until he cleared his throat. "There's one other thing—"

She shook her head. She'd meant to do so much, ask all these questions, play the detective, sort out right and wrong. Instead she'd been steered around a bunch of ruins like a tourist. It was plain weird. She wondered if she could tell Ty.

"Go riding tomorrow—come through the fence. There's an old

church over the third hill. There's something there you should
see—"

"No—"

"One o'clock." He lifted his hand and she reached for the door.

"Forget it. I'm not coming."

"You'll come if you care about what's happening—"

Her legs were shaking as she climbed into Ryder's truck in the
parking lot, and she had to squint to make her eyes focus on the traffic of early evening shoppers as she drove over to park so she could
do the grocery shopping she'd promised.

At the tall freezers of frozen vegetables, where she searched for
the promised okra, she saw herself reflected in the glass and quickly
rubbed at the dark eyeliner smears under her eyes.

She almost missed the turn-off for the ranch road, and met Ty's
truck halfway. He pulled alongside and looked at her with an expression of worry and anger. "I thought something'd happened
to you—"

She hoped he couldn't see her eyes clearly, and she bit her lip and
ducked, then made herself smile. "I went to the library and forgot
about the time. Sorry." How was she going to explain where she'd
been, what she was trying to do? He was so jumpy these days, he'd
misinterpret everything.

He nodded. "Ryder's been asking about you all afternoon. 'Bout
drove me crazy." He stared at her again. Maybe he saw it, maybe he
smelled the other man, like a dog pissing on a tree higher than the
others. He looked away into the dark shapes of hills around them. "I
still got chores to do." He eased the truck forward until he could
turn around and followed her back to the house.

Christmas in three days, she thought. Merry Christmas, Ty. She'd
wanted to do something to help him, help both of them. She had to
figure a way to get at Harney. Forget Cody and his spooky shit. It
wore her out, whatever it was. Her exhausted body felt flat and
buckled, like a cardboard box left out in the weather.

She made spaghetti and meatballs for dinner and could barely eat
anything. She kept catching Ryder looking at her. Ty just ate and
went up to bed. Something was wrong with him too, but she didn't

have the energy to ask. She crawled into bed next to him at nine after Ryder's assurances that he was all right, he wanted to watch a movie instead of talking for a change. Maybe he'd told her everything he could think of, she thought as she drifted to sleep, her back wedged against Ty's, holding the second pillow tight against her chest and between her legs, the cold just beginning to loosen its grip on her thighs in the radiant heat tenting his body.

⨍ Chapter Twenty-two

She told herself all the next morning she wasn't going to go, but after lunch she grew more and more impatient, waiting for Ty to come
in from cleaning the barn he'd started on, and snapped at Ryder
when he tried to insist she play cards. She apologized and said she
needed to go for a ride. It was almost three before she found herself
on Noah, trotting up the pasture with the house quickly receding
before she realized that she'd not made the actual decision, she'd let
the momentum carry her along instead.

The tiny white wooden church surrounded by cedars and an old
graveyard was right where Cody had said it was. She tied her horse
with a halter and rope she'd brought and went inside, where she
could see her breath. A huge cross made of cedar limbs lashed together hung on the wall facing the door, and an antique pump organ
stood across from a large wood stove, which would provide the only
source of heat aside from the bodies that would line the plain white
wooden benches that served as pews on Sunday mornings. There
was a border in red, yellow, and turquoise running along the tops of
the four walls.

"I painted this." Joseph Starr's voice startled her, and she turned to
see him standing behind her in the doorway. "That red bear with the
lightning through its body was for Bob. We're cousins. Bob and I
came out here last summer when he was trying to quit drinking. We
spent the afternoon hanging out, watching a pair of hawks hunting

mice in the hills. We were sitting out front when way across the valley this big buck walks around the hill and stops. Soon as we noticed him, he lifted his head and we stared at each other for a good twenty minutes." Joseph walked to the wall and touched the flaking red paint of the bear.

"In the old days, people had to be real careful hunting deer. The white-tail could turn itself into a beautiful woman and seduce hunters, who mostly went crazy or died afterwards. The black-tail they couldn't even kill and if a hunter tried, he usually went crazy. Only a very strong man could survive."

Dakota looked at his face, the eyes shiny with memory.

"Then Bob went back to drinking and I went back to work. We didn't run into each other again until a month ago. Last time I saw Bob was the night before he got killed. He was playing pool and drinking at the Corner Bar in town. Decided to go up to the Res and find his sister, who just got back from Sioux Falls. She's got a good job with an insurance agency there. Bob thought she'd give him some money. Things got a little crazy though. Guess he ended up sleeping in the back of some car in the driveway of his brother-in-law's house. Last time I saw Bob, he was snoring with his mouth wide open, using a dirty pair of pants for a pillow. I don't know why he took his pants off, but it made me laugh."

Joseph kicked at the pew and the wood rang like metal in the cold. "Bob always made me laugh. He was a pretty good guy."

"I'm sorry," she said and put her hand on his arm.

"Would you just sit here with me for a while?" He indicated the pew he'd covered with a couple of blankets. They sat side by side, their laps covered with two ragged gray wool blankets that gave off a damp dog smell every time one of them shifted their legs.

"Thought you weren't coming," he finally said as the sun began to tint the white hills pink through the wavy glass of the church windows.

"Why am I here?"

"Thought you needed to know the kind of man Ty Bonte is—"

"I *do* know." She plucked at the ragged gray edge of a saucer-size hole in the blanket.

"The kind of man could ruin another's life on a whim?" Joseph continued as if she hadn't spoken. "You're a good woman. You should go home. There's nothing for you out here. You could get hurt—"

"I thought it was *Ty* I had to worry about—now it's *you*?" She threw the blanket off and stood up. "You're *all* wrong about him! It's *Harney Rivers* you should be dragging around this godforsaken countryside, not me and Ty!"

She started toward the door but stopped when he called, "Wait!" She could hear him collecting himself behind her as she stared at the red bear painted on the wall over the door, traveling west, following the arrow of lightning through his body. She could see so many men in that figure, men on the run from themselves as much as her. But with Ty it was different—days and weeks where they worked side by side, and too tired to speak or even make love at night, they would climb into bed and fall to sleep, wrapped in the safety of each other's flesh. For the first time in her life, she was coming to see what a gift that ordinariness could be. She wasn't going to let that go—no matter what mistakes he'd made in the past.

Then the door blew open.

"He loves me," she said.

"He's in trouble—"

"I know." She turned and watched him sit in the pew next to her.

"He didn't run down your cousin," she said. "We were at the ranch together. It couldn't have been Ty. It was all Harney Rivers with the knife too. That's the truth. The God's truth." She felt stupid saying that last thing, but she had to convince him.

Joseph shook his head. "But Ty was there."

She gripped the back of the bench to keep her hands from shaking. "It's driving him crazy. He's going to kill Harney over this unless I can stop him."

The old man leaned back with his arms folded across his chest, watching her with neutral eyes.

"The other man—is he still here? The other man they beat that night?"

"He moved to Minneapolis right after that. I sent word for him not to come back."

She told him about Harney Rivers coming to Kansas and trying to kill Ty, and about the phone call she'd overheard with Logan Woods.

"Maybe it's better they find each other then."

She shook her head. "One of them's going to die if that happens."

"Somebody already has," he reminded her. "Maybe these white men deserve to kill each other."

"You don't know Ty. None of you know him—"

"Do you?"

"Better than you—why don't you all just leave us alone, for God's sake!" She ran outside to her horse, who was looking anxiously toward home as the sun flooded the hills with apricot light. Tightening the cinch, she was just swinging on when Joseph came out, a dark figure against the splendid orange light spilling across the gravestones around him. She shaded her eyes and took one long last look as he leaned against the door frame and watched her ride away. All the way up the hill and over the other side, she could feel his eyes like silent tongues cursing her with words he'd never uttered.

"Ty," she whispered and lifted the gray into a lope as soon as she was through the fence. If she were lucky, if she were lucky, she kept thinking, he would get through this and they could go back to the way things were before. But as the lights of the ranch appeared below her, she knew that was another lie between them.

"He's not here—" Ryder said as she came expectantly into the kitchen. "That Kya Bennett came over right after you left and drove him to town." Ryder was eating pink Jell-O, thoughtfully licking the spoon between bites. He was wearing a fairly new-looking red-and-black plaid wool bathrobe over the pajamas. She'd probably have to get him some more pajamas if he was going to be living in them.

"She's a helluva woman, isn't she?" His eyes held the kind of malice she'd only seen used on his son so far.

The band at the Buckboard started at nine, with the kids home for the holidays drinking pitchers of beer to get their courage up to spill out onto the dance floor by ten. There was an anxious rowdiness and good humor about the big room, filling up with families and young people. Kya and Ty watched from the corner, slowly drinking and picking at the food they'd ordered. Kya's long legs were stretched on the extra chair in front of her as if she were in her own living room, and Ty noticed how she seemed to possess everything she came in contact with—the furniture as well as the people. She was too much for him, that he knew immediately after they'd matched shooter for shooter a couple of hours ago. Now he tried to force himself to eat to keep the liquor down and sober up.

The steak sandwich tasted dry in his mouth, and the fries greasy. Kya reached over and punched his shoulder. "Not feeling sorry for yourself, are ya?"

Those eyes were reflecting off the evergreen velvet shirt she wore, even in the newly dimmed light of the bar. She was like a fancy horse he couldn't afford. He buttered another roll and finished it in two bites, washed down by beer. At least the bread would soak up some of the booze. He didn't even have a way back tonight. Couldn't trust Kya. She wanted something, and it wasn't sex. He'd missed Dakota, had half a mind to saddle up and track her when Kya had shown up. Coming to town with her had seemed like the thing to do at that moment. But what was Dakota up to? Maybe she was off talking to that Joseph Starr or Latta or—then he thought he knew—

"Come on." He shoved the chair back and stood clumsily, catching his foot and jarring the table so the glasses slopped over. It was Cody. She didn't look like she'd been to the library yesterday. She looked—"Aw shit!" He kicked the chair out of his way, and Kya grabbed his arm and led him through the gathering crowd and outside to the front sidewalk.

He was getting madder and madder. He wanted to hit something—he looked around at the brick wall of the Buckboard and the metal sign post.

"Let's go down to Diamond Dave's—it's quieter." Kya dragged his arm until he fell into step. He shoved his cold hands in his jeans pockets and she put her arm around his shoulders like they were just cowboys out for a good time.

At the Diamond, they sat at the bar in the grim brown light with three other drinkers, listening to the loud music and shouts from below.

"What's going on?" he asked when the bartender refilled their glasses.

"Dancer downstairs—"

Kya slid off her stool and pulled on his arm. "Let's take a look—"

"No—" What he wanted was to go home and confront Dakota.

"Come on. Just a peek, then we'll go, I promise."

"You'll drive me back?" He stood and drained his beer.

"Sure—" She headed toward the stairs.

They descended to the windowless basement, dimly lit by lavender fluorescent lights half-hidden along the low ceiling of the black painted concrete block walls that seemed to pulsate with the heavy bass of rock-and-roll. They sat at a wooden table along the wall, facing the floor-to-ceiling mirrors that framed the tiny black plywood platform, bisected by a grimy brass pole, where a nearly naked woman in her early twenties was gyrating half a beat behind the music. She ignored the cowboys leaning against the bar with their half-bored eyes and snickering grins, and danced only to the image of herself in the mirrors, cupping her breasts, playing with the tassels at the tips, running her hands down between her legs, and following the sequined strap up the curves of her buttocks as she bent over and looked at the room from between her legs. She smacked the creamy white of her buttocks and licked her lips. With her straight, thin brown hair sweeping the floor and her unfocused expression, she resembled a young girl hanging by her knees from the schoolyard jungle gym. She jumped up and pretended to mount the pole, sliding down with her eyes closed. When she reached her knees, she tongued the pole while her body pumped against it.

"Jim Beam straight up and a glass of water." Ty practically had to shout to make himself heard by the waitress, who was older and plainer than the girl on the floor.

Kya switched to Coke and he looked at her. She smiled and flicked her attention back to the dancer. Leaning across the table, she said loudly, "I heard that someone caught the sheriff's new deputy with her last night in the alley behind here. He had her handcuffed to the telephone pole—"

He squinted in the smoky darkness. "So what do you want?"

She shrugged. "Get to know you, I guess. Latta said you were an okay guy. We're neighbors—"

"Nice place for the Welcome Wagon—" He nodded toward the dancer and Kya slid her chair around the table next to him. He rested his arm on the back of her chair and noticed how big-framed she was compared to Dakota. That brought the extra pain of jealousy again and he lifted his arm away. Maybe he'd blown it. Hell, he'd blown everything. He couldn't ask her to wait while he went to jail.

They drank for a while, watching the dancer put on a black see-through net peignoir, tied with a ribbon at the neck, after her set was over and go to talk to the cowboys at the bar stretched along the opposite wall. The bartender turned down the music so she could speak to the men, but not one of them got up and offered her a seat, although someone did buy her a drink. She went from one to another, making them laugh and touching them on the arm or leg, but they kept their hands and extra dollars to themselves. After a while she gave up and started emptying ashtrays. It depressed him so much, Ty dug out a five-dollar bill and walked over to give it to her. When she looked at him in surprise, he could see how big and dilated her pupils were, and how the smeared mascara made her face look hungry. She'd go off with one of these men, get roughed up some more like last night, and never know the difference. He flinched at the thought of Dakota, another young woman loose in the world, having to come to a place like this, take drugs, and dance naked for a bunch of indifferent cowboys.

When he returned to the table, Harney Rivers was there, just getting ready to sit down across from Kya. Ty lunged for him and they banged against the table and fell onto the chairs, then rolled off and crashed into the supports under the table. Harney, who was heavier, ended on top and jammed his forearm against Ty's throat. "Better stop," he panted. "Sheriff's deputy's coming down the stairs."

The arm released and Ty gasped for breath while Harney lifted off of him. By the time he extricated himself from the table, Harney was slapping the deputy on the back. "Man was so glad to see me, knocked me over—" He put an arm around Ty's shoulders. Ty had to stop himself from smashing his face. The deputy grinned and went to the bar.

"Sit down, Ty." Harney smiled, his fleshy features a mask on the verge of melting in the blue neon glow.

Ty reached for Harney's expensive tan leather sport jacket, but Kya grabbed his arm.

"The sheriff's deputy is sitting there at the bar watching us," she hissed and he sat down.

"Like old times, huh? Drinking and looking for a fight. Or, in your case, drinking and looking for pussy. Missed ya, buddy." Harney held up a finger and made a circle for drinks.

"You mean I'm alive—" Ty shoved at Kya's nails digging into his thigh.

"Just wanted to say there's no hard feelings, Ty." Harney laid a twenty on the table when the drinks quickly arrived and waved off the change.

"You gotta be kidding."

"Pay back, man. You had my horse—horse stealing's illegal, you know—" Harney tasted his drink and frowned. "This isn't JD— cheap bastard." He put the drink down.

"What about Dakota? I told you that was her horse."

Harney nodded. "And I thought about what you said, I did, and I do have another horse for her. Soon as I heard you were in the hospital, I thought it was the least I could do. Figured you'd show up sooner or later. But we can settle that issue. Tell her the new horse is twice her old nag."

"Fuck you—"

"But not in front of the lady. You need to come get it, Ty. Already told the sheriff I had a stray I was tired of feeding. Hate to send it to the killers, you know."

"I'll tell the sheriff the truth." Ty drained the glass of whiskey. He really should just follow this son of a bitch and kill him tonight.

"Think he'll believe your word against mine? Who the hell are you? Some bankrupt drunk, just like your old man—"

"I can still tell him the truth about what happened that night—plant some doubt. Just a seed maybe, but who knows what kind of tree will grow outta that—"

Harney's eyes went dead. "You do that." He stood and walked back to the bar and spoke to the deputy, who got up and followed him.

"What's going on, Ty?" Kya's voice was soft and coaxing under the music that picked up a throbbing beat as the dancer took off the peignoir and began to stroke herself between the legs in the mirror's reflection, even further behind the beat than before.

He had to get out of here, go someplace alone. He staggered upright, pushing against Kya's hands trying to guide him. His father had guns. Hell, he had guns in his truck. Now, why hadn't he brought them to town with him? He could have nailed Harney right here, it'd be all over. Then the deputy would nail him, it'd be done, gone—he pushed his way up the stairs and outside.

When the cold spiked his face, he remembered how much trouble it was to drink too much, especially when you had something important to do. He looked up and down the street, lined with trucks and cars parked in the dirty snow, the fake Christmas greenery draped tiredly overhead. God, he hated this holiday. The last good one was the time Ronnie got the boots he wanted, smallest man's size they carried at the western store. Finally he was out of the childish boy's versions he'd objected to, even though he had to stuff the toes with newspaper for a real fit. Ty had saved for a year for those boots, and personally taken his little brother in to shop for them. As always, the lady clerks had all taken a turn at helping the little boy and wishing him the best, he was such a favorite. "Tell your brother to feed you," they said to Ronnie, glancing at Ty with disapproval in their eyes. How could he explain what it was like out there at the ranch with their father, and then Ronnie running himself ragged trying to compete with grown men? Maybe if he'd been wearing his sneakers that day, his foot wouldn't have slipped off the brake, and the tractor wouldn't have rampaged into that hole and tipped over.

"Oh Christ—" Ty leaned against the side of a building.

"Ty—" Kya tried to drag him toward the street, but he jerked away.

"Leave me alone—what do you want, anyway—"

She stood there, his height, hands on hips, her long hair tangled down one side of her chest. "I want the truth—"

"Leave me alone!" He pushed at her, but she backed up and he almost fell down.

Two cowboys paused outside the bar and watched in case she needed help.

"It's all right—" She waved them on, and they shrugged and walked away. "You didn't do it, did you? Joseph says you were there, you might have used the knife, but I know you couldn't do that. You ran though, after you helped them, why? Why didn't you come back and testify against him, Ty, he would've gone to jail. Attempted murder on reservation land, it was a federal case— You're still covering for him. Come on, we'll go to the sheriff together—"

"I can't," he said, trying to wave her off him.

"Yes, you can. Tell me—tell me!" She grabbed his coat and shook him hard and when she let go, he staggered against the brick wall again.

"You people—" he panted.

"You people? What the hell is that? Some racist bullshit now?" She balled her fist, ready to punch him, and he held up his hands to stop her.

"It's between Harney and me, Kya. Tell Joseph I'm sorry, I never meant for anything to happen like it happened. I mean—I thought, I mean, we were just supposed to find some drunk Indians and beat 'em up—no excuse, it was a fucked thing to do—I ran. Never meant for that boy to get hurt so bad, or die—" He couldn't look at her, but reached a hand toward her. "Now just leave me alone—all of you—"

"We're not done yet. Not by a long way." He heard her heels hitting the sidewalk with sharp clicks as she walked away.

He leaned over, waiting to throw up or pass out, and when he straightened she was gone. He tried to look down the three blocks to where they'd parked her truck, but he couldn't focus that far.

He was still standing there twenty minutes later, trying to figure out what to do when the police car swung into the empty space in front of him and the deputy got out, his billy club in hand. Ty watched him with little interest and allowed himself to be hand-cuffed and shoved in the backseat without a word. He leaned his head back and closed his eyes. At least it was warm. They drove around for a while, which was fine with Ty, who only wanted to sleep. Although his arms cramped and his wrists and hands hurt, he figured he was going to get beat up or worse and he didn't much care at this point.

Finally the car pulled up in front of the police station and the deputy started talking to him without turning around, just watching him in the rearview mirror. "Mr. Rivers told me I could use some baton practice. Suggested I take you south of town, but I have to tell you the truth, I went to school with your sister. My wife and I go to the same church as your mother. I don't know your dad but to look at him on the street, heard he's an old hell-raiser, but he's not given any trouble since I got hired. Neither have you. So this time? I'm letting you spend the night in jail." The eyes in the mirror shifted away, then came back. "But I was you? I'd stay out of Mr. Rivers's way. He's got a mean repu-tation, and a bank to back it up now. And in case you're wondering, Sheriff Moon has that warrant sitting right on top of his desk."

They called his mother and she bailed him out as soon as the bank opened. He stank of vomit and urine, and as soon as they got out of the car at her house, she told him to go right upstairs and shower and put on the clean clothes he'd find there on the bed in Ronnie's room. That's what she still called it. He soaped himself and let the water run over him until it began to cool. He had a vicious headache. She had two aspirin and coffee waiting when he went down to the kitchen. The clothes were new jeans and a cream color western-cut shirt, but he didn't think anything about it until she looked him over and said, "Merry Christmas, you're wearing your presents." He thanked her and sat down at the table while she served him breakfast.

"I'm not going through this again after your father," she said over her cup of coffee. He nodded, unable to look in those cool gray eyes of hers.

"I mean it, Ty. You came back here looking for trouble, I don't know why, but I won't have it again. You understand? You can leave right now if that's what you have in mind." She didn't sound sad or anything, and he realized that she'd never seemed to regard him with any feeling at all. He was a fact to her. He could understand that. And surely didn't want to trouble her, although inside of him, very, very far inside someplace he could hear but not locate, there was a small indignant voice saying "That's not fair," as he ate the yellow clots of scrambled eggs.

"I don't know what you're mixed up in with that Reservation priest, either. A man came to the door the other day. Monday. Said his name was Joseph Starr and it was his cousin you knew who got killed last week on the Reservation. I told him I didn't think you knew any Indians, but he acted like I was either lying or mistaken. It made me very uncomfortable, Ty."

Her voice warned him that he was crossing the line they'd drawn between them years ago. Early on in his life, he'd learned that her state of mind was fragile and must be treated like a precious glass object. So when Ronnie died, he'd waited for her to break apart, crash and splinter. He'd been prepared to lift and hold her, carry her where she could rest, guard her until she was well if need be, but she hadn't needed him at all. She'd stood perfectly straight all through the funeral, crying her little tears and drying her face, then pouring the coffee from the silver service at the reception here afterwards, taking condolences, her trim little lips smiling in what he could only think of as a grimace for years afterward.

"I'm sorry, Mother. I'll get you the bail money as soon as I can—" He had no idea how that was going to happen. Maybe sign the truck and trailer over to her. Sure, she'd have a real need for a hot rig. He finished the eggs and bacon and drank more coffee.

She put her cup down, smoothing the flowered cloth napkin on the table beside her. "Listen, Ty, I want you to call me when Ryder—" She looked around at the spotless cabinets and shiny stainless steel sink she dried with a towel to keep from spotting. He'd seen her do it.

"I will—but I think you're jumping the gun. He's not going anywhere soon." Ty pushed away from the table.

She shook her head and started to say something, but stopped and stood up. "I'll get the rest of the presents and drive you home."

He started to protest, but stopped. Wasn't his problem. Ryder would probably die of a heart attack seeing his wife twice in the same week after spending most of his life alone out there. Ty walked into the dining room and through to the living room, inspecting the artificial tree, its stiff green limbs studded with red and pink flocked bows that seemed to march off the tree and continue along the picture rail on all four walls, outlining the fireplace mantel and crossing into the hallway to follow the staircase up. Everywhere he looked there were Santas and reindeer and snowmen in some sickeningly happy pageant. She'd even set up Ronnie's old train under the tree and when Ty knelt and turned the switch on, it promptly chugged around the little oval, hauling three box cars, on the top of which rode a tiny sleigh full of gifts, pulled by tiny brown reindeer he wanted to snatch up and throw across the room.

"Oh, don't run that, dear—" His mother walked quickly across the room and unplugged the cord before he could turn it off.

He got up slowly, careful not to let her see his face as he went to the front door. She'd made him leave his jacket outside, draped across the wrought iron railing to air the jail stink out, and when he slipped his arms in the sleeves, it was like putting them in ice water. He shivered and went back for the box of presents.

It wasn't until they were halfway to the ranch that he realized he hadn't gotten his mother a present this year. When he was still at home, his father had usually given him money and instructions for buying her present. Later, on his own, he'd called an 800 number for flowers or candy to be sent to her every Christmas Eve. Now he had nothing for anybody. It was Christmas Eve and he was broke. He felt in his pocket for the twenty dollars he hoped he still had. What he pulled out was a wad of two fifties along with the twenty. How the hell? He thought for a moment that maybe he'd stolen it, though he didn't remember.

His mother glanced over at him. "Figured you needed some money." She looked back at the road, keeping her car at a steady 62 miles an hour, just over the speed limit, as if it were some test of will in the up and down of the Sandhills.

"Thanks," he said and looked away. Maybe he could steal one of Ryder's credit cards and still get her something—pay the old man back with this money. Then there was Dakota. Shit. He was going the wrong direction for shopping.

"God, I was so worried—" Dakota's swollen eyes said the rest as he helped her make the coffee and fill the tray with cookies for his mother and father, seated in the TV room.

"I couldn't call."

She slammed the sugar spoon down extra hard next to his thumb and he jerked it away.

"All right, you want to know the truth? I was in jail. My mother bailed me out this morning. Gave me these clothes 'cause I stank." He spread his hands.

"Ryder told me you went off with that woman," she said and almost scalded his hands with coffee she was pouring past the rim of the cup.

In the back of his mind, there was something he'd realized last night about her and—but he couldn't remember except that it made him mad at her. Now he was the one needed to be sorry and he was.

"All we did was get drunk." Her face relaxed and he took a deep breath. "Had a run-in with Harney too. That's why the night in jail."

She set the coffeepot down and looked at him. "You didn't do anything to him, did you?"

"No. I wanted to, but Kya stopped me. He said he's got a horse for you though. I have to go and get it, I guess."

She rubbed the side of the metal pot with her finger. "Don't go." She picked up the tray. When she looked him full in the face, her eyes were so scared it made him want to do anything to comfort her. "Please? For me?"

It struck him then that she loved him. Truly loved him, and he was exhilarated but exhausted at the same time, because he didn't want to think of any way around killing Harney.

His mother and father were laughing at something on the TV, and it made Ty stop in the doorway and watch while Dakota served them as if she worked here. His mother nodded her thanks and Ryder didn't even acknowledge it. Some things never change, he decided bitterly, and followed Dakota back into the kitchen. Since when did those two ever get along? The old fart still knew how to play his cards, and his mother, well, there was absolutely no accounting for anything she felt or did. One thing for sure, her real and only son died years ago. Ty was just the hired man, the stand-in extra for whatever family she'd constructed for herself out of the one she was given. Suddenly the money felt bad, like he was being bought off, a tip or bonus for showing up and helping out and he wanted to get rid of it, spend it as fast as he could, although he'd be broke if he did.

"Let's go to town, get some food for tomorrow. Christmas shop, maybe—my mom gave me some money. Come on, let's go." He took Dakota by the shoulders and spun her toward the door before she could object that she needed to get dressed or stay and watch Ryder. While she put on her coat and boots, he hollered in to his parents that they'd be back in a while. Maybe he'd pick up some wine for tomorrow too, Dakota would like that. He had to try and make her as happy as possible while he still could, that was the best he had to offer in exchange for what he'd seen in her face a few minutes before.

∞ Chapter Twenty-three

Although it was Christmas Eve and a holiday reprieve seemed to settle into the house when Ty and Dakota returned from town, Ryder was so tired at supper he could barely eat. It took both Ty and Dakota to lead him back to the study so he could go to bed. While they cleaned up the dishes, Ty kept sneaking looks at the woman beside him, trying to memorize details. She had a wart on her forefinger she sometimes rubbed, and a scar on her eyebrow. He meant to ask her how she got it. And there were freckles sprinkling her arms and face from the years in the sun. A mole on her neck where it cupped with her shoulder he leaned over and placed a kiss in, which made her squirm and laugh and threaten him with the soapy dishrag. She'd bought some liquid detergent, and the hard greasy skin was finally disappearing from the pans and dishes. He put a drop in the mashed potato bowl and ran hot water into it until the bowl filled with bubbles he blew at her the way he used to do with Ronnie. She filled her hands with bubbles from the sink and threw them at him. When soap bubbles landed in her glass of red wine, he drank them off the top, grabbed her and kissed her, transferring half to her mouth before she could stop him. They drank more and shared it until it was gone and their shirts were stained. He was grateful that she chose not to mention the fact that he was drinking.

After the dishes, they checked on Ryder, who was sleeping for a change, filling the room with loud gurgling snores that overrode the constant noise of the television. Back in the kitchen, they looked out the little window over the sink at the clear night sky and the light of the rising moon flowing across the snow like an invisible river.

"Let's check on the horses." Ty kissed the top of her head and took a deep breath of her hair, which smelled like celery, a sweet light green he would never forget. He nuzzled her shoulder again and thought he smelled the thickness of vanilla, maybe almond. Earlier, when they were grocery shopping and stopped to check out the magazine rack, she'd read him a list of smells that turned men on— lilac and apple pie were the only ones he recalled. He liked *her* smells and hoped she never changed them. Maybe he should tell her that—tell her all these things he thought about before it was too late. He kissed her throat and worked his way up to her ear, pressing his lips deep. Had he told her he loved her? He'd told Logan, but had he ever said the actual words? He meant to. He thought she knew. She must know. He knew. He turned her face slightly and kissed her, soft at first, then harder and deeper until he felt her moan and twist in his arms to come fully against him.

When he pulled back and laughed, she clung to him and he loved how he could feel her nipples through their shirts. "We better check on the horses first, darlin'—" he murmured.

The snow squeaked under their boots, and the barn door groaned, breaking loose of the frost as it slid open. One of the horses nickered low at them and another stamped a hoof against the stall when Ty flipped on the lights. The buckskin in the nearest stall slowly got to his feet and, dropping his hindquarters, stretched his neck out and, starting with his head, gave a shake that moved down his whole body before he straightened. Then he eyed them with the suspicion of a seasoned cow pony.

"Relax, we're not putting you to work—" Ty laughed and reached over the stall to scratch around the ears, which this horse particularly liked. The buckskin put his head down and nudged in closer to the hand. When the fingers dug deeper, the horse closed his eyes and lifted his upper lip, baring his teeth in pleasure.

"Here—" Dakota held out one of the carrots she'd brought with her. The horse dropped his nose and sniffed it suspiciously. She took a bite and chewed noisily while he watched, then she broke a piece off and slipped it in the corner of his mouth. He moved it around on his tongue, testing the taste, then crunched tentatively. As soon as he had swallowed, he grabbed the rest of the carrot out of her hand with his teeth and pulled his head back in case she tried to take it away.

"Now he's hooked," Ty said.

"If he sees carrots he might come when you call instead of making you chase him with a rope." Dakota went to the next stall, where the gray was still lying down, too lazy to move. Dakota opened the stall and went inside. Kneeling beside him, she scratched up under his chin and down his throat. He groaned with pleasure, making deep sounds of satisfaction in his chest and belly. She laid her face against his head and put her arms around his neck.

"I hope he doesn't expect you to move in," Ty said.

"They all want me to move in, the place is so clean now." She straightened and offered him a carrot, which made him grunt and roll into a more upright position, with his legs folded under him. He chomped the carrot greedily, choked on a piece, coughed, swallowed, and immediately began searching her pockets and hands for more.

Going down the line, she gave every horse a carrot. When she was done, they were all standing at attention, their heads hanging over the doors, bobbing impatiently for more food.

"See what you've done?" Ty said. "Okay, I s'pose a Christmas treat would be in order. Give them each a handful of corn while I toss them some hay," he instructed. By the time they were through, they were warm enough to unzip their jackets. They sat on the stack of hay bales lining the wall and leaned back. He tucked Dakota under his arm, while she wrapped her arm around his waist. The horses pulled pieces of hay loose and hung their heads out so they could watch the activity while they chewed. There was something comforting in the slow grinding punctuated by an occasional slurp of water or stamp of hoof. The scurrying claws of a mouse scratched over the top of the big steel grain bin behind them in the dark, and occasionally a sparrow in the rafters overhead fluttered and gave a tiny, indignant peep. Outside the night was still except for the creak and snap of wood and metal in the cold. From a distant hill the sound of a coyote howl was more peaceful than mournful.

"This is what it used to be like when I was a kid out here," Ty whispered. "When Ronnie was little, he heard a story at school about how the animals got the gift of human speech at midnight on Christmas Eve. He started begging to stay up and come out here to the barn so he could talk to the horses and dogs. One time a pet chicken he got from somewhere. And the barn cats, of course. He was convinced." Ty smiled and snugged Dakota in tighter, putting his other arm around her waist.

"A couple of times, I had to come out and bring him back in after he'd fallen asleep in the hay waiting. Who knows, if the animals wanted to talk, they probably would have talked to Ronnie."

"He sounds like a wonderful little boy," Dakota said sleepily.

Ty nodded and smiled. "I'm glad he never found out the truth." For once the thought of Ronnie didn't make him angry or sad. For the first time in months, the complications were locked outside while he was here, snug and warm with the woman he loved. Maybe this was the best he'd ever felt in his whole life. He hugged Dakota against his chest and kissed her hair. Celery, definitely. Her breathing deepened and slowed and he could feel the spot where her mouth was getting hot and damp. He could stay there forever.

It had snowed again by the time they woke up late on Christmas morning, and when Ty went to feed the animals, the outside horses pranced and played before collecting to eat in the hard, bright sunshine. The cattle crowded the truck and pressed his body in a friendly way. The sky was that impossible bright winter blue, so optimistic that Ty even threw some corn out for the crows that had collected in the cottonwood trees by the barn. Once he was safely out of the way, the big black birds sailed down and walked with little mincing steps to snatch up the grain. They were the only birds he ever thought of as having arms—either in some much earlier evolutionary stage or some distant future one, but whenever he looked at them, he saw arms where the wings were.

He was just heading back to the house when his mother's dark blue Escort pulled up. He quickened his pace as the door opened and she climbed out, then ducked back inside. Maybe something was wrong; she never ever came out here on Christmas morning. By the time he had reached the driver's side, she was bending down, tying a big red plastic bow on the collar of a dog. The dog squatted fearfully, as if it expected to get hit when she didn't pat it.

His mother straightened and held out the thin rope she was using as a leash. "Here, can you take it? She's going to activate my allergies—had to drive here with my windows open as it is. I'm half-frozen to death."

Ty took the rope from her and stared at the dog, who was sneaking glances at his big rubber boots and manure-splashed Carhartts. He bent and patted her, noticing how the tail picked up a small wag and the nose touched his leg briefly before she ducked again.

"Where'd you get her?" he asked.

"Oh, it belonged to a family that got stranded on their way home to South Dakota for Christmas. Their truck was packed with little ones and presents, and the dog had been car sick since they left yesterday morning from Topeka. They came to the church to wait for the garage to finish with the truck, poor things. Hardly a dime to their names." His mother gestured toward the dog as if it were the one responsible for the family's poverty.

"Well, there was no question about it. Our pastor asked us to help them, and we pitched in the best we could. When the father saw what we were giving them, he broke down. With the clothes and food added in, there really wasn't an extra inch of room, and this dog was no traveler, I can attest to that. Lucky she hasn't eaten anything this morning, only messed the backseat a little bit." His mother actually smiled and looked around at the barnyard as if she were pleased to be here.

"I thought your father might enjoy having a dog again. She can keep him company since he can't—" She stopped and glanced at him quickly, something in her eyes he hadn't seen in a long time.

"Anyway, the dog will do fine out here. Just don't put her in a vehicle." She began to walk toward the back door. "He's up, isn't he? I just want to wish him Merry Christmas."

Ty was a little unsure about how his father was going to feel about this skinny, chewed-up-looking cross between a coyote and a bird dog. Odd patches of yellow fur sprouted from its neck and legs, as if there were some lion blood in there too, although the rest of the body was covered in a nondescript brown and tan.

On the porch, Ty stooped and pulled the pieces of hay from the dog's coat and tried to brush down the bushy yellow fur. He'd have to take the clippers to her. His mother knocked on the glass and simultaneously opened the door as Dakota was serving Ryder the first waffles off the iron. He waited for his mother to announce herself, then followed with the dog, which wagged its skinny tail once at Ryder.

Ryder looked at the dog, looked at his wife, then looked at the dog again. "You want a waffle, you'll have to wait your turn," he said to the animal, who promptly flopped beside his chair, with her head between her paws, eyeing him.

"Merry Christmas," Ty's mother said, and he dropped the rope beside the dog. Ryder nodded and quickly chewed so he could breathe, and Dakota patted his wide, bony shoulder.

"Well, it looks like you have everything under control here." His mother glanced at the food on the table, gave one of her quick smiles, and was out the door before anyone could invite her to stay.

Ty washed his hands and sat down, then realized he was expecting Dakota to wait on him and got up again. "I'll do the rest," he said and gently pushed her toward a chair.

"There goes breakfast," Ryder muttered, looking at the dog.

"Didn't bother you before," Ty said and overpoured the batter on the iron so it spilled down the sides.

"Didn't have a lot of choice then. Now I got the best darn little cook in Nebraska." He grinned and peeked at the dog again.

Ty pulled the top of the waffle iron up before the light went out, and the waffle split in two, half stuck to the top, half to the bottom. He slammed the lid down again, and poured himself a cup of coffee.

"This dog says she's hungry," Ryder said.

"I'll get it—" Ty motioned for Dakota to sit still while he prepared a bowl of last night's roast beef.

"Need to get her some dry food next time you're in town," Ryder commented.

Ty filled another bowl with water. Stooping beside the food, he called the dog. She lifted an eyebrow and glanced at Ryder, then Dakota.

"You go on over there and eat now. Don't embarrass him in front of his people," Ryder said, and the dog slowly got up and inched her way to the food. "Give her some room, boy."

Ty got up and went back to the waffle iron.

When they were all finished eating, they sat for a while at the table, watching the wind blow the snow off the cedars and tops of the fence posts under the intense blue sky. For a little while nobody said anything, and again Ty felt the kind of peace he remembered from his early boyhood and later from a day out working cattle or hunting in the hills, when the silence and the space seemed to cure whatever was troubling him. It never lasted though, he remembered, as Ryder stood up and began shuffling his way toward his TV. The dog stood and looked anxiously back and forth between them and the retreating figure. Finally Dakota unsnapped the leash and told her to go on and she trotted sheepishly after him.

"She knows," Dakota said.

"Think he likes her?" Ty asked.

She looked at him as if she couldn't believe how stupid he was sometimes and shook her head. "You don't have a clue, do you?"

He thought about the neon yellow western shirt he'd bought her and knew she was right. He wasn't even sure it was the right color. He should've gone for the red or blue. Thank goodness he'd settled on the poinsettia for his mother, nice safe choice at the grocery store. Buying the food had about wiped him out. Turkey, he hadn't had a Christmas turkey in years. Usually he and Ryder would have venison or beef roast and spend the day watching football or sleeping. Dakota had already started the stuffing the night before.

The dog walked back in with nails clicking on the linoleum and stood by the back door, wagging its tail. "Needs to go out," Dakota said and Ty opened the door for her.

"Think she'll come back?" he asked as she trotted out the yard toward the barn.

"She knows where the food is."

He put his arms around her as they watched the dog following her nose along the ground.

"What'd you do with my dog?" Ryder's voice surprised them.

"She's out doing her business," Dakota said and turned back to cleaning up the dishes in preparation for stuffing the turkey.

"Well, you folks come on in here for a minute then." He walked a little faster to stay ahead of them and they could hear his wheezing. By the time he reached his chair, his chest was heaving with the effort and it took him a few minutes to catch his breath. Dragging on the oxygen, he pointed a trembling finger at a square white box with a silver ribbon on it sitting on the TV tray set up beside him, then pointed at Dakota. Ty understood immediately and picked it up and gave it to her.

Being careful not to break the ribbon, she tugged it off and opened the box. Inside was a heavy gold necklace and matching bracelet in scalloped seashell links. "Ryder—" She breathed and picked up the necklace. "Thank you, it's *so* beautiful—" She started to fasten it around her neck and Ty had to lift her hair and finish the catch while she snapped the bracelet on her wrist. She turned her wrist back and forth so the light played on the expensive gold, then went and kissed the top of Ryder's head and brushed his hair back. "Thank you, this is the nicest present anyone's ever given me—" Her eyes were shiny as she looked quickly at Ty.

Ryder put down the oxygen and gestured toward the gun case. "Why don't you pick out the rifle you want and consider that your present, son."

Ty hesitated. It was an awkward moment. They rarely if ever gave each other presents. Then he shrugged. He'd always admired the custom-made .12-gauge shotgun. He took it down, noticing that the old man had kept the engraved barrels shiny and clean. The blond maple stock fit perfectly against his shoulder. He nodded at Ryder, who wore that small, satisfied smile that so irritated him most times. Now he wasn't sure he cared so much.

"That dog needs letting in—" He gestured to Ty. Taking the gun with him, he left, aware that they began talking the minute he was out of the room.

Ty felt cheap giving Dakota the ugly shirt he'd chosen, and decided he couldn't give her that after he opened the door for the dog, who was shivering patiently on the top stair to the porch. He wanted to be mad at Ryder for upstaging him, but in all fairness, the old man did owe her something, and it wasn't his father's fault Ty was too broke to do something nice for her. Then he thought of the gray horse. Bobby was dead. He had told himself this morning that he'd get up and go after Harney as soon as Christmas was out of the way, and hell, he wasn't sure he'd be coming back. Best to make sure she got the gray now. He looked around for some paper and a pen, or a card if he was lucky. In the pile of mail, he found a blank sheet of paper, scrawled a greeting, signed his name, and stuffed it in a slightly dirty white envelope he found in the bottom of the odds-and-ends drawer next to the fridge. It looked terrible. He remembered a couple of Ronnie's old crayons in the drawer, pulled them out, and tried to decorate the envelope with black-and-red trees and hearts. By the time she was coming back into the kitchen, it was too late to start over, he realized with despair as he looked over the scribbled mess. He was too embarrassed to give it to her.

"What's this?" She leaned over and picked up the envelope, the heavy gold bracelet clanking on the tabletop before he could stop her.

"It's for you." He stood to pour himself another cup of coffee, wishing for the first time in two days that he could open a bottle of whiskey to cut it with. He had to stop drinking. He didn't even know why he'd started again. Actually, he'd used part of the money from his mother for a fifth of the cheapest he could find, and hidden it in the truck. He could go out and get it now, but he shouldn't. Not now.

"Interesting decoration." She laughed, turning it over and over. As she read the paper, a strange expression came over her face, then she reread it and held it out to him. "Read this."

He took it and read: "Merry Christmas. I hereby bequeath the gray horse to you. Love—me."

"Bequeath?" She smiled. "Are you planning on dying soon or something?"

He felt his face grow hot.

"Thank you, Ty, really. I really appreciate it. Just wasn't expecting a horse, I guess." She put the braceleted hand on his arm and he felt embarrassed. Should've given her the ugly shirt. See, this was why he hated Christmas so much.

"Wait here," she said.

When she came back, she handed him a big box wrapped in blue-and-silver paper. He set it down on the table, really not wanting to touch it. He hated opening presents in front of people.

"Go ahead, open it."

He shrugged and picked at the end with a broken fingernail. She'd sealed every seam with tape. Finally he succeeded in getting a flap loose and peeled back the paper.

"I didn't have any ribbon—" She stood grabbing the back of the chair, rocking on her heels.

Inside the box was a pair of the ugliest maroon-and-gray dress boots he could imagine. He touched the marbled leather of the needle toes. Christ on a crutch, they must have had a celebration the moment these boots walked out the door. "They're nice—"

"Aren't you going to try them on?" She pulled one out of the box. "Try them on—"

"Yeah, okay." He sat and tried to tug them over his socks, but they wouldn't go. The leather was stiff and the cut all wrong for his foot. He held them up and smiled. "Have to save these for special occasions. Thanks a lot."

There was a moment of awkward silence before they burst out

laughing and hugged each other. Then he ran upstairs and retrieved the shirt. When she opened the box and gasped at the lemon neon, he grinned. "I guess this wins the prize, huh?"

They kissed and she pushed him away. "Go on out and torture some animals now—I have cooking to do."

He got into his Carhartts, coat, and boots. At the door, he said, "Thanks a lot, Dakota," before he went out.

He pulled the whiskey out of the truck and slipped it in a deep pocket of his coat before he walked to the big barn. With his luck today, the poinsettia he'd given his mother would probably drop dead at noon. Next year, he vowed, he was not going to do this. He was going to ask Dakota for a list. Hell, next year he might not even be alive.

Looking around the barn, he thought of the neat, fussy one at Latta Jaboy's. His place in Kansas would be suffering the cold now. The horse bodies had kept it warm enough during the winter—he hadn't had to worry so much about frozen water pipes, but this year, when it stood empty through extreme cold, the building would suffer.

He'd gotten these stalls mucked back down, hauled the old manure out to a pile he found in back. In a couple of days, he'd spread it for fertilizer over the one hay meadow they'd cut last summer. He'd cleaned out the garbage too, and dumped what he couldn't burn in a washout they'd been trying to fill since he was a boy, but the erosion kept eating away. He planned to haul larger things like tires out to some places Ryder had told him about. But when was he going to do all this? Going to Harney's tomorrow or next week might mean the end of his work here, and what would happen to the ranch then? What would happen to Ryder?

He took a drink of whiskey, liking how it cleared his head. Sometimes he could really understand how the old man had needed to drink all those years away. Probably quit as soon as Ty took off, because there was nobody left to deal with.

The horses were waiting for him, nickering as soon as they caught sight of the man in the dusky aisle. Ty opened the stall door for Noah and clipped a lead on the halter. He was a good, sturdy animal, lucky the bowed tendon had healed so well. He thought of the horses that had disappeared that day. The lame horse from Dusty's was probably Alpo. The heavey horse too. Some of the others might have survived. Maybe the App he'd gotten from the track. He had a lot of flesh on him, but he was kid-proof and soundproof and not completely ugly. Good starter horse, anyway.

He tied the gray and picked up the curry and brush, going over the tall horse with circular motions to loosen dirt and dead skin and scraping the loose hair out of the implements every few minutes. He should pull shoes today. He looked at the angles on the gray. Too much heel, needed to align the bones and hoof for the continuous angle. Last shoer had filed the toes to make the shoe fit and now they were a mess. And when he lifted the front hooves, it looked like there might be a bruise from the shoe cutting in too far at the heel. Noah nuzzled his back pockets, using his teeth to pull at the handkerchief. "Here—" He batted at the head behind his back, and the horse grabbed his coat sleeve and pulled. Ty let the hoof down and looked at the horse, who—aside from having the coat caught between his teeth—looked perfectly innocent.

"Yeah, you're a real joker, now let go—"

He used the nippers to cut the heads off the nails and pry the shoes off. Then he took the curved hoof knife and began to cut off the old growth of the sole until it shone white, then trimmed the edges so he had nice clean lines. There was a small bruise on the first foot, but it didn't look like it was festering or sore, so he trimmed it up and checked the angles and length, then went on and trimmed the other front foot. The back shoes were so loose that he pulled them off without having to snip off the nail heads, and had to inspect for damage. Aside from a few torn and chipped places, the hooves were pretty healthy for a gray horse, notorious for weak, white hooves, and he simply had to smooth them off.

While he worked, he thought of Kya and how she must see him as some racist shit because of what he'd done. He'd been a kid, he didn't care who they were beating up. He wasn't like Harney. He really didn't give a shit about Indians or white people. Truth of the matter was, he didn't give a shit about anybody back then. Not even himself. But something had changed inside of him when he saw the blood on the snow and drove off, leaving those boys to die. Something had made him go back, though he'd cursed all the way, and made him drive them to the St. Francis and made him actually care when one of them died, even now, all these years later. Kya had told him about Bob being the drunk haunting the streets of Babylon these past years. All that, the man went through all that, and died anyway. That was the wrong part here. That was the unfairness—for a person's life to be erased so easily, so negligently. It made his own life seem worthless now too. He couldn't explain it. That's why he couldn't talk about it, no matter who wanted to know. That's why he wasn't just going after Harney for himself.

He worked quickly and efficiently, and had all five of the most broke horses trimmed and back outside before he took a breather and got ready to face the youngsters, who would give him trouble. Being used to him, his chestnut colt hadn't given him any trouble, but Ryder's horses looked wild-eyed every time he came near them.

Well, he had it to do—he sighed and roped the first, a big paint with a thick neck and equally thick legs that hinted at draft horse ancestry. God only knew where Ryder'd gotten this one, and from the stubborn glare in its eyes, he had his work cut out for him. They argued about picking the hoof up and keeping it still while it was worked on until Ty drew the opposite hind leg up with a pulley system he'd seen an old shoer use years ago. With only two legs to balance on, the horse figured it out pretty quickly and contented itself with snapping its teeth whenever Ty got within striking distance. This thing wasn't such a youngster, he decided upon closer inspection. The feet were seedy, the pale crumbly hoof below the white legs about what you'd expect to find. He found evidence of some foundering in the ridges a fever sometime in the past had made on the outside of the hoof and felt more sympathy for the horse. Probably in pain from rotated coffin bones. He needed shoes desperately to get the weight off those heels. Pads over the soles too. He left as much heel as possible and promised the horse new shoes before he turned him loose with a handful of corn so he'd remember something pleasant. The paint grabbed the corn, trying for a few fingers in the process, and trotted off, limping slightly.

The other horses were just ignorant, and settled down fast enough so he could finish the job. By the time he was headed back to the house, it was afternoon, and both his ribs and his back ached pretty good. He was looking forward to a long soak in the tub and some whiskey to ease the soreness away.

"Trimmed the horses' feet," he said to Dakota's back as he took off the barn clothes, remembering that he had to smuggle the whiskey upstairs somehow as he hung up the coat it was stashed in.

"How were they?" She pulled out the rack and basted the turkey, which smelled wonderful.

"Okay. Have to shoe the paint—it's been foundered." She was paying so much attention to the turkey, he figured now was his chance. He lifted the bottle out of the coat and held it down along his side as he walked out of the kitchen. "Going to take a bath—" he said as he headed for the stairs.

"Ty," his father called and he turned the corner and left the bottle on the stairs before going to see what the old man wanted. The whole house smelled like roasting meat and his stomach growled.

"Trimmed all their feet," he announced.

"They give you any trouble?" Ryder kept his eyes on the football game in progress on the TV.

"That paint's a pain in the ass. Where'd you get him?"

Ryder looked up. "That's Turbulence, that roping horse went to National Finals three years running?" When he noticed his son's blank expression, he added, "Forgot. You were gone by then. Nielsen loaned him to a fellow the fourth year while he stayed home, and the jackass foundered him. Hasn't been worth spit since. I told Nielsen he could come out here and live, boss the babies around. Surprised he let you at his feet. Even Nielsen's given up trying it without a tranquilizer. He comes out a few times a year."

"Well, he sure needs more than that. I'll shoe him tomorrow. Think we got a system worked out he can stand, long as I stay outta the way of his teeth."

Ryder laughed and wheezed and the dog beside him thumped her tail. "You got a lot more ambition than me, son—there, you see that? Son of a bitch's been throwing interceptions all afternoon—" He pointed at the TV and Ty left.

That night a big storm blew in from Wyoming and collided with another storm, coming down from the Dakotas and drove snow in huge drifts across the ranch. By morning Ty was fighting a hangover and eight-foot drifts to get feed to the animals, which took hours, with the wind whipping new drifts to replace the ones he was trying to plow. The people in the house did the only thing they could do then, hunkered down and waited for the storm to blow itself out, praying the electricity would stay on. Although there was a small generator in the basement for emergencies, Ryder hadn't had it on in years. They slept and ate and played cards and argued. When Ty went out that evening to move the horses into the barn, he almost got lost. He managed to bring in three that time, and went back to get Dakota and some heavy-duty flashlights and rope to finish the job. Making a moving corral with the rope between the two of them, he pushed the horses against their will toward the open back doors of the barn. They kept stopping and hunching, their backs to the wind, unwilling to move until Ty hit them or dragged them by the halters forward again. When they got close enough to see the light coming from the barn and hear the other horses whinnying, the horses stampeded for the door, smashing against each other in the effort to get inside. There they crowded into empty stalls together and kicked at each other, making things dangerous for Ty and Dakota trying to sort them out. By the time they were ready to close the door, they had to clear a drift. With the howling wind locked outside, they looked at each other, frosted and red-faced.

"We better hurry," Dakota said, "we shouldn't leave Ryder alone for this long."

"He knows where we are—" Ty put a scoop of corn in the buckets they'd lined up for the horses tied across from the stalled ones, and began to distribute hay. It was warming up in the barn, and the horses were already steaming as the snow began to melt and slide off their backs. "Grab a sack and rub them while I finish haying—"

She took off her gloves and began work on the paint, who flattened his ears and lifted a hind foot.

"That one's pretty sour." He dropped a bale of hay and spread it out among the three tied horses. The stalled horses nudged their buckets and kicked the stall boards in case they'd been forgotten.

"Hope the cattle'll stay put. They start wandering in this storm, pushing through the fences, getting out there where we can't get hay to them, we could lose a lot." Another burst of wind shook the windows in their frames and blinked the overhead lights. "Remind me to ask Ryder when we're due to start calving, okay? Some of those cows look pretty big. Just hope he didn't decide to try January calving or some dumbass idea like that. Couldn't get close enough to check all the udders, but I thought it looked like at least one of them was starting to wax up—now, that would be a real mess."

He grabbed a burlap bag and started on the stall horses, quickly rubbing to increase circulation and speed of drying. That's all they needed—bunch of sick horses. He thought about going to see Harney, it'd have to wait a few more days. Maybe after New Year's. It would be his own personal resolution. He stopped rubbing on the horse and looked across the aisle at Dakota, who was standing on her tiptoes next to the buckskin to get the hips good. Suddenly he was humbled by her sticking with him. It wasn't fair for her to be mixed up with this thing that got started between Harney and him so many years before.

He finished the horse and went to the next stall. His arms felt like lead and all he wanted to do was go back to the house and sleep. They might not even make the house with the blizzard. That was just wishful thinking, he realized; he'd tie them together with a rope and use the flashlights. They'd left the house lights on too. But it took them half an hour struggling in and out of drifts and redirecting their path to get to the porch. Ryder was waiting in the kitchen with hot soup and tea for their chattering teeth and stiff, half-frozen flesh. "Snowing out there, huh?"

"When are those cattle due to calve?" Ty asked as soon as he could talk again.

"Now that is a problem—" Ryder looked out the window obliterated by the snow piling up on the sill. "If we had sold and shipped last summer like I planned, see—"

"How many?"

"Two hundred head. I was trimming back the herd, thought I'd sell 'em for early calving—heard there was more interest south of here for that—"

"They said on the radio this morning this could be the worse winter on record," Ty said.

The old man nodded. "I know. We're in trouble—"

↶ Chapter Twenty-four

The first calf came right after the new year, before Ty had a chance to dig out the cattle from yet another storm, sort them, and move them closer to the feeders. He found it that morning, encased in ice, its eyes never opened, the mama bawling over its shiny red-and-white form, her udders painfully swollen. When he tried to take the calf, she pushed and butted him until he roped and dragged her to the fence, where he left her tied. The temperature had plunged and threatened to stay well below zero for the next week. He was probably going to lose more, he thought, as he fastened a rope around the calf and pulled it to the hay yard. The deer had started tearing up another stack. He'd have to get out there with a gun and scare them off. Maybe give that new dog a run at them, though she seemed content to hang around with Ryder, pricking her ears and looking at him with those sad watery eyes as if she understood every single word the old man was saying. Ty couldn't remember there ever being a dog allowed indoors. Any animal for that matter, except for the occasional snake or toad Ronnie snuck upstairs.

He'd saddled the paint, and with the new shoes and the bottom of the pads greased so snow didn't pack up, the old horse was quite willing to work cattle. Ty was trying to move the most pregnant cows into the smaller pens so he could keep track of their calving. He also wanted to keep the weanlings close enough that he could pull a feed sled to them. He'd almost asked Dakota to help him, but he'd left her in the house, listening to the old man rambling on about some bullshit or another. Added to everything else, Dakota had been too quiet the past few days, and that worried him. Maybe she was going to leave. Ryder always said that Sandhills ranching was too hard on women. That woman in Texas had gotten quiet, then she was gone and he was left with a pile of dirty clothes and a bad attitude.

He tried to think his way past Harney, plan how he'd take up the rest of his life, return to Kansas, rebuild his business, but he couldn't make his mind go there. Everything came to a halt at Harney Rivers and here, as if his own life had been in parentheses between that night years ago and now. He remembered as a boy riding to the top of the tallest hill on the ranch, 2,200 feet, and looking out across the broad emptiness, uninterrupted as far as he could see by buildings, billboards, or roads, with the sky a pale erased blue overhead. He'd believed that if he could just get away from here, his life could be as open and limitless as that view. Now he realized that he had lived only one small piece of life, in a single deep valley from which he could only look up and imagine the endlessness beyond.

When he'd come in from chores last night, he'd found Dakota on the phone. She'd looked at him with this startled expression and quickly hung up. Neither one had said anything about it, and Ryder was having a bad enough night with pain in his back and legs, struggling for breath and demanding the breathing treatments early, so Ty had let it go.

Working his way through the cattle, he found another fifty head whose udders were waxing up. He'd have to start checking on them a couple of times a night. Even then, he wondered how he'd keep the newborns alive unless he could crowd them all into the barn somehow. As if in warning, the cow that had lost her calf moved to the fence closest to the hay yard and set up a steady chorus of bellering that sounded close enough to a human sob that a couple of times he caught himself looking up to see if maybe a person was there.

At noon, when he went in to warm up, Dakota was pulling on her snow boots.

"Soup's on the stove. You need to wait for Verna. She should be here in another hour or so. But in case she doesn't get here, he needs a breathing treatment in exactly one hour. Don't forget, it's really important to keep him on schedule, okay? I have to go to town." She stood and reached for her coat as he wiped the frost off his eyebrows and rubbed at his icy earlobes.

She took out her gloves, then shoved them back in her pocket and finally looked at him. "I have some errands to run."

He nodded and shrugged. The soup smelled good, but he didn't want her to go. "How about a sandwich?"

She sighed. "I have to go, Ty."

Something in the way she said it worried him, what if—but she was taking his truck, surely she wouldn't run off with that. "I'm ass deep in pregnant cows out there, can't it wait? I could really use some help."

She stared at him. "Verna said she'd be out after this new family she has to go see. Just don't leave him alone, okay? And don't forget about the breathing treatment. He's not good today, Ty." She kissed his cheek and zipped her jacket.

He had this impulse to grab her hands, hold her in his arms so she couldn't go. "Looked the same to me this morning." He turned his back to her, willing her to leave before he stopped her. He had this awful feeling that he might not see her again once she stepped out that door.

"Bye." She opened the door.

He heard it shut with a soft whish, and then the porch door and her feet on the steps, the truck engine chugging awake, and the truck slowly crunching across the barnyard snow and down the road. He looked out the little window over the sink in time to see the exhaust rise and hang in the frigid air in miniature rose-shaped clouds over the road.

After he ate, he went to check on his father. The dog lifted her head and eyed him mournfully, then sighed and dropped back, her eyes shifting between his stockinged feet and the recliner Ryder occupied.

"How you doing?" he asked, but the old man didn't answer. Ryder was watching the burgundy-and-tan clock on the shelf next to him and writing something down with a pencil on a long yellow legal pad. Without appearing to spy, Ty got up and went to the gun cases, checking the tablet over his father's shoulder. It was filled with numbers in descending order, apparently counting something down. The TV show was on mute, and the colorful flashes reflected in the glass of the gun cases like a cartoon. Ty knelt down to search the lower shelves of the cabinets for the pistol he remembered Ryder keeping around for varmints. When he came up empty, he opened the drawers, finding nothing but old photographs and the foot of Ronnie's first jackrabbit. It was gray and moth-eaten from years of being packed around in the boy's pocket and then living in the dark drawer afterwards. When Ty picked it up, most of the hair fell off into his hand, making the foot look naked and somehow obscene. He dropped it and shut the drawer.

He turned to ask his father about the pistol, but the old man was asleep, his mouth ajar, his head crooked uncomfortably, the pencil still clutched in his hand. Ty didn't want to wake him, so he tiptoed out.

He was working on the logs, trying to get a better sense of the calving and the cattle he'd ship next week when he heard his father gasping his name. Running in, he glanced at the big clock. Shit. Almost two hours. He'd missed the treatment and Ryder was strangling, holding the oxygen tube up to his nose with shaking hands and trying to force more air in while his chest heaved. Ty panicked. He hadn't paid enough attention, he'd been relying on Ryder to tell him how to set up the medicine and the breathing tube. Now the old man couldn't, and his face was turning deeper red as he struggled and fought for air. The dog leaped up and barked and ran from one end of the room to the other.

"Where is it? Where's the stuff?" he yelled and Ryder waved toward the TV tray set up against the wall, which held the little vials and wide plastic tube. "How do I do this?" He shook the vial at his father, whose eyes were wide with panic.

"Help—" he whispered.

"Oh shit, here, is this the way?" Ty tried to force the vial open and broke the top, so the medicine spilled out in an obnoxious-smelling stream. He grabbed another vial and ran to the kitchen for a knife or something to make a hole in the top. He looked at the plastic apparatus in his other hand and couldn't remember how to make it work. Somehow it had to produce the fumes that delivered the medication to his father's lungs, shrinking the swollen tissues, opening the airways so he could breathe. Behind him he could hear his father choking for air and the dog barking. He took the cleaver out and hacked the top off the vial with a loud bang just as the back door burst open.

"Hello?" Verna Stromme called out in a singsong that disappeared as soon as she saw Ty's face. "What's wrong?"

"He's dying—" He held up the breathing equipment and the useless vial.

"Give me that!" Verna grabbed the plastic tube and marched out of the room. Without taking off her coat and hat, she inserted a new vial and administered the treatment, soothing Ryder's panicked breathing with her calm, soft voice while Ty looked on helplessly. After he'd settled into it, she gave him a shot. "This isn't going to make you sleepy or anything, Mr. Bonte. It's to give your lungs an extra boost, clear some of that fluid that's making it hard to breathe. You need your treatments on time, though, you need to remember that. It's dangerous to let it go this far." Ryder wouldn't look at him, and Ty felt his face go red. "Now take that dog out of here," she ordered.

"It was my fault," Ty said and took the dog's collar and together they slunk off to the kitchen. Was he trying to kill his father? Did he want him dead that much? No, he'd been busy, and he thought the old man looked tired, needed to sleep. He complained all the time about not being able to sleep. But maybe he did want him dead sooner than later. He couldn't be sure.

After a while Verna came in and took off her coat and hat, and put a hand on his shoulder. "He wants to see you."

He didn't want to face his father with what he'd almost done.

Ryder's face was pale and still, as if he were simply too exhausted to make any expression. He motioned Ty to stand closer, with the dog at his knee whining. The old man put his hand on the dog's head to quiet her. "It's okay, son."

"I'm sorry—I didn't mean to—"

"I know." Ryder closed his eyes and Ty felt the immediate release of shame, for which he was truly grateful. He couldn't remember feeling this kind of gratefulness before, not with his father, not ever. He started to put his hand on the old man's hand, but stopped himself and quietly left the room.

Dakota found Mrs. Bonte in the basement of the Evangelical Brethren Church, reading Bible stories to a group of small children stretched out on little mats for their nap time. In the room she'd checked first, several older kids were trying to solve mathematical translations of the dimensions of Noah's ark into modern terms. She'd been told by a woman dismantling the Christmas tree in the vestibule that theirs was an alternative school staffed by the minister, his wife, and volunteer parishioners. Mrs. Bonte was very good with the younger children, and could be trusted to fill in when Eugenia, the minister's wife, had to see her dentist. She was having one root canal after another. Dakota could tell from the way the woman jerked the ornaments off the tree limbs, spraying dry needles, that having bad teeth was borderline sinful in some people's eyes.

She watched Mrs. Bonte's mouth, hoping for a glimpse of her teeth. Ty's were okay, big and solid with the usual fillings. He could brush them more often, but they weren't as bad as some. Eddie had always made a big deal of keeping his teeth white, said it sold a lot of horses. So did drugging them and sleeping with the clients, he should've added. It was good to be away from him, but looking around the grim room, with the gray painted walls and the worn gray-and-black flecked linoleum floor, she had to admit that maybe this deal wasn't much better.

She'd come to talk to Ty's mother about Ryder and Ty. Somebody needed to do something—hospitalize the old man, hire a good lawyer for Ty—and she wasn't family. She wished she could talk to Latta Jaboy, but Dakota couldn't think of a way to approach her. Besides, it meant dealing with Cody again, and that was too weird. Then Joseph Starr had called two days ago, asking her to meet him up in St. Francis. She'd tried to say no, but he'd said he had news about Ty's case she should hear. Looking at the small children, whose eyelids were starting to flutter sleepily, she wished she could go to sleep too. Or call her own mother for a bus ticket. She thought of the hurt on Ty's face and knew she'd never leave him, no matter what happened. There was something about spending the night with him, his worried arms clutching her tightly in his dreams. When he woke her with his angry mutters, it took only a few soft words from her to calm the dream. She'd never felt such healing power in her life. She thought of her own mother and father, how once they had probably been able to soothe each other too, before the losses piled up between them like a thistle fence.

Mrs. Bonte closed the book, looked at Dakota as if she had a hard time placing her for a moment, then stood and came out of the room into the hallway, leaving the children asleep on the floor. They agreed to go down the street for coffee until Mrs. Bonte had to go to her other job, at the home for "my boys," as she called them.

Walking the three blocks from the church beside the tall, thin woman Dakota wondered what his mother thought of her living out there with those two men. These hyper-Christians scared her. She'd avoided the churches in Divinity, partly to stay away from the wild kids who used the youth programs as a way to spend time messing around with each other, and partly because she found herself virtually unable to believe a single word that came out of those ministers' mouths. The cross on top of this church even wore a lightning rod. But sometimes she read Genesis, letting the generations lull her into a sense of well-being, believing that no matter what happened, life went on and on and on and on, and so a tiny part of her must too.

They passed the library she'd lied about going into, and she thought maybe she'd come back there later, even though the one-story blond brick building didn't look big enough to hold many books. Then in the second block they passed the drugstore, the Harmony Gift Shop and Vacuum Cleaner Repair, whose windows were filled with colorful yarn dolls and tissue box holders, a Christian bookstore; a store that sold pets, musical instruments, CD's, tapes, and magazines; a deserted pizza place; a pinball and video arcade; and a bar. On the next block, they passed a furniture store, a bar, a clothing store, and finally reached the café. Apparently the place had once been an old-time drugstore, Dakota decided when she saw the long marble counter with the low stools and the high, dark oak booths. The floor was made of black and white hexagonal pieces of marble, and the tin ceiling was yellowed with smoke and grease. Bottles of alcohol on a shelf lined the mirrored wall behind the counter, and below the shelf stood the malt machines and canisters for hot fudge and toppings. Greasy smoke hung in the air and nudged against them as soon as they sat down in a booth. The thin, dark woman behind the counter put her cigarette down and blew smoke toward the closed door before she came around and asked them what they wanted.

She must be Native, Dakota realized as the light brown hands quickly set their table with glasses of water and then coffee. Her straight ponytail was the black-brown color of Kya's hair, and her eyes lifted up at the edges in that slightly Asian way.

Mrs. Bonte sipped at her coffee and stared out at the street, apparently unwinding from her class. Dakota couldn't think of a way into the conversation she needed to have, so she sipped at the slightly bitter afternoon coffee too.

The waitress picked up her cigarette and began smoking again as she leaned back against the work area and looked out the front windows.

"Well, I'm sure you didn't come here for the coffee." Mrs. Bonte tore open another packet of sugar and dumped the contents in her cup, followed by another shot of milk. "I should have asked how long this has been sitting." She sipped at the cup, made a face, and sipped again.

Dakota blew on the surface of the cup and drank. Black and bitter. Ty would've loved it. "I guess you know Ryder's getting worse—"

The other woman nodded, watching her with those perfectly guarded gray eyes.

"I'm not sure what you want me to do—I mean—" She stopped because Mrs. Bonte looked over at the Native woman smoking behind the counter. Since they were the only customers, there wasn't anything else to do.

"I wish she'd stop smoking." Mrs. Bonte's voice was loud enough to carry across the small room. As they watched, the woman sighed and put out her cigarette, then walked to the double doors leading to the kitchen and disappeared.

Mrs. Bonte drank some coffee. "I understand that my husband is dying. I've urged him to make his peace with the Lord, but knowing Ryder, he won't. There's nothing else I can do, is there?"

No wonder Ty left here. Dakota wanted to get up and walk out. She couldn't even look at this woman. "I'll stay with him, but that may not be enough. You may want to think about some other options for him. He should be in a hospital or nursing home. I don't know how long Ty's going to stay. They don't seem to get along so good, and Ty's in trouble himself. He needs a lawyer, and I was hoping—"

"I am not getting involved, I told my son that already. He made the bed he's lying in, and that's all I have to say to him. He's too much like his father. My other two children were more like my people—the Bontes, well, the less said about them the better. I don't know what my son has told you, or what the two of you are mixed up in, but I'd prefer it if you'd either keep it out at that ranch or take it back to Kansas."

She put her cup down and stood. "Now I have to go to the group home and take care of my boys. I hope we understand each other—" The woman stared long enough to get her message across, then glanced toward the street with such a look of longing that Dakota understood something she hadn't before: how much Ty's mother wanted to avoid anything that would bring her feelings bubbling to the surface again.

"Well, thanks for your time. I'll get this—" She pulled two dollars out of her pocket and rummaged in her coat pocket for change as Mrs. Bonte walked away. Sitting there, sipping at the coffee while it cooled, she tried to think about what to do next.

"She coming back?" The waitress held the glass coffeepot to one side as if she'd pour it on the older woman's head if she appeared again.

Dakota shook her head.

"She's always complaining." She held the pot over the cup and Dakota nodded. "I don't know why she bothers coming in here if things are so bad. All those people from that church are like that except for a couple of them. The preacher's wife is okay. She at least tips. Those people come in here of an afternoon and sit around wanting all kinds of service for their measly coffee and donuts and leave maybe a dime between all of 'em. I told Mary to put a CLOSED sign up the minute that school of theirs lets out. She won't though."

She put the pot down and dug in the pocket of her apron for her cigarettes. "I'm Lisa."

"Dakota."

"Mind?" She gestured toward the opposite bench and Dakota shook her head.

While she lit up and took a deep drag she blew across the aisle, Dakota noticed the darker brown of small scars and bruises on the woman's arms, as if she'd led a hard life.

"You're not from around here."

"Iowa originally, then Minneapolis and Kansas." The coffee was lukewarm, but she didn't want any more.

"Hitting all the high spots, huh?" The two women laughed. "I'm from Pine Ridge, but my boyfriend in high school was from Rosebud, so when I got pregnant, I moved. Used to work at the Pizza Hut, but I got tired of the organizational bullshit. Mary here is good to me. When my kids are sick, we can usually work something out, you know. You married?"

Dakota shook her head.

"Saw you with that Cody Kidwell before Christmas." She didn't look at Dakota, but tapped her ash off on the floor and scraped at it with the toe of her sneaker. "His sister's up on the Res all the time, telling women to keep their hands off him. She's mean, you better watch it."

"Yeah, well—we just met—" Dakota couldn't look at the other woman.

"Uh-huh. Where you staying?"

Dakota hesitated. "A ranch south of here." Lisa's silence made it clear she was waiting for more. "The Bontes' place—"

"Figures." Lisa stood and put the cigarette in the corner of her mouth, so she had to squint as the smoke rose up. "You were talking to the old lady." She picked up the coffeepot.

Dakota wanted to say that he didn't do it, but she could feel the wall come up between them. It wasn't just the two of them, it was the whole community's wall she faced. A community that in this case, white and red alike, was beginning to surround them on all sides, to isolate and keep Ty and her out.

"Thanks." Dakota stood and left without looking at Lisa again. That made two people in the space of fifteen minutes she wouldn't be speaking to ever again. At this rate she'd finish the whole town in less than a week. Harney's bank stood across the street overseeing the corner with its faux bell tower and glass brick windows, as out of place in the old Sandhills town as the Pizza Hut at the far end of Main. When she got home tonight, no matter how tired he was, she was going to make Ty sit down and figure out this Harney deal.

∞ Chapter Twenty-five

When Dakota finally found St. Francis, she slowed for the sign to the Indian School, then because she was early, kept driving slowly past the Outpatient Alcohol Treatment Center, housed in a long, long trailer painted with Native American designs on the front, and a trading post with three sullen-looking men lounging out front. A middle-aged woman bundled in layers of thin, ragged coats, black sweat pants, blue-and-red scarf, and a pair of men's green rubber boots moved achingly slowly toward the post. In her hands she clutched some letters to be mailed. A large black-and-brown dog followed close behind, glancing anxiously around, but the woman ignored him. As Dakota passed, she saw that the woman had a fleshy, almost pouchy, scarred face. A new maroon pickup squealed around the corner and sped past her, going in the opposite direction. Three young Lakota men with long hair and sunglasses were crammed in the front seat. They looked over at her, said something, and laughed.

It was two blocks to the other side of town, where she turned around. She took the first left and ended up in a neighborhood of single-story houses with practically every window broken and mended with plastic, boards, or duct tape. Large black garbage bins on wheels blocked driveways and sidewalks or stood half in the street. Plastic children's toys, bottles, cans, old tires, and trash poked through the snow in the yards. She could see no one outside walking, or even peering at her from behind the pulled torn curtains and shades. On the corner was a burned-out trailer, its black greasy insides erupting into the crusty snow. She drove slowly as if she were in enemy territory, permitted to pass through only by a brief truce. A couple of dogs stood in the road smelling something squashed flat, and she braked, not daring to honk at them. They glanced at her with casual indifference and trotted off to the edge, where they stood waiting for her to pass so they could return to their find.

Coming back to the highway, she took the next turn and drove onto the Catholic school and church grounds. She kept going until she came to the cemetery and stopped. It was surrounded by a high security fence topped with strands of barbed wire, as if the dead were especially violent prisoners. Inside, half the grounds was crowded with white wooden crosses placed so closely together it was as if they were for dolls. The markers puzzled her, as if the dead were so insignificant they could be buried almost on top of each other. Then suddenly she understood—this was the school cemetery. For the Indian children dying here at school, homesick, heartbroken, fevered, and coughing, far from their families, then put here in long, tight rows like dormitory beds. There was nothing to distinguish them as Native American children, nothing to distinguish them as individuals at all. It reminded her of the national military cemeteries. She looked away to the nearest maintenance building, whose missing panes of glass seemed to gaze like empty eyes at the scene across the road. She turned the truck around.

Joseph Starr was waiting outside the cream masonry church when she pulled up, and they stared at each other for a moment until he came around and got in the passenger side. Rubbing his hands in the blowing heat she switched on, he smelled like wood smoke and something else, denser and sweeter, herbs maybe. He shoved his hands in his jacket pockets and looked at the building set back a little beside the church.

"That's a museum. Not open now, but you should come back in the spring. It's a good place. The ladies who run it know a lot of things. They'll take you on a tour of the church too. They love showing off the old priest vestments. Whole inside of the church was repainted in the twenties. A young Native woman did the designs." He glanced over at her, but she couldn't see anything through his highway-patrol mirror sunglasses. "She was a relative too.

Dakota nodded, thinking he must be related to half the Reservation. He pulled the shoulder strap on the seat belt out and struggled to fasten it until she helped him find the latch.

"We going someplace?" she asked, with her hand on the gear shift.

"Turn onto the highway going north—to your right. We need to run over to Rosebud."

On the far side of the town of Rosebud, Joseph directed her to pull into the parking lot for the Rosebud Tribal Police and Court. It was the first thing he'd said since they left St. Francis. Her heart thumped unevenly as she read the sign, and she gripped the steering wheel hard.

"What's this?"

"I want to show you something." He climbed out of the truck.

She waited until he was almost to the plate glass door of the court before she followed. Her eyes blurred with panic, she hardly noticed anything as they were led into a small consulting room with a white man in a navy blue blazer, white dress shirt, blue jeans, and cowboy boots. His head was shaved clean like a basketball player's, making him look more distinguished, even handsome, she noticed, when Joseph introduced him as Kyle Langly, the Rosebud public defender.

"This isn't about those nephews of yours, is it?" Kyle asked after they shook hands and settled around the small table.

"The assault case on my cousin? You were helping me with the paperwork?" Joseph took off his mirror glasses and squinted. He rubbed each of his bloodshot eyes in turn.

"You were one of my clients, I'd say you were smoking too much dope, Joseph." The lawyer laughed.

"Too much cedar smoke in my trailer this morning," he said. "Think I'm getting allergic or something."

"Probably pissed off one of the spirits," Kyle offered and rapidly tapped the pen in his hand against the table. "Say, I was driving up here to work early this morning? Sun just coming up? Suddenly right in the road in front of me were three deer. What is that, some kind of sign, do you think?"

Joseph looked at him with a serious face, thought for a moment, then nodded. "It's a blessing."

Kyle lounged in his chair, grinning like he'd just won a new car. "Yeah? What sort of blessing?"

Joseph rubbed his right eye again. "I s'pose you could call it a blessing you managed not to hit 'em."

"Very funny." Kyle glanced ruefully at Dakota and shook his head.

"Okay, let me get the papers for you." He left and returned so quickly she didn't have a chance to ask questions.

"You file this and we serve the two of them. Then it's up to them whether they want to come up here and deal with it or not." Kyle set the papers in front of Joseph. "You need to sign here and here." He turned to Dakota. "Are you the witness?"

"No." She looked from one man to the other. "What's going on here?" Kyle raised his eyebrows at Joseph, who shrugged.

"Well, Mr. Starr here is suing Ty Bonte and Harney Rivers, who tried to murder his cousin. I don't know how he thinks he's going to get them up here, but he seems to believe he can do it."

"Forget it." She stood and pulled the truck keys out of her pocket.

"Wait," Joseph said. "Let me finish reading this—"

She stood by the door, confused between feeling this sudden fury and wanting to cry from fear. Was he setting her up somehow?

"You need to bring Ty up here. He'll pull Harney along. They won't let the other one come alone—too worried about a one-sided story," Joseph said. "Trust me, this is the best way for Ty to clear himself."

"Why don't you just admit it—you're trying to put him in jail!" She tried to grab the papers but he caught her arm and held it until she relaxed. She rubbed at the place where his fingers had gripped it like metal claws.

"If he's innocent, he'll be fine. All you women have about con- vinced me of it. Now I need Ty's help to make Rivers pay." He looked at her, but she felt his focus someplace on the wall behind her rather than on her face.

"Why should I help?"

"The sheriff in Babylon isn't going to serve the warrant on Ty. At least not until Harney Rivers can put enough pressure on the prosecutor. Or worse, until one of them gets up the nerve to shut the other one up for good. Think about it. That's all Ty can do unless he runs again, and that's all Harney can do if he wants to live around here and stay in business. You say your boyfriend's not a killer, then help him prove it. Bring him up here to court. He can bring a lawyer." He shifted in his chair. "Right, Kyle?"

Kyle nodded, his sharp gray-blue eyes holding no sympathy for her, she noticed.

"Why can't you just subpoena him or something? Serve him and make him come yourself?" she asked.

"A white person has the right not to answer our court here, even if he's committed a crime on tribal land. If it's a bad crime like murder, manslaughter, rape, kidnapping, he'll likely be charged under the Indian Major Crimes Act and go directly with the FBI to federal court." Kyle took the papers, glanced through them, and put them down. "This court is more a psychodrama than anything. Hardly anyone gets sentenced to jail or does much time. Mostly six months to a year maximum. That's for aggravated assault, domestic abuse, drunken driving, arson, things like that in criminal court, which is essentially a misdemeanor court like children's court."

"Why don't you use criminal charges then?"

Joseph crossed his legs and looked at his hands folded in his lap. "We thought about it. Kyle here says there's no double jeopardy between concurrent jurisdictions." He smiled grimly at the lawyer. "Have to put a different kind of pressure on Harney. He'd walk out of twenty-year-old assault charges. And we don't want to convict Ty alone." He took the lobe of his right ear and caressed it between thumb and forefinger.

"You want to use Ty—I won't do it." Dakota crossed her arms and shook her head.

"I think you better." Joseph locked his eyes on hers and she felt cold and helpless. "You care about him, you should try to keep him alive."

"I do care, and I'm gonna try to keep him away from here, that's for sure! And don't try serving any papers, I'll be waiting with a rifle and an attack dog!" She yanked the door open and ran outside to the parking lot, but her truck was blocked by a black Explorer out of which that Kya woman was climbing.

"Get out of my way!" Dakota screamed and had to stop herself from kicking the driver's door of the Explorer.

"All right, calm the hell down—" Kya threw her cigarette on the snow-packed ground and climbed back in. Gunning it, she spun the tires and slid around so Dakota's truck had enough space to inch by.

Joseph and the lawyer were watching Dakota's departure when Kya stomped into the office, leaving grids of snow from her boots and flooding the air with cold and smoke drifting from her clothes. She picked up the top document and quickly scanned it. "Guess I missed all the fun—"

Looking at Kyle, she said, "Keeping out of trouble?"

"Trying to." He looked away, blushing.

The secretary told Dakota to wait, Mr. Rivers was with someone. That was good. She needed a few minutes to calm down before she confronted him. Sitting on the overstuffed gray leather sofa facing the gray-and-burgundy lobby, she watched the ranchers come and go with their small transactions. They seemed slightly ill at ease with the lush contemporary carpeting, drapes, and wall coverings. Everything else about this town was straightforward, from the pickup trucks and battered Reservation cars to the bars on every block.

There was a reserve too in the bodies that came to lean tiredly at the teller windows, and in the faces that looked her over without hesitation and only a little curiosity. She'd grown up around rural people, but these were different, as if they understood how tenuous their hold on the land was, as if they accepted that all their efforts would eventually be buried in the hills threatening to slide across their puny ranches and towns. There was a uniform colorlessness about their clothes and expressions, along with a stubbornness that refused to resign itself to the inevitable. She recognized it in the Bonte men too.

As she looked back toward Harney's door, it finally opened. A tall, heavy-set man walked out in front of Harney, turning at the sec-retary's desk to say something else and shake hands. There was something familiar about him, the mouth or eyes, but she couldn't place it. When they both came to where she was sitting, their size made her feel like a child, but they were standing so close she couldn't get out of the too-soft sofa without bumping into them.

"Arthur Bennett—Dakota Carlisle—" Harney said as if they were at a cocktail party. It bothered her that he knew her last name.

"Miss Carlisle—" Arthur bowed his head at her in an old-fashioned gesture that seemed to go with his suit and string tie.

"She's staying at the Bonte ranch," Harney said.

"How's Ryder doing?" Arthur asked.

"He's pretty sick," she said and regretted it. These were the kind of men Eddie used to say you never gave information to unless it benefited you, because they sure as hell would make it benefit them if they could.

"Sorry to hear that." He looked so familiar somehow.

"Dakota's quite the horsewoman." Harney smiled as if the two of them were much more intimate than they were.

"We'll have to get you out to the Bennett ranch then, take you riding. We have some very pretty land, you know. I've come to appreciate it in the winter especially, with my hay fever—" He touched his nose and chuckled.

She tried to smile but felt shaken and drained by the size of these two men, towering over her. She leaned forward as if to rise. Arthur took a step back, but Harney held his ground, trapping her in the sofa.

"We're almost neighbors, anyway," Arthur continued. "Our place is on the other side of Latta Jaboy's—" The corners of his mouth turned down, and he began to put on his overcoat. "Have to go down to Ainsworth again. Still trying to dicker with that old man for his motel, but I'll check back the beginning of the week. And don't worry, we'll be able to cover the whole casino deal. It'll be worth the wait." He clapped Harney on the back, nodded at Dakota, and walked away.

"You're waiting to see me?" Harney asked and held an arm out toward his door.

When they were settled in his office, which was surprisingly simple, he swiveled in his chair and looked out the small, smoked-glass windows that gave him a view of the side street. The only wall decorations were four big oil portraits of men with varying shades of white hair and enough family resemblance to be Harney's forebears. The furniture was tan saddle leather, in contrast to the hunter green carpet and neutral walls, but despite the color, the room held no warmth or personality. A small silver-framed picture of an ordinary-looking woman rested on the ornate cherry desk that might have been passed down through the generations of the men on the wall. Dakota sat uneasily on the edge of her seat, refusing the too-soft chair that would again keep her at a disadvantage. She'd driven off the Reservation in a rage, then worked to calm herself. With a dangerous man like this, she didn't want her anger to blind her. The bloody images of Ty and the horse threatened to settle over her like wet flannel, and it took some effort to push them away so she could stay alert. Watching the disarming way Harney studied the street, chewing at his lower lip, shoulders tense with thought, she felt like a barn mouse stilled just before the bull snake jaws snapped it up.

Finally he turned back to her. "What can I do for you?"

Don't give in to the anger, she warned herself. "You owe Ty. He's kept his mouth shut—now give him the bridge loan for the ranch."

He looked surprised. "Ty sent you to—"

"That's bullshit, and you know it."

At the first sign of her emotion, Harney smiled. "Look, Miss Carlisle, I'm awfully sorry about the Bontes' troubles. But the fact is the ranch has been mismanaged for so very long I can't in good conscience allow this bank to loan them any more money." His face was bland, unremarkable, like the blunt edge of a steak knife.

"This isn't about that—"

He waved off her words. "Don't waste your breath."

They stared at each other for a moment until she broke and he looked out the windows again. But it was enough for her to see the blue liquid deadness sitting empty there. She made herself return to the bloody images of Ty, which resurrected enough angry strength that she could stand and walk to his desk.

"You owe him! And you'd better pay up or I'll—" She picked up the glass paperweight with the iridescent blue butterfly trapped inside.

He was so quick he was able to grab her wrist and turn it until she bent across his desk, gasping but refusing to cry out.

"You'll what?"

"Testify!" she panted and gritted her teeth.

He twisted a bit more, making the ache in her elbow and shoulder stab sharper, like something was about to tear and break, and she had this desperate moment when she realized nothing was stopping him. Then he released her.

"Testify, huh. Don't even think about causing trouble here—" He rubbed his own thick wrist like he'd hurt it instead of hers. "Tell Ty he'd better keep his mouth shut too and stay the hell away from me. Now get out of here before I call the sheriff."

IV

Every Form of Refuge

◯ Chapter Twenty-six

When she'd told Ty where she'd been and everyone she'd spoken with, he grabbed her shoulders and shook her so hard she bit her tongue bloody. When he let go, she swung at him and missed. The pain in her arm from earlier made her cry out and admit what Harney had done. It took her threatening to leave for good to keep Ty from driving straight to town. She'd tried several times during the past two weeks to explain her interference further, but he was too exhausted to talk, sleeping in the barn now to be on hand if a cow needed help with calving. This morning he'd come dragging in, dark hollows under his eyes, unshaven, hay and manure sticking to his clothes, and asked her to help him with something. They'd had to use a chain to pull a calf out with two broken legs from being twisted, and the cow had almost bled to death before Ty could stop it. What Dakota would always remember from the scene was the grunting of the cow and the hoarse staccato breathing of the man as they worked against each other, Ty finally wrapping the chain around a post for leverage. Then bloody to his elbows and cursing in a steady mind-numbing stream, he put the pistol to the calf's head and pulled the trigger. After that, she'd come back in and spent a long time showering, then soaking in the tub to get rid of what she felt until she realized that it was the sour smell of blood, manure, and brains in her nose.

Ryder spent his days moving between the recliner and Ronnie's bed they'd finally brought down to the study for him. He seemed to sleep as much as he was awake and his skin was getting grayish yellow and loose. Although she made the recipes he'd taught her, she couldn't tempt him to eat more than a few bites at any meal, and she'd almost given up trying to invent new treats. Yesterday Verna told her that he was beginning to show signs of oxygen deprivation, and that eventually the build-up of carbon dioxide in his blood would make him hallucinate and then drop into a coma as his lungs gradually filled with fluid and he drowned, if his heart didn't quit first. They could hospitalize him or they could take care of him at home. A few minutes ago Dr. Wilkes had shown up, and his voice could be heard booming from the other room.

She was standing at the kitchen sink waiting. There wasn't anything else to do these days. The house was as clean as she could get it without painting the walls and throwing out the old furniture. She had the feeling that she'd done all she could here, but she couldn't leave. In the past when a man pouted or cut her off for a few days, she'd have packed and been gone before he had a chance to blink. Now she was trapped, because for the first time in her life she loved a man she didn't think she could do without.

"Well, I've given him something else for that back pain." The doctor walked into the kitchen as if they'd already been having a conversation. "It has to be mild, but just don't let him take too much at one time, no matter what he says. I'm sending out some stronger steroids for his breathing. Verna'll bring them tomorrow." The doctor stopped and looked out the window on the porch door. "He's a tough old bull."

"How long?" She hated the question, but it had to be asked.

He shrugged and rubbed the back of his neck. He was a tall man with a pronounced belly that rode high and hard like a melon on an otherwise thin frame. "Seen cases like this go in a couple of weeks or six months." He began to tug on his boots.

"But he *is* dying."

His narrow face turned toward her. "Well, we all do eventually—"

"No. I mean he's dying *now*. It's important that we know." She couldn't keep her hands from knotting against the cupboard drawers behind her.

He nodded slowly. "Yes. Anything we do now is to keep him comfortable. If we're lucky, if *he's* lucky, he'll slip off in his sleep in the next few weeks."

"You tell his son then. He needs to know that. He doesn't believe—"

"You can say I—"

"No, I can't. You need to tell him, he's out calving in the barn. And you need to get someone out here to stay full time. Tell him that."

He slipped his arms tiredly into his big brown parka. He was an old-fashioned man who still wore a dark blue suit doctoring, although it was shiny and threadbare from use.

"Hard to find someone who'll come all the way out here." He put on his black-and-red checked wool hat with the earflaps down.

"You find someone." She turned her back on him and fiddled with some silverware in the sink.

"Whatever you say." He sighed and clumped out onto the porch, then outside.

Turning back, she watched him walk to the barn, each big boot landing clumsily as if gravity were about to fail, the way astronauts walked on the moon. After a while, he reappeared from the barn, shaking his head as he walked to his Jeep Waggoner and drove away. She watched until he was out of sight. She didn't know why she'd said that to the doctor. Something had to change though, and it looked as if it was up to her to make that happen. What was odd of late was her impulse to call her mother, ask her advice, and pour out her story—although she hadn't called, because it was something she'd been careful never to do in the years since she left home. It was these hills, she thought, looking out the kitchen window at the snow going lavender blue in the failing light. These hills made you realize how alone you really were in the world and turned you back toward anyone you were ever connected to while the string holding you together thinned and frayed. But her mother wouldn't understand this place or her daughter's life. Dakota had given up on that years ago. She could imagine the words her mother always said, "Come home, dear." Come home, as if sleeping under the eaves in her little single bed with the musty plaid wool-backed comforter would solve the adult problems of her life. She thought for a while longer, then looked up a number in the local phone book and dialed.

For dinner she made beef stew, loaded with potatoes and carrots and peas, and served it with a black raspberry Jell-O studded with fruit cocktail. Having saved out some cherries, she arranged them in a face on the surface of Ryder's portion. He only looked up briefly from his tablet of numbers and scrawls when she came in the room, but she set the tray down beside him. "I can read to you later," she offered. He nodded and told the dog to go eat its supper. "Try to eat something yourself," she urged and left.

Ty surprised her by coming in and heading upstairs. Twenty minutes later, when she was finished with her dinner, he came in clean-shaven and bathed, wearing fresh clothes. He'd lost weight, she noticed, from the way his jeans hung on his hips and bagged in the seat. When she got up to get him a plate of food, he caught her at the cupboard and leaned his hands against the counter on either side of her.

"What's going on?" he asked with his face close enough to kiss her, but holding back.

"Nothing."

"Oh really." He put his arms around her and hugged her body carefully.

He took the plate and dished up some stew, sat down at the table, and ate quickly without speaking. Then he got up for another plate and some bread. This time he ate more slowly, chewing thoughtfully, with his eyes on her. She wished she hadn't called Latta and poured out her troubles.

The dog came in and shoved its head onto Ty's knee. He patted her and slipped her a piece of stew meat. She gulped it noisily and went to the door. He was halfway out of his chair when Dakota stood and let the dog out. "You need to hire some help," she said to their reflections in the dark glass of the door.

"Why would you say a thing like that?" he asked when she sat back down and picked up her fork to poke at the Jell-O that was suddenly too close to the color of the blood drying on the straw under that cow. He dragged a piece of bread through the gravy and stuffed it in his mouth. His big hands were rough and raw red from the cold and work, the fingernails still holding rinds of dark grime.

She shook her head.

"What's going on?" His voice got soft.

"I need you back here in the house—"

His eyes got hard and his eyebrows raised. "Can't you handle it? I got calving in the middle of winter, I got that old man on my back all the time, now you want company? Jesus—"

"We need help here. You're working yourself stupid. I can't— your father's dying, Ty, please—we can't *both* of us go twenty-four seven. And nothing's being done about—"

"What? You got more for me to do?"

"I asked you to talk to Joseph Starr, to talk to a lawyer so you could take care of yourself. I don't want you killed, don't you see that? I *saw* Harney, Ty, I *know* what's going to happen. You're going to throw yourself away for nothing!"

He slammed down the fork in his hand, stood, and grabbed her shirt and hauled her to her feet.

"Let go!" Her face and body stung as if he'd hit her. "I'm going to tell your father everything."

He picked up his plate and threw it crashing into the sink. The remaining stew flecked the window and cupboards.

"Tell me what?" Ryder leaned against the doorway, the oxygen tubing snaking behind him like a leash.

Outside they could hear the dog barking and scratching to get in. Dakota turned and slammed out to the porch and the dog bounded in ahead of her, but quickly dropped to its stomach in front of Ryder.

"Tell me what?" The old man's tone carried its old authority and harshness despite the panting breath that surrounded the words.

"She's—" Ty pointed his finger at her.

"We need to get somebody here to help us." Dakota glared at Ty.

"Wonder what took you so long." Ryder limped off into the dark shadows of the dining room.

"Fine. You're right, hire whoever you want." Ty wiped his face tiredly and began picking up the pieces of plate.

Two days later Verna showed up with a suitcase in one hand and a case of Diet Coke in the other. Dakota shrugged and led her upstairs to Ty's sister's room. For some reason, she couldn't bring herself to put the other woman in Ryder's room. Verna looked around critically as she plopped the suitcase on the bed. "No TV," she said and sighed.

"Just the one downstairs with Ryder." Dakota looked at the dead flies and dust on the windowsill she'd forgotten to clean. "So, do you need anything?" She hugged her arms around herself as Verna inspected the room once more and shook her head and sighed again.

Verna released the tarnished brass suitcase locks with a dull snap. "I expect it's going to be pretty lonely out here."

"Is that Verna I heard thumping around upstairs? I've had bulls walked softer than that woman." Ryder put his tablet aside and pushed his hair off his forehead. She'd meant to cut it yesterday.

"Is Ty giving you fits—that why you moved that infernal woman in here?"

She shook her head and looked at his hands, with the fingernails turning blue-white. Another sign of oxygen depletion, Verna had told her.

"A person could do worse than hooking up with my son. He's a hard worker when he puts his mind to it. A little soft, maybe, but I tried to toughen him up. Takes things too hard. Never got over his brother. Like his mother, I guess, in that one respect."

His mother had claimed Ty wasn't like her at all. She took a deep breath. "He doesn't want anyone's help."

"Never did." Ryder's face flushed pink and his mouth tightened. "You aren't leaving, are you?"

"I'd never do that—"

Ryder nodded and coughed in short, painful gasps for a few minutes. After she offered him water, he leaned back and closed his eyes. She thought he was falling asleep until he spoke. "My son has a lot of faults, but he'd never hurt you, Dakota. That, you can count on. Granted, he doesn't know a helluva lot about women—hell, I don't either. But whatever else his failings are, he's not the kind who'd hurt anything he didn't have to. I know the calving business is hard."

"No—" She wanted to talk the whole thing out with him, but it would just be cruel to get him excited and worried when his time was so short. By the time Ty had to deal with Harney, Ryder would probably be—

"Well, make sure you keep your promise now. Don't want me going to my grave cursing you for leaving me alone with Verna Stromme." He turned his head toward the shelves of books and she closed her hand over his for a moment.

Getting up to leave, she looked out the windows toward the barn in time to see Ty dragging the carcass of another dead calf out to the place beside the burn barrel, where the last one was still smoldering, filling the cold brittle air with the rancid smell of singed hair and charred flesh. It was so cold that the smoke clung to the earth, refusing to rise up.

∞ Chapter Twenty-seven

The next day a lawyer from Rosebud drove up and handed Ty notification that he was being sued for assault and wrongful death. He threw the papers in the pile on the dining-room table and stomped out to tangle with the paint horse, who needed shoes again. He knew better than to work on horses when his temper was up, and the paint reminded him with a hoof to the thigh that left a big bruise when he got careless pulling the pads and shoes off. He found himself cursing Joseph Starr, Dakota, Latta, his father, Jesus Christ, and just about anybody else he could think of.

Then he stopped and laughed at himself, in a brief respite from the depression and anger that had been working on him lately. The one thing he intended to make clear when he had time was that he did love her, and that was why he couldn't let her get in the middle of this mess. It had scared the hell out of him when she went to see Harney. As long as he knew she was safe, he could stand anything that happened to him. Maybe he should send her away. The idea made him careless with a nail and he almost quicked the paint, who yanked the hoof out of his hands and stomped the side of his boot with it.

"All right," he muttered and patted the horse.

Back at the house, Ryder kept watching him and waiting for him to say something, but Ty was used to that from the old days, so it wasn't hard to slip back into the usual resistance he met his father with. It just hurt this time, where it used to feel good to be so stubborn. Verna Stromme fussed around enough it irritated both men and occasionally united them in a quick glance or shake of the head. Several times Ty saw a strange truck parked outside the house when he came back from working cattle, fencing, or town. He had no idea who it was, but it was clearly planned for when he was away. For the first time in his life, Ty felt so utterly trapped he couldn't imagine his next step. He simply could not picture his life a year from now, and it haunted him as he worked through the long late-winter months fighting storms, cold, and calving.

In mid-March Verna announced that she was going on a week's vacation to Las Vegas with her husband, and she was gone the next morning. Ty remembered his panic the last time he was alone with his father in crisis. As soon as Verna left though, Dakota handed him a nursing schedule. When he tried to object, she held up her hand, put on her coat, and left in the truck. He had first shift today. Forget cleaning stalls and checking fences.

Ryder hardly ever got out of his recliner now except to go to the bathroom or lie down in the bed. Ty went in to sit beside him in case he needed anything. There was a couple of days' lull in the calving if his calculations were right, and the doctor said he'd come out that afternoon. He half-hoped that Dakota would come home early.

Ryder's words had a hiss around them as if they rose out of steam or vapor when he spoke. "I think you and your sister should run this place together. Put a package together for the bank and buy another place, the way Arthur Bennett is doing." He lifted his hand and dropped it on the remote, causing it to flip channels silently. The mute button was always on these days.

Ty nodded. His father was coming up with one scheme after another, none of which was possible. Maybe they were things the old man wished he'd done.

"You got to quit having parties in here at night too."

Ty's head jerked up. "What do you mean?"

"The nurses spilled their drinks on my toes." Ryder was smiling.

"Okay." Ty decided the old man was clearly going crazy, so he'd better humor him.

"So what'd you do to that little girl sent her off this morning so I'm stuck with your sorry attitude?"

Ty looked around for something to distract his father. "Want me to read to you?"

"No, I do not. Never particularly liked the sound of your voice. That Dakota, now she's got a fine reading voice."

"Just let it go."

When he looked at Ty, there was a yellowish tinge in his eyes, but it didn't disguise that old, familiar hardness. Here it comes, Ty thought.

"You ran out of here like a scalded dog, stole my truck and saddle—left me that sorry excuse of a note like some raggidy-ass cowhand. What happened to you, boy? When did you turn into such a little coward?" Ryder was gasping after his short speech.

"It's none of your goddamn business what I did or do. When the hell did you ever care?" Ty stood up and paced to the TV, flipped the sound on, then off, trying to control his anger.

Ryder laughed and the familiar caustic sound stopped Ty. "You think this is funny? You laugh at everything, don't you? Goddamned comedy routine. Ma leaves, funny as hell. Ronnie dies, you're grinning at the funeral."

Ryder coughed and dragged shallow breaths on his oxygen. "You leave your brother out of this—"

"Not laughing now, are you? Isn't it funny now you're dying, isn't that hilarious?" Ty leaned both fists on the recliner arms, putting his face close enough to the old man's to smell the rotting thrush on his gums.

"Git—" The frail hands pushed at the thick wrists, but couldn't budge them. The dog lying on the other side of the chair sat up on her haunches and looked worriedly at them.

"Okay—" Ty lifted his fists and straightened, then, looking once around the room, he turned and walked to the kitchen intending to go outside, but something made him stop and return to his father's side.

"What now?" Ryder sounded exhausted.

"Ronnie."

The old man shook his head.

"Why didn't you just let him be a kid?"

Ryder sat still, his eyes closed.

"You know what?" This terrible urge to hit his father rose up in him. He wanted to smash that face with his fists, batter that ugly mouth until it bled. "Of all the things I felt that afternoon lying out there beside my dead little brother, one thing made me happy—just like you every time something bad happens."

Ryder shook his head and squeezed his eyes. "Don't—"

"The only thing I have ever been able to feel good about is that for once, for once in your life you got to reap exactly what you sowed. You killed Ronnie, and you were going to live with it for the rest of your life. It wasn't the tractor killed him, it was you, you god-damned stubborn, hard, bitter, heartless old bastard. You. And we both know it. You couldn't wait for him to grow up, you had to break him like you broke me. Only he wasn't as strong as me, and Mother wasn't here to stop you, the way she'd stopped you before."

The tears starting down the white-stubbled cheeks enraged Ty—what right did that old man have to grief? "That day I knew he'd died to make you sorry, and I was *glad.* You got what you deserved." Ty's heart was pounding so fast he couldn't catch his breath and he had to bend over while the room swayed.

"You hated him, Ty, you could've stopped him from getting on that tractor—you wanted him out of the way—" Ryder whispered.

"That's a lie! I loved Ronnie, God, I loved him—" Ty fought his own tears.

"You never loved anything or anyone, Ty. I watched you. You're just like me."

"No! Don't you say that—I'm not like you, I loved my brother—I wished it was me that afternoon, me that'd died, not him—or you, God, I wish you'd die."

Everything was silent around those words, which landed and scattered like dark feeding birds between them. Ty couldn't take them back, and his father couldn't bear their weight.

Finally the old man rubbed his forehead with a shaky hand and opened his shiny eyes. "Well, it looks like you're going to get what you want this time. Got anything else to say while we're clearing the table?"

Ty didn't want to say the next thing, but he couldn't stop himself any longer. "You were glad it wasn't me out there, weren't you? 'Cause I carried a man's work—couldn't afford to lose me, could you? Eight-year-old boy wasn't so bad though—"

Ryder stared at him for a moment. "You know so much, you figure it out."

"Fuck you, old man, just fuck you to hell." Ty slammed the palm of his hand against the door frame so hard it rang out in a loud clap as he spun away.

"Won't be too long for that either," Ryder said to the retreating back.

Ty was putting on his coat when the phone rang. Logan's voice sounded cautiously upbeat when he asked how things were going.

"Perfect. Just perfect," Ty said and told him about Ryder's deterioration. When he told him about the lawsuit due to come to court in April, they both grew silent.

"Want me to come up there?" Logan finally asked.

Ty thought for a minute. After what had just happened, it would be good to have someone else to sit with his father, but he couldn't inflict that on a relative stranger. "Maybe in a few weeks—I could use some help branding and moving cattle around then."

"Okay. Ty? You're still holding up, aren't you? I mean, you aren't planning anything—"

Ty shook his head. "Wish I was—"

"Don't go off half-cocked now. See this thing through with your dad. Get a lawyer, and we'll figure out the rest when I get there. And *do not, do not* go after Harney on your own."

"I'll try." That was all he could bring himself to commit, because he could feel this pressure swelling against the seams of his mind like an infection. He wouldn't make it another couple of months, let alone a couple more weeks. And he wasn't going to let himself be dragged through court. He'd had enough of that bullshit as a kid.

"Call me before anything happens, I can be up there in a day."

"Sure, okay, I gotta go now." Ty listened to Logan's good-bye and quickly hung up the phone. He was going to have to do something before too long, even if it was just hassling Harney. He couldn't let his enemy get too far away, that's when he would get dangerous again. And while he was cleaning house, he might just go over and kick the crap out of him. The thought made him happy until he caught the reflection of his smile in the window over the sink and realized how much it made him look like his father.

He was cleaning out the barn, staying close enough to the house so he could check on his father, when he saw Dakota drive up, climb out, and pull two bags of groceries into her arms. He threw down the pitchfork and headed for the house.

When he slammed the door shut, she jumped and turned from the open refrigerator, a carton of orange juice in her hand.

"Why didn't you tell me you were going to the store?" He grabbed a bag by the top and it ripped and dropped, spilling cans and bananas onto the floor.

She pushed the refrigerator door closed and kicked at a can rolling her way. "That was brilliant."

"You take off without warning. What if Ryder needed something?" Ty dropped his hat down on the table.

"Verna gave me a list of what was needed while she was gone. God, you are such a—" She bent to pick up the bananas sitting precariously close to his duct-taped boot.

He opened his mouth, then shut it and went to the sink. Grabbing a glass from the pile of dirty dishes he hadn't washed after she'd gone, he filled it with water and drank with his back to her. She picked up the rest of the groceries and put them on the table.

"I'm not going to fight with you, Ty." Her voice sounded sad and he turned to look at her. She was running her fingertips over the label on a can of stewed tomatoes Ryder had asked for.

"Dakota—" He stopped when she looked at him.

"What?"

"Logan called. Said he wanted to come for a visit. In a couple of weeks, I guess." He wanted to say that he missed her in bed and wanted her back.

"That'll be nice." She picked up the can of tomatoes.

"I hate those things." He nodded at the can.

"Yeah well, they're not for you, are they?"

"I'm not cooking 'em either." He regretted the words as soon as he said them and saw the annoyance on her face.

"Do you have to be so selfish all the time?"

"You—" He started to say that she didn't understand what there was between him and his father, but changed his mind. "They make me sick to look at. I know he likes them—I just have trouble fixing them is all."

She began sorting the items on the table.

"Look, I'm sorry." His voice dropped to a whisper. When she turned and hugged him, he felt grateful enough to offer to stay with his father the rest of the day. They went to check on his father. Ryder was dozing with his mouth open, snoring, a rind of white crusted along his lower lip. The room stank of medicine, rotting gums, and something else, close to urine but more acrid. Ty tried breathing through his mouth but stopped when the taste showed up on his tongue.

Dakota watched him trying to work the spit around his mouth. "You have to take some time off, Ty. Go to town or something. I'll stay—"

He kissed her hair. "Maybe I could return those boots." They'd agreed on exchanges Christmas Day. She smiled and pushed his hair behind his ears. "Be nice to have dry feet this spring." He hugged her and went upstairs for the box.

Merkel's Western Wear traded the boots in without an argument, and he put the remainder of the cost on the ranch charge. The sun, which had been shining earlier, had disappeared behind a thick layer of dark gray clouds. Ty walked across the street to the Buckboard for some lunch and a beer. Just outside the door, he looked across the street and down to the corner at Harney's Suburban parked in front of the bank. Maybe he'd visit his bank account after lunch.

Since it was well past the noon hour, the restaurant was almost empty and the service exceedingly slow, with most of the activity loud voices and clattering dishes coming from the kitchen. Ty drank the first beer quickly and had to wait ten minutes for the waitress to appear again. "They lost your order," she said. "Then they ran out of the special—"

He ordered one of the all-day breakfasts, two more beers, and a couple of shooters. No point in wasting all this time, he told himself. Retrieving a refolded copy of the *Omaha World Herald* from the next table, he tried reading while he drank and ate, but found himself unable to care about the stories of city violence or international politics. He noticed two teenage Indian boys taking turns at coming out and circling the dining room while they pretended not to be watching him. Since he was the only person eating now, it was pretty obvious. He almost said something, but decided to ignore it.

When he couldn't put it off any longer, he paid and left. The rain had started with a quiet mist, carried by the wind shifting to the northwest. With any help at all, it would start freezing, he decided as he looked toward the truck. He should really get home before the roads glazed over. Then he looked back down the street toward the bank. Maybe he should go see his mother before he left town. They hadn't spoken ten words since the holidays except for hello and good-bye when she called to check on Ryder and he handed the phone over to his father. He went to his truck and climbed in. The alcohol was rushing his head and giving him too many decisions, so he started up, backed into the street, and headed toward the bank and his mother's church. He'd let the truck decide.

His new boots slammed on the brakes at the corner and he turned left and parked. Then he remembered the promise to both Logan and Dakota. And he wasn't really one hundred percent sure he'd be able to stop himself from killing him once he was inside. He stood on the sidewalk outside the bank, rubbing his wrists in the rain, which was starting to come down in hard, icy slices pinging against the hoods of cars and trucks and clattering on the sidewalk and pavement. His arms and hands ached from holding back the anger that wanted to send Harney through his bank windows.

Ty looked around for something big and heavy to throw through the bank's plate glass doors, but when he noticed a couple of pickup trucks slowing and the drivers looking him over carefully as if he might be going to rob the place, he realized what a stupid idea that was. It didn't feel right to go home though, so he turned and walked back across the street to the corner bar where he'd been that night with Kya. Patches of ice were already starting to coat the walk and the slick soles of his new boots slipped a couple of times before he made it inside to the stale afternoon twilight of smoke and beer. It wasn't much, but it was better than facing Ryder and those damn cows again.

There were high windows along the street side that he could just see out of if he turned sideways on his stool, but he didn't. Instead he drank steadily, ignoring the comings and goings of the few stray cowboys having a beer before heading back to their ranches, and the two regulars who carried on a slow, witless conversation at the far end of the short bar. Behind them in the dark, dirty room a small scuffed dance floor glowed palely between the empty black wooden booths lining both walls.

Occasionally the owner, a man named Franklin, whose right forearm had been hacked off by a Japanese colonel in the Second World War, punched in some Hank Williams or Patsy Cline on the jukebox. "For days the sun don't shine," he told Ty, who nodded and wouldn't look above the hooked arm that swung casually over the glasses and clinked against the bottles. Discouraged, Franklin went to talk to the two men who leaned heavily on the bar nursing mixed drinks and cigarettes like professionals. Ty could hear their conversation plainly as they began to discuss Harney.

"Heard the Rivers boy's about run that bank into the ground. My wife's sister is a teller there?" one of the regulars said. "She says he had to go to the board about a week ago and explain some big loan he made to himself."

The other man smirked. "That's why I keep my money under the mattress."

"Don't that bag of quarters keep you up at night?"

They ordered another round and Franklin poured liberally, with a quick glance at Ty's glass. "Another?"

Ty nodded.

Franklin filled the glass, knocked off the foam, and filled it again to the very top. He set it down in a ring of wet and drifted down the bar again.

"Heard he might lose the Cessna plane too. Imagine, no more quick trips to Denver for dinner," Franklin said. "The old man was a businessman. This Harney, he plays too fast and loose. Has no reason to mess with those casino people. That's his trouble."

As the men continued to talk, Ty's spirits lifted. Although he knew better than to trust this phase of drinking, it felt good to have his mind swinging slowly from one thing to another, breaking the usual connections and pictures and finding new logic and memories. While not all of them were pleasant, he could count on them floating off after a while, and that was as good as it got.

It was dark out when the three Native boys came in and settled around him at the bar, but he was too drunk and absorbed to notice anything unusual about it until one of them bumped his shoulder, spilling the beer he was drinking into his lap. When he just stared at the bubbles disappearing into the dark of his jeans, the kid apologized and bought him a new beer. Before long, they were talking about football and cattle and weather like old friends.

"So what did the elephant say to the naked guy?" the kid to his left asked. Ty shook his head.

"How do you eat with that thing?" The three boys burst out laughing while Ty tried to puzzle it through.

"Get it?" they kept asking. "Do you get it?"

It surprised Ty that he felt like conversation, but the words didn't hook up into sentences well enough for him to follow, so it didn't seem to matter whether he actually paid attention or just seemed to, while the three boys around him laughed and told more jokes and drank their beer. He doubted they were old enough, but if Franklin didn't mind, he didn't. After all, this was where he and Harney had done their underage drinking too.

He was starting to nod out when the boy next to him said, "Come on," and slipped an arm around his shoulders. Before he could protest, he was stumbling out the door with them, and being half-shoved into the backseat of an old Monte Carlo with peeling green paint and a crumpled front passenger's door that was roped shut. A green plastic garbage bag held in place with duct tape covered the missing window. The fresh air cleared his head enough that he started to wonder what he was doing with these boys, who rode one on each side of him with only the driver in front. The way they laughed and glanced at him out of the corners of their eyes, while the car slid down the icy street blasting rock-and-roll, scared him.

"Shit," he mumbled and closed his eyes, but had to open them immediately because the car tilted too hard.

The kid next to him leaned his head close to his ear and said, "What?"

"Where we going?" he slurred.

"Don't you worry about that—" the kid on the other side said and suddenly punched him on the side of the head, splitting the scar at the top of his ear and making his head ring.

"What the hell—" He started to struggle toward the door, but the two boys in back clamped their hands and legs over him.

"Shut up!" the one who'd punched him said and shoved a smelly glove in his mouth so far he gagged.

"Don't let him barf in the car, man! My brother'll kill me," the driver yelled and the glove was removed.

His ear stung, and the blood was flowing freely down his neck inside his collar, but that was good because the punch had started to sober him up. The car was hurtling up the dark highway toward the Reservation as far as he could tell. When they got to the Rosebud Casino, they pulled into the parking lot and around to the back door. The driver stopped and got out. "Hold him a minute, I promised my brother I'd pick him up." He sprinted away.

"You sobering up?" the kid who'd punched him asked.

When Ty nodded, the kid said "Good" and hit him as hard as he could in the thigh with an elbow, cramping the muscles in a tight, painful knot.

The driver returned and spun the car around. "We have to go back to town, my brother's down there."

"Fuck that man," the hitter said.

"He'll tell my dad if I don't show up," driver said.

Ty tried to get his mind on a straight track he could fight back from, but it kept wanting to go to sleep instead. Who were these kids? He looked carefully at the silent one to his left, whose hold on his arm seemed weaker. Both boys in back wore their straight black hair almost to the shoulders, and there seemed to be a family resemblance between these two, with the same round faces and darkish skin with almost a violet cast to it in the dome light periodically turned on by the driver to change the tape. The hitter was thicker-bodied, with a short broad nose and big dark eyes, while the other one was skinnier, with small even teeth and light brown eyes. The driver had light hazelnut skin and dark reddish-brown hair with a wave he kept flattening down with the palm of his hand.

"Do you want some money?" Ty asked, trying to relax his body so the next punch wouldn't hurt so much.

"Money?" hitter mocked and laughed. "Oh shit yes, let's see what he's got, Henry—" He dug his thick fingers into Ty's jeans pocket, tore the fabric, and pushed at his side so he could pull out the bill-fold. "This is pretty pathetic—" The kid fanned the seven dollars in his face. "Not even a credit card? Big tough white guy must have to beat up Indians for the money, huh?" He flashed his wide fist in Ty's face and laughed when he flinched.

"Seven dollars, and with what we got left, we could get a case," the thin one said.

"What do you think, Jerry?" Hitter thumped the top of the driver's seat. "Beer?"

"Have to keep it in the trunk until I take my brother home. He don't want me drinking."

That was when he got hit again, this time a clip on his shoulder hard enough to send a shock of numbing pain all the way down his arm. At least they were leaving his stomach alone, probably so he wouldn't throw up in the car. He knew what they wanted now. That damn lawsuit probably had half the Res looking for him. Harney was smart to stay in his bank, out of sight.

After the beer stop, the kids shoved him in the trunk, with his feet resting on the case and his head on some oily rags and coils of thick, greasy chain. The cut ear he was lying on throbbed, and the stink of the oil rags was so strong it leaked down the back of his throat to his stomach and he almost threw up. There was so much junk under him he was being poked from every angle and couldn't straighten or seem to roll his body. For a moment he panicked, then made himself start to feel around for something he could use as a tool to break out with. His fingers found a hub cap, set of jumper cables, five empty oil cans and two full ones, what felt like a small fabric doll that crinkled like it was stuffed with corn stalks, something with fur on it, a smelly old quilt, a piece of rubber hose, some newspapers, but nothing useful like a tire iron or wire clipper or hammer. Bouncing around in the dark trunk sobered him up a little, making him understand that he was screwed. When the car stopped again, for the brother, he presumed, he banged on the trunk lid and hollered for help, but the kids cranked the music so loud he knew he couldn't be heard. Then he decided to keep quiet. He didn't want to give them a reason to beat him up before he figured how to get out of this mess.

It was cold in the trunk, and he tried to scoot down into the rags, but there wasn't enough to cut the icy wind and water coming through the series of rusty gunshot holes in the side panel and trunk lid. The car was going too fast for the freezing road again, and the back end kept sliding around, then it turned and the beer shifted and the car bounced around so much they had to be on a dirt road. Then they slammed to a stop. The trunk flew up and the hitter grabbed the beer while his brother held a hunting rifle on Ty.

The gun changed everything.

"Here, have one on you." Hitter laughed and threw a can at him. He caught the beer in his hands and thought about opening it, but changed his mind. He'd had too much already. Hitter slammed the trunk lid. As the car spun around, rocking his head and cut ear against the chain, he knew what he was going to do. There was a ragged, rusted-out place low on the side panel. By lying on his back, he was able to draw his legs up enough to kick at it, although not very hard. It took a few precious minutes until he felt his boot break through and he had to twist his foot around to get it back. He kicked again and again until the hole was big enough he could clearly see the pavement they were on again, shiny with freezing rain. When he'd busted out all the rotted metal, the hole still wasn't big enough for his whole body to go through. He stopped for a moment, the noxious fumes of the exhaust clouding in on the rain now, and the music pounding its hyperbass into his skull.

"Do or die time," he whispered and scrounged for the jumper cables. With great effort, he twisted and worked his body around so his head was at the hole and he could look directly down at the wet pavement and tire spinning water up into his face. If he could hit the tire and cut it—he tried banging it with the jumper cable clamps but they did nothing. He'd have to cut it. He'd left his boot knife at home because he was buying new boots today. But the silver trophy belt buckle he was wearing had an edge he'd sharpened years ago. If the tire was old, the buckle might cut the rubber, especially going at the speeds they were. Using the clamp on the jumper cable to secure the buckle, he stuck his arm out and managed to hold the buckle against the tire's sidewall, making himself keep it steady despite how his arm ached all the way up to the middle of his back. The worst part was the time it was taking when he couldn't tell whether it was making a difference or not.

He was about to take a rest when the tire suddenly popped and disappeared as the car swapped ends and flipped slowly across the road, rolled down an embankment, and came to a rest upright, straddling a barbed-wire fence. The horn bleated for a while, then died with the music and headlights.

Ty woke up in the dark and couldn't remember where he was, but when he tried to sit up and bumped his head on the trunk, he knew. He rolled onto his back and kicked at the trunk lock as hard as he could. The lid sprang up with a dry creaking and for the first time in hours, he could take a deep breath of air free of car exhaust and oil. Outside the icy rain was freezing over everything in a thick coat. He looked at the side of the embankment they'd rolled down, and the field beyond, where gray humps of uncollected hay bales squatted forlornly. There were about three feet between the car bumper and a fence post, both glittering dully with ice in the thick darkness that had the feel of coming dawn. He felt something warm on the back of his head and probing gently with his fingertips found the golfball-size lump with the freely bleeding cut. He thought about wrapping the rags he'd been lying on around his head, but then he remembered the boys.

He hated this next part. Climbing out of the trunk, he had to stand for a minute to let the dizziness pass when his feet hit the ground. Maybe someone would come along, he thought, looking up toward the highway. Not at this hour of the night. Using the car to balance himself on, he staggered to the back door and tried to look inside. The glass had shattered but not fallen out, so he pulled at the door, which wouldn't budge. With the almost crushed roof, it'd be a miracle if any of the doors opened, he realized, as he tried the driver's. On the other side, though, he fumbled the knotted rope loose and pried the passenger door open. He hesitated, took a deep breath, and bent down to look inside. The driver was lying across the front seat with a gash in his forehead that had stopped bleeding. At first Ty couldn't tell if the kid was still breathing, but holding his fingers over the mouth and nose, he felt the warm air. It wasn't as strong as it should be, but it was something. He twisted around and managed to see the other two boys jammed against each other. Hitter seemed to have a broken nose and maybe an arm or shoulder from the way it bent, while the smaller one's leg looked wrong. Both boys were bloody from the rear window, which had popped and thrown glass across them. He thought he saw both their chests going up and down with irregular flutters, but he wasn't sure about the smaller one, Henry. Then hitter's eyes opened, saw Ty, and shut again as he groaned.

Maybe he should try to get them out, he thought, as he pulled back and stood again, clutching what was left of the roof to keep his balance while a spell of dizziness passed over him. Bit of a concussion, he decided, but he'd ridden rodeo broncs and bulls in worse shape than this. He thought about going to the trunk for a beer to take the edge off the hangover he could feel settling in his body, but decided against it when he realized what he had ahead of him.

Climbing the embankment wasn't as easy as it looked. The ice-coated ground kept tricking him, and the clumps of dead grass he grabbed at either pulled out of the ground or refused his hold on their icy stems. Finally he crawled over the top and stopped on his hands and knees, catching his breath and letting the dizziness pass again. Okay, he told himself, and stood up. He couldn't tell exactly where he was and there wasn't a single light from a house as far as he could see in the rolling hills. When he squinted, though, the sky to one direction had the faintest gray to it that meant it was east, so he headed west, having to keep to the icy gravel, which at least helped some to keep his feet under him. As it was, he slipped to his knees several times before he developed a system of dragging his feet along to turn the gravel and sand enough for traction. His head hurt like a son of a bitch, and after a while he peeled off his shirt, ripped off a sleeve, put his jacket back on, and wrapped the sleeve around the cut to stop the bleeding. Although the compression made the lump throb, it helped the headache. He was damn lucky, he reminded himself every few yards and tried to make himself keep a steady pace by picturing the kids back in that car.

The graying sky behind him reached out and pushed the dark farther and farther ahead of him, but he still couldn't see any signs of people. Figuring he was on the Reservation, he might have to go ten or twenty miles. Even then, they might not listen to a white man. He couldn't blame them. Maybe he should've taken one of the kids' billfolds or something to identify them. Then he remembered his own billfold, with the driver's license and picture of Ronnie in it.

The utility vehicle burst over the top of the hill and bore down on him like he was a rabbit in the road. He stopped, shielded his eyes from the headlights, and waved. When it didn't slow, he stepped into the road and slipped to one knee, but kept his arm up.

It pulled to a stop beside him and he stood. Someone got out of the front passenger door and came around.

"Joseph Starr," Ty said.

"Where're my nephews?" the older man demanded.

"If you mean those boys who stuck me in the trunk of their car, they're back there." He tipped his head in the direction he'd come from, suffering a stab of pain for his trouble. "I was coming to get help. They rolled the car, but they're all alive as far as I could tell."

"You okay?" Joseph stepped closer and peered into his face.

"Just a bump on the head." He followed Joseph around and climbed in the backseat. Kya looked at him over her shoulder and stomped on the gas. "It's just down here a ways, spun out on the ice, then flipped and rolled down this embankment. Landed right side up though. Lucky. Might want to call an ambulance." Kya looked at him in her rearview mirror and shook her head slightly.

"Faster to take 'em ourselves if we can," Joseph muttered. "Lot of accidents last night. Carload of people gambling at the casino crashed head-on with a cattle truck half hour ago. Everything's tied up."

"How'd you get mixed up with the boys?" Kya asked, slowing as the rising light glinted on the ice-covered pavement.

"Met at a bar. I was getting pretty drunk, next thing I know, we're in this car driving all over hell and gone. Things got a little ugly and they put me in the trunk. Probably saved my bacon."

"Gerald's brother said the kid never showed to take him home. My nephews, the other two boys, were due back at ten. We been out half the night looking for them. Talked to every bartender in town. Franklin finally told us he'd served 'em. Greedy bastard. Told us they left with some twice-drunk white guy he didn't recognize."

"We were scared for them," Kya said. "How much farther?"

Ty rolled down the window and looked closely for landmarks. "Over the next hill, I think—"

The driver was still out, and they laid him carefully in the cargo area in case he had a head injury. Hitter, whose name turned out to be Horace, was coming around and indeed had a broken arm, which he cradled against his chest but didn't complain about, though tears streaked his face. His broken nose needed packing, but he didn't seem to notice that as much as his younger brother, who seemed not to recognize anyone. Kya and Joseph carried Henry, who had a broken leg, and laid him across the seat with his head in Ty's lap. Joseph put Horace in front next to Kya and began to check him out as they drove to the hospital.

Although she was driving more carefully now, to keep from jarring the injured boys, Ty had to hold his head with his hand to keep it from throbbing with every bump.

She looked over her shoulder. "You okay?"

"Just this cut," he said, discovering that speaking also hurt his head. What he wanted most was to sleep. Felt so good to—

"Ty." She shook his leg. "You don't want to be sleeping with that bump, come on, stay awake now."

"Okay," he mumbled, "I'm awake—" He forced his lids open for a few minutes, then she was shaking him again, making his head stab viciously. That woke him up. They went through the routine all the way into Babylon.

The nurses decided he was as much hungover as concussed and finally let him sleep for a couple of hours before they woke him with the news that they were releasing Joseph's nephew Horace, but keeping Henry and Gerald overnight. Staggering into the reception area, he had no idea how he was going to drive himself back to the ranch, feeling as he did. Arm in a cast, nose taped, and with two black eyes, Horace was sitting in a chair beside his uncle and refusing to look at Ty, who stopped at the desk to ask them to bill him at the ranch.

Kya came by while he was waiting for the printer to spit out the long summary of charges, though basically they'd only stitched his cut and given him two aspirin and let him sleep.

"Horace backs up your story." She put her hand on his shoulder and smiled. First time anyone from around here had given him a friendly look in months, he realized, and nodded.

"The man you're charged with assaulting was their cousin."

Ty watched the paper inch out of the groaning machine, and tried not to show the chill her words put in him. "They had a rifle," he said.

"They're only kids." Her hand slipped down his back and rubbed up and down.

He sighed. "Yeah, I guess." She was worried he'd go to the sheriff, and maybe he'd let them think that for a while to get some peace and quiet.

"I'm driving you home," she announced when the clerk handed him the printout.

He cringed at the figure and remembered his billfold again. Stopping in the reception area with Kya, he asked Horace for his billfold. Without looking at him, the boy grudgingly pulled it out of his jacket pocket and handed it over. "I'll expect that seven dollars in the mail," Ty said and the kid blushed.

"Don't you have something to say?" Joseph asked Horace.

"Yeah." The kid bit his lower lip and studied his blood-spattered boots. "Thanks," he choked out.

Joseph held out his hand to Ty. "Goes for me too." They shook hands. "Takes a *real* man to do what you did." He turned a scowl on his hangdog nephew.

Joseph dropped them at Ty's truck, still parked at the bar. Climbing in the passenger seat, he looked back at the bank in time to see Harney pausing by the door to his Suburban to watch them. As they drove past, Harney made a gun with his fingers and shot him.

Kya glanced at him but kept silent, which was fine with him because he was drowsy again and it felt good to lay his head to the side and close his eyes now that the aspirin was kicking in enough to send the throbbing pain behind a distant wall. She turned on the radio but kept the sound low, and he drifted in and out of country songs all the way home.

As they pulled up beside the ranch house, he remembered that he hadn't called to tell Dakota anything. He had to wait for the wave of dizziness to pass until he could walk straight, and Kya put her arm around him when he stumbled on the ice and almost went down. He was surprised by the sudden weakness, but knew it would be gone in a couple of days. That's the way concussions were. Dakota pulled the door open before they had a chance to turn the knob.

"Where have you been?" she said, then whitened at the blood spilled down his shirt. Kya pushed past her and led him to a chair.

"He was in an accident," Kya announced. "He needs some tea. Can you put on the hot water?" She dwarfed Dakota in a way that made Ty smile a little. He'd like to see the two of them go at it sometime.

Dakota banged the kettle down on the stove and the noise made him wince.

"Take it easy, he's got a concussion," Kya warned. "Is there any food in the house?" She went to the fridge and started rummaging despite Dakota's obvious displeasure.

"Ryder and I were worried sick—" Dakota said.

He closed his eyes against the throbbing the commotion was creating in the back of his neck and ear. He'd forgotten about the split ear, and touching it he discovered the neat row of stitches. He must've been out for that one. Little shit had done a job on him.

"You feed him his stewed tomatoes?" he asked.

She ignored him and poured the water over the tea bag in a cup. "Here."

Kya pulled out a loaf of bread, and jars of peanut butter and jelly and proceeded to make sandwiches.

"You didn't wreck the truck, did you?" Dakota asked.

"No." He picked up the cup and tried sipping at the too hot liquid, which tasted like bitter water. What he wanted was coffee, but he wasn't about to argue with Kya, who thrust a sandwich at him. He really just wanted to get away from the images of the unconscious boys lying in the glitter of glass and ice, blood darkening on their faces.

"Ty—" Dakota took the sandwich and redistributed the ingredients while Kya watched, chewing with her mouth partially open.

When he'd eaten half the sandwich, Dakota sat down next to him. "So what happened?"

"A misunderstanding. I'm fine. Everything okay here?"

"Your father hasn't slept at all—kept the country music channel going all night long. Thought he was on the phone too at some point. I called Dr. Wilkes, but he says there isn't much more he can do. Can't help with the pain in his back anymore. Brittle bones are going to break, but he can't give him anything strong enough to stop the pain because it'll suppress his breathing and strain his heart. Ty?"

He looked at her face, full of sympathy for his father, and wanted to ask her to forgive him for whatever he'd done, because he needed some of that sympathy too. "Yeah?"

"He's not going to last much longer. It could be any time now. Do you want to take him to the hospital to—" She leaned over her hands, clutched together on the table. Kya stopped chewing and watched them.

"What does he say?"

"He wants to go at home." Her voice dropped almost to a whisper.

He sighed and laid the other half of the sandwich on the plate. "That's it, then. It's his to say."

"But can we handle it?" Her eyes searched his face, and he wanted to say no.

He shrugged. "Not a lot of choice, is there?"

"I guess Verna will be back in a week." Dakota glanced at Kya as if she'd forgotten the woman was there with them.

He looked at Kya sucking jelly off her fingertips. "Thanks for bringing me home, but how are you going to get back?"

"Already called Cody for a ride."

"Found the trouble you were looking for, huh?" Ryder said when he saw the dried blood on his son's clothes. His voice was so much weaker that it shocked Ty, who was bracing for another go-round.

"Car accident on the Res," he said and collapsed into the chair along the wall where he usually sat in his father's sickroom now.

His father looked at him for too long, and Ty was the first to drop his gaze.

"For some reason that woman cares about you."

"It's not really about her."

There was another long pause, filled with his father's shallow breathing and the hiss of the oxygen. "Maybe you better tell me about it then," he said finally.

More than anything in his whole life, maybe even more than wanting Ronnie back, Ty found himself wanting to tell his father the whole story, but fear of the disapproval and disgust on the other man's face stopped him. "I can handle it," he said and made himself stand, forced himself to suck up all the longing for understanding and forgiveness he felt at that moment and stuff it away where his father wouldn't see the weakness and use it against him like he always had.

He thought he saw relief in his father's face as he nodded and closed his eyes.

Ryder lived for two more weeks, during which the two men never referred to anything personal again. On the second of April, Ryder began to fail so quickly Ty called his mother and the doctor while Verna and Dakota sat at the bedside, patting his hand and watching the heart monitor while he struggled with quick, shallow breaths.

He was slipping in and out of a coma by the time Mrs. Bonte arrived. Dr. Wilkes was on his way as they stood beside the bed, the recliner now thrust back beside the silent, dark television.

They couldn't tell if he was conscious or not until he said, "Comb my hair, Muriel, will you?" His wife picked up the comb on the table beside him and dunking it first in the glass of water began to comb the strands over to the side, replicating their wedding picture she'd brought for him, which now stood on the table next to Ronnie's.

"You look so handsome, Ryder, just like the day we met, remember? You were the most handsome boy in the county. You still are." She leaned down and kissed his cheek and kept combing.

"I'm sorry, Muriel, I'm sorry for all of it." He grasped her wrist and she nodded. "I forgive you too," he croaked.

She stopped combing and held his hand, rubbing it while he struggled for breath and tried to talk.

"Dakota? Forgive me?"

"I forgive you, Ryder." She put her hand around the foot that stuck up at the end of the bed.

"Verna, I'm sorry." He looked at the nurse.

"Of course, Mr. Bonte. You been a very good boy, now it's time for you to go to sleep. You're all done in." She dabbed at the corners of his mouth where the white crust was forming, and fought back her tears.

"I'm ready," he announced in the tired voice.

Ty marveled at how his father was being made back into a child, letting himself be coaxed and taken care of by these women. He wasn't going to say anything to his son though, not now, it was too late. As Ryder closed his eyes, there was regret in Ty that he hadn't said more, spoken up while there was a chance. It was all going away so fast. He stepped closer to the bed and put a hand on his father's thin arm.

Ryder opened his eyes and stared at him from a great distance, then seemed to know who he was again. "Son—" He lifted his hand a couple of inches and Ty took it gratefully. "Forgive me," his father said with tired thick words, "forgive me."

"I forgive you," Ty said, wondering that it was so easy to say.

"And I forgive you too, you kept making me forgive you over and over, six times, Ronnie, but I did, every time." He closed his eyes. "Good night, son."

"Good night." Ty held the hand that was going limp in his, trying to fight the idea that his father had called him Ronnie. Did that mean that he didn't forgive him, but his brother instead? Was the whole thing a sham? Something the old man had read about and decided you have to do when you die so you don't go to hell? It was too damn easy, it couldn't be this easy.

"Night, Verna." The voice got younger.

"Good night." Verna patted his cheek and pulled the covers up to his chin.

"Night, Muriel." It sounded almost like Mama, and she leaned over, rubbed the broad forehead, and kissed it, wiping away the tears in her eyes before they could fall on her dying husband.

"Good night, dear, sleep well. Tell Ronnie I love him and I'll be there as soon as I can," she whispered and his jaw went slack. The dog they'd been ignoring for the past two weeks whimpered and crawled under the bed, refusing to come out.

The coma lasted two days, during which they all took turns sitting with him, the women rotating their sleep in the beds upstairs while Ty used the sofa just around the corner in the living room so he could be close. They couldn't bring themselves to sit in Ryder's recliner. The end came while Ty was in the room alone. First the breathing got hoarser and louder, then it simply dribbled away in longer and longer intervals. The silence was shocking, like the aftermath of a furnace or pump quitting. Ty stood beside his father, noticing how impersonal the face had become as the skull bones appeared under the sunken ivory yellow skin. It could be anybody in the bed now, but they had died and that was something terrible indeed. A great loss, a life gone— He waited beside his father for tears, but they didn't come until he finally leaned down and kissed the top of the head, something he'd never done in his whole life, and said "Good-bye, Dad. I love you."

○○ Chapter Twenty-nine

They buried Ryder next to Ronnie in the tiny family cemetery south of the house. The heavy snows had brought out hillsides and valleys of tall, yellow golden pea and the squat white primrose, and an abundance of others Ty didn't have names for. His father had his own personal vocabulary for the flowers and grasses on his land— *stinkweed* for a tall plant with blue flowers that appeared in the cow pastures in July and August. *Dumb flower* for a plain little white blossom they found in the hay meadows in wet years. *Ears* for the short cactus that grew where the soil was getting worse and worse. Ty wished he could remember more of the names. The soapweed was always just that, one thing his father agreed with the rest of the world about. Somehow it resisted being included in his father's own personal scheme of things. There was plenty of it out here, looking so damn perky with leaves brighter and harder green than the new tentative spring grass on the hills. Ty paused to listen to the service, but the minister, who clearly had never met Ryder, was praising him to God.

The headstones were beginning to tilt precariously on the lip of the hill, which had once been rounded but had been cut by erosion into horizontal terraces. A community of sand muhly grass was just getting started in the barer places. If Ty didn't do something pretty soon, he'd have another blowout on his hands. To keep his eyes off Ronnie's gravestone and the hole Ty and two men from his mother's congregation had dug this morning, he made a list of what he had back at the barn—slabs of wood, tires, sheets of roofing tin to lay along the hill to save the cemetery from erosion. Actually, Ryder had requested that there be no service, but his wife had shown up with the preacher early this morning, and Ty had simply loaded the coffin on the wagon and pulled it with the tractor, as she instructed.

His eyes kept being drawn back to Dakota, standing with Verna on the far side of the grave and facing Ty and his mother, with the minister and the two strangers on the other side. Dakota looked leaner and whiter from being indoors with Ryder all winter, and she was wearing a blue dress he'd never seen. It seemed a little big, but he liked it overall. Then he remembered that one night at dinner, Ryder had announced that blue was his favorite color. He'd gone on to claim that both Ty and his mother were colorblind. Look at this robe, red-and-black plaid, he'd complained.

His sister, Charla, hadn't been able to come, too busy with classes. Even more than Ronnie, Ty realized, Charla was the one missing in action. She didn't want to be connected with a single one of them. She'd sprung free and nothing was going to bring her back here. That made her the smartest person in the family.

As soon as everyone had gone, he began filling the hole. The wind shifted and took up a cold edge that blew his hair into his eyes, momentarily stinging them, but by the time he was finished, the wind had changed direction again, scudding away the few high clouds as the sun began to warm the ground. He threw the shovel in the wagon and fastened the tailgate, and was just about to swing up onto the tractor when out of the corner of his eye he caught the flick of sudden movement a few feet away. He paused in case it was a rattler, but hearing no sound, he turned and saw a small hognose snake with a broken spine lying in the middle of the tire track from the minister's station wagon. The snake flattened its head and neck at him, hissing loudly and trying to strike at his boots. When that didn't work, it created a couple of weak convulsions, opened its mouth to let the tongue hang out, and tried to flip itself over on its back, to expose the yellowish belly to play dead, but couldn't. The odor from the feces it had released when it was run over still stung the air around the snake's short, thick tan-and-cream-spattered body.

Ty went back to the wagon for the spade. The snake was still trying to writhe away when the shovel bit the head off. Ty stood there for a few moments, watching the muscles continue to contract, then scooped the snake up and brought it back to the grave. Placing the snake on the raw, sandy dirt mound, he waited a moment to watch the blood soak the pale soil dark before he turned and left so he wouldn't be tempted to stop for Ronnie.

At his mother's reception, the people he opened the door for were almost all strangers from her church or The Home. There were a few old-time ranchers who grabbed his hand and nodded as they took off their cowboy hats, but the reception was really for his mother. He had been in a state of efficient numbness since he'd kissed his father good-bye, but looking around at the people crowding his mother's neat, polished rooms with talk and food, he had the urge to yell something about the snake he'd just killed or about his mother, who never let her husband in this house. He wanted—he didn't know what. He wasn't hungry, certainly not for the pans of brown meatloaf with blood red sauce, purple bruised-looking Jell-O with big, dark, too sweet cherries, or pink fleshy ham. The smell of perfume and food mingled with the spices of the hot cider and the image of his father's flesh sinking before his eyes those last hours. Only bones and skin. Even his genitals that time the covers had slipped. Shrunken, hairless, and sad, the size of a boy's. He'd hurried to cover them up again.

Something writhed inside him. He could feel it as he threaded his way through the bodies and mouths saying words of "Sorry" and "For the best," and made it to the kitchen, ignoring the women busy with platters and containers and talk about shopping and weather. Dakota pulled his arm, and he turned and there was Arthur Bennett with Cody and Latta and Joseph Starr and Kya. They were standing in the doorway, looking at him with some kind of expectation on their faces. It was Arthur who put a hand on his shoulder and half-pushed him out the back door to the yard, where several of the older men stood around smoking.

One of them saw Ty and slipped a pint from his suit jacket pocket. "Ryder Bonte," he said and drank.

The next man took it. "Best bronc ride I ever saw," he said to Ty and drank.

"Here, boy." One of the old men, bent at the middle with arthritis, handed him a fresh pint of whiskey, then turned his back to him. The men went on with their ritual, ignoring him, except for Arthur Bennett, who waited until he'd drained half the pint.

"Your mother said that now Ryder's gone, the ranch might be too much and you're probably anxious to let go of it, head back to Kansas. She sent me out here to talk to you—" Arthur was clipping the end of a big cigar with a silver cutter. Something about the way he stuck it in the middle of his mouth with the band still on and gripped it between his wide lips made Ty dislike the man. The matching silver lighter clinched it.

"No." He drank again, tasting the smoky flavor for the first time because it boiled back up his throat from his empty stomach and he had to swallow again.

"Your mother—" Arthur took the cigar out of his mouth and tapped at an imaginary ash.

"Has nothing to do with it." Ty was as surprised as Arthur by the statement.

"Oh?"

"Have to get the ranch back on its feet before we do anything." Ty looked around for his mother to back him up.

"I think you're mistaken. Harney Rivers told me—" He stopped as Ty pushed past him and headed for the back door, the pint bottle in his hand. The women in the kitchen hushed when they saw him, but picked up whispering immediately in his wake. His mother was standing in the far corner of the living room head to head with Harney.

"Ty—" Dakota grabbed his arm, but he twisted loose without looking at her.

"You get the hell out of here, Harney!" he yelled and heads

snapped up. People dropped back and opened the space between them.

"Ty." His mother's tall, spare form stepped in front of him as he reached for the other man. He was about to shove her aside when she slapped him hard enough to make his eyes sting. "You will not do this in my house. There will be no more, you hear me, no more of these scenes. Ryder is dead. This kind of behavior is buried with him." It was the cold glitter in her eyes more than the blow that stopped him, and a hand behind him took the bottle he readily let go of. She hated him. He was so thoroughly one with his father in her mind that she'd probably never loved him.

"We're not selling the ranch." He could only speak by looking away from her eyes and focusing on the thin, arched brows.

"Mr. Rivers has been holding off on the mortgage until after your father—now he needs to call it in. We have to sell, Ty. There's nothing left to do." Her tone became conciliatory, but he'd seen her true feelings.

He shook his head. "You always hated the ranch and everyone tied to it. Your husband, your children—no, you don't—" He grabbed her arm before she could strike him again.

"You're nothing but a small, bitter woman."

"Shut up, Ty." Dakota punched his back.

"No, it's true. She wants to sell the ranch to get even with all of us, she—"

"I want you to leave. You're dishonoring your father with this behavior. I'll see you at the lawyer's tomorrow, we'll settle this ranch business then. Nine A.M. After that—I never want to see you in this house again. Now get out." She wasn't yelling, but he could hear the shouting behind her words. He wasn't the one, he kept telling himself as he collected his hat and coat, it wasn't his fault. Somewhere below all his self-righteousness though, he had this sliver of doubt.

He was dirty and unshaven when he climbed the narrow flight of stairs and walked into the lawyer's office at nine forty-five. He'd barely had time to grab coffee at the gas station. His mother was already seated on one of the two wooden chairs in the little office. She looked at him quickly and turned her face toward the window.

"As I said, Mrs. Bonte, and I'll tell your son here." Quinn Yount slipped his narrow body into the plain oak chair behind the big oak library table he used as a desk. As far as Ty could see, he was the same man who had defended him years ago, except now his hair was gray instead of brown. Ty sat down quickly next to his mother.

"As I said, Ryder did make some changes in his will last January after his son came home." He looked at the two of them expectantly, but they simply stared back.

"Since you were well provided for already and had signed the previous agreement of separation, he put the ranch in your son's name alone, with the stipulation that your son make a monthly payment to you as long as you lived or until he chose to sell the ranch. Then he is to make a cash settlement, not to exceed twenty-five thousand dollars, or one half of the net. You see, it's in your interest, therefore, for your son here to keep the ranch working. You stand to gain, let's do the math for a moment, a great deal more income that way." He handed them each a copy of the document.

She waved it at him. "What about our daughter, Charla?"

The lawyer's narrow mouth grimaced as he leaned back, dropped his chin, and folded his hands on the desk. "I believe she's taken care of with a small amount of cash, her choice of furnishings from the house, and his very best wishes."

Ty wanted to laugh. Ryder at his finest. Screws over his own daughter.

His mother shook her head. "I know they weren't close, but—" She let the hand holding the will collapse in her lap. "I warned her he'd do something like this if she didn't at least call or come see him. But she doesn't want to have anything to do with the family—" She wiped at the corner of her eye with the palm of her hand. "I suppose I can't blame him either. It hurt him, his pride, that she ignored him." Then she glanced at Ty. "You came home just in time, didn't you?"

The implication that he had manipulated his father was there, but Ty had bigger things to deal with than the momentary sting of her words. "So I can do what I want with the ranch now?" he asked and the lawyer nodded.

"Just pay your mother her stipend or make the cash settlement if you sell." The lawyer looked at them both, then at the papers on his desk again. "You're certainly capable of making you and your mother a good living on that ranch. Too many young people sell out and leave the Sandhills these days. I hope you'll stay."

While his mother said her good-byes to the lawyer, he waited by the window. When he saw her on the sidewalk in front, he turned to the other man. "She doesn't have much use for me." The other man sighed, and it embarrassed Ty that it was so obvious. "I waited for her leave because I—I'm in some trouble—"

By the time he finished, he had hired Yount to represent him, but only after enduring the disgusted head-shaking and silence he knew he deserved. Now that Ty owned the ranch, Joseph Starr could go after him and see something for his troubles, Yount warned him.

"As your lawyer and Ryder's executor, I need to know exactly what is going on with you and Harney Rivers." He looked at him with the kind of no-nonsense expression Ryder used to wear when the boys were young. "Every single thing."

Ty knew that opposing the Rivers family over the years had cost Yount a lot of business and money, and that Ryder had used him because he was the only lawyer in town who wouldn't cave in to local politics.

After listening to the story of the night with Harney and the two Native boys, the lawyer nodded and wrote some things down. Ty didn't know what to expect next, but it surprised him when the man said, "Your father came to me years ago with his suspicions about your leaving right after the assault Harney was arrested for. Then the warrant was issued and Harney was released. Ryder wanted to know if there was something he should do. I told him that as long as you stayed away, he should keep quiet. He never believed the story Harney told, putting it all on you."

"I fired the gun, you know. Just never knew if I hit anything."

Both men looked out the window at the sparrows flitting in and out of the brickwork along the top of the building across the street that housed the J C Penney Catalog Store. "So he knew the truth," Ty said finally, depressed that he'd let his father die without assuring him that he hadn't been the one with the knife.

"He mentioned it again in January when we drew up the new will, but I advised him to let sleeping dogs lie." He turned back and stared at the writing on the pad. "Looks like I might have been wrong about that one." He picked up the mechanical pencil he used for notes and clicked more lead down, watched it crumble off, and clicked it again and again until he was satisfied. "He was afraid of losing you again, Ty."

Ty stood and went to the window, leaning on the middle sash. "He never said a word. Just acted the same as always. I would've told him—" But he knew he was lying. He'd worked hard to avoid anything personal with Ryder, except that time about Ronnie. He banged his fist on the woodwork. "This is so screwed up—"

"Don't do anything to Harney Rivers, Ty. Leave him be. Things have a way of working out for people like him."

Ty spun and faced him. "Yeah, for the best. No. That's all I'm going to say. I don't want you to be involved. Hell, I didn't want my family in this either, that's why I left."

"Well, maybe you should have trusted your father, Ty. I can't say. But don't do anything to compound the trouble now. You have a fair amount of property now—both a ranch here and your place in Kansas, and you have a life you can live. I'll see Harney about the mortgage on the ranch, and start to arrange for other financing with some people I know in Valentine and Ainsworth. He won't get the ranch, you can count on that."

Ty started for the door.

"One more thing—"

"Yeah?"

"Clean yourself up. You're not doing yourself or your family any favors with your behavior of late."

Yount closed his eyes and held up his hand to stop Ty's protests. "And I think we should answer that lawsuit up on Rosebud. I know a couple of the judges up there and I think you need to try to clear your name." He stared at him through his wire-rim glasses. "Unless maybe you like being dragged all over the Reservation in the middle of the night."

Yount knew everything, then—probably defended those little shits himself a couple of times. Like he had in Ty's early years. "What if we lose?"

The older man stared at him for so long, his thin lips pressed together, that Ty felt his face and throat redden. "No reason why we should, is there? If you're telling me the truth?"

Ty shook his head, but didn't believe it himself. Hell yes, he could lose—the whole thing might come down to handing over his family's ranch, his Kansas place, *and* what little was left of the Bonte name. Dakota—could lose her, too. He wiped his mouth and tried to look Yount in the eye.

"The sheriff doesn't seem much interested in serving his warrant, or you'd be in jail right now. This is your chance, then. It's a civil case. That's good. The wrongful death issue won't fly. You can answer the assault charge to some degree. I'd say our best strategy is to get Harney Rivers to court too. I'll go to work on that. Meanwhile, stay out at the ranch. Avoid coming to town. Avoid trouble of any kind. And try to think of some character witnesses."

"Guess my mother doesn't count." He smiled grimly, but felt reassured.

Yount didn't bother acknowledging his comment.

"Well, thanks."

Standing on the sidewalk again, Ty felt a momentary reprieve that opened the day to him. Maybe he didn't have to do anything about Harney. He'd convince Dakota to live with him on the ranch. Hell, he'd even marry her. Things could work out after all. As soon as he got home, he'd call Logan to come help with the cattle. And he'd quit drinking again.

A young ranch wife pulled up in a dusty pickup and three small kids spilled out of the passenger side before she could climb down. He touched the brim of his hat to her and she gave him a brief smile that was almost a grimace and hurried after the children, who were arguing over who would pull open the heavy plate glass door to the western store and saddle shop. He breathed deeply, stuck his hands in his jeans back pockets, and looked up and down the quiet, sunny street. On such a beautiful spring day, the only people in town were picking up supplies or having repairs made on equipment. Above and beyond the small town buildings was a pale cloudless blue, as if someone had thrown bleach water across the sky.

Ty took another deep breath, rocked on his heels, and nodded. Okay then, it was going to work out after all. First he'd go to the grocery store, then pick up some salt blocks, order the new pipe for the broken windmill, grab a new rope and the antibiotics for branding. He'd have to hit it if he was going to get through spring in any shape at all, and by the time he was finished calving and branding and culling, it would be haying time. For the first time since last summer, he began to feel optimistic again. When the ranch woman came out of the western store in a flurry of children, he held the door open and tipped his hat again. He could see himself with children of his own maybe, and Dakota taking them down the street for ice cream. They'd have sturdy legs and minds from playing and reading and enjoying their lives, he vowed, and they wouldn't do a man's work until they were grown.

V

In Heaven's
Unchangeable Heart

"It's going to take all summer at this rate." Logan coiled his rope and leaned a forearm on the saddle horn as he watched Ty pull the piggin string loose from the calf's ankles. The calf lay there stunned for a moment, then scrambled up and ran bawling back to its mother, who nuzzled and licked at the new brand.

"Not much I can do about that." Ty put the branding iron back in the charcoal heater and loaded a new bottle of antibiotics on the syringe. He put the notching knife in the jar of bloody pink alcohol. "Ryder never liked the squeeze chute."

"Can't you call around and find some day workers at least? I mean, Christ, boy—" Logan packed his cheek with chew, a luxury he couldn't practice around his wife. He made a loop with the rope and touched his horse with the spurs. "Least you got me a decent horse here—" The paint with the founder was digging into the work like he missed it, and after Logan cut the next calf out of the bunch they'd corralled, the horse chased it down and slammed on the brakes so hard as soon as the loop settled around the calf's neck Logan almost fell off. When it was Ty who ran to the thrown calf before it could climb back to its feet, the horse craned its head around and gave Logan a disgusted look. "Not my job," Logan said, patting the paint's neck. "He thinks I'm slacking off." Ty wrapped the calf's ankles and set to work branding, notching the ear and shooting it with broad-spectrum antibiotics.

At first Ty had tried to breathe through his mouth, until the stench of burning hair and blood soaked into the morning air enough that he didn't notice it. His hands were covered with blood, dirt, and ash, and he could taste the bitter penny residue on his lips, which he kept licking in a nervous habit he shared with his father. Both men always had problems with cracked, bleeding lips during periods of heavy work. He'd think about his father in moments like this and actually feel himself missing him. Well, not him precisely, but some of the moments of work. The shared part. How they'd rub the small of their backs and at the end of the day be fairly hobbling with stiff and sore bodies from the battering the cattle gave them. If Ryder had left him anything of himself, it was the knowledge that a man could feel satisfied from a long, hard day's work. Hard, physical work could blot everything else out of a person's mind. Ty had been using that lesson all his life. Finished, he squatted on his heels beside the calf a moment and looked at the other man.

"Maybe you're right. Ryder always hired a couple of extra men this time of year, even though the two of us could turn a fair number a day if we pushed it. Hard on the herd to hold them off their pasture this long. They need the spring grass, need to fatten up before the really bad fly season hits." He pulled the piggin string and the calf stood and shook itself, glared at him, and sauntered back to its mother. Ty and Logan laughed. "Maybe we'll keep that one a bull. Got good depth in the flanks and body. Not too rangy. We can wait a year on him. He's got more attitude than we've seen all morning."

"We get to eat, riding for this outfit?" Logan spit a brown stream to the far side of the horse.

Ty went to the buckskin he'd tied to the fence and mounted. "You bet. Food coming up." Together they trotted to the barn, unsaddled the horses, put them in stalls, and threw them hay.

When Ty looked at himself in the bathroom mirror, his eyes were ringed with dirt that streaked his face and gave him a mustache. Maybe that wouldn't be a bad idea, he thought as he washed. Then he wondered if Dakota would object—and had to stop himself. The only thing bad with the past few weeks was the idea of her spending so much time over there at Latta's, helping out since Juanita got so sick instead of being here with him. Soon as he finished today, he was going to drive over and surprise her. He looked at his clean, wet face in the mirror and toweled it off, then looked again. He had to be honest. He didn't want to die now. He didn't even want to go to jail. He combed his hair back. It was getting so long he used a rubber band to hold it now. Maybe he should cut it before they went to court. He frowned at himself in the mirror and hung up the towel, splotched with brown and red. He'd have to do laundry pretty soon. This was the last clean towel in the house.

"You should call around tonight for some help. What about the neighbors? Dakota said the other day that you had some decent people next door—" Logan pushed a plate of bologna and cheese sandwiches at Ty as he sat down.

"They're pretty busy too." Ty pushed a quarter of a sandwich in his mouth and chewed briefly before swallowing. They couldn't waste much time and he was starving.

"You fighting with people these days?" Logan drank some cold coffee he'd put ice cubes in and finished the sandwich he was working on.

Ty shook his head and tried to concentrate on the dirty dishes lining the counters. If they had someone else in, they'd have to clean up and feed them better than this. He and Logan had been working so hard they were living on Dinty Moore canned stew, eggs and bacon, and bologna sandwiches.

"You want me to ask Dakota?" Logan asked.

Ty picked up another half sandwich and put it down again. "What exactly did she have to say the other day? You been on me ever since—" He drank the last of the milk from the carton. Logan liked it for his coffee, so someone would have to make a town run before tomorrow.

"Said you two hadn't been talking much since your father passed away."

Ty waved a hand. "Too busy." He wasn't exactly telling the truth. In fact, he was still worried by her contact with Harney. It was better having her occupied at Latta Jaboy's, where she could be protected—something he wasn't sure he could do. So he hadn't been pressuring her to come home. The pink bologna on his plate sud-

denly took on the fleshy look of the ham at the funeral reception a
few weeks ago.

"Maybe the three of us should sit down."

Ty pushed the plate of food away. "I'm gonna ask her to stay on
here—"

"Then what the hell were you thinking this winter?" Logan drank
some coffee and smacked his lips.

"I guess you could say it was more what I was drinking."

Resting the glass of coffee on his chin, Logan stared at the scared
face across the table. "You must of been riding it pretty hard, Ty.
She doesn't strike me as the kind'd shut down on a whim."

"Maybe not riding hard enough."

Logan put down the glass. "You got more attitude than that
cocky bull calf out there, Ty. Better lose some of it fast, or you'll
lose her."

Ty pushed at the table and stood. "We working or talking?" He
stomped out the door.

Logan watched him all the way to the barn, then consulted the
list of phone numbers penciled on the wall beside the kitchen
phone. Latta Jaboy picked up after ten rings. Upon introducing himself and explaining, he extracted a promise of two days' worth of
help. After that he called home and left a message for Marlys on the
machine. He was going to stay another week, and if he couldn't get
things straightened up by then, he'd have to head home anyway.

They finished the bunch of calves earlier than expected and Logan agreed that he'd move the group of cattle out to pasture while
Ty ran to town for food. At first Ty was going to go without cleaning up, but a quick inspection in the mirror told him he'd better
shower and put on clean clothes. He'd go to Latta's and ask Dakota
to stay on for good. Did he have to have a ring of some sort, then?

The wind creaking the porch door reminded him of Ryder's dog,
which ran off right after the funeral. That made two dogs he'd lost
since they met—not much of a track record.

He was trying on one of the white western-cut shirts with pearl
buttons she liked when the phone rang.

"We're going to court tomorrow," Quinn Yount announced in the loud voice of a person talking across wide spaces. "Rivers's attorney promised he'll be there too. I'll meet you up there at nine."

"I'm in the middle of branding," Ty said.

"Can't be helped. Get cleaned up and be on time." He hung up.

Great, now he'd have to put off seeing Dakota.

Everybody has secrets, Dakota told herself as she watched the parade of plaintiffs and defendants in the tiny Rosebud tribal courtroom. The complaints were small ones: debts owed, acts of vandalism due to feuds, assaults on name and character and body. Every form of failure in ragged performance. The horse was lame, the cow not pregnant, the car broke down, the windows fell out, the food was rotten, the house burned down. Beside her Latta shifted and looked again toward the door. Dakota took a paperback from her purse and began fanning herself. With no windows, the air in the hot room seemed to stick to the skin. Was the lighting dim to keep tempers calm or to save money?

"Oh," Latta whispered, and Kyle Langly, the public defender Dakota had met in the winter, came through the door, followed by Joseph, his nephews and brother, Ty's lawyer, and Ty. Before the door could fully close, a group of Native men and women, many of them elderly, pushed in and shuffled along the wooden benches to form a solid wall across the room. The smell of sweet grass smoke gradually filled the air. The judge gave judgment on the case before Ty's and announced that there would be a fifteen-minute recess.

"I wonder where Harney is," Dakota said.

Latta shrugged. "The important thing is that Ty's here, but I thought Kya was supposed to come."

"God, I hope this works—" Dakota hunched forward and looked down the bench just as the door opened and Logan came through. When he saw her, he lifted his eyebrows and motioned for her to scoot over.

Sitting down, he put his cowboy hat under the bench and reached his arm around her shoulders and squeezed her. She brushed his cheek with her lips. "Thanks for coming—"

She started to introduce Latta, but since they had already talked on the phone, they acted like old friends. While they discussed the logistics of finishing the branding in the next couple of days as if the case would be easily resolved, Dakota stared at Ty's straight back and stiff neck, willing him to turn around, but he merely dropped his eyes to his hands, folded in front of him on the table. The spectators and witnesses talked quietly, as if they were in church. Ty's lawyer, Quinn Yount, was deep in discussion with Joseph's attorney, Kyle Langly. Just as the judge reappeared, Ty turned around and caught Dakota staring. She smiled. He smiled back. She nodded and thought his shoulders lifted a little. When he stood, his body looked a little more at ease. She could almost feel it on hers again and the thought made her scalp and neck shiver.

Harney and his attorneys appeared just as the judge was reading the charges in the assault and wrongful death suit. Without pausing, she glanced at them over the top of her black-rimmed glasses and concluded by asking if the defendants still wanted to waive a jury trial. In contrast to Ty's black dress pants shiny from wear and gray wool suit jacket tight across the back that came from his father's closet, Harney was wearing an expensive western cut tan gabardine suit, with a white shirt and string tie that perfectly set off his blond hair and tan skin. Harney paused in the aisle and shook hands with a couple of Native men attired in expensive Stetsons, tailored jackets, custom boots, and heavy turquoise-and-silver watch bands. One of his lawyers, Francis Waverly, the former county prosecuting attorney, was wearing a navy blue blazer and gray flannel trousers, while the other lawyer, a petite woman, was wearing a short red dress and a necklace of heavy gold beads that looked real. Her dark brown hair hung loose in wide waves and loose curls. Ty's lawyer wore a poorly fitting black suit and plain black cowboy boots with a dull finish. It was as if Harney's two lawyers were working extra hard to establish their difference from the other defendant. The judge eyed the legal team when she was done talking. Nothing in her expression conveyed an opinion of this crew showing up late in her court, but Dakota hoped she was offended. She certainly seemed smart enough not to be taken in.

"That's Mary Mott, prosecuting attorney in a county just south of the hills, with Harney. She has quite a reputation," Latta whispered as the clerk shuffled papers and tapped on her computer keyboard until she found what the judge needed next. "Keeps files on all the prominent citizens and an enemies list that would put Nixon to shame. Must be trying to spread her influence statewide. Cody got caught speeding in her town one time? She almost had him sent to prison before Arthur and I could pay her and the cops off."

"But this is South Dakota and a reservation," Dakota whispered.

Latta shrugged. "Depends. She can always go after the judge's family—she's sure done that before—and she must have ties with the feds or she'd be in jail by now. We'll have to see—"

The judge lifted her head to see where the noise was coming from as Dakota grabbed Logan's hand and squeezed. The attorneys waived opening statements and Joseph's attorney called the first witness.

The two tribal policemen testified that they found Bob One Pony on such and such a night last December, apparent victim of a hit-and-run. Waverly challenged some of the assertions but did little more than clarify what the police had observed. After that the county coroner certified that Bob had died from severe trauma to the body and head due to being struck by a vehicle.

"Well, the poor son-of-a-bitch is for sure dead. Let's get on with it—" Logan muttered.

Ty stared at the men as they took turns on the stand, while Harney swiveled in his chair and looked around as if he were merely an observer in court. Once Dakota caught Harney watching her and she quickly looked away. He scribbled something on a legal pad and pushed it toward the woman next to him. She nodded and wrote something back. This went on for a few minutes. Latta tapped Dakota's knee and frowned with a tilt of her head toward Ty, who was looking over his shoulder anxiously in her direction. She smiled and nodded and he turned back to face the next witness called, who turned out to be Jimmy Short Knife, the other man involved in the assault all those years ago, according to his statement. When Waverly stood and protested, Joseph's lawyer, Kyle Langly, said that he was laying the groundwork to show how and why Bob One Pony died. The judge ruled in favor of the plaintiff without hesitation; Waverly sat down to confer with Mary Mott and Harney.

Quinn Yount did nothing but take notes while Ty stared at the man on the stand. He was trying to find the beaten, unconscious boy from all those years ago. He glanced at the hands settled on the man's knees, and remembered the small fingers that had seemed so fragile with their dirty fingernails. They had reminded him of Ronnie. Now they were clean and trim. In fact there was little about this man in his short haircut, light blue cotton sweater, and khaki slacks that could be associated with the boy from that night. As Ty examined him, the man looked back with the same lack of recognition in his eyes.

"Are you employed, sir?" Kyle spoke from his chair, keeping his eyes on the yellow tablet of notes.

"Yes, I teach elementary school in Minneapolis, Minnesota."

His face showed some of the scars from his early life, but aside from those, there was a sense of calm and control in his expression and body now that had little to do with what he had been.

"How long?"

"Eight years."

He answered in a low, courteous voice, keeping his words simple and neutral. It was almost more damning to Ty, who half-wished the man would stand up and take a swing at him. He deserved it. As soon as this was over, he would apologize. No matter what the outcome, he would say he was sorry, as he had wanted to do all those years ago.

"And you were present the night of the assault on Bob One Pony?"

"Yes."

"Again, I have to protest, Judge." Waverly raised his pencil. "This other boy was drunk, then passed out during the events. This is all hearsay."

The judge stared at him until he lowered the pencil. "I'll hear the testimony, if you don't mind, Mr. Waverly."

Ty could see the flush blotching the lawyer's neck. Harney raised an eyebrow at Ty and flicked his eyes toward Jimmy Short Knife, the boy Ty had beaten.

"Tell the court what happened that night, Mr. Short Knife," Kyle said. "As well as you can remember."

Jimmy fixed his eyes on his hands, folded in his lap, opened the thumbs and closed them again. "Bob One Pony and I had hitched a ride to town around noon." He took a deep breath and let it out slowly. "We drank a lot in those days, and Bob had stolen a new quilt his grandmother had just made. We could usually sell the quilts in Babylon."

"For drinking money?" Kyle asked.

"Yes. It took an hour outside the grocery store, by then we were freezing cold so we went straight to the Corral and did shots until we warmed up. After that, we played pool and drank the rest of the day and evening." His voice was barely audible, and no one moved for fear they'd miss something in a whisper of fabric.

"You were pretty drunk when you left the bar then?"

"We could walk, and we did once we got to the road into the Reservation. That sobered us up, I remember." For the first time he lifted his eyes to stare at Ty.

"How drunk were you?" Kyle asked.

Jimmy shifted his gaze to Kyle. "We were mainly cold and sick from not eating. We didn't have enough money for both, and drinking was more important in those days. I remember wishing we'd kept the quilt. It was a nice one—yellow starburst—and we could've wrapped it around us and kept walking. Not have to take a ride from someone we didn't know."

"How cold out was it that night?"

"Your Honor—" Waverly lifted a file and slapped it down.

She waved her hand at him to be silent.

"Ten or twenty below. We'd wrapped some rags we found in the trash behind the bar around our heads and hands, but we were nearly frozen when those boys showed up in the car."

Ty glanced out of the corner of his eye at Harney, who was staring at the witness as if he too were hearing the story for the first time.

"Can you describe the car and occupants?"

Jimmy shrugged. "The car was new, black and shiny. I've never paid much attention to cars." He grimaced and spread his palms. "The boys inside though—I remember the one in the passenger seat very well. The other one—the driver—I—"

He looked at the judge. "I have a less clear picture of the driver," he said quietly.

Harney's lips twitched as Ty's chest pounded flat.

Kyle walked Jimmy through the identification process and what few details he could recall of his own beating. He remembered little after it because of the concussion he suffered during the assault.

At the end of his testimony, Kyle asked if there was anything he wished to add. Jimmy looked first at Ty, then Harney, and said, "Yes, Bob told me that it was Harney Rivers who stabbed him."

Waverly lept up. "Hearsay, that is hearsay."

It was Ty's turn to stare at his hands and the further denouncement in their scarred history.

While Harney's lawyers continued to wrangle with the judge and went through the cross-examination trying to make the witness confess that he couldn't really identify his assailants, Ty had to force himself not to look down the table to where Harney sat. Off and on, Ty could feel those eyes trying to sting him, but he refused to look, like being the window glass a wasp bounced against over and over. Nothing Harney said or did could ever reach inside him again, he vowed.

Yount had warned Ty to sit still, look interested, and not to react. For once, he intended to do what he was told, except for writing a quick note to Yount telling him to make sure they had Jimmy's address. He resisted asking him how it was going.

At four o'clock they wound up for the day. Ty and Quinn went to Babylon to consult over supper while Logan and Dakota drove back to the ranch for chores. The fact that Jimmy couldn't actually identify Harney had put a huge dent in Ty's defense.

"My next witness is Donna Allen," Kyle announced the following morning, and this time it was Mary Mott who stood and protested that they hadn't taken a deposition from either of these witnesses, smoothing down the front of her skirt, which had folded almost to the top of her panty hose.

"Again, we're making the argument to tie these two men to the assault and subsequent death of Bob One Pony, Your Honor. We gave our witness list to the defendants. They had ample time to depose them. If they chose not to, that's not our fault."

"Proceed with the witness," the judge said. Mary made a show of pushing her chair and rearranging it before sitting down. Ty thought he saw a glint of amusement on the judge's face as she watched.

Donna Allen had plumped up pleasantly since high school. She now wore small, contemporary glass frames on her small, round face and had dyed her short hair black. She smiled self-consciously at Ty and wouldn't look at Harney as Kyle Langly shuffled papers and cleared his throat.

First he established that she knew both of the defendants, but that she was only with Harney the night of the knifing. Amid a flurry of protests that had even Harney sitting up straight, there was time for Ty to turn slightly and catch Dakota's eye again. She gave him an okay sign with her fingers.

Again, the judge ruled in favor of letting Donna tell her story, and Ty let out a breath he didn't know he was holding as she began.

Both of Harney's lawyers protested but remained seated, as if they'd figured out the lay of the land and weren't going to waste much energy until their turn came.

"I was asleep, but the door to my brother's house on Sheridan was unlocked, so Harney just sneaked into my room like he used to do when we were sleeping—seeing each other—a few months before." Donna's lips pursed as if the older adult woman were sitting in judgment of the younger one.

"We were just friends by that time, that's what I told him whenever he brought it up. He just seemed to like talking most of the time anyways. He was a year older than me, and my brother didn't like him. None of my family did." This time she looked at Harney, who smiled.

"He used to like scaring me—doing things like clamping his hand over my mouth to wake me up, said it gave him a charge to see the fear in my eyes." Her eyes dropped to the hands cupped in her lap. "I guess I didn't take it serious enough. You know how kids are—it just got boring after a while.

"I asked him what he wanted and told him he wasn't getting in my bed." She squirmed in her seat and glanced sideways at the judge.

"Then what happened?" Kyle prompted.

"We smoked a cigarette and I remember thinking what a slob he was, letting the ashes fall on my comforter. I made him put it out in an empty Coke can I kept sitting on the table beside the bed. He had this way of holding the smoke in and letting it out in rings or this real thin stream like he was on TV or something."

"What did Harney want?" Kyle asked, keeping his tone even and encouraging.

"He wanted me to take a ride with him. I intended to make it short, so I just put my parka on over my pajamas and stuck my feet in a pair of my brother's Sorrels. It was dark and I was still half asleep.

"Harney was driving his mother's Buick, not his Firebird like he usually did, and so he spun the car by accident when we were driving down Main. See it was so icy and all and the back end slung into a light pole and there was a kind of crack sound and he stopped and got out but all there was was some red plastic from the shattered taillight in the snow, so we went on. His mother wouldn't ask, he said. 'She's so out of it, she'll think *she* did it.' He'd taken her Buick because his Firebird sucked in the snow.

" 'I've got something to show you,' he kept saying.

"We pulled off the county road onto an isolated ranch road and slowed down, it made me real nervous. I asked him what was going on and he acted like he was looking for something.

"First he couldn't find what he was looking for. Had to make a U-turn and almost got us stuck. Then he saw this spot where the fence was down and he stopped. 'Sons a bitches got away,' he said and looked around. He told me to come on and get out of the car." She pulled a tissue from her skirt pocket and wrapped it around the fingers of her right hand.

"I didn't want to follow him. He was being too weird and I was scared.

"Then he said, 'Come on, you big baby—this is cool—' and started around the car. I got out and stood shivering there in the cold while he climbed across the small snowbank, stepped over the fence, and stopped. 'Aren't you coming?' His voice had this little boy sound that made me feel sorry for him.

" 'Okay,' I said. He waited until I caught up, then took my hand and led me down the slope to a big dark place on the snow." Her voice dropped, but the room was so silent she could still be heard.

"He dropped my hand and circled the dark place, his hands punching at each other. I was supposed to see something, but what? The clouds overhead thinned and scutted out of the way for the first time and the moon came out, making what was on the snow glisten. I knelt down, and almost touched it before I jerked my hand back. 'This looks like blood,' I said. 'Harney, what is this? Is this blood?' There was a whole lot pooled there, a whole lot, as much as a butchered hog. I stood and backed away. 'Harney, what *is* this?' I yelled, and looking at him in the moonlight, I noticed the dark stains on his clothes and hands for the first time and quickly rubbed the hand he'd touched on the front of my coat. *'Harney!'* I yelled again. He wasn't acting right, bouncing around the stain again, excited as a kid with a new horse.

"He kicked some snow at it and danced a couple more steps. 'Almost took that sucker out. Didn't lay a finger on me, either one of them.' He was practically singing it. I couldn't look at him, but I couldn't look at the pool of frozen blood either. And I couldn't figure out what that smell was, like a dead animal in the sun—had he actually killed someone? Then suddenly I was so cold, shivering all over and hugging myself to get warm. I don't think it was only the cold, but I told him to take me home.

" 'They're all right,' he said as we pulled onto twenty, heading back to Babylon. 'They got a ride to the Res. Probably getting drunk again for the umpteenth time today.'

"Sure, I thought, after spilling enough blood to stock the Red Cross. I was watching the side mirror, praying nobody was following us, like the relatives of those men or the men themselves. I kept asking myself why I had let him talk me into coming out there."

She took a breath and a drink from the glass of water beside her. Kyle nodded at her.

"The car came over the hill moving a lot faster than we were and it scared me. Then the flashing lights jumped on and the siren started wailing.

"He smiled and pulled over to a stop. Reaching beneath the seat, he pulled out a big wide-bladed knife. It was like one of those ranger commando knives you see on TV. He handed it to me, saying, 'Hide this, will you?' It was sticky with dried blood and I almost screamed. I didn't know what to do with it, the cop was walking toward us—I panicked and stuck it in the wide top of my boot just as the cop came up to the driver's window, one hand on his gun, one hand holding the flashlight he poked around the car with.

"The cop had noticed the broken taillight and was going to cite us, he said, and went back to the squad car where we could see him with his head down writing. For some reason, he hadn't noticed Harney's bloody hands and clothes. Harney fooled with the tape player for a few minutes, smoked a cigarette half down and tossed it out the window, then clicked his door open. 'I'm going to speed things up,' he said, getting out of the car.

"The blood was so clearly visible in the dome light, I wondered why the cop hadn't noticed it before. When the headlights showed the bloodstains off like new paint as Harney walked back toward the cop car, I panicked again and called out the window, 'No, Harney—' But he was already standing at the cop's window with that smirk on his face."

Donna stopped and wiped the corners of her eyes with the wadded tissue. This time she didn't look at anyone as she continued in the hushed courtroom.

"We spent the rest of the night in the Babylon sheriff's office, being questioned, first together, then separately. A priest from St. Francis had called in the stabbing and assault. At first Harney told the cops some jokes and laughed a lot while I sat there with the knife bumping against my ankle every time I shifted my weight in that hard chair. I didn't know what to do. I was still in high school and my brother was going to kill me when they called him. I kept hoping they'd let me go, just smile and let me go, say it was all a mistake. But the deputy said something about it being a federal crime, since it happened on reservation land. Finally Harney's father showed up, talked to Mr. Waverly there, who was the prosecutor, and got us released, and drove me home at dawn. I snuck in at first light and went to bed, sticking the knife between the mattresses." She whispered the last words and had to take a deep breath, as if she'd run out of air in the telling.

"But my sleep was all screwed up by these dreams where the knife kept slamming up through the layers of fiber to catch me in the stomach and hold me there until I was swimming in a pond of my own blood, gasping, unable to reach the edge of the bed and safety. I still have those nightmares.

"Late the next morning, my brother pounded on my door, saying I had a phone call. It was Harney's father's lawyer, Red Tibbetts, wanting to know about the knife. Did I still have it? He'd like to come and get it so they could make sure it was turned over to the proper authorities. He sounded like he knew what he was doing, so I agreed to give it to him. He was a lawyer, what else was I supposed to think? When I got off the phone, I noticed there was a dark line of blood on the cuff of my pajama leg, and I just started bawling and didn't stop until that lawyer took the knife away."

"And what happened to the knife?" Kyle asked.

She twisted the tissue in a tight rope. "I never saw that knife again. I don't think anyone else did either."

There was a long silence as the people in the court let the chill of the story sink through them. A few of the elders looked over at Harney for the first time. The judge was busily writing notes until Kyle said that he was through. Quinn Yount finally stood and asked a question. "And Harney Rivers never mentioned Ty Bonte that entire time?"

"No, he did not." This time Donna glared at Harney, who didn't bother looking up from the tablet he was doodling on.

Ty knew he was going to take the stand and describe what his part in the assault was, but he was relieved that at that point in time with Donna, Harney hadn't yet shifted the blame to him. He'd been too full of pride to share.

Francis Waverly and Mary Mott spent the next hour trying to discredit Donna's testimony.

"It's true that you were angry with Harney for dumping you, weren't you? And you were really with someone else that night, that's true, isn't it? Maybe even someone in court here today?"

Her face reddened; she glared at Harney's lawyers and loudly announced, "No!"

"Now Donna, tell the truth. A man's livelihood and reputation are at stake. Those were times of wild, youthful indiscretions. You were pretty well known at that time as a girl with an alcohol and drug abuse problem, weren't you? Maybe *you* were driving that car used to pick up those boys that night. Maybe *you* helped hurt those boys, and you've waited all these years for some childish payback, haven't you? The court in Nebraska didn't believe you, so now you're trying to peddle it up here, aren't you?" Waverly smiled at her benignly, as if she were still a teenager he had to discipline and forgive.

Tears started down Donna's face as she shook her head, sniffed, and said, "No—I'm telling the truth—I am—"

She looked at Ty and shook her head, a motion Waverly and everyone else in the courtroom caught. There was a restless shifting of bodies, and the judge cleared her throat.

"I wasn't close to *Ty*." Her voice rose.

"It's okay," Waverly said in a soothing tone as if he'd caught her in a lie.

Watching her, Ty felt despair in a thin, dizzying buzz seep down his scalp.

The rest of the day's session was called off because the old priest was giving last rites to an elder in White River. Ty stayed in town with Yount again so he would be able to make the 9 A.M. start.

The next morning, the ancient priest from St. Francis hobbled down the aisle with a cane and had to be helped into the witness chair. His account of the night Ty brought the two victims in went pretty much the way he remembered it, and Yount reinforced the humanitarian angle as best he could with his questions. "He was a good boy at heart," the hoarse voice said. "I knew he'd been in the fight, but I could tell he was sorry. Tried to keep up with him over the years by calling his mother for news. Always felt like he'd turn out all right if someone gave him half a chance. Same is true of most of the boys I see—" He let his watery eyes rest on Joseph's nephews, who bowed their heads. Hearing those words, Ty felt a sudden gratitude that he hadn't had the boys arrested.

Harney's lawyers wisely kept their protests and cross-examination to a minimum, but managed to show three different facts about current political affairs the old man confused to discredit him as a person whose twenty-plus-years memory could be trusted. As he passed, the old priest paused and put a shaky hand that was even more like a claw than before on Ty's shoulder and gave it a surprisingly firm squeeze. He almost thought he could feel those hard fingernails dig like talons through Ryder's gray suit jacket.

The plaintiff rested and the court adjourned for an hour lunch break. Joseph Starr remained seated in conference with Kyle Langly while most of the people got up and trailed out to their cars for the sandwiches they'd packed. Over the past few days, word had spread across the Reservation and now the parking lot and blacktop were crowded with cars and spectators gathering to see if Joseph Starr could really bring the white men to justice. The crowd was quiet though, as if prepared better to accept the blow should it come as it inevitably did in such matters.

Ty and his lawyer went to the conference room with sandwiches Quinn had brought in his briefcase to discuss the morning. Although they were both named in the suit, Harney's lawyers had been keeping themselves as separate as possible and went out to a new maroon van with dark windows to confer. While Yount reviewed his notes of the morning and made more notes, Ty kept hoping Dakota would try to find him, but the door stayed shut until Mary Mott slipped in, her small heart-shaped face as alert and sharp as a fox's.

Chapter Thirty-one

"We have to start sticking together. Mr. Rivers stands to lose a great deal more than a few dollars here and he's willing to make it worth your while—" The idea of money obviously excited her. She pulled an envelope out of the square black leather purse hanging from her shoulder by a strap. "The mortgage on your ranch!"

"That's okay." Quinn stood and pushed the envelope and her hand back toward her purse. "We've made other arrangements."

Her face whitened and then hardened as if the skin had lost its elasticity. The transformation from warm-blooded animal to reptilian in her eyes fascinated Ty, who had no idea what Quinn was talking about, but he would've lost the ranch rather than make a deal to save Harney's skin.

"I wouldn't do this, Quinn," she warned.

He shrugged and smiled, his hands spread wide. "Take your best shot."

When she slammed the door behind her hard enough to shake the cheap wallboard, he shook his head and chuckled. Glancing at Ty, he said, "I found you a new mortgage from a bank in Omaha. Friend of my brother's. So don't worry."

There was a small knock, the knob turned slowly, and the door opened a few inches. "Ty?" Dakota called.

Quinn opened the door and stepped aside, smiling. "I'll wait for you inside."

Dakota seemed smaller when Ty wrapped her in his arms. "Are you okay?" He tilted her chin up with his thumb.

She nodded. "How are *you*?"

He quickly kissed her parted lips, then licked the raspberry taste of gloss left on his own. "You taste good—"

"Ty!"

"It'll be a relief to finally talk about it." He paused, wondering if he should say the rest. "But I'm not sure Donna did us much good. She took a pretty good hammering—the fact that the earlier jury thought she was lying doesn't help."

Dakota glanced toward the closed door. "But the details—" She shivered.

"Could work just as well for me being the one, like Waverly said." He dropped his arms. "I don't know if you should stay for the rest—"

Dakota put her hand on his cheek. He turned and kissed the fingers.

"Shhh—" She pressed her fingers against his lips.

The door opened and Harney stepped quickly into the room, shutting it firmly behind him.

"Get out—" Ty said, putting his arm around Dakota.

"Listen to me, both of you!" Harney's voice had a ragged breathlessness, and his hands were clenching and unclenching at his sides. "This is important—that little bitch telling those lies doesn't help either one of us, Ty. We have to get our stories straight fast. His eyes shifted from their faces to the walls and windows of the tiny conference room as he quickly unfastened and refastened the metal band of his watch three times.

"You tell your version, I tell mine?" Ty dropped his arm, shifting his body so Dakota was standing slightly behind him.

Harney rocked back as if from a blow. "No, you dumb bastard! Look, you owe me—my life was fine until you stole my colt and fucked my insurance claim. I could lose the bank— Everything! *Everything* depends on this stupid court—but those Indians are such dumb fucks, all you have to do is say you weren't there—neither one of us was there—we don't know a thing about it—except your Good Samaritan deal on the way home—"

Ty shook his head. "Uh-uhn."

"Yes! Goddamit! Just do me this favor, Ty, and I'll—" Harney stopped and stared at them, his fingers on the clasp of his watch band, apparently hearing the reality of his words. There was a subtle shift in his face that stilled the emotion. "Do it or I'll kill you—both of you." He closed the door with a careful click.

"Ty?" Dakota whispered.

Ty and Dakota entered the court just as the judge was stepping up to her chair. Harney watched Dakota with such unrestrained interest that Ty couldn't help but notice. Quinn Yount leaned over and asked Ty what Harney had said, but the judge called Harney to take the stand. Quinn glanced at Waverly, who smiled smugly and rose from his chair. Ty had been supposed to go first. When Ty wrote a ? on his tablet and showed it to Quinn, the lawyer just shrugged.

Meanwhile, Waverly was leading Harney through a series of questions designed to establish his prominence in the community. "So you designed a program to invite Native Americans to open free checking accounts at your bank?"

Harney said yes. He sat in the chair with a benign authority that suggested he took the proceedings seriously but knew he'd done nothing wrong.

"What else have you done for the Rosebud community?"

"I sponsor a baseball team every year, help fund a head-start program, provide free turkeys and hams at Thanksgiving to a number of deserving families, and offer job training to high school seniors." Harney's eyes were opaque blue marbles as he surveyed the spectators.

"So you obviously have no animosity toward the people in this court today?"

"Or any other people." Harney glanced at Ty and smiled. For almost the first time, Ty wondered if he really dared tell the truth, if anyone would even believe him. And if they did, would Harney carry out his threat? Ty looked over his shoulder at Dakota, whose face reflected the same worry.

"Your Honor, since you asked us not to take up the court's time with the ten character witnesses wanting to testify on Mr. Rivers's behalf today, I am simply submitting their written testimony." Waverly gave a thick sheaf of papers to the clerk.

"Would you please proceed, Mr. Waverly?" The judge took off her glasses, wiped them on a tissue, and laid them down.

"Could you tell us then, Mr. Rivers, what you were doing the night Bob One Pony was the victim of a hit-and-run?"

Harney shifted in the chair, focusing his bland face on Joseph's family. "I was meeting with my lawyers until nearly midnight."

Quinn leaned over to whisper, "You're both clear on the wrongful death, but we still have the assault—"

Langly wrote something on his pad of paper and showed it to Joseph, who responded and pushed it back.

"Mr. Rivers, Harney, I'd like to ask you a few questions about the assault that occurred twenty years ago," Langly said.

Waverly protested, but the judge waved him down and instructed Harney to tell his version of that night.

"I can't tell you much." Harney shook his head apologetically.

"Why's that?" Langly asked.

Harney spread his hands with the palms cupped up. "I wasn't there."

"What about the previous testimony we heard here today?"

"Well, since Donna was Ty Bonte's girlfriend too, I can only guess that she was trying to protect him."

"The bloodstains on your clothes the police noted?"

"Donna and I did run into each other at the Quik Stop late that night, and she did convince me to take her back out to this place on Rosebud. The blood was pretty obvious in the snow. And when I knelt down to check and make sure, my foot slipped and my knee and hands were covered with blood, which I then tried to wipe off on my jacket and pants. Typical teenager, I guess—" Harney smiled and looked at the spectators for the laughs that never came.

"The rest of the story is pretty accurate except for the knife. I never even saw a knife. If there was one, Donna must've been holding it for Ty or something. I've never liked knives—not even as a boy, so I'd never *have* one—" Harney looked at his hands, folded in his lap.

"It hurt that Ty and Donna tried to set me up—shift the blame— but I realized that maybe they weren't my friends after all. I was still young enough to make mistakes like going out to the scene of a crime in the middle of the night. I hope I can be forgiven for that piece of poor judgment. As for what followed, I've tried to be a good citizen who contributes to the well-being of *all* people, red and white, black and brown."

Ty noticed a couple of heads nodding in agreement.

"So you didn't even *know* Bob One Pony?" Langly asked.

Harney shook his head. "No, I *did* know him—the same way everyone in Babylon knew him. He'd stop me from time to time for spare change and I took him to the Buckboard for a meal or two. He had a severe drinking problem, and I hated to see him so sick."

"*Really,*" Langly said. "According to my information, you and Ty were together a number of times when there was some form of violence in those days. Let's see, everything from underage drinking and vandalism to assault."

"Your Honor, my client's juvenile records are sealed, and there is no evidence to suggest he's done more than any other boy his age— unlike Ty Bonte." Waverly spoke with weary authority, including the judge in his circle of wisdom.

The judge turned to Harney. "Did you and Ty Bonte have trouble with the authorities as teenagers or not?"

Harney smiled and shrugged apologetically. Looking her in the eye, he said, "A couple of times. Once we shot holes in a stop sign. Another time we tried to buy some beer. We were just bored kids then. I tended to go along with Ty. That is, until he did this other thing. All that blood—" He shook his head. "That was a wake-up call. I didn't need anyone to tell me how sick he was after that. I straightened up. I remember being so scared by it." His voice pitched a notch higher so he sounded like a kid again, in awe of his own near fatal mistake, but Ty saw the tip of the tongue flick out to taste the lower lip, always a sign Harney was lying. "You can check my record," he added.

For a brief moment, Ty wondered if Harney had overplayed his hand, but the judge offered a brief smile to replace her usual frown. Across the aisle, Joseph shuffled his feet and loudly cleared his throat, dispelling the apparition of the repentant boy.

"So let me confirm what you've testified here," Kyle said. "You were *not* with Mr. Bonte that night. It was *not* your mother's car used to pick up the boys. You did *not* assault the two boys in question. And you did *not* run down—"

"Your Honor, do we have to keep going into this wrongful death issue?" Waverly said.

The judge nodded and waved at Kyle to continue.

"So is this correct? This is your sworn testimony?" Kyle raised his voice enough to wake people dozing in the hot room.

Harney nodded. "I wish I could help you here, but honestly, it wasn't me. Ty must have had someone else with him. You'll have to ask him. I'd offer a witness as to where I was during that time, but he's dead."

Langly nodded. "Isn't it true that you beat and stabbed Mr. Bonte last fall though?"

Mary Mott stood and protested and the judge told Kyle Langly to stick to business. Harney glared at Ty. Mary helped Harney reinforce his story some more. When Quinn had no questions, he left the stand.

Looking at her watch, the judge noted that they had time to start Ty's testimony, even if they had to continue to the next day.

Taking the stand, Ty kept his eyes on Dakota to see what she thought he should say. Tell the truth and risk their lives or not? He still hadn't decided when Quinn began to walk him through the facts of his life over recent years, which sounded pretty paltry compared to the previous array of civic accomplishments. His father and the Bontes before him had never trusted the legal system, why should he? He looked at the people watching him: Joseph Starr and his nephews, the boys on the straight and narrow again. If he lied, what would that say to them? Logan would still be his friend, but he'd be disappointed. Latta? She'd probably seen and heard it all from Jaboy, her first husband. But she'd been kind to him all those years before, could he let her down to save his neck? What about Ronnie—if he were alive? There were the faces of the Native people too—men and women—maybe he owed them something for coming on their land and attacking one of theirs. Certainly Ryder Bonte believed that when he found a trespasser, they owed. And Dakota—once he started talking, she'd hear from his own lips the kind of man he was.

"Ty, I want you to tell in your own words exactly what happened that night." Quinn folded his arms and leaned against the table, waiting. When Ty opened his mouth, he only intended to say he couldn't remember, but instead he heard the story begin to unravel to the moment the fight started. He stopped, almost panting, and took a long gulp of water, spilling some on the chair arm and brushing at it with the sleeve of his coat. The pull of the material across his back reminded him of his father. He could almost hear the old man's derisive laugh—here he was in court again.

"Ty? Please continue—" Quinn urged. "Who began the assault?"

"It was Harney started kicking Jimmy, who was on the ground curled in a ball, but it had to hurt. Harney had on cowboy boots—he always wore those when we were looking for a fight."

Waverly objected in a bored voice and Quinn continued.

"You didn't try to stop him, though, did you?"

Ty shook his head and grimaced.

"What did you do?" Quinn's voice was neutral.

"I went after Bob, hit him twice in the stomach before he started puking."

"How'd that feel?"

"Stupid. They weren't putting up a fight. I was turning away when he sprang up and lunged at my knees, taking me backwards. I fell with him on top, crushing the gun I was carrying. Smashing my ear."

"You were carrying a gun?" Quinn asked.

"Yeah, I was that night. I didn't use it though—" He was certain he'd just convicted himself.

"Let's get back to that night," Quinn prodded him.

"Bob surprised me, he was so strong and quick and hit hard too. I connected with his cheek and started on his body. Then Harney had him in a hammer lock, telling me to hit him some more. I remember him saying to 'hit him good.'"

"Then what happened?"

"My ear was bleeding all over and that made me really mad, furious, so I slashed at his head, which Harney held up by the hair. Broke his nose all over his face. Heard a front tooth snap. He opened his mouth, but he didn't make a sound. Just blinked away the tears in his eyes and stared at me in such an infuriating way that it made me even madder. I kicked him in the mouth. I kicked him again in the head and his eyes finally closed. I stepped back and wiped the blood from my own face with the sleeve of my coat." Ty stared at his scarred hands.

"Is that all?" Quinn asked.

"Then I just wanted to get out of there. I got in the car and started to close the door, but Harney wasn't moving. That's when I knew he hadn't gotten enough."

Waverly shot to his feet. "*Objection*, Your Honor. If we have to listen to this fairy tale, let's at least keep some semblance of procedure—" Waverly had overstepped himself now, according to the judge's expression.

"*I* determine the procedure in this court, Mr. Waverly. You chose to submit to the Tribal Court, now you will please sit down and be quiet so I can hear this testimony."

"What happened next, Ty?" Quinn asked with a quick glance at Waverly scrawling something across his notes.

"Harney reached under the driver's seat and dug around until he pulled something out. He smiled at me as he straightened with the long knife in his hand. 'Bring your gun,' he said."

"Can you describe the knife?"

"A long, wide blade notched on the back. A Rambo knife, like from the movie."

"Then what happened?"

"I was scared. We were miles from anybody who could help. It was really black, only light was from the snow. Nobody was going to stop him. I'd been stupid earlier showing off the gun. I didn't know what to do. Then I heard a moan and got out. Jimmy was still passed out or unconscious. He was breathing, I checked. I looked up and down the road for Harney and the other Indian, but they were nowhere. I worked the pistol out of my pocket. Then I heard another moan and looked over the snowbank into the pasture. They were just over the crest of the hill, a few yards away. At first I thought they were fighting again, but then I saw an arm come up and the knife glinting in the hand."

"You saw the two men fighting over the knife?" Quinn interrupted.

"Yes—so I yelled for them to stop. I figured the sound of the gun might divert their attention so I squeezed off a round over their heads."

"Did that help?"

"No. As I got closer I saw puddles of blood on the snow, and when the Indian on the ground got back up, I could see his face and shirt covered with blood and he had a knife in his hand also. They were too far gone to stop, I guess. Harney did pause and look at me for a second, and then holding the knife at his waist, he crouched and came at the Indian again, angling for another try."

"So you did not try to stop the fight?" Quinn said as Waverly opened his mouth to object again.

"I yelled again and waved the gun. Short of shooting them, it looked like nothing could stop it, though. As the Indian's knife nicked Harney's cheek and they grabbed onto each other, I did fire over their heads. The Indian slumped."

"Had you shot him?" Quinn asked.

Ty shook his head. "No, well at first I thought I might have, but I knew I'd aimed above them. No, he was stabbed. Harney cut him pretty bad. I threw down the gun and jumped Harney from behind and dragged him up the slope. By the time I threw him in the passenger's side, he was giggling hysterically."

"Would you say he *was* hysterical? Unaware of what he'd done?"

Waverly popped up. "Objection—"

The judge ignored him until he sat down, then she said, "I am aware that this is a personal account, a version of events. I do want to hear it all so I can compare the versions as they're presented, Mr. Waverly. Your client's included." She nodded to Quinn to continue.

"Did Harney Rivers seem capable of understanding what he'd done?" Quinn asked.

Ty paused and looked over at Joseph, who wore the expression of a person faced with a choice between hunger and eating rotted flesh. Ty understood the deep revulsion mirrored in his own heart.

"Harney wanted more. It excited him. Like a kid on a birthday or something. I remember him punching my arm, asking over and over, 'Did you see that?' as I backed down the road as quickly as I dared, trying to keep an eye on the bloody knife Harney was holding.

" 'We probably killed him,' I said when we hit the highway again." Ty released the chair arms he'd been gripping.

"What did Harney say to that?" Quinn asked in a soft voice.

"He said, 'I hope so,' then cranked the window down, stuck his head out, and yelled into the cold wind until I grabbed the neck of his jacket and yanked him back in."

He paused again, watching as Harney mouthed, "You're dead."

"So you two drove off and left the two injured boys to freeze to death out there?"

"Yes," Ty mumbled.

"Did *you* want them dead too?" Quinn's dry tone left no doubt as to his disgust with his client's actions.

"No," Ty whispered. "I was sick about it, but I knew Harney would finish them if I didn't get him away. Their only chance was for us to leave them—"

"That's pretty sorry—" Quinn laid his palms flat on the table.

"Yes, it is. Everything I did to those boys was stupid and wrong. I know I deserve to be punished."

The room seemed to draw a breath, and the judge frowned.

"You're prepared, then, to accept responsibility in this case?" Quinn sighed.

Ty nodded. "Yes. I did not run Bob One Pony down, but I helped mess up his life that night. His and Jimmy's, and if I could change that, I would. I have no excuses. I've relived that night a thousand times. I wish it had been me who was beaten and stabbed. In a way, I've come to realize that each of us left a part of ourselves we'll never recover. We all died up there that night. I *am* sorry. In my heart and in my soul."

The judge glanced at Harney and his lawyers busily writing notes to each other.

People rustled uncomfortably in their seats until Quinn asked Ty to describe what happened after that. Confirming the priest's story, Ty told of going back for the boys. He saw Dakota's shocked face but knew that there was nothing else he could have said. And now he was sunk because he had confessed and Harney had managed to cover his tracks again.

When he was done, Mary Mott stood and asked, "Isn't this just a pretty piece of fiction to cover up what you did?"

"No," he said, "it's the truth."

She glared at him, opened her mouth, closed it again, and shook her head. The moment was gone.

What he wanted to do when the judge dismissed him was walk out, grabbing Dakota on the way, and drive off the Reservation forever. Ryder had been right. It was a mistake for any white man to come here—but he was wrong too—Ty *had* lost something up here.

"Do you have any redirect?" The judge asked Kyle Langly after consulting her watch.

"Yes. I'd like to recall Jimmy Short Knife."

Waverly whipped around as Jimmy came forward, manuevering between the chairs from the plaintiffs crowding into the aisle.

When he was seated in the witness chair, Kyle said, "You stated earlier that you could not absolutely identify the driver of the car that night. Is that correct?"

"Yes." Jimmy appeared more relaxed this time, his hands resting on his knees, and almost a smile tugging up the corners of his mouth.

"You testified that you could not give a complete description of the car either."

"Yes, that's correct." Jimmy leaned forward.

"But you *do* have evidence that can identify the car and the driver that night, don't you, Mr. Short Knife?" Kyle rested his elbows confidently on the table as the courtroom erupted in fierce whispers.

Waverly stood. "Your Honor, we object. There has been nothing placed in evidence in this case, nothing—"

The judge raised her eyebrows at Kyle. "Mr. Langly?"

"Allow me to continue and you'll see why that was impossible, Your Honor."

She looked at Jimmy, then nodded. "All right, please present the evidence—"

At a nod from Kyle, Jimmy pushed up the left sleeve of his blue cotton sweater and held out the underside of his arm, where a sequence of clumsy numbers could be seen etched in pale scar tissue.

"I object!" Waverly jumped up and the courtroom became a din of voices. The judge banged the gavel and motioned Waverly down.

Ty glanced down the table at Harney, whose face had suddenly reddened.

"Please explain, Mr. Short Knife," Kyle said.

"I *was* beaten and concussed that night, but I *did* wake up while they were working over Bob. I didn't know whether we'd make it out alive, but if we did, I for sure wanted to go after those two. So I took my pocket knife and scratched the license plate number in my arm. It was all I had." He ran his fingers lightly over the scars. "When the first trial failed, even though I kept telling him that this day was coming, Bob gave up." Jimmy looked at Ty and Harney. "He should have waited—I wish he had—"

"And whose license plate number is it?" Kyle asked.

"It belonged to Harney Rivers's mother's car. But she wasn't the one driving that night—"

"And the car was never reported stolen—so *someone* in the Rivers family drove it up the road to Rosebud, picked up two half-frozen, exhausted drunks, and nearly beat and stabbed them to death." Kyle purposely avoided looking in Harney's direction. "Do you have any idea who that might have been?"

Jimmy shrugged his shoulders and pulled down his sleeve. "Harney Rivers."

There was an explosion of noise in the room, and it took the judge a few minutes to restore quiet so that Kyle could next call the old priest, who testified that he had noticed the bloody numbers the night the two boys had been brought to St. Francis for medical treatment.

Waverly's questions only worked to reinforce the story until he gave up. Sitting down, he pushed away the tablet Harney was frantically pushing toward him.

Quinn Yount wrote "Thank God" on Ty's tablet and collected his notes for summation.

Because the judge wanted to finish hearing testimony that day, they started closing arguments at four-thirty with Kyle summarizing the points of his case. Harney with some help from Ty had tried to murder the victim in the first assault. There was a history of bad blood there. Donna's statement proved that Harney had done the stabbing and bragged about it. Harney was involved in business dealings on the Reservation that made Bob One Pony's continued presence, in light of Ty Bonte's return, a threat and a hazard. Both men had the motivation and the wherewithal.

Then Quinn Yount went, emphasizing Ty's compassion and regret, and stating that "in fact he was at the family ranch when the man was killed. Ty left twenty years ago, not fleeing the warrant, but wanting to start a new and better life, away from the bad influence of Harney Rivers." Yount paused and rested his hand on Ty's shoulder.

"Ty freely admits what he did and that it was wrong. He deeply regrets his part in the beating of those two young men. There is nothing but Harney Rivers's testimony to suggest that Ty was the main instigator of that violence. He is a respected businessman who is more than willing to take responsibility for his part, his part in an assault two decades ago, not the untimely death last December."

There was a brief murmuring among the spectators that made Ty wonder if they were getting ready to rise up and walk out on the white men denying justice to a fallen brother. He tried to see the expressions on the faces of the people along the benches behind Joseph Starr, but couldn't.

When it came to Harney's lawyers, Waverly stood and delivered an eloquent list of all the ways in which the plaintiff had failed to establish Harney Rivers as the person behind the wheel of the hit-and-run vehicle. He carefully avoided mentioning the assault or attacking Donna's or Jimmy's testimony. He simply repeated in a multitude of ways that "Harney Rivers was not there when it happened. Not unless every prominent person in the community is lying."

When he sat down, Ty had to admit that it had probably worked. Although he knew firsthand what Harney was capable of and had wanted to testify to that despite Quinn's warnings not to muddy the waters with the attempted murder in Kansas, Ty had never really believed that Harney had killed Bob One Pony with a car. It probably was an accident, which the driver fled for any number of reasons. But that wasn't the point here. Joseph Starr wanted to make someone take the burden of the death, someone who had severed what future his cousin had twenty years ago. Ty understood.

"It may take her a couple of days, so don't get too worked up," Quinn leaned over and whispered in his ear.

The judge spoke briefly to her assistant, sorted some papers, wrote some things down, and cleared her throat. Leaning into the microphone for the first time all day, she said, "I'm ready to give judgment." She cleared her throat again and Ty looked quickly at Yount, who raised his eyebrows and grimaced. The court grew silent.

"Given the history of bad blood here that hastened the end, I find both Ty Bonte and Harney Rivers responsible in the assault and wrongful death of Bob One Pony." When the crowd began murmuring, she raised her hand. "Please—therefore, I am awarding the plaintiff twenty-five thousand dollars and court costs. Ty Bonte, since I find you less responsible because you took responsibility for your actions and continue to suffer remorse, you are to pay ten dollars of this judgment. You are also to get to know Bob's family and begin to pay back with your own time and resources, as best you can, some of what has been taken from them through his absence. I trust that being the man I see here today, you will do your best."

When Ty heard the verdict, he slumped back in his chair. Ten dollars for the twenty years of guilt and grief. Ten dollars for another man's life. There was a mixture of relief and outrage and sorrow he could barely swim clear of to listen. He looked over at Quinn, who sat perfectly still, his eyes focused on the judge.

"Harney Rivers, you clearly hold the greatest responsibility here. Having lied once to the court, sir, you are now a liar. Nothing you have to say can ever be believed. Therefore, you are to pay the remainder of the judgment. And Mr. Rivers, I want to suggest that it would be very wise of you never to set foot on Rosebud Reservation again. I'll make sure the police have your license plate number and picture in case you feel tempted. Court dismissed."

Ty sat dazed for a moment while all around him people were talking and jostling each other. Harney's lawyers remained seated with their client, heads together in conference. Ty climbed to his feet, shook Quinn's limp hand, and thanked him. Turning to find Dakota, Ty bumped into Joseph, who caught his shoulder and turned him around to shake his hand. The two nephews shuffling behind their uncle had to be pushed forward to shake Ty's hand without ever looking up from their feet. Weaving his way outside, he found Dakota standing with Latta and Logan.

Ty grabbed Dakota in a big hug. "You coming home or do I have to manhandle you here?" Breaking away from their kiss, he saw Harney pausing before the two casino men. Although Harney had his hand out, the two merely turned away and began talking to others. There was a new expression on Harney's face—rage twisting the features while people bumped past him as if he had ceased to be alive now.

∽ Chapter Thirty-two

Ty was riding the buckskin, who thought he could tolerate the picnic basket, and Dakota was on the gray, who had decided in an unusual act of temperament that the small lemonade cooler and blanket strapped behind the saddle were almost more than he could bear. He was dancing and shaking his head as they cut up past the cemetery on their way along an old cattle trail to the sod house. Ty hadn't thought about that place in years, and only remembered it this morning when he'd ridden to the southernmost pasture to check the windmill and water tank. There it was, on the edge of a small marsh that became a pond in wet years.

The spring hills were more beautiful today than he remembered them ever being from his early years out here or maybe now he could finally appreciate what it meant when a breathy new green began replacing the tan, yellow, and mauve winter grasses. New bald face calves were nursing and sleeping and trying to reach grass between their spraddled front legs. And across the marshes and hay meadows, the land was alive with birds, mating, building nests, taking off and landing. As they wove past a pond edged with rushes, a small flock of yellow-headed blackbirds took off, swirled once around, and settled back down. When they rode by a small lake, he pointed to the end where the pelicans floated, some with young riding on their backs. They stopped to let the horses drink and watched while overhead a migrating flock of geese wheeled and spun up into the sun, appearing and disappearing like knife edges as their bodies turned.

"This is part of the great flight way down the middle of the country," Ty said as they started out once more. "Next spring we'll go south to the Platte and watch the Sandhill cranes arrive. In the winter we can go up to the Niobrara and see the bald eagles hunting in the river valleys. Once in a while you see a golden eagle too." He stood in his stirrups and stretched to see the far side of the lake, but the gnats found their horses' ears and eyes and they had to jump into a lope to escape.

Trotting down into the small flat valley the Loup River made as it wound true to its name in and out of the Sandhills, they found the air felt fresher here, and for some reason they'd left the gnats behind. Around and then over the next hill, they came to the small marsh, with a bath mat size spot of blue water showing, and next to it the little sod house he'd built Ronnie as a surprise that last spring when his brother had been reading about Nebraska pioneer life in school.

After they dismounted, unsaddled, and hobbled the horses, Ty took Dakota's hand and led her to the tiny dark house.

"What is this?" She hung back as he worked the door handle and finally pushed the door open with his shoulder in a creaking rush and went in. There was a scurry of nails on the floorboards and something flew out of the glassless window facing them. She backed up and folded her arms across her chest. "Ty?"

"It's a sod house—" He came out brushing the cobwebs off his shirtsleeves and hair. "See?" He picked at the side and some of it crumbled away. "I had to use black sand sod instead of dirt the way they did south of here. Doesn't last as long—although this one's held up pretty good. Roof has a hole in it, but the walls seem okay. It helped that I used wood for the roof and was starting to stucco the walls when—" He'd explain that another time.

She stepped close enough to rub her fingers over the gritty side of the house. "How do you keep it from growing?"

"I cut the pieces in squares, my brother told me how to do this part, then turned the grass side down to dry it and kill anything growing. That's for the walls. The roof they'd just leave the grass alive for protection. Here, look here—" He grabbed at something and held it in his fist. When she looked closer she saw a small garter snake wriggling to get loose.

"They live in the walls along with mice and insects—like a little town, I guess—see all the holes?" He walked to the side of the house and let the snake go in the deep grass.

"Could it be lived in now?" Dakota shivered at the thought of a night with all those creatures dripping on the bed while a person tried to sleep.

"Needs some work—they shift over the winter, so every spring they'd have to be shored up again. I don't think I'd like it much—how about you? Want to spend our wedding night out here?"

She pushed his shoulder and went to spread the blanket and unpack the food.

They sat on the grass, while the horses pulled hungrily at the new grass. Overhead, a pair of hawks drifted across the valley hunting, two black scissors against the pure spring blue sky, undiluted by the summer heat that turned it almost white on the brightest July and August days. They were far from any road and there were no power lines or houses or people. Living in Kansas Ty had forgotten about the quiet out here, how it stretched the land, made spaces larger. He lay down in the new grama grass and listened to the buzz of insects sawing around him. A meadowlark sang its musical scale and waited for an answer that didn't come, then it tried again. Ty turned his head to see what Dakota was doing.

Without saying a word, she scooted so she could lean over him, shading his face against the sun. "How're you doing?" She played with the top button on his shirt.

"Feels good out here."

She nodded. "If I ever left, I think I'd miss this now. Iowa's so—I mean, I liked it there, but it's so orderly, everything in its place. Here, you feel yourself, nothing is so owned yet, I mean, it's still reaching out for you, for everything that's alive. You notice life in a place like this. Almost a desert, people might say, but it brings you back to the smallest thing to be here." She looked embarrassed. "Know what I mean?"

"Yeah. Hadn't realized I missed it so much until I came back. Kept thinking of the hills as Ryder and Ronnie—not this—" The water's quiet slippage against the grass seemed to make the air sway and shimmer around them for a moment. "Dakota—" He reached for her and she caught his hand and they fell softly into each other.

"We should talk," she whispered, "nothing's settled—"

He sat up surprised and ran his hand through his hair, which was so long he could tuck it in his collar now. "Of course it is—Harney's finished, the trial's over—"

"No." She sat up too and lined her legs together, pointing the toes of her boots toward the sod house. "That's not what I meant."

He looked at her a long moment, noting the blade of grass stuck in her hair. "Oh, you mean—"

She nodded and pulled some grass and tossed it away.

"I just assumed you were staying—"

"You haven't asked—"

"Asked?" He wiped his mouth. "Oh, *asked*, you mean, *asked*—"

She pulled more grass, pretending to concentrate on separating the blades while she sneaked a glimpse of him out of the corner of her eye. "Ty!" She threw the grass at him and he caught her hand and wrestled her down beneath him. Sitting back on his heels, holding her arms at her sides, he smiled.

"Finally, some real power!" he gloated.

She laughed and wriggled but not hard enough to dislodge him.

"So will you stay? Get married and stuff? Maybe?" he stammered.

"That's a reassuring way to put it."

"Well?"

"I will stay the summer." She closed her eyes so he wouldn't see the lie—that he'd have to drive her away with a gun if he ever wanted her to leave.

"What about the other part?" He leaned close and brushed her lips. She smelled the cinnamon coffee cake they'd had for breakfast on his breath.

"Do you have a ring?"

He shook his head.

"Let's take care of business first, then you want to propose, you get a ring." She could hear her mother in her voice, but shrugged it off.

He kissed her, circling her mouth with his, pulling her up against him so she felt small and protected against his broad chest. "You sure turned into an old-fashioned girl all of a sudden," he murmured into her hair.

She smiled secretly. Ty would never understand that he was the one who had brought them back to this place, where it seemed perfectly reasonable to dream small, ordinary lives that took up the land and gave it back at the end. To live here she would be able to measure her happiness and sorrow, and she would have a share of each, she knew, and if she were lucky, if they were lucky, there would be just enough of each so that they never grew too careless of the good times, nor too bitter from the hard times. The extravagance in life, she finally understood, was being able to love, being able to survive the dream of loving. She must never let Ty see how fragile that dream could be. He must work hard and love completely. He was a person who made another person's dreams real. The sod house for Ronnie, the gray horse for her. The ranch for all the Bontes before him and all those after. To be with him, she must work hard also, keep their lives from igniting like paper, keep him from coming to the ruined dreams that haunted their parents.

"What about the Kansas place?" she asked.

"Do we *have* to do this now?" He rocked back on his heels and let go of her arms. She slid out and sat up, putting her hands on his knees.

"There's a heck of a lot of work to do if we're going into business here, and we're already getting a late start."

"Okay," he sighed. "You're right. Let's make a list. First, sell the Kansas place. Or should we try to rent it out in case things up here don't pan out?"

"You can't lose the ranch, Ty, so let's not do it halfway. What about moving the horse business here?"

"I suppose we could use the money from the Kansas place to put up an indoor arena. That might help get us back in shape with the cattle too, a little operating capital, or we can get a bridge loan now that Harney's out of the picture."

"Is he?" She looked across the empty hills.

"Sure, he can't show his face now. The bank examiners were there yesterday and removed him bodily. What's he got left? His casino deal fell through the day the verdict was announced."

Dakota shivered. "I don't know—"

The discussion continued until late afternoon, when the horses began to stamp anxiously for home. Just as the sun was melting yellow-rose into the horizon, a small plane circled overhead, then flying low over the hills, disappeared, leaving only the engine growl to hang in the air. The horses lifted their heads and snorted at Ty and Dakota hurriedly saddling.

As soon as the barns appeared in the distance, the plane they'd seen earlier circled the hay meadow and drifted gracefully downward like a large bird. The nose dipped though, and the wheels caught in the marshy ground, and just as gracefully the plane flipped end over end.

"Ty!" Dakota pushed the gray into a gallop. Although she was still too far away to see who was crawling out of the plane, Ty guessed. He caught up with her as the figure ran toward the barn and disappeared from sight.

"Wait a minute—" He pulled up next to her and she slowed to a trot. "Stop! It's Harney. Wait here—let me go ahead."

"Harney?" She looked at the serene barnyard before them. "Are you sure?"

"Yes—so don't get any closer. If you hear gunshots or anything, ride the hell away." He rode off before she had a chance to argue. He had it to do. Trotting down the hill, he pulled to a walk by the corral, where the horses were milling anxiously, heads flung up and nostrils wide as if they smelled the danger. They snorted at him and spun their bodies in a curving wave around the enclosure, spooked by the loud banging of metal shoes smashing wood that was coming from somewhere deep inside the barn. Dismounting, he let the reins trail in case he needed to jump on fast. The buckskin knew what to do and dropped his head to tear at a clump of grass next to the barn, careful to avoid stepping on the reins. He was banking on Harney wanting to talk before he did what he'd come to do.

"Okay—" Ty called into the brown light of the barn and waited. It sounded like the paint he'd left stalled for Logan to use was kicking its stall down. Then it stopped and gave a whinny that ended in a high, colty questioning tone, followed by another rattling kick that splintered yet another board. Ty ran down the aisle. If Harney had hurt another horse—

Flinging open the paint's door, he saw Harney half-shoved into the next stall, bloody body wedged by the broken boards, head twisted and hanging at an odd angle. His usually neat yellow hair was a greasy tangle, his skin strangely blotched as if the blood underneath were about to burst through. His clothes were wrinkled and there were greasy spots on his chinos. And his wash blue eyes now stared into the empty air. When Ty knelt to check the body while the paint blew loud and kicked the opposite stall boards, he found a bruised dent in the partial curve shape of a horseshoe at the temple. A wide-bladed knife rested on the straw at his feet.

Calming the paint, Ty ran his hands over its body until he found a cut on the dark spotted flank. A few inches lower and Harney would have cut the hock ligament. Probably what he had intended to do. The paint had defended itself as if from a wild dog attack.

He was leading the paint to another stall when Dakota grabbed him.

"What happened?" She looked in the stall and jerked away. "You didn't—"

"He was like that when I got here. He cut the horse, and it kicked him to death."

"It's over then."

Ty nodded, and for a moment he could hear his brother in the cool darkness of the barn, brushing the air free of what clung to him.

A PENGUIN READERS GUIDE TO

THE WEIGHT
OF DREAMS

———

Jonis Agee

An Introduction
to *The Weight of Dreams*

The endless, rolling prairie of the Nebraska Sandhills seems just like the kind of place to escape to, a place where life is simple and unsullied, untouched by technology and noise and the complications that other people bring. *The Weight of Dreams* lays bare the realities of life on America's last frontier—a life that even at the end of the twentieth century can be difficult and lonely but that can also be beautiful and redemptive.

The Nebraska Sandhills cover nearly 22,000 square miles of grassy sand dunes and include the largest and least populated county in the nation. Each cattle ranch averages 8,000 acres and while the Sandhills remain a beautiful and sometimes unspoiled land, only a few hearty individuals—like Ty Bonte and Dakota—can survive here. And, as one would expect in a region where life is based on a single industry—ranching—there is an ongoing economic crisis. As a result, the gorgeous landscapes of the Sandhills are interrupted by dreary prefab houses, fast food stops, and empty storefronts cropping up in places like Babylon, Ty's hometown. There isn't much reason for young people to stick around, and it is difficult for ranchers like Rider Bonte to pass their land on to subsequent generations. People like Ty and Dakota are the exception; ranching as a way of life is just too hard for most of us.

In a place where you measure the distance between you and your neighbor in miles, not yards, community can seems like an abstract concept. Yet the acres of empty land that separate the inhabitants of the Sandhills also encourage its inhabitants to huddle close to one another, like cattle bracing themselves against a prairie blizzard. And Ty, after returning to his family's Sandhills ranch to face up to his checkered past, feels the weight of his neighbors' judgment on his back. The townspeople are also a heavy presence, bringing out the worst in him, leading him back to the behavior that drove him away from Babylon in the first place. On the Rosebud Reservation, with its trash-strewn lawns, decrepit houses, and the alcohol treatment center, he is considered a murderer, just one more reason for the red and white communities to mistrust and fear each other.

Through her portraits of Ty and Ryder Bonte, Dakota Carlysle and Harney Rivers, Cody Kidwell and Latta Jaboy, Joseph Starr and Jimmy Short Knife, Jonis Agee shows us that the Nebraska Sandhills are experiencing the same social crisis as culture at large. And with their lives dictated by weather, nature, and the land, their existence is tenuous, perhaps more tenuous than life in a crowded city or a sprawling suburb. Indeed, *The Weight of Dreams* illustrates that life on the frontier is far from simple. But for the people who do choose to live there, the Sandhills offer both solitude and freedom.

A Conversation with
Jonis Agee

The Nebraska Sandhills figure largely in this and other novels you have written. What is it about the landscape and its people that inspires you? What was it like for you to live there? How have the Sandhills changed over the years and where is this region headed?

One of the real pleasures of Sandhills driving is to top one of the hills, having not passed another car in an hour, and encountering one of the marshes or lakes thick with swans, pelicans, ducks, and geese in the spring or fall. Not only is there a raw, unspoiled beauty in the land, there is a tough individualism bred in both the white ranchers and the Native Americans of the region. Two reservations, Pine Ridge and Rosebud, sit just across the Nebraska-South Dakota border and there is a long history of racial conflict in the region. Both peoples experience on a daily basis what it means to live physically close to the land, to rely on it for spiritual, communal, economic, and social survival. These are the most basic elements of human existence and the most important issues of our lives spring from them. For a fiction writer this is a perfect place.

You write of heartbreaking cruelty inflicted on horses by trainers, riders, and dealers. Is this treatment common in the horse business? How did you do your research for this aspect of the novel?

The minute an animal such as a horse becomes the means to convey wealth, power, and prestige, a few ruthless individuals will be attracted to the business. Cruelty to horses is not common among the amateur owner/rider, but it does exist in all areas at the professional level where the reputations of trainers are based on their ability to win prizes for their clients. In the mid-nineties, there were a number of news stories about the scams perpetrated by some very wealthy and unscrupulous owners and trainers in which valuable show and race horses were murdered for the insurance money. Sometimes the horses, bought at overinflated prices to begin with, failed to perform to the expected level and needed to be discarded. Sometimes the horse had been injured, and was no longer able to win in the show ring, and thus an "accident" would be arranged so the owner could purchase another animal with the insurance money.

I have been involved with horses most of my life and in recent years showed dressage and hunter. For this novel, I interviewed stable owners, veterinarians, trainers, grooms, owners, riders, judges, and stewards in many divisions of the show world. They told me stories of other kinds of unscrupulous behavior: severing the tail nerves of quarter horses so they will lie still during competitions where steadiness is valued; using ginger and hot peppers in the anus of Saddlebred horses to make them more excited and brilliant in the showring; growing the hooves to twice their normal length on Morgans, Saddlebreds, Arabians, and any horses shown in park classes to create higher action, even though horses live in thier stalls as a result; bleeding horses to quiet them before classes where they are judged on manners. Part of my intention in including this material in the novel is to suggest that the ruthlessness that we accept as part of sports and economic life exacts a terrible toll.

Do you think Ty Bonte's experience of growing up and working on a ranch and of feeling isolated from the town and its people typical of other Sandhills adolescents?

Yes, except that with the advent of satellite television and radio, adolescents are finally experiencing a much vaster communal culture and fleeing the hills as soon as they're able. The kids who move to town for the school year to live with their mothers, another relative or family friend, of course, have the advantage of some socializing process, but the disadvantage of being part of a broken family, essentially fatherless.

Is Harney Rivers's character a good representation of the kind of people who are encroaching on the American west?

Harney Rivers is the type of ruthless entrepreneur we have seen in this country since the first white man traded some worthless junk to a Native American for a chunk of land that wasn't owned to begin with. I don't think we've necessarily seen an exponential growth of greed and rapaciousness in this country; we've just grown more aware and we're finally beginning to examine the cost of what our national ethos has created. Is Harney the new Westerner? In some sense, perhaps, but I prefer to think of him as the American businessman with a bit of sadism thrown in. He's just getting around to exploiting places like the Sandhills—now that he's run out of other places.

This novel shares a number of characters from your second novel, Strange Angels. *How are the two connected? What led you to return to this earlier work now?*

I returned to the characters and setting from my first Sandhills novel, *Strange Angels*, in part because I am now planning a trilogy of books set in the region. It was actually exciting to go back to the Sandhills in the new novel, to pick up the lives of characters I'd grown so found of, to see how far they had progressed along the road. When Cody and Latta, the main characters of *Strange Angels*, started having marital troubles, I was not surprised since they'd had such a rocky time to begin with. However, I began to worry that Cody might become one of those middle-aged philandering men so I now have to go back and take a look at him again in another novel. Also, I wanted to see how Joseph Starr's work in Native medicine was going, along with his emerging relationship with Cody's half-sister, Kya. It's almost like going to a family reunion every five or ten years to revisit one's characters, and I discovered that I've missed them. One of my plans is to continue to bring in characters and places from the first three novels into the next ones as a means of building a real sense of life in the Midwest, which cannot be looked at through one place alone. Contrary to popular belief, the Midwest is a very diverse region fraught with complex landscapes, populations, and issues, comparable to the South. In my next novel, I am weaving in characters from the first and third novels. I want to move the novel away from the idea of a work of fiction being isolated in time and place.

You write often of families and their emotional legacies. Is the family dying in the American West?

No, actually in areas where people are dependent on one another for physical, economic, and social survival, the family remains intact to some degree. Nonetheless, now that the Sandhills and the remote areas of the West have been invaded with popular culture, these places now share in the current divorce rate, etc. Also, the necessity of dividing the family for the children's education places great stresses on the family, as I suggested in the novel, and the fact that the children often leave these areas as soon as possible continues to fracture the extended family.

How does the idea of family—its importance and prevalence—differ between the Native Americans and their Anglo neighbors?

During the nineteenth century, white political leaders instituted policies that prohibited traditional religious worship, destroying the core of Indian life. If a person was caught practicing any Native devotional rituals, the entire family was deprived of food allotments for a month. Furthermore, Indian children were routinely taken from their families and educated in special boarding schools where they were forbidden their language, religion, and culture. Every effort was made to exterminate the basics of Indian family life. The real miracle is that any family and communal life could survive at all on the reservations, especially today as poverty, alcoholism, and drug use take their toll. Comparing the two groups' dedication to family, one could only say that all human peoples have children, loved ones, at the heart of their community life, and that white culture has yet to be tested to the extreme degree that Indian culture has been.

Describe the process you underwent in creating the Native American characters in both The Weight of Dreams *and* Strange Angels.

As a white writer I worried about how to create Native American characters and cultures. The tendency is to idealize "the other" or to make the other exotic—either one being untrue. What I did was to concentrate on the qualities that all human beings share, and to portray the essential dreams of people as individuals. I tried to create an actual history, not downplaying the social ills or problems, yet not creating stereotypes based on those either. Ultimately, I chose to construct the Indian characters in the same manner as the white: as complex individuals with successes and failures, dreams and desires, good and bad memories, etc. It's never an either/or proposition with characters, for me. I have to know their little crimes as well as their great hearts, their darkest dreams as well as their shining ones. And I see everyone as a composite, in differing proportions, of such qualities. All of us engage in a lifetime war within the self to combat the urges toward doing wrong, toward being utterly self-interested, and that's what intrigues me.

Can you comment on the title, The Weight of Dreams?

We take for granted that our lives are driven by dreams. In the novel, every act is the result of someone's dream, and every horror and achievement is the outcome. Also, I intended to show how we carry our lives like a weight upon our backs—and that our relationships are complicated weavings of memory, dream, and reality. To be dreamless is a terrible, devastating state, but to have dreams is a dangerous experience that requires great responsibility and strength.

Tell us a bit about your other Sandhills novel, Strange Angels.

Strange Angels looks at how the patriarch of a family forced his children's lives into shapes of his own choosing, which caused great divisiveness among them—yet they had to learn to co-exist in order to survive after their father's death. It began my exploration of the Sandhills and the historical conflicts between Native Americans and whites.

Your fiction has been likened to the work of Larry McMurtry, Cormac McCarthy, and Tom McGuane. Do you feel that these comparisons are apt?

Yes, in the sense that I'm dealing with men and women who live closely with the land, whose livelihoods are dependent on the land, whose spiritual and social values are derived from the land, and who register a deep resistance to the erosion of traditional life founded on physical engagement with the environment.

What writers have influenced your work?

Faulkner, because of the language and because his characters are always filled with desire; Flannery O'Connor because of the metaphors and because she dared to speak of the spiritual as if it mattered; mystery writers like Raymond Chandler and Dashiell Hammett because they could use language in original ways while they kept a plot churning; Charles Dickens because of his narrators' voice and humanity; Eudora Welty because of her language and her excessive characters who care with passion and suffer when they don't; early Joyce Carol Oates because her characters want so much and suffer anything to have it.

As a woman writer, how do you think your evocations of the American West may be different from some of the male authors who focus on the same region?

I probably create female characters who are strong in their own right, and who are not necessarily looking for relationships with men to complete their world, even though that is something they definitely would rather have than not have. But most of my women characters are unwilling to settle for less or for having a life that is not shaped by their own hands. Although Latta, in *Strange Angels*, had a bad early marriage where she was something of an exotic ornament, as soon as she gets free, she makes a world very much her own. The same can be said of Dakota in this novel. While she tries to compromise, she refuses to compromise herself or her horses simply in order to have a man. She has a kind of internal moral force about her that helps Ty find his.

QUESTIONS FOR DISCUSSION

1. Compare the characters of Ty and Dakota. How do they handle their emotions? What consequences has their past had on their ability to be in a loving relationship? What do they learn from one another, and how does each change over the course of the novel?

2. How does Ty fit into the stereotype of the American cowboy? Do you think this stereotype is accurate?

3. Discuss your feelings about Ryder Bonte. Without knowing about his own childhood, how much is he to blame for Ty's unhappy adolescence? What is there to like or admire in Ryder? Do you, ultimately, forgive him for his treatment of Ty?

4. What do you think of Ty's mother? How is her life in town different from Ty's and Ryder's on the ranch? Do you blame her for realizing that she couldn't endure the latter? Do you think she and Ty should try harder to forge a positive relationship?

5. What impact has the death of Ty's younger brother, Ronnie, had on Ty's life? How does the piecemeal way Agee gives us information about the death affect our understanding of the incident, and of the kind of men Ty and Ryder have become?

6. We learn about Ty and Harney's assault on two Indian hitchhikers in a similar fashion—through a series of flashbacks that gradually reveal the truth. Do you like or dislike this narrative technique? How would the novel be different if the entire incident were revealed in one scene, at the beginning of the book?

7. Do you think Ty's ultimate sentence for his role in the crime—a nominal fee and a commitment to repairing the emotional damage to Bob's family—is sufficient? How might it be argued that Ty has already "served time" for the assault? How do you think his life might have been different if he had owned up to his part in the crime instead of running away?

8. Compare the scenes that take place in Minneapolis compared to those set in the Sandhills and in Kansas. How does Agee make use of the novel's settings—both out on the prairie and in the town of Babylon—to convey the novel's themes and moods?

9. Compare the courtroom scene that opens the novel to the courtroom scene that takes place on the Rosebud Reservation. How has Ty changed? What is significant about the fact that the first scene takes place in a U.S. court of law, and the second in a court presided over by Native Americans?

10. What has Agee's novel taught you about the plight of Native Americans in our country? What have you learned about life on a reservation, and about the relationships between the Indians and ranchers that inhabit Nebraska's Sandhills?

For more information about other Penguin Readers Guides,
please call the Penguin Marketing Department at (800) 778-6425,
e-mail at reading@penguinputnam.com or write to us at:

Penguin Books Marketing Dept. CC
Readers Guides
375 Hudson Street
New York, NY 10014-3657

To access Penguin Readers Guides on-line, visit Club PPI on our
Web site at: www.penguinputnam.com

FOR THE BEST IN PAPERBACKS, LOOK FOR THE

In every corner of the world, on every subject under the sun, Penguin represents quality and variety—the very best in publishing today.

For complete information about books available from Penguin—including Puffins, Penguin Classics, and Arkana—and how to order them, write to us at the appropriate address below. Please note that for copyright reasons the selection of books varies from country to country.

In the United Kingdom: Please write to *Dept. EP, Penguin Books Ltd, Bath Road, Harmondsworth, West Drayton, Middlesex UB7 0DA.*

In the United States: Please write to *Penguin Putnam Inc., P.O. Box 12289 Dept. B, Newark, New Jersey 07101-5289* or call 1-800-788-6262.

In Canada: Please write to *Penguin Books Canada Ltd, 10 Alcorn Avenue, Suite 300, Toronto, Ontario M4V 3B2.*

In Australia: Please write to *Penguin Books Australia Ltd, P.O. Box 257, Ringwood, Victoria 3134.*

In New Zealand: Please write to *Penguin Books (NZ) Ltd, Private Bag 102902, North Shore Mail Centre, Auckland 10.*

In India: Please write to *Penguin Books India Pvt Ltd, 11 Panchsheel Shopping Centre, Panchsheel Park, New Delhi 110 017.*

In the Netherlands: Please write to *Penguin Books Netherlands bv, Postbus 3507, NL-1001 AH Amsterdam.*

In Germany: Please write to *Penguin Books Deutschland GmbH, Metzlerstrasse 26, 60594 Frankfurt am Main.*

In Spain: Please write to *Penguin Books S. A., Bravo Murillo 19, 1° B, 28015 Madrid.*

In Italy: Please write to *Penguin Italia s.r.l., Via Benedetto Croce 2, 20094 Corsico, Milano.*

In France: Please write to *Penguin France, Le Carré Wilson, 62 rue Benjamin Baillaud, 31500 Toulouse.*

In Japan: Please write to *Penguin Books Japan Ltd, Kaneko Building, 2-3-25 Koraku, Bunkyo-Ku, Tokyo 112.*

In South Africa: Please write to *Penguin Books South Africa (Pty) Ltd, Private Bag X14, Parkview, 2122 Johannesburg.*

	DATE
DEC 0 5 2001	
DEC 2 0 2001	
JAN 1 7 2002	
FEB 1 2 2002	
MAR 1 2 2002	
MAR 1 9 2002	
APR 1 0 2003	
JUL 0 7 2003	
AUG 2 2 2003	
MAY 0 4 2004	
SEP 2 0 2008	
JUL 2 3 2010	